For King & Country

Robert Asprin
&
Linda Evans

FOR KING & COUNTRY

This is a work of fiction. All the characters and events portrayed in this book are fictional, and any resemblance to real people or incidents is purely coincidental.

Copyright © 2002 by Bill Fawcett & Associates

All rights reserved, including the right to reproduce this book or portions thereof in any form.

A Baen Books Original

Baen Publishing Enterprises
P.O. Box 1403
Riverdale, NY 10471
www.baen.com

ISBN: 0-7434-7168-7

Cover art by Larry Elmore

First paperback printing, November 2003
Second paperback printing, November 2003

Library of Congress Catalog Number 2002023216

Distributed by Simon & Schuster
1230 Avenue of the Americas
New York, NY 10020

Production by Windhaven Press, Auburn, NH
Printed in the United States of America

A TIME-SENSITIVE MISSION

Stirling mopped his face with one hand. Christ, he'd needed more sleep before facing this. *Cumann Na Mbann*, that was the last thing he'd wanted to hear. The women's arm of the IRA, the most secret part of the whole terrorist organization and the most efficient as well, damned near impossible to infiltrate. *Cumann Na Mbann* members had done everything from running guns and messages in their babies' prams to gunning down British dignitaries. A more ruthless, clever opponent, Stirling could not imagine.

"Right, then. I'll have to go back in time after them."

"*You?*" Indrani Bhaskar gasped. "But you're not trained! You don't know the first thing about the time period—"

"And those two *do?*" Stirling interrupted her, gesturing at the too-still bodies of McEgan and Banning lying shrouded beneath the wires of their time-transference headsets. "They're not exactly historians, Dr. Bhaskar, although I suppose it wouldn't take a great deal of historical training to assassinate Henry II before he has the chance to invade Ireland."

Dr. Bhaskar gave him the rest of the bad news. "They didn't go to the same time Dr. Beckett did. They're not at Henry II's court, not anywhere close to it, in fact."

"All right," Stirling grated out, "where *have* they gone?"

Her eyes, still wet from her shocked weeping, reflected a fear of not being taken seriously. "Well, Captain, you see . . . They've set the equipment for this region, right here in Scotland."

"This region?" Stirling echoed. Uneasiness stirred, worse than before, in the pit of his stomach. "Granted, Scotland's been the site of a number of historic battles, but major enough to upset all history? What could McEgan possibly be after, *here*, that would benefit Northern Ireland?"

Indrani's lips worked. Her answer came out as a ragged whisper. "King Arthur."

For David James Hollingsworth,
the sunshine of our lives.

My deepest thanks, as always, to Robert R.
Hollingsworth, military historian and battle
choreographer (whose wonderful archery post
graces the cover) and to his lovely wife Susan
Collingwood, whose discerning eye keeps me
on track. Thanks to them, as well, for the loan
of their libraries and their highly limited time!

I owe special thanks to Susan Gudmundsen,
for climbing the immensely steep slope of
Cadbury Hill, just to take photos for me. The
weather was raw and thoroughly disagreeable,
but up she went, into the wet clouds, to get
my 360-degree panorama, which illuminated
the whole climactic ending of the novel.

And another special thank-you to Patricia
Grohowski, for her tireless cheerleading,
for pointing me in the direction of that
wonderful little shop where I found the books
on Glastonbury Tor, for lending me half her
fascinating library, and for always finding
a way to make me smile, in the midst
of all the howling.

I couldn't have done it without them!

—Linda Evans

Chapter One

~

The election should have made things better.

Would have, in fact, if held virtually anywhere else in the world. But this was Belfast, the blazing heart of Northern Ireland, where sanity was a concept seriously out of fashion. With the election only twenty-four hours old, the Irish "Troubles" were heating up again, threatening to spiral as badly out of control as they had in the middle decades of the previous century. And Captain Trevor Stirling was caught in the middle, a place where no self-respecting Scotsman had any business to be.

Worse still, it was his ruddy birthday.

Stirling stood gazing down at the cake for long moments, its multitude of candles a disquieting sight against the backdrop of the grim barracks. The dip and flare of the flames echoed other fires, causing Trevor to recall stories about the explosion of '69, when half of Belfast had burned. He'd lost a great-uncle in the fighting, an idealistic Scots lad sent in by Britain to keep the peace. Young Trevor McArdle, his mother's only uncle, had been caught dead in the cross fire.

Now it was Trevor Stirling's turn.

Memory replayed, cuttingly, the moment four years previously, when Trevor had come home to his mother's cottage an hour outside Edinburgh, bursting with the news.

"I've just joined the Special Air Services!" he'd shouted, jubilant to be following a good half of his male progenitors.

She'd run into the bedroom, weeping.

He hadn't really understood why—until his unit was posted to Belfast.

Stirling glanced up from the cake to see Murdoch, cavorting as usual in his underwear and trading ribald jokes with Balfour and Hennessey, who were shouting out punch lines above the blare of music. Good men to have at one's back in a place like this, among the best in his command, in fact, and they hadn't forgotten his birthday, despite the rising tensions and sporadic outbreaks of violence. He supposed there were worse situations in which to find oneself. Nor was he afraid of the job he'd been sent here to do. He just wished somebody else had been sent to do it, since he couldn't see either side in the centuries-old feud backing off or seeing reason.

Stirling squinted back down at the flaming cake, attempting to count the improbable number of lit candles, and had just come to the conclusion there were seven too many, when Colonel Ogilvie sent the barracks-room door crashing back into the wall. Laughter and party uproar chopped off. Someone killed the music even as Stirling snapped around, blazing cake already forgotten. He blanched at the look on Ogilvie's face.

"We've got riots heating up in West Belfast, boys,"

the colonel growled, voice harsh with strain. "God-damned Paisleyites are burning down Clonard Gardens and ten blocks surrounding Divis Street, and the IRA's not having any of it."

They scrambled for riot gear amidst a clang of slamming locker doors and thudding boots. Candles guttered out on the forgotten cake, puddling into rainbows of melted wax across the frosting. Chairs went crashing in the rush. Stirling prided himself on being first out the door, shoving all civilian concerns back into a little-used corner of his mind. On a job like this, anything less was suicide. Murdoch and Balfour were right on his heels, Murdoch still struggling with zippers and Velcro on hastily donned battle gear. A convoy of armored vehicles waited outside, engines idling in the muggy June heat.

Stirling stood by the barracks door, directing the lieutenants and sergeants who reported to him while other sections down at the next barracks did the same into a second line of troop transports. Stirling's men were counting off their squad members as they jumped into the lorries. One hundred twenty strong, in four-man fire teams, with lieutenants and sergeants shouting out their counts, the loading went smoothly, at top speed. Once the squads reporting to his section had called out their readiness by the numbers, Stirling flung himself over the tailgate of the final transport, mashing his radio send button to signal their readiness to move out.

Lieutenant Ian Howell and Sergeants Griffin and Everleigh, with their respective teams, plus the men of Stirling's own squad, had piled willy-nilly into the armored lorry's rear compartment, slamming loaded magazines into Browning Hi-Power pistols, SA-80 rifles, and MP5 submachine guns. Stirling was glad to have an MP5 in his hands, rather than the service Patchett regular troopers were issued.

As the lorries jerked into motion, Hennessey snarled

over his SA-80. "Wish to bloody hell Ministry of Defense had never adopted these useless bits of trash. IRA's got AR-180's, why the hell don't we?"

Lieutenant Howell muttered, "I'd like to see you try clearing snipers out of a building with those old SLRs some of the other units train with. Be bloody glad you've got an SA-80, not one of *those.*"

Nobody answered. They all knew exactly what Howell meant—the SLR was a good hundred and twenty centimeters long, a full meter and a third of another, impossible to take down a hallway without hanging up the muzzle on *something*. Hennessey growled obscenely again at the faulty magazine latch and shoved the loaded magazine in once more, ruthlessly ramming it home until it caught properly.

"What I wish," Murdoch muttered, finally righting his uniform, "is for those johnnies in the M.O.D. to pick somebody *else* for riot duty. Let the RUC handle things and send us home."

"Royal Ulster Constabulary, my arse," Balfour shot back. "Bunch of Paisleyite Orangemen, is more like, joined up after the Ulster Defense Force was outlawed, and the IRA jolly well knows it."

Stirling just grunted. The history of conflict in Northern Ireland was twisted enough to give even the slipperiest of diplomats a raging headache. *Nobody* understood Ireland. Except, of course, the bloody Irish. "Might've waited a few minutes longer," he grumbled under his breath. "Would've enjoyed at least blowing out the candles."

"Tough luck, Captain," Lieutenant Howell thumped Stirling's shoulder as the armored lorry jounced and jolted through Belfast at top speed. "And that lovely bird we hired hadn't even jumped out of the cake yet. Right raver, too, blonde and stacked, wearin' nothing but buttercream icing . . ."

"Prat," Stirling grinned. "And if you think Ogilvie'd let a stripper past security . . . Like as not, she'd be some Provo sympathizer, or worse yet, *Cumann Na Mbann,* and that'd be the end of us, right quick, now wouldn't it?" The SAS had learned the hard way how things worked in Northern Ireland. Up here, the Official IRA based out of Dublin—touted by London as *The Enemy* for most of the twentieth century—counted for nothing. It was the Provisionals, a splinter of the Officials born in the violence of '69, calling the shots in Belfast.

Literally.

Mostly out of Armalite rifles. And that wasn't counting all the little splinters who'd left the Provos in the '90s, at least three main groups of them, all hating the Protestant Orangemen with a peculiarly Irish virulence that spanned centuries. The newest IRA splinters made the Orangemen's paramilitaries look like schoolboys—and the Orange terror squads proudly claimed kinship with Attila the Hun.

And every man—and woman—jack of 'em, Protestant Orange or Catholic Green, hated the British military. Impartially and with a cold, calculating violence aimed mostly at SAS troops sent in to contain the damage. As a seasoned SAS captain with a full year's experience in Belfast—during which he'd watched seventeen of his mates shot and blown to pieces—Northern Ireland gave Trevor Stirling nightmares. It was little comfort that Northern Ireland's Troubles gave London's ministry types nightmares, as well.

They heard the riot and smelled the smoke long before the lorry ground its way to a halt. A hasty roadblock had been thrown across Percy Street. The ugly sound of shouting, of sporadic gunfire, smashing glass, and the unmistakable roar of a major fire blasted into the lorry right across the open tailgate. A stink of gasoline fumes, gunpowder, and burning buildings choked the blockaded road. Stirling jammed his helmet down tighter, gripped his MP5 in a sweaty fist, and jumped down into the middle of the hell sweeping through Clonard.

He peeled sharp left, taking up position along the wall their lorry had stopped beside, and directed his section out of their transports and into position along both sides of the street. In his own command squad, Balfour exited right, followed by Murdoch, who moved ahead of Stirling, then Hennessey, who took up position ahead of Balfour. The lorries lurched forward a few meters, giving them cover and spilling out other squads farther along the street, under Stirling's terse radio instructions. Static sputtered in his ear as more of his section reported taking up position.

Stirling swept the area with a quick, careful scrutiny, looking for trouble spots. The Catholic neighborhood consisted mainly of rundown flats, in grubby, multistory buildings owned by Protestants who refused to grant their tenants basic civil rights, never mind ordinary maintenance and upkeep, but charged rents triple the going rate across the border in the Irish Republic. Most of the windows in Stirling's line of sight were pouring black smoke and lurid flames, the classic trademark of the Orange paramilitary terror squads. Women and children ran like screaming ants, carrying whatever they'd managed to salvage and trying to stay clear of the gun battle raging from street to street. Sporadic weapons fire cracked like distant fireworks, the sharp reports of handguns and small-caliber carbines overlain by the deeper crashes and crumps of heavy rifles.

Stirling's hundred-twenty-man unit hadn't even finished piling out of their lorries when a howling mob of Orangemen burst into view from Divis Street, lobbing gasoline bombs through broken windows and raking the corner of Divis and Percy with small-weapons fire. Two women and several children, including a copper-haired little girl barely five years old, crashed to the pavement, screaming and writhing or bent at grotesque angles, ominously still in the glare of the flames. Then someone else opened fire from near the roof of a building three blocks distant and four Orangemen crumpled to the street, gut-shot.

The mob scattered, burning and shooting as they went. Stirling clenched his jaw and gripped his MP5 until his knuckles whitened, aching to fire into the thick of those bastards, but he was not about to shoot live ammunition into a crowd with women and children scattered through it. His radio sputtered with Ogilvie's voice, shouting, "The police are trying to contain them before they reach St. Peter's church and the school! Move out by sections and drive those damned Orangemen back, trap 'em between the police barricades and our guns! And for God's sake, watch the rooftops, we've got IRA sniper fire coming from everywhere, they're likely to take potshots at us for the sheer fun of it!"

"Bloody lovely!" Balfour snarled as their section ran forward in a flanking movement toward the Orangemen, leapfrogging their way under whatever cover was available. "The election of the century, they call it. Catholics claim they finally got a majority, while the Orangemen are claiming fraud, and bloody Sinn Fein's all set to vote in reunification with Dublin, like the IRA wanted for years. And now we've got the bleeding *Orangemen* bombing us. Goddamned Ministry of Defense would've done better to let us wipe this country down to bedrock!"

It was a common enough sentiment in the SAS, one that Stirling didn't share, as it happened; but he understood it, only too well. "Button it, Balfour," he snapped. "Before some Orange bastard blows your head off! You can't do a job while you're complaining! And put your bloody respirator on, we're about to pump CS at them!"

He jammed his own gas mask on, then they were in the thick of it and there was no time for anything but survival. They moved down Percy Street in relays, with McCrombie driving their armored command lorry at a slow crawl to provide cover wherever possible. Every doorway and window offering possible cover for gunmen brought sweat prickling out beneath Stirling's body armor. Unpleasant trickles ran down his brow and dripped stinging salt sweat into his eyes under the rubber mask, an added misery courtesy of the sticky, hot June weather. He blinked furiously to clear his vision, cursing the heat and the bloody "Troubles" that made tear gas necessary.

The Orange terror squads fell back under a steady hail of tear gas canisters fired into the mob, along with rubber shot and so-called baton rounds, thick oblongs of rubber fired from 37mm grenade launchers. They fired into the street just in front of the mob, sending the rubber projectiles cannoning like super-balls hurled with enough force to break bones.

The rioters melted into side streets to fight pitched battles with Catholic youths throwing rocks, broken bottles, and flaming gasoline bombs of their own. Orangemen shot back with pistols ranging from great-grandfather's Webley revolver to smuggled-in Makarovs manufactured three months previously in Russia, passing through three or four hands before ending on the streets of Belfast.

Surprisingly few IRA guns answered back. The price, Stirling realized after a moment's puzzlement, of keeping guerilla weapons scattered, part of the IRA's effort to keep its arsenal out of police and army hands during neighborhood sweeps. The IRA excelled at planning terrorist hits in advance, but responding to a sudden emergency was more difficult, given the level of searches these neighborhoods routinely underwent. It was ironic; the very reason the IRA had armed itself so heavily in the first place was situations exactly like this one, starting back in '69, with Orange terror squads burning Catholic neighborhoods, shooting civilians, and the ruddy police and outlawed B Special squads helping them do it. That was the whole reason the British army had been activated, to keep Orange-controlled police and their mates in the marching societies and paramilitary units from wholesale massacre of Catholic minority neighborhoods.

Not much had changed, since '69.

As homemade Molotov cocktails ran short in supply, lit car flares took their place, arcing through the air, crashing through windows and igniting curtains, upholstery, anything combustible in their path. If the fire fighters weren't brought in soon, all of West Belfast would go. Stirling's section left Percy Street under cover of their armored lorry, moving down Divis Street in an effort to drive the rioters into the police barricades set up this side of the school and neighboring church. Through his gas mask, Stirling caught sight of the police squadron at last, firing lead-filled, CS-coated bean bags from their grenade launchers into the melee, bringing down combatants from a distance of several meters. A couple of the constables gripped shotguns, as well, firing shot shells loaded with miniature rubber batons.

Unfortunately, the constables were firing indiscriminately at both Orange raiders and Catholic defenders, drawing the attention of someone with a high-powered rifle. A constable near the edge of the confusion screamed and went down, clutching his gut and bleeding between tight-clenched fingers. An instant later, a gun-wielding Orangeman suffered the same fate, sprawling under the rear bumper of a burning car.

"Got us a sodding sniper!" Murdoch shouted, ducking down. "Anybody see where he's firing from?"

Stirling scanned windows in a frantic effort to spot him, while the constables broke and ran—straight for the SAS lorry they were using for cover. "Bloody *damn*—"

He ate pavement as the constables skidded in. Bullets whined off concrete walls and window casements as the sniper tracked them. Policemen were shouting, "Do something! *Do something, goddammit!*" and Murdoch was screaming at them to shut up and keep out of the way. A stiff wind had sprung up, fanning flames and sweeping away clouds of CS gas. Stirling snatched off his gas mask, which was impeding his view, and raked the windows with a frantic gaze, looking for their hidden IRA gunman. He tracked movement at a broken fifth-story window—Christ, a ten-year-old kid without enough sense to hide, watching the riot like it was a thriller on the telly. "I don't see a thing, curse it!"

"Maybe he's broken through a roof somewhere, shooting through a hole in the roofing tiles? They've done it before, often enough."

Another constable went down less than a meter from Stirling's position, screaming and badly wounded. Orangemen were in retreat, firing at every window in sight, blasting away at shadows. The IRA sniper was driving them back from the church, at least, but there was no way to contain them as long as the sniper kept Stirling's section pinned, as well. "We've got us one savvy, trained sniper, here," he snarled. "Knows enough to keep back from the window, so we can't see spit!"

He rolled prone under the fender of their stationary lorry, where McCrombie had the advantage of bulletproof glass. Stirling craned his neck into contorted positions, trying to see the uppermost windows and rooflines without exposing himself to sniper fire. He was studying windowpanes in the building across the street from their riot-happy ten-year-old when he saw it. Reflected movement showed the boy leaping back from the window. The reflection also showed a flash of light from deeper inside the room: muzzle blast from their IRA gunman.

"Got him! Fifth floor, third window along from the corner! Bastard's using the boy for *reconnaissance*." God, putting the child between himself and the guns of the SAS . . . Irish Republican Army ruthlessness occasionally horrified Stirling.

One of the constables crowed, "Marvelous! We'll get that stinking gun out of his hands and off the streets!"

Stirling shot the copper a disgusted glance. "Isn't the bloody gun that's dangerous, mate, it's the man behind it. Stop thinking like a copper for a change, eh? These lovely blokes are trying to kill us, last I noticed, IRA and Orangemen alike. Take all the guns you can carry, they'll still kill you with rocks and bombs and bottles full of petrol."

While the copper sputtered, Murdoch growled, "We'll have to take him out, curse him. Can't get across there with him shooting at us and we can't contain those bleeding Orangemen, sitting on our bums!"

"If we had a Scorpion, like we keep asking London," Hennessey put in disgustedly, "that'd make quick work of it. Those 30mm cannons would take care of our IRA man up there, right handy, like."

"Yeh," Stirling shot back, "along with his neighbors and the building next door and the county over the border, besides. The very last thing those ministry types want is tracked vehicles rampaging through Belfast. Might look bad on the telly, come election time."

"So pump a CS canister in with him!" the constable snarled. "Isn't that what you SAS types are supposed to do? Control the bleeding snipers?"

"That'd be grand," Balfour growled, "if we hadn't shot the last canister three blocks back."

The constables were out of CS rounds, as well.

And none of the other squads in his unit could get close enough to resupply them, what with the emergencies under way all around them and the very sniper they needed to take out controlling the entire street. Stirling cursed long and loud. "Right, then. I'm in command of the entry team, so it's my job, isn't it? I'll circle round the block, get in from behind while you draw his fire. Murdoch, you're with me. Lay down a covering fire, mates. And try not to hit the boy, eh? I don't want careers ruined and good men jailed for shooting the lad, no matter what his Da's using him for, up there!"

"No, no, don't bloody well shoot at *all*!" one of the constables yelled, even as Stirling took to his heels, running at a low crouch, MP5 held at the ready, and calling in his situation over his command radio set, keeping his own commander and lieutenants informed. Unfortunately, two of the constables were following Stirling and Murdoch, howling like a bunch of disappointed soccer fans.

"Dammit, you'll tip him off, tell him we know where he is! He'll jump ship before you're even close—"

A rifle bullet snapped past Stirling's ear, striking sparks along the brick wall. He ran faster, trying to gain the corner, and cursed the interference of bloody, stupid coppers and their fixation on taking the guns and capturing the shooters, rather than stopping the immediate threat. The rest of the unit finally opened up with a withering hail of fire, clearly having won the argument with the balance of the coppers. The heavy barrage drove the sniper back, giving them a clear chance to cross the street. Stirling speeded up, racing across the open road for cover on the far side. Fierce heat from a blazing tenement blasted down an alleyway, then they were past and running for the corner. Behind them, a steady rattle of semiautomatic fire chattered, most of it coming from Stirling's pinned-down squad, with periodic shots from high overhead, where the IRA gunman held them off.

He skinned over a wall in a rollover, never lifting more than his shoulder blades above the top, and dropped into a dingy yard where a couple of cats huddled under a scraggly bush. Murdoch was over in a flash, darting ahead to kick out a window. The coppers came over the wall awkwardly, heading automatically toward the rear door.

"Get down, you bloody fools!" Stirling snapped. "Never use the doors, they expect that!"

Murdoch was already inside, through the broken window. Stirling followed, motioning the constables back when they tried to follow too closely. Stirling and Murdoch eased across the room, weapons held at low-ready position, butt-stocks tucked into their shoulders, muzzles pointed toward the floor. Easing round a corner with a rifle at low ready, a bloke didn't advertise his presence, whereas carrying it the way chaps did over in America, snout up, the first thing round a corner was the muzzle. Jolly bad form and a good way to die, trying that in Belfast.

The lower corridor was clear. They raced for the staircase, moving fast and low, coming around corners at a crouch, down where the average man wouldn't be expecting them. On the third-floor landing, screams erupted from several flats and a rush of feet came charging down the corridor.

"What the devil—" one of the constables began.

A pack of women, many of them carrying small children, stampeded into the stairwell, running wild-eyed past Stirling, Murdoch, and the panting constables. One of the girls, fifteen at a glance, snarled at them on her way past.

"What the hell are you doing in here, eh? Chasing the only man with guts enough to shoot back at those butchers? Why don't you British bastards go after the Orangemen for a change?" She spat in his face, then fled down the stairs.

It wouldn't have done any good to tell her they would *already* have gone after the Orangemen, if the sodding IRA sniper hadn't pinned them down, preventing it.

Meanwhile, smoke poured down the stairwell in the wake of the fleeing women. Stirling cursed under his breath. "Upstairs, double time, he'll make every shot count, now the building's been torched." If he hadn't gone already, running for safety in the confusion.

Two more flights up, twisting round the landings, and they'd gained the fifth floor. Doors stood open, flats abandoned by panic-stricken residents. A chatter of gunfire sounded through broken windows from the street below. The sound of return fire from the IRA gunman was unexpected music in Stirling's ears. Their sniper wasn't as well trained as he'd thought. He was still in the room, shooting. A fully trained IRA man would've bolted the moment he saw two SAS soldiers leave their squad to head his way. Stirling motioned for the constables to stay back, then eased forward, listening intently with every step. Murdoch crept from doorway to doorway, checking each room along the corridor before slipping past. They leapfrogged cautiously down the hall, then it came again: the crump of a heavy rifle firing, three doors along, and a male voice saying, "Keep your bloody head down, lad, bastards down there'll shoot it off!"

Bullets were ripping into the hallway, slapping through the hollow-core door and punching like icepicks through thin, poorly constructed walls, embedding themselves into the ceiling. Stirling's section was doing a marvelous job of pinning him down so he couldn't run without exposing himself worse than he was already. He keyed his radio and whispered, "Cease fire, we're going in," then nodded silently. Murdoch nodded back, exchanging ready signals. The firing from the street stopped and they entered with a diving roll through the smashed-down door. Murdoch and he fired simultaneously. The sniper jerked wildly and went down with a gurgling cry, hit at least five times. In one corner, hiding behind a bookcase, the boy crouched with both arms over his head, screaming.

"Get out of here, boy," Murdoch snarled, jerking him up from his corner by one thin arm. "Building's burning round your ears!"

"You shot me Da!"

"Life's tough, mate," Murdoch bit out, dragging the boy along. "He was trying to kill us, last I noticed. Move it, lad, or we'll leave you to burn with him."

"Easy, Murdoch," Stirling pulled the boy out of the younger man's grip, "he's a scared kid who's just watched his father die. C'mon, lad, you can't stay here. Where's your mother, then?"

The boy shook his head. "Orangemen shot her."

Wonderful. Another orphan who'd grow up hating Protestants and blaming the British army. It never ended. "I'm sorry about that, lad. Come on, now, before we're trapped by the fire." He glanced around for the constables and swore under his breath. They were ransacking the flat, snatching out drawers, dumping contents across the floor, rifling the gunman's pockets.

"What in hell are you doing?"

"Looking for evidence! Lists of his mates, telephone numbers—"

Murdoch grabbed the nearest by the shoulder and roared, "Leave it, you bloody stupid bastards! It's a battle zone out there and the building's on fire! Worry about arresting the IRA when the smoke clears!"

They cursed, but complied, stuffing handfuls of the dead man's personal papers into their own pockets on the way. Murdoch radioed down that they'd cleared the sniper and Stirling picked up the terrified boy, carrying him. He managed to snag a family photograph on his way out the door. "There's a good lad, hold this." He shoved the photo into the boy's hands and set out for the stairwell at a fast jog. They left the tenement considerably faster than they'd entered, plunging down the smoke-filled stairwell past blazing corridors and other fleeing refugees. Stirling saw a woman carrying nothing of her own.

"Here, take the lad, would you? He's just lost his dad and mum."

She took the boy wordlessly, fleeing ahead of them down the stairs.

They exited the way they'd come in, through the rear of the building, only to be met by a howling mob of Orangemen, emboldened once more by the silence of the sniper. "Get the civilians out of here!" Stirling shouted at the constables, then he opened fire with a three-shot burst of full-auto fire, bringing down a man pointing a pistol at them. The mob checked its forward momentum, dispersing instants later under a hail of live fire, giving the women and children time to get clear, running down an alleyway. "Bloody bastards!" Stirling growled, slamming another magazine home. "I've had just about enough . . . of Northern Ireland's *Troubles!*"

"Amen to that," Murdoch agreed, firing at another gunman who'd paused to snap off shots in their direction. "I'd give all the money in Threadneedle Street to be sitting in some pub in Cheapside, right about now!"

"Tell me one I don't know, mate. It's my bleeding birthday."

They cleared the remaining Orange mob, driving them into the fringes of a bottle-throwing pack of young Catholics bent on vengeance. For once, Stirling was inclined to let them settle it amongst themselves. At least the Orangemen would be too occupied to torch any more flats.

He and Murdoch had just reached the corner again, trying to rejoin their section, when a delivery van skidded round at high speed, plowing straight toward the melee of rock-throwing Catholics and, coincidentally, toward the rest of their unit and the embattled constables who'd taken cover with them. Halfway there, the driver skidded the brakes, bailing out as the van slewed and slowed. The man ran back toward Stirling and Murdoch at breakneck speed while the van careened in a spinning turn toward the SAS position.

Realization struck instants too late.

"Bomb!"

The concussion hurled Stirling five meters through the air. The whole city block erupted in flame. Murdoch slammed into a parked car, flung like a doll by the force of the explosion. Buildings to either side crumbled into the street, smashing down in a ruin of bricks, mortar, and twisted pipe. The rock-throwing Catholics vanished in a blazing rain of debris. A heavy tiled roof crashed down across Stirling's entire section,

burying them under a belching avalanche of flame and
broken buildings. Then Stirling smashed into something incredibly hard and the whole world faded into
dim grey chaos.

He roused briefly into an unwanted reality where
the only sensation was a throbbing mass of pain the
length of his body. Some unknown stretch of time after
that, a rosary swung into his field of view, dangling
above his face. Urgent voices floated to him where he
lay at the bottom of a very deep pit.

"Is he still alive, Father?"

"Yes, God be praised, help me carry him to an
ambulance. . . ."

They lifted him from the pavement, instantly rousing
all the demons of hell in a vengeful dance. They stampeded *en masse* from Stirling's skull to the toes of his
combat boots. He tried to scream and mercifully lost
consciousness, instead. He had no idea how long he'd
been out when reality finally firmed again, piecemeal.
Bits of him hurt worse than others and his ears didn't
seem to be working properly. Sounds came in a
confused jumble of voices and meaningless noise.
Gradually Stirling differentiated various sensations as
the tug of bandages, a sharp ache from an IV feed in
the crook of one elbow, a plaster cast around one wrist,
something stiff, a brace maybe, around one knee, and
the tug of stitches along his face, down one arm, and
across his torso. Stirling's hearing cleared up next,
bringing order from the chaotic noise. He made out
the sounds of monitors beeping softly, a rattle of glassware, hushed voices in a corridor somewhere nearby,
sobbing voices farther off, and somewhere in close
proximity, a very young child screaming in endless,
mindless agony . . .

Hospital, Stirling realized fuzzily. *They got me to*

hospital through that mess, that priest and whoever was with him. Gratitude prickled behind his eyelids and thickened his throat, making him long mightily for the strength to blow his nose. Instead he lay quietly, trying to recover the use of more of his senses. Vision cleared at last, revealing a stark white ceiling, equally stark walls, and the steel railings of a hospital bed. He lay in a casualty ward, with gurneys stacked in the spaces between the regular beds, all filled with badly injured civilians. In the corridor just beyond, Stirling could see harried doctors and nurses performing miracles of triage, routing the worst cases into surgery. He wondered how long he'd been here. Whether any of his command had survived that car bomb. If *his* commanding officer knew where he was.

He tried not to wonder how badly injured he might be.

Time stretched out in that endless way it does when the body is too traumatized to move, but the mind is too alert to sleep. Stirling was left with no activity to distract him, save listening to the unfolding chaos out in the corridor. More wounded were arriving every minute, giving him all too grim a notion of how badly the riot had spread through West Belfast. Eventually, footsteps entering the ward roused him to greater attention. Stirling focused on three figures approaching his bed, one dressed in hospital whites, one in the unrelieved black of the Catholic priesthood, and the third in badly stained battle gear. Surprise registered when he recognized Colonel Ogilvie. The look crackling through the colonel's eyes told Stirling the most important news of all. None of his section had made it out of that street alive. God, a hundred and twenty good soldiers, snuffed out in an instant. And who knew how many innocent civilians with them . . .

" . . . captain is very lucky that Father McCree, here, pulled him out of the rubble," the doctor was saying.

"I'm afraid we weren't able to reach the others," the priest said in response, an exhausted note of horror wavering through his voice. "The whole block of flats came down, buried the whole of Divis Street in burning rubble. The entire SAS unit was under it, along with at least a dozen constables and a whole crowd of boys, most of them no older than sixteen."

Ogilvie nodded sharply. "I'm grateful to you, Father, for rescuing at least one of my lads." Ogilvie's radio crackled and he listened, then spat orders. The next moment, he'd reached the bedside. "Stirling, it's good to see you. Doctors tell me you're bloody lucky, son."

"Sorry, sir," he croaked out, horrified by the rasping, watery whisper of his voice. "Orange bastard drove a panel van past us, cram full of explosives. Didn't twig to it, not until it was too bloody late . . ."

"Easy, son." Ogilvie pressed his shoulder with one calloused, grime-streaked hand. "It's no use blaming yourself for a suicidal maniac. They've set off half a dozen other car bombs of the same type, set to blow on timers. Run 'em into a big crowd of Catholics with a margin of a few seconds for the drivers to get clear. There's no way anyone could've stopped it. Believe me, we've tried. Shooting the drivers doesn't stop the bloody bombs ticking and they're on too short a timer to defuse 'em."

Stirling wanted to be comforted by the news, but all he could see was Murdoch slamming into that parked car, buildings toppling down across his men, crushing anyone who might've survived the initial blast. Maybe Balfour had been right, after all. Scouring this place to bedrock seemed a sane solution, in light of the Orange terror machine's latest atrocities. Stirling had never expected to understand the IRA's hatred of the Orangemen as thoroughly as he did now. Not that the IRA was any better, for all that they didn't torch Protestant neighborhoods the way the Orange paramilitaries torched Catholic ones. They preferred blowing up crowded shops and pubs, instead, and SAS facilities, vehicle checkpoints and RUC stations, or executing prominent Protestant politicians, government officials, and members of the British Royal family. The worst of it was, he couldn't see any way to end it. Not with both sides demanding total capitulation to mutually exclusive goals. The hollow feeling in his chest terrified him.

Ogilvie squeezed his shoulder again. "Rest for now, Stirling. We'll talk again when you've recovered a bit more. The doctors will take proper care of you."

"Yes, sir," he whispered, utterly empty inside.

He faded into sleep while the doctor was still telling him about his injuries.

Chapter Two

The sway of the train and the steady clacking of wheels across joints in the track might have lulled Stirling to sleep, if the dull throb of pain from wrist and knee hadn't kept up a steady counterpoint to the rhythm of the rails. He'd sat stiffly upright and correct in his seat for the first quarter of an hour out of the station, before giving up all pretense of appearances and simply eased himself into the least uncomfortable position he could manage. The newspaper he'd picked up in London lay in untidy folds on the seat, unable to hold his interest despite articles on Northern Ireland's continuing Troubles and some archaeologist's claim that a major volcanic eruption on Krakatoa in the middle of the sixth century A.D. had disrupted worldwide weather patterns for more than a decade, triggering the worldwide failure of agriculture, the mass migration of various peoples and a spread of plague throughout Britain, all across Europe, even creating population upheavals in Ireland. The bloke quoted in the article even blamed the eruption for the Dark Age's collapse of European civilization—including the defeat of King Arthur's Britons by Saxon invaders.

Somehow, he couldn't work up much enthusiasm about events from the year 538 A.D. when his body ached from still-mending injuries sustained in a firefight he should never have been involved in, in the first bloody place. He had, at least, come a long way since his initial discharge from hospital. Belfast to Blackpool by military airlift, down through Manchester and Derbyshire by rail to London and a battery of surgical specialists to repair his knee, then from London to York and points north by rail, on his way to a new posting he didn't particularly want. In fact, the only good thing he could find in the assignment Ogilvie had handed him, his first day out of rehab in London hospital, was the location.

Trevor Stirling hadn't been home in four years.

He'd forgotten how much he loved the dour Scottish hills until the train plunged over the edge of the Southern Uplands, revealing Edinburgh spread out in the late afternoon, golden light spilling across the Lothians and the Pentland Hills which swept down to the very edge of town. A storm front was moving in, scudding low over Arthur's Seat, an achingly familiar mountain that lifted its brooding black profile well above the prominence of Calton Hill. The Palace of Holyroodhouse and Edinburgh Castle dominated the skyline along the rocky spine known as Royal Mile, which ran slap through the heart of Old Town. The train roared its way across the high spans of the Forth rail bridge, far above the glimmering waters of the Firth of Forth, while the leading edge of the storm obscured all but a smudge of the Highland ranges in the distance.

Stirling leaned back against the seat, abruptly

exhausted by the hours-long train ride up from London. His wrist, broken in several places beneath the cast, ached and his newly repaired knee had swollen up and gone stiff inside its brace. It had needed surgery to repair damaged cartilage and torn ligaments. He wouldn't be seeing combat for a good, long while yet, a prospect that both dismayed and relieved him. Lying about in hospital with far too much time on his hands had eaten ragged holes in his self-confidence. When finally released, he'd left the hospital with a cane, a bad limp, and a gnawing fear that he'd be useless to the regiment.

And Ogilvie, never the fool, had spotted the trouble at once. His final debriefing flashed through a memory still raw from his own inadequacy: the slow limp toward a chair, the stiff knee and the stiffer scotch Ogilvie poured and pressed into his hand, the embarrassed flush of awkwardness, easing himself down into the chair.

"I've been giving some thought to your future with the regiment, Stirling," Ogilvie said quietly, steepling his fingertips. "Your record is exemplary, your loyalty unquestionable, which is why I'm considering you for special assignment."

Stirling lowered his glass cautiously. "Special assignment, sir?"

"We've had a request from the Home Secretary's Office for someone with experience in Belfast. Seems the IRA's been showing interest in a research facility they've tucked away in a nice, quiet little spot in the Scottish Lowlands. They want someone up there who understands the IRA. I've recommended you."

Dismay rose like bile in his gorge. "Research facility? Are you fobbing me off with an assignment to guard a bunch of ruddy scientists?"

Ogilvie grinned. "Pegged it straight off, didn't you?

I know what you're thinking and you're not far wrong. This business has shaken you, lad, whether you admit it or don't, and frankly, I can't afford to send anyone up there who's not already sick-listed. We're short-handed until we can bring in replacements. You can't function on the streets with a partially rehabilitated knee and a broken wrist, but you're certainly up to handling this little job. Think of it as a holiday, if you like. Or call it a belated birthday present from your colonel. I think," he added with a quirk of the lips, "you'll rather fancy the research site."

"Oh?"

The colonel chuckled. "You hale from the Highlands, don't you?"

"Stirling, actually," he nodded, "gateway to the Highlands. Straddles the only mountain pass between the Highlands and the Scottish Lowlands." Stirling Castle, whose walls overlooked seven major battlefields, including Robert the Bruce's resounding victory over England's Edward II at Bannockburn, was legendary in the annals of Scottish history. And if legend were to be trusted, even King Arthur had understood its strategic value, wresting a much older fortress on the site from a Saxon army. "My ancestors go back a ways," he added with a wry twist of the lips. "There've been Stirlings in Stirling since time immemorial."

"That's grand, then. You'll be familiar with the countryside and the locals will trust you as one of their own. It's a delicate situation, calls for a man good with people. I've half a dozen other men sick-listed that I might've recommended for this job, but they haven't either the people skills or the Scots background we want. You're the man for it, no mistake. Study the file on your way up," Ogilvie added, handing over a sealed manila envelope. "Your train leaves for Edinburgh in two hours, the best transportation I could manage on short notice, since you're in no shape to be driving, and I can't commandeer military transport for one man. Wouldn't send the message we want, anyway. We're not taking them over, at the lab, we're protecting them. You'll be met by a car from the research site when you reach Edinburgh. Stop in and say hello to your family for a few days, when the job's done. You've earned that much, at least."

"Yes, sir," he said, trying to conceal the glum disappointment settling over him. Sent packing to stand watch over a gaggle of scientists . . . "Thank you, sir," he added unhappily, finishing the scotch and accepting the envelope with his new orders.

Ogilvie just grinned and clapped him on the shoulder.

Two hours later, he had limped aboard the train, found his seat, and rumbled northward through a wet English morning, heading home for an assignment no SAS man in his right mind would have volunteered for. *Bloody holiday, my arse,* he thought uncharitably, scanning the dossier on the so-called research facility. *What in hell's the IRA thinking, to be interested in a crackpot scheme like this?* Come to that, what was the Home Secretary's Office thinking, to be funding such a thing? *Time travel,* no less. Bloody lot of nonsense and a frightful waste of taxpayers' money.

They hit a delay on the line when the train was forced to stop while crews worked to clear wet leaves from the rails. The weight of trains crushed the leaves into a gluelike sludge so slick trains had literally slid through stations, on occasion, unable to brake and ending derailed with passengers injured. The bane of British rail travel, thousands of pounds of fallen leaves every year required work crews to strip the rails by hand with sandpaper and cleaning solvents.

Accustomed to military transport, Stirling had forgotten how frustrating such delays could be, particularly when he was tired and hurting.

They finally jerked into motion again, houses and familiar landmarks flashing wetly past. Castle Rock, the Scott Monument with its Gothic spires, and the porticoes of Greek-style art galleries . . . By the time they finally chugged into Waverly Station at city center, depositing Stirling on the pavement along with the rest of the bleary-eyed flotsam spilling out through the station doors, the storm front had rolled across the city. A cold rain was pouring, typical of Scotland's weather, although Edinburgh's was generally drier than Glasgow's, farther west.

Limping through the station, Stirling fought a running battle just to keep his eyes open. *Should've slept on the run up from London* . . . Belfast had robbed him of the ability to fall asleep in public places. Maneuvering through a crowd with a duffel over one shoulder, one wrist in a splint and the other braced through the cuff of a crutch-style cane, all in a stinging downpour, wasn't a great deal easier than threading through a riot in Clonard. Several people jostled him painfully, muttering brief apologies to the injured bloke in uniform before hurrying on their way.

He finally reached the curb and scanned the line of cars queued up there, squinting against drenching gusts of rain, hopeful he wouldn't have to wait long. He spotted an ancient Land Rover, allowed his gaze to slide past, then snapped it back with a rising sense of dismay. The driver, a boyish chap who at second glance might have been as much as thirty, was leaning patiently against the battered fender, holding a ratty umbrella and a hand-scrawled sign that said, innocuously enough, STIRLING. Whether it was meant to identify him by name or point out their destination hardly mattered. The driver caught sight of him next moment and hurried over to take his duffel.

"You'd be Captain Stirling, then?"

"I would," he allowed.

"Marc Blundell, project liaison and dog's body. If anything wants fetching, I'm the one to do it." Blundell eyed the wrist cast and the crutch-cane with a dubious glance. "Training accident?"

"No." It came out stiffer than his knee. "Clonard."

Blundell's eyes widened. "Bugger, you say? The *election riots*? Bad luck, mate."

Stirling didn't bother to respond. No civilian could possibly understand, anyway.

A flush crept up Blundell's neck. "Right. Well. Let's be off, shall we? Beastly weather, it usually is." Blundell hunted through pockets for keys, unlocked the doors, and tossed Stirling's duffel into the backseat. "Put yourself in the passenger's seat, Captain. Would you be needing to go the messages before we leave town?"

Stirling paused in the midst of wrestling one-handed with the door latch, surprised into a faint smile. Scots dialect, its English idiom influenced to an improbable degree by past ties to France, sounded at once alien and the most heartwarming thing he'd heard in four years. "Thanks, but no, I did my shopping in London before the train went."

Blundell gave him another quick, narrow-eyed once-over, followed abruptly by a cheery grin. "You're a Scots lad, then? No lowland Englishman would've understood that."

Stirling finally wrenched open the passenger door with a scream of rusted hinges, legacy of Scotland's eternal damp. The interior of the Land Rover smelled of mildew and stale pipe smoke; the pipe lay upended in the ash tray. He eased himself into the seat. "I was born in Stirling, as a matter of fact. Took a university degree from Edinburgh before signing on with the SAS."

"A university man, now?" Blundell muttered, brows twitching upward as he slid behind the wheel. "That's one we didn't expect. What was it you studied?"

"History, as it happens. Military history, mostly."

Blundell's second once-over was even keener than the first. "You'll fit the bill better than we thought, then. Belt yourself in, Captain, and we'll be off. It's a bit of a drive to Stirling and the weather's supposed to worsen toward evening."

That, at least, was no surprise. The Land Rover roared away from the curb with a surprising burst of speed which spoke of careful maintenance to the engine, whatever the condition of the chassis and hinges. Blundell negotiated afternoon rush-hour traffic with ease while the windscreen wipers played a slap-swash melody against the glass. As he made the turning onto the M9 Motorway northwest out of Edinburgh, Blundell said, "The site is well away from town, between Culross and Stirling proper, so make yourself comfortable."

Stirling grimaced. "Right." He eased his leg into a new position.

"There's coffee in the thermos, if you want it," he added, nodding toward a large canister between the seats, along with two plastic cups. "Might warm you up a bit, after that drenching rain."

Given the lack of heat emanating from the Land Rover's vents—simple openings onto the engine block, not a proper heater at all—Stirling poured coffee and gulped it gratefully. Not as satisfying as tea, but warm and chock-full of caffeine, which he needed rather badly.

"Were you posted to Belfast long?" Blundell asked at length.

"Long enough. A year."

"Not a good one, this last year. Bit of a mess."

There wasn't much point in answering.

Blundell glanced his way again "You've experience with the IRA, at least. We'll need that."

Stirling studied Blundell's profile. Despite his apparent youthfulness, the skin around his eyes was taut and the muscles along his jaw had bunched into corded knots. "Trouble?"

"Not yet. We're expecting it, though. Leastways, I am. Some of the others . . ." Blundell paused, reddening slightly. "You'll see when we arrive, I'm afraid. Security is a joke."

Much like the project, Stirling thought uncharitably. *Time travel . . .* He'd be a laughingstock when word got round the regiment. He could hear it now: *Have you heard about Stirling's latest conquest? Went haring off into the bloody Lowlands, chasing terrorists who've better sense than fall for a hare-brained scheme like time travel. Poor bugger, never was the same after Clonard . . .*

"I brought along employment dossiers," Blundell interrupted his glum maunderings. The project liaison was rummaging in a file box behind the thermos. "Thought you might like to get started," he added with an uncertain smile, "since it's a bit of a drive up and there's not much to see, with this rain."

"Thanks." He hoped it hadn't come out quite as dryly as he feared.

Blundell glanced rather sharply at him, then switched his attention back to the road, which flowed like a creek with runoff from the storm. "Don't mention it. I'll leave you to study our profiles, then."

The chatty project liaison fell silent at last. Stirling opened the first file as the tires whined along the broad motorway, skirting the long reach of the Firth of Forth estuary. Paper rattled and crinkled as he read through the dossiers, the sound quiet against a backdrop of drumming rain and occasional rumbles of thunder. The staff were a mixed lot, which he already knew, of course, having read Ogilvie's files, but the employment dossiers gave him a different slant on the resident scientific team. At the very least, the files drew his attention away from the aches in wrist and knee.

The first on his list was Terrance Beckett, project director and quantum physicist, with degrees from Oxford and an American university called MIT. His chief assistant, London-born Zenon Mylonas, obviously of Greek immigrant descent, had advanced degrees in quantum mechanics and theoretical mathematics. They jointly supervised the work of graduate student Fairfax Dempsey, another quantum physicist. All three men haled from England, with unimpeachable backgrounds, and all three had been with the project for more than a year. Irma Hubert, the only female mathematician among them, had joined the project six months previously, and Wilbur Rosswald, physicist, had come aboard five weeks ago.

Cedric Banning, one of the six senior scientists, was involved with an unlikely field called psychoneuro-immunology, with a specialty in bioenergetic plasma fields, whatever those were. He, too, supervised a graduate student, a fairly recent addition to the staff. Jill Dearborne had been recruited by Terrance Beckett himself, three weeks previously. Banning had been with the project for two months, replacing a plasma-field specialist killed in a motor crack-up, victim of a blinding rainstorm and wet pavements. Banning hailed from Australia originally, but had been raised in Manchester, according to his security clearance paperwork.

Marc Blundell, intent on his driving and fumbling

tobacco into his pipe, might not look the part, but
evidently was a quantum mechanics genius, thus prov-
ing that appearances had very little in common with
talent. He was the official project liaison with the
Home Secretary's Office, as well, which suggested
shortcomings in Terrance Beckett's personality. Indrani
Bhaskar, Whitechapel native, had won a scholarship to
Oxford, where she had distinguished herself to the
point of winning a professorship of history early in her
career. Clayton Crandall and Amber Darnell served
Bhaskar as assistant historians.

, Quite a mixed bag, and he hadn't even reached the
bottom of the pile.

Norvell Mann was resident computer programmer,
working with Elsa Maynard, computer hardware technician. Then there was Edsel Cuthbert, data analyst;
Leo Hobart, who performed complicated computer
modeling scenarios; and Sergio Donatelli, computer
data tech. The entire computer technical staff hailed
from London. Not one had reached their thirtieth
birthday, yet. Twenty-odd was plenty of time to develop
clandestine connections, of course, but none seemed
to *have* any connection to Ireland.

In fact, there was only one person on the entire
team who *did* have such a connection: Dr. Brenna
McEgan, whose work in physiology and psychological
biochemistry sounded as much like gibberish as bioenergetic plasma fields. She was even newer to the
team than Banning, having arrived only four weeks
previously. McEgan, too, was a replacement. The crack-
up that had killed Banning's predecessor had also
killed the team's physiologist, leaving two critical holes
to be filled in the senior research team. McEgan had
been educated in Dublin, according to her dossier,
but her birthplace was Londonderry, a Catholic
stronghold of Northern Ireland. She had inherited an

assistant named Cameron Blair, who served as medical technician.

Stirling narrowed his eyes. He wanted a word with Mr. Cameron Blair. Several words, in fact. Although he disliked snap judgements, the leading candidate for IRA activity was clearly Brenna McEgan. He frowned and pulled thoughtfully at his lower lip. There were plenty of other newcomers to the staff, of course, and the IRA certainly wasn't above paying someone to do their snooping for them, although it wasn't their usual *modus operandi*. He'd have to thoroughly investigate everyone, while working up new security procedures. A prickly problem, right enough, with too many unanswered questions simmering in his mind and a staff so large, any terrorist in the neighborhood could drive a bloody lorry through the possible security holes.

He read them through twice, then set the last one aside, fishing through pockets for an anti-inflammatory which he swallowed with coffee from Blundell's thoughtful thermos. He sipped, grateful for the warmth. As they rounded a long, sweeping curve in the road, he said, "You haven't included the peripherals in these dossiers."

"Peripherals?" Blundell echoed, eyes widening in uncertain surprise. "What d'you mean?"

"Cleaning crews, groundskeepers, maintenance men, what have you. Peripheral staff."

A look of utter chagrin stole a march across the liaison's boyish face. "Hadn't thought of that."

Stirling held back a sigh. "How many?"

"Let's see . . . Four—no, five. A charwoman, she comes every day for the cleaning; the groundsman and his assistant, they come round weekly; the equipment technician, he comes every five days or so for adjustments and spot checks. Then there's the lady who runs the concession, she comes in every couple of days to fill the machines. Oh, make it six, some days she sends her eldest daughter. Girl's sharp as a razor, but a sweet little thing. Completely wasted filling machines with candy bars and suchlike. Ought to be at college, someplace, but they haven't the funds and her father's that sick, her mother needs her at home."

A good candidate for bribe money, then, from any IRA mole wanting access or information. "Any of them housed on site?"

"Not the peripherals, as you call them. Not all the staff, for that matter. Team's grown, these last few months, and we haven't enough space in the cottages to accommodate everyone. McEgan lives off site, so do Banning and Mylonas, from the senior group, and most of the assistants rent rooms, as well."

"There's a gatekeeper, surely, acting as a security checkpoint?"

Blundell's chagrin deepened visibly. "Well, actually, we haven't needed any such precautions. Until now." He cleared his throat. "We're accustomed to civilian status, y'see. It's only recently, with the Home Office's interest, that we've realized there might be military or terrorist applications to our work."

Stirling sighed aloud this time. Blundell was right. If this were their notion of security, it *was* a joke. Civilian scientists, too myopic to comprehend realities like Belfast . . . It'd been too long since the IRA had bombed London or Manchester. Riots and bombings in Clonard notwithstanding, people outside Ireland— with the exception of the London ministries—were beginning to forget the dangers of civil disturbances spiraling out of control.

It was nearly dark by the time they turned off the main road, several kilometers short of Stirling, with its century-spanning history of warfare and its high cliff where Stirling Castle sat—if legend was correct—atop the remains of a Dark Ages stronghold that had been named as one of King Arthur's fortresses, possibly even ranking as a "second Camelot." Caerleon and Carlisle, down in the border counties, vied for the honor of "first Camelot."

The familiar, much loved countryside stirred long-forgotten memories, adventures with schoolmates, playing rough-and-tumble war games up the slopes surrounding Stirling Castle, pretending he and his mates were knights of the Round Table. No remains had been found, of course, but neither he nor his mates had cared one whit for archaeological evidence. It was the romance of it that mattered.

As he glanced out the Land Rover's windows at the rain-darkened slopes, Trevor Stirling allowed himself a slightly bitter smile. What fools they'd been, playing at war in these hills. Warfare in the sixth century had doubtless been a bloody business, as grimly devastating to civilian populations as it was in the twenty-first century. Stirling was no longer interested in the tales which both his grandfathers—Scots and Welsh—had recounted, of brave British chieftains holding back incursions of barbarians from Saxony, from Jutland in Denmark, from Ireland and the Pictish Highlands.

Fighting a sixth-century war would've been bloody hard business, even against more favorable odds than the Britons had faced. When all was said and done, what had Arthur really accomplished? A delay of the inevitable for a few decades? Stirling closed his eyes. God, he was tired of the fighting . . . Which was exactly why Ogilvie had sent him up here, rather than posting him back to Belfast. He wasn't fit for duty any longer.

As the Land Rover's headlamps picked out the rough asphalt track Blundell followed up into the mountains, Stirling's low opinion of security dropped even further. There *was* a fence, but no one guarded either its perimeter or its gate, which stood wide open. He didn't see so much as a watchdog. No cameras, either. Maybe the Home Office thought the project was as loony as he did? In which case, why bother to fund it?

A row of cottages stood along the access road, pre-fab affairs lacking any remotely attractive features, just dull little buildings of concrete where some of the on-site staff lived. "That largest cottage, there," Blundell pointed, "is Terrance Beckett's. You couldn't pry him away from here with all the whiskey in Whitechapel."

"What, he never goes into town at all? Doesn't he fancy a night at the pub now and again?"

Blundell grinned. "Oh, aye, now and again. But with the Falkland Arms just a few hundred meters down the road, why go all the way to Stirling? The Falklands run a nice pub, the local girls are pretty enough to suit, and the fish and chips better than any you'll find in Stirling proper."

"Yes, I know the Falklands, by reputation at least. We didn't move in the same circles. Where do your people stay, then? Surely not Stirling?" he added, eying the map.

"No, the Falklands rent rooms in some cottages that were put in last year, catering to summer tourists, birders and fishermen and the like. Everyone who lives off site stays in the Falklands' cots. We'll settle you there, as well."

"Huh." Stirling wondered just how friendly the local girls were and what sort of security risks they might pose. He probably knew a fair number of them by sight. Stirling found himself hoping the Falklands' cottages, at least, were a bit more picturesque than these drab concrete huts.

They swung round a final bend and Stirling got his first good look at the main facility. It was a larger version of the squat concrete cottages, but window-less, with steel security doors and a sizeable power plant visible off to one side. Rain squalls slashed across ugly walls and rooftops, racing past with a storm-lashed rhythm before writhing across the mountain slopes beyond.

He knew the valley, from childhood summer excursions. High, cloud-shrouded ridgelines, all but invisible in the rainy twilight, fenced the facility in, with only one access road leading out. If they'd bothered setting a gate guard, the place might have been virtually impregnable, by dint of sheer isolation. It was at least two kilometers from the nearest major huddle of farm cottages, a fair distance to hike through mountainous terrain with a load of unpleasantness strapped to one's back, but not far at all to come by car bomb. He wondered how amenable the researchers would be to the changes he intended imposing.

Not that he thought much additional security would prove necessary, but having come all this way, he might as well do a proper job of it. The Land Rover halted near the main doors and Stirling sighed, extricating himself gingerly with crutch-cane and compressed lips. There was, at least, a card reader at the front door, so no one could simply stroll straight in. Blundell swiped his identity card through it and the heavy steel door clicked open. "We'll get you a card, first thing," Blundell assured him as they stepped through.

"Second thing. Where's the bog? It's been a long drive and I drank most of that coffee."

Blundell grinned and pointed the way to the men's room, where Stirling took advantage of the sink and mirror to repair the worst of the travel damage and wash grit and sleepiness from his eyes. Ten minutes later Stirling was in the project director's office, with Blundell making introductions.

Terrance Beckett was a stringy sort of fellow one might have called rangy, had he possessed any decent physical conditioning. He glanced around at their entry, a scowl flickering into existence beneath a hawksbill nose. He glared down the long length of that nose, clearly resenting Stirling's intrusive presence in the lab's affairs as much as his more famous namesake, the Archbishop of Canterbury, had resented the intrusive presence of Henry II in the church. Come to think of it, Henry II was directly responsible for the present mess in Ireland, since he was the English king who'd first invaded the Irish.

This Beckett gave Stirling a long look, his glacial, blued-steel gaze sweeping across the wrist cast, the knee brace, the crutch-cane. "I see the Home Office has dispatched its best, as usual."

Stirling produced a nasty smile. "I often question the wisdom of the Home Ministry."

Beckett reddened, then bit out, "You'll want the tour, I suppose?"

"Bit of a problem designing security measures without one."

"Well, there's no one here tonight, so you'll bloody well have to wait. Gone to the damned pub, they have, bunch of lazy bastards. See to it our *Captain*," the emphasis he laid on the word made it an insult, "receives the grand tour in the morning, Blundell. Now get out. I'm much too busy to be bothered. And see that he doesn't touch a single, bloody piece of equipment on his way through the door!" Whereupon Beckett presented his back and became reabsorbed in his computer screen, which presented the disgruntled physicist with what amounted to colorful gibberish, as far as Stirling could determine.

The moment the door was closed, Blundell started to apologize.

"No, don't bother," Stirling waved off the flood of embarrassed words. "He doesn't want me here any more than I care to be here myself, so we're even on that score. Show me round the place anyway, then we'll stop at the Falkland Arms and meet everyone, shall we?"

Blundell's worry faded at once. "Right. Frightfully glad you understand about Dr. Beckett. He's a bit of a stickler, you see, utterly dedicated, doesn't see the need for all the security fuss."

"Let's hope he's right," Stirling muttered.

Blundell gulped, quivering like a frightened rabbit, then escorted him on a bizarre tour of an utterly empty facility, allowing him to memorize the laboratory's layout, the location of every door—particularly those left unlocked—and the placement of each piece of equipment. He was careful to ask which equipment required outside maintenance. The laboratory wasn't much to look at, really, just a lot of computers, an innocuous enough hospital-style ward with several beds and a cabinet for medical supplies, and a tangle of high-tech equipment that might have come straight out of some American science fiction film. If there were a time machine hidden amongst the jumble, he couldn't place it by sight.

When Blundell attempted to explain what each item did, Stirling's eyes crossed.

"You can give me the detailed explanations tomorrow," he muttered, vowing to get a decent night's sleep before attempting to comprehend the science behind this crackpot setup. "I'd like to meet the staff now, if you please."

"Of course, Captain."

A quarter of an hour later, the battered Land Rover pulled to a halt in a muddy carpark outside the brightly lit pub where Stirling had occasionally stopped for a pint on his way to and from university classes at Edinburgh. Blundell set the brake and shut off the engine. "We'll speak to Mrs. Falkland about a room at one of the cottages, shall we? Get you settled, then join the others?"

"No," Stirling shook his head, "introduce me round, then speak to Mrs. Falkland yourself, while I'm busy making everyone's acquaintance. I'd rather make my impressions of them before they've a chance to make them of me, which won't happen if I arrange lodgings first. Get a room as close to the road as possible, even if it means shifting someone else, so I can keep track of comings and goings."

"Very well." His request clearly disgruntled Blundell, who probably didn't relish being spied upon any more than the others would, once they found out.

The roisterous interior of the Falkland Arms public house hadn't changed much in four years. A wave of nostalgia washed over him, accompanied by the scent of ale and bitters, chips in the deep-fryer, tobacco smoke, and spiced curry and popadums, a London import. The pub was full to capacity, mostly with tourists who'd come for the region's favorite outdoor pastimes. The roar of voices talking incessantly about the fish, the weather, the grouse, and the golf, was punctuated by spurts of laughter and the clink of glassware. The research team comprised the largest group in the pub, occupying one whole corner, tables scooted together to accommodate a clutter of empty dinner plates and an impressive collection of glasses.

It looked to Trevor Stirling like a major celebration was under way.

"Ah, there they are." Blundell spotted them at least sixty seconds after Stirling did.

Stirling navigated the crowded pub with care, not wanting to trip himself up with the crutch-cane, which would leave a fine first impression. They'd nearly reached the table when one of the women, a graduate student, Stirling realized, placing her from her dossier photo, spotted them. Young and pretty, her whole face lit up. "Blundy! You're back!"

Marc Blundell turned red to the roots of his hair.

The curious stares leveled his way led Stirling to a singularly unpalatable conclusion: nobody had told the research staff they were to be saddled with SAS security. *Lovely*.

"Where've you been, old bean?" one of the men asked in a teasing tone. Cedrick Banning, Stirling nodded to himself, the Australian—decked out in the polo-snobbery variety of high style, with a paisley silk scarf tucked into his shirt collar and some fraternal pin Stirling didn't recognize decorating his lapel. Christ, another bloody colonial from the outback, trying to prove how very English he was.

Banning grinned in a friendly fashion. "You've ruddy well missed all the fun!"

"Fun?" Blundell blinked uncertainly.

"Beckett's Breakthrough," the Aussie chuckled, capitalizing both words. "Couldn't tear the old bastard away from the lab tonight with an atom bomb. We," he swept a gesture at the gathered team, "decided to celebrate in style, since he won't." Banning's friendly gaze landed on Stirling, and the Aussie greeted him with a cheery grin and an outstretched hand. "I say, old man, frightfully good to see you. SAS, isn't it? Jolly good, a captain, no less. Bit of a cock-up with that leg, eh?"

Christ, the man sounded more like Oxford than Outback. Must have an inferiority complex a kilometer long. Stirling shook his hand, anyway. "You could say that," he allowed tightly. "Belfast."

Banning's eyes widened and several of the women

emitted sharp little gasps and cooing sounds of sympathy. Stirling's gaze, however, was riveted on Brenna McEgan, whose admittedly lovely mouth had tightened at mention of Belfast. One of the dark-haired brand of Irish women, with a complexion like cream-colored silk, sparks of suppressed anger jumped in her eyes—and she wasn't at all shy about returning his narrow gaze. Her own was as cold as glittering sapphires. "I see you ran afoul of our Orange brethren," she said coolly. "At least, they're claiming the victory from the fighting, aren't they?"

Dismay ran like lightning round the conjoined pub tables, as party mood abruptly gave way to realization that the unpleasantness occurring across the Irish Sea might well overtake *them*.

"In my experience," Stirling said quietly, holding those chilly eyes in a steady gaze, "Belfast has no winners."

A vertical line twitched into existence between her brows. "How very odd. An SAS captain who actually understands Northern Ireland?"

Blundell cleared his throat nervously. "Captain Stirling will be joining us for a bit. He wanted to meet everyone, this evening. I'd love to hear about the breakthrough, Ceddie. I'll, ah, just go and arrange the captain's lodgings, then rejoin you."

Blundell fled, leaving Stirling to cope with social niceties on his own. He shook hands all round as introductions were made. Brenna McEgan watched him narrowly as he greeted each team member in turn. It took a concentrated effort to study the others, distracted as he was by her disturbing attractiveness, combined with her equally disturbing connections to Belfast. Stirling scolded himself for attempting security work while short of sleep and concentrated on the half-dozen senior staff, promising to sort out everyone else later. *Might at least have kept their bloody staff to a decent minimum,* he groused. *Security bleeding nightmare.*

"Sit down, Captain," Banning invited, leaning over to hook an empty chair from a nearby table. "Name your poison," he added, waggling fingers to gain the barmaid's attention.

The barmaid took one look and broke into a broad smile. "Trevor Stirling! Whatever brings you home, luv? Does your mum know?"

"Ah, no," he cleared his throat, aware of stares from every quarter. "I'm on duty, as it happens. How've you been, angel?"

Cassiopia McArdle had blossomed in his absence, filling that barmaid's uniform to an improbable degree, looking, at eighteen, like a soldier's favorite wet dream. He remembered her in braids and orthodontic braces. She winked. "I've been lonely. You look to need a bit of R and R, Trevor. I'm off at eleven. Pint of stout?"

"You *are* an angel. Give my best to your mother."

She grinned and went in search of his pint. He held back a sigh and met the surprised stares of the scientific team. "Well, then, what's this about a breakthrough?" he asked too brightly.

Cedric Banning recovered first, although his eyes continued to blaze with unspoken curiosity. "Beckett's Breakthrough. Yes. Old Terrance has finally done it, is what. We're no longer a theoretical concern."

"Beg pardon?"

Fairfax Dempsey, one of the graduate students, leaned forward eagerly. "He's done it, Captain! Went back in time! Full translation for sixteen minutes, right into the court of King Henry II, he said. He listened to Henry discussing the invasion of Ireland with his privy council! Beckett's bloody well made history today!" The young man chuckled as he realized the double meaning. "Twice, in fact. Once going *into* it, once making it."

"Why he chose *that* time and place to visit," Brenna McEgan muttered, "baffles me. Henry II, for God's sake, bloody-minded butcher . . ."

Stirling scarcely heard her, wondering if the sickening lurch in his gut were disbelief or terror. "D'you mean to say, you've actually *perfected* time travel?"

"Perfected it?" Brenna McEgan echoed, her tone droll. "Hardly. Beckett very nearly died, before we managed to retrieve his consciousness." Stirling gave her a sharp stare, which she returned with uplifted brow, faintly amused at his shock. "Dr. Beckett may have succeeded in testing his apparatus today, but we are a very long way, indeed, from running a full-bore field test. Naturally, that is precisely what he intends to do, first thing tomorrow morning. He wanted to go again today, but we managed to veto the notion. His heart did not cope well with the first translation—and he was gone only a quarter of an hour. Frankly, the last thing we need is for Beckett to drop dead."

Stirling tried to digest that, while wishing the room would stop lurching about as his equilibrium played catch-up. "Perhaps," he cleared his throat and tried again. "Perhaps someone had better explain all this in more detail?" Like it or not—tired or not—he needed to absorb the science *now*.

Zenon Mylonas, who'd remained silent until now, nodded. "Very well, Captain."

Dr. Mylonas was one of those perpetually mournful-looking chaps one expects to find in a mortuary, but seldom does. Sitting in the crowded pub, with his lesser colleagues ranged about him, he reminded Stirling of a gawky adolescent, all elbows and knobby shoulders and a discomfited awareness of not quite fitting in properly. His eyes held the look of a man who's faced the worst humanity has to offer itself and has not come up on the winning side.

Realization struck like an electric shock: Mylonas was utterly terrified. *By his own research.*

The implications were sickening, like a bottomless hole opening out under his feet, when he hadn't expected so much as a crack in the pavement. What the IRA could do with *real* time travel . . . The crowded pub crashed back into Stirling's awareness with a roar of voices raised in laughter and snatches of drunken song, the perpetual clink of glassware, the blue haze of cigarette smoke, all combining like the clattering of an unseen train roaring past in the fog. An ominous tremor began in the pit of his stomach, worse than pre-combat jitters. Stirling unfroze long enough to completely drain his glass in one long gulp, before gesturing for another. "All right," he finally managed. "Give me a lesson in time travel, professor."

"We'll begin with the basic physics of the project," Mylonas leaned forward, rolling his own empty bar glass between his hands. "You understand, surely, the concept of infinite potential futures? If I do x instead of y and you respond with b instead of c and so on, multiplied by all the physical factors in the universe? A crushed butterfly that robs some bird of its dinner, which prevents the offspring from transmitting a fatal disease that would have wiped out half of Asia. Or a supernova or meteorite being taken as a sign from God, prompting someone to invade a neighbor, abandon a revolution, or engineer a new religion which in turn kills several million people under the guise of saving their souls. If one accepts this as fact—or, perhaps I should say, as unchallenged hypothesis, as we are all scientists laboring under the scientific theory—then one must also understand there are an infinite number of potential *pasts,* as well. I didn't do *x*, but did *y* instead, you didn't respond with *b*, but rather did *c*."

"Well, I suppose so," Stirling frowned, "but look here, this doesn't make logical sense. How can *both* *x* and *y* have happened, when clearly, only *x* *did* happen?"

"It's a matter of quantum physics," Mylonas said patiently, "or rather, a matter of *fractural* physics, which is not something even your average quantum physicist has begun to grasp."

"*Fractural* physics?" Stirling echoed. "What the devil is that?"

"A bloody Nobel Prize," Cedric Banning grinned, raising his half-drained glass in a salute.

Mylonas shot Banning a quelling glance. "Quite. *If* the Home Office will ever allow us to publish our data." The haunted look in the man's eyes deepened. Stirling narrowed his gaze, realizing abruptly that Mylonas *wanted* the Home Office to keep his work classified. Oddly, none of the others appeared to be so deeply rattled. Rampant delight was the operative word at this table. What did Mylonas know, that the others hadn't glimpsed, yet?

"Go on, please," Stirling said quietly, sipping from his second glass of stout. "What *is* fractural physics?"

"A mathematical way of describing, of accounting for, the impossibilities in observation which neither quantum physics nor its mathematical system can explain. Surely you knew, already, that the simple act of observation literally brings a thing into being, at the quantum level? Observation equals creation. If you ask the right question, in other words, the universe obliges you by providing a previously nonexistent answer. And if a thing exists, it can be fractured into something else; time is no exception. In fact, without fractural physics, nothing would—or could—exist."

It sounded barmy to Stirling, but then, he'd barely

squeaked past subjects like tensor calculus and non-Euclidian geometry, never mind quantum relativity.

"What we've done here," Mylonas nodded toward the distant research lab, "is the elementary work of understanding how fractural physical laws operate. And what we've discovered is both infinite futures and infinite pasts, all coexisting in fractured planes, sliding over and past and through one another, a bit like a child's kaleidoscope, where the patterns and colors shift as the colored pebbles tumble about. Fractural physics provides the only scientific explanation of psychic phenomena, in fact. The human mind has billions of neural connections hardwired into the nervous system and the senses. We haven't manufactured an instrument, yet, of that complexity.

"I rather fancy that precognition occurs when an individual with particularly acute senses encounters the intersection of fractural planes and is abruptly confronted by two possible futures. Two or more. There are people attuned to the future of fractural planes, just as others are attuned to a fractural plane's past. You might think in terms of one set of instruments tuned to ham radio frequencies and another tuned to microwave transmissions. People who have learned to shift their own consciousness from one plane to another—so called astral projection or out-of-body experience—are actually moving the pattern of their consciousness from one plane to another, or to some other referent point on their own plane. What *we've* done is engineer a way to hook the conscious portion of a human mind, which is, after all, merely a pattern of energy which can be codified and transferred from one point to another, through the endless shifting of fractural planes—"

"Wait, slow down!" Stirling resisted the temptation to massage aching temples.

Mylonas halted, brows climbing into his receding hairline. "What don't you understand? It's perfectly simple, at least in concept. It's the engineering that's a bit tricky."

"May be simple to you," Stirling muttered, "but it's perfectly impossible from where I sit. Look, perhaps I'll grant you that bit about consciousness being a shifting energy pattern. I've seen some pretty odd things, ran across a fellow once who swore on stacks of holy treatises he had yearly out-of-body experiences, and he wasn't a candidate for the loony bin, either. So maybe, for the sake of argument, I'll buy your story about projecting someone's consciousness some*where* else. But some*when* else? I'm not a credulous fool!"

"Neither am I," Mylonas said very quietly. Stirling was struck again by the depth of fright in those dark eyes.

"Suppose you explain it again. Pretend I'm a newspaper reporter or some chap on the dole, with no more science education than, say, that keg of ale can lay claim to. On second thought, perhaps you'd better leave off telling me *why* it works and just try explaining why it could prove dangerous in a terrorist's hands?" He had to fight the impulse to glance at Brenna McEgan.

"They might well be interested," Mylonas said patiently, "because of the potential for *change*, which is inherent in the shifting of the fractural planes. Changing a variable, even a minor one, could have drastic consequences. I have tried to warn Dr. Beckett against rushing blindly ahead, before proper precautions can be taken, but he won't be stopped. Not by anything short of dying, anyway. Who do you think requested help from the Home Secretary? It was *not* Dr. Terrance Beckett. God help us, if terrorists ever get hold of this work."

The level of tension at the crowded table rose abruptly, like a nasty miasma over a swamp, compounded of equal parts suspicion, fear, and anger. More than one set of eyes flicked uncertainly toward Brenna McEgan. She sat cool as a queen at her corner of the table, sapphire eyes focused on a speck of dust that floated somewhere over the center of the untidy tabletop. When nobody broke the awkward silence, Stirling cleared his throat.

"Surely there's no way to actually change anything in the past? It's already happened, with no way to undo it. And even if you could, wouldn't paradox destroy any possibility of changing things, stop you before you got started?"

Mylonas shook his head. "You're forgetting the infinite pasts part of the equation. If you projected the energy pattern of your consciousness into *a* past—say, the court of Henry II, as Dr. Beckett did, or even further back, to the time of King Arthur—"

Cedric Banning snorted into his pint of bitters without quite laughing out loud. One of the graduate students dug her elbow into his ribs. As Mylonas reddened, Indrani Bhaskar put in mildly, "There is a great deal of evidence to suggest that King Arthur was quite genuine. Not a king, perhaps, but a real historical figure."

Stirling grinned. "Yes, Dux Bellorum, and all that. Sixth century A.D., wasn't it? Last of the great Romanized Briton Lords of Battle."

"Quite," she smiled. "I see you're a well-read man, Captain Stirling. Mind your manners, Cedric."

Banning laughed, clearly unrepentant, and lifted his glass in a mock salute.

Mylonas cleared his throat. "Yes. Well. If you project yourself into *a* past, along the fractural plane that resonates most closely with your present, you then find yourself in a new present, with an infinite number of potential futures stretching out before you. Should you take an action contrary to the ones taken on your plane of origin, call it Fractural Prime, then your consciousness will slide into a *different* fractural resonance, perhaps close to your Prime, perhaps not, depending upon the magnitude of difference between the two."

"Then it isn't changing history at all, is it?" Stirling's mind had filled with images of vast sheets of multihued crystal fragmenting and crashing into one another, until the universe resembled a pile of shattered quartz, pulverized under a geologist's hammer. The longer he thought about it, the more the image disturbed him.

Mylonas sighed. "It's a bit of both actually. It isn't as simple as you imagine."

"What do you mean by that? Either it is or it isn't."

"Not in fractural physics. The key word is *resonance*. If you switch from one fractural plane to another, the law of conservation of energy—among other things— *requires* a transfer of resonant energy between them. If the two resonances are sufficiently dissimilar, a dissonance is created. An energy embolism, if you will. Depending on how far back the dissonance occurs, it may have either negligible or very serious consequences in your Fractural Prime. The resulting embolism may produce a minor bruise, or it could produce catastrophic damage."

"Catastrophic?" Stirling blinked. "What, exactly, are we talking about here? What scale? Do you mean the traveler's energy pattern is violently disrupted? As in, fatally? Or do you mean something else? Something . . . worse?"

"That," Mylonas said tiredly, "is precisely what we do *not* know. The traveler could die, yes. Maybe. Unless the dissonance only affects things *after* the energy pattern's shift between planes. *You* might be spared, while everything else fractures around you. If the dissonance is set up in the new fractural plane, you might destroy the future of that plane, rewrite it, so to speak. You'd start with a clean slate, from your perspective, although you might well be killing off billions of people in the secondary plane's future. No way to tell, of course, subjectively, from the traveler's viewpoint.

"But suppose the dissonance affects the old fractural plane, the Prime you originally came from. This one." Mylonas rapped bony knuckles against the tabletop. "What do you have, then? Your action in moving from Fractural Prime to Fractural Secondary destroys both the present *and* the future of your plane of origin. Shatters it to bits, in fact. By setting up the dissonant energy pattern in the past of one fractural plane, you utterly destroy at least one future, possibly both. Not a terribly attractive situation for scholars, but *frightfully* attractive to some madman bent on vengeance. Or a terrorist bent on political blackmail."

"Dear God," Stirling whispered, staring into Mylonas' haunted eyes. "You're talking about the murder of *billions* of human souls!" He didn't know precisely how many people there were in the world, but it was an appalling number to snuff out in one fell swoop.

"Yes." Mylonas swallowed. "That is the reason the Home Office insisted on sending a chap who understands counterterrorism."

Stirling struggled to reorder his entire view of the tactical situation. Indeed, his view of the entire universe. He glanced around the table, finding stunned eyes and expressions of rising horror. Clearly, none of them had fully grasped the project's lethal potential until now. Unless, of course, one of them *was* a terrorist, someone who would have realized exactly what could be accomplished using this project. Getting himself—or herself—onto the team wouldn't have been easy, granted. But there was that fatal motor crackup, which had killed two members of the senior research team. The realization left Stirling's insides shaking. Brenna McEgan was staring bleakly into her own ale glass, fingers clenched white. Her sapphire eyes were nearly as haunted as Zenon Mylonas'. How much death had she seen, coming up from a place like Londonderry, where explosive violence and terrorist murder was nearly as common as it was in Belfast?

Stirling cast back over those dossiers he'd read, both Colonel Ogilvie's and Marc Blundell's, trying to recall everything documented on Brenna McEgan. There hadn't been much, which left him cursing the incompleteness of the material. Dammit, he needed to know how many times the people at this table had wet themselves in their prams, and the Home Office handed him a synopsis measured in thirty-second sound bites. *Was* Brenna McEgan the evil *djinn* in the bottle? Or was she simply too obvious a candidate?

Whoever his terrorist proved to be, if there even *was* a terrorist, once the *djinn* was loose . . . Several billion souls, destroyed instantly. It was *unthinkable*.

Stirling shuddered.

Northern Ireland's madmen perpetrated the unthinkable every day.

Chapter Three

Brenna McEgan left the boisterous warmth of the Falkland Arms pub to enter to a cold and wet night. The rain and wind and scudding clouds were as full of foreboding as she herself was—not a pleasant feeling for a woman in her position. Her cover story would not stand up to the kind of scrutiny Captain Trevor Stirling would shortly bring to bear. The SAS, for God's own sake . . . As Brenna unlocked the driver's side door of her car, she was as close to blind terror as she'd been since leaving Londonderry, all those years ago. The phone call which had come, tracing her to her Dublin flat and her new life, had not frightened her precisely, only filled her with a nameless dread which had all too quickly found its familiar shape and hue.

Orange terror tactics. *Again*.

Indeed, what else?

It was the reason she'd left Londonderry, the reason she'd never married, unwilling to bring a child into the madness, to inherit the hate and the killing. She still woke up some nights, drenched in cold sweat, watching her older sister and niece dissolve into blasted bits of human flesh not a dozen paces in front of her, coming out of a little shop where she'd agreed to meet them, planning to lunch together after their shopping was done. She'd joined, right afterwards; and had left for almost exactly the same reason, five years later: a Protestant woman and her child caught by an IRA car bomb, with a young girl on her knees beside them, tearing at her hair and screaming.

"I left a long time ago," she'd told them over the phone lines. "I'm not active and you bloody well know it. And the reasons."

"There isn't anyone else."

"Don't give me that—"

"Brenna. At least hear us out. Arlyne is coming to Dublin to see you."

God and thunder, her own grandmother . . .

Worse and worse.

And it *was,* the worst news ever given a member of *Cumann Na Mbann.* The whole future of humanity at stake, if they were right, and she the only operative—former operative, she insisted forcefully— with the credentials to get inside, to trace the Orange mole, identify and stop him.

"Brenna," her grandmother had leaned close, holding her and rocking her slightly, "I know, child, why you left us and I respected that, you know I did. But we need you, child, and it isn't just *Cumann Na Mbann* or the Provos trying to stop it. The leadership of the Orangemen came to us, to the Provos, I mean, to say one of their own had gone off the deep end and disappeared, vowing to destroy Britain."

She stared at her grandmother, eyes wide.

"Aye, love, it's that serious. He doesn't want the

elections to go forward, knows the Catholics have a majority this time around, and he's vowed to unleash genocide, not only against the Irish Catholics, but the British, as well, for betrayal. The Orangemen are frightened, love, and they can't find him."

"But you did?" Her voice came out whispery, little-girl frightened.

"We did. And, child, if there's truth in the rumors about the laboratory he's joined, he can destroy all of us, and I mean everybody on this bloody planet, billions of innocent lives."

She'd sat in her grandmother's arms for a long time, shaking, listening as her grandmother explained everything they'd learned, why they couldn't just hit the bastard with a standard IRA hit team. No publicity, not even the breath of publicity, nothing that would look even remotely like anything but pure accident— and before they could do even that much, they had to know. Was the threat real? Was the research viable? And if so, how far away was the team from success? And literally the only person in all of Ireland who could infiltrate that team as the Orangeman had done was Brenna McEgan.

"They'll pull strings, child, our own people and the Orangemen, both. They're afraid of him, Brenna, terrified of the man they've created and now must stop. They can't do it on their own. They've no one with the credentials to get close to him. And even if they did, he'd recognize them in a flash, drop them off a cliff somewhere. Together we'll get you inside that lab, Brenna. From there, it's you and no one else must discover the truth and stop him."

It was, ironically, the first time in the Catholic-Protestant history of the island that the Orangemen had voluntarily worked *with* the IRA Provisionals. All it had taken was the realization that they'd unleashed a creature so deadly, he would risk destroying the entire world—including the Orangemen who'd turned him into a weapon—to take his vengeance against Catholics and the British who'd "betrayed" him.

Cedric Banning—not his real name, but the name of his carefully constructed cover persona—was ruthless, brilliant, and utterly mad. To refuse the mission was unthinkable. He *had* to be stopped. So she'd come to Scotland, with no idea how many strings had been plucked to get her there, and she'd identified Banning, and she'd assessed the threat level—utterly deadly— and now she had an *SAS captain* on the job, who knew none of this, whose every glance tonight had shouted plain as daylight that she topped his suspect list.

How could she not? She was Irish, wasn't she? Reason enough for any self-respecting Brit to hate and distrust her, given the circumstances. By the end of Mylonas' hideous little lecture, every colleague at the table had been shooting her furtive, unhappy little glances. *The IRA,* those looks said, *the IRA's threatening us and ours, and you're by-God Irish.* It would have done no good to stand up and say, "You're absolutely right, mates, I'm IRA to my bones, and I'm the only thing standing between you and a disaster so enormous, you can't even comprehend it."

Admission would only earn her a one-way ticket to prison—and leave the man she'd come here to stop with a free and easy road to success. A very powerful intuition was screaming at Brenna that her enemy—all humanity's enemy—would waste no time, now that the SAS was on the job. It wasn't logical, not even remotely. Logic said he'd simply sit back on his own forged and impeccable credentials and smile while the SAS locked her up. But intuition said otherwise. Intuition whispered, *He'll move now and throw blame on you, Brenna, so what are you going to do to stop it, eh?*

She turned the key in the ignition and put the car into a smooth reverse in the crowded carpark, then set out for the lab. Whatever he planned, he would do it tonight. Sitting at the pub all evening with a crowd of eyewitnesses would get her an alibi, but what good was that if he blew the entire future to hell while she earned it? She thought of Terrance Beckett, alone in a silent lab office, working like a fiend to prepare them all for the next trip into time, and shivered.

There was a gun in her cottage, the most illegal thing she owned, urged on her by her own grandmother, for safety's sake on a mission like this. Not for assassination, no. Her job was to identify the Orange mole, so that others could take him out—under circumstances that would not throw suspicion on the IRA. This was a covert ops job of the most delicate kind ever undertaken by the Irish Republican Army Provisionals and one of the very few where publicity was the very *last* thing they wanted. Enough to get the job done.

But the bloody SAS had thrown everyone's time-tables into disarray.

Brenna was torn between the desire to drive back to the cottage to slip the gun into her pocket and the equally powerful desire to drive to the Firth of Forth and throw it into the bay. An impossible situation. It had been from the outset. And dithering about it would do no one any good. *Get on with it,* she told herself fiercely, hating the tremors in her hands.

She drove carefully, swinging off the main highway onto the access road, windscreen wipers slapping with futile energy at the downpour hammering the glass, and finally pulled to a halt beside her temporary home, the drab and repulsively ugly cottage assigned to her by Terrance Beckett. None of the others had returned from the pub, yet. Only Beckett's car was visible, in front of his own cottage, the one closest to the main lab building. No way to tell if he were in bed or still working, since the lights in his cottage were off and there were no windows in the lab to reveal a telltale glow.

She shut off her car and dashed across to unlock the cottage door, wiping water from her face despite the overhang protecting the door from the elements. She switched on a single light and stood irresolute for a moment, gazing bleakly at her belongings scattered through the room. There was less of her personality in this cottage than there had been in her dorm room at University. Old habits, consciously set aside for the move to Dublin and the declaration of independence from the organization she'd finally found the courage to repudiate, had returned to haunt her, as familiar as her own skin and far more disturbing. Brenna's face twisted, half bitter recrimination, half grief. Once *Cumann Na Mbann* . . . They had you for life, whether you willed it or no. Insanity, to stand here wishing like hell she'd walked a different road as a girl.

Pride and hatred. They solved nothing. Unfortunately, neither did walking away from the trouble. God knew exactly how hard she'd tried *that*. What, then, was the answer, when the other side refused to put down its weapons and be reasonable? When, backed into a political corner and snarling like a wounded dog, the other side viewed your very existence as a threat to their survival? Who could win a war like that? She'd told that SAS captain no more than God's honest truth. *Nobody* won in Northern Ireland. Brenna slid open the drawer, hands trembling as she gazed down at the gun hidden there.

A Russian-made 9mm Makarov, sleek and semiautomatic, sixteen centimeters long. Small enough to conceal in a sturdy coat pocket, large enough to pack a lethal punch. Smuggled in from God alone knew where

and brought south across the border into Dublin by
her own grandmother. And carried in her luggage from
Dublin to Scotland, reminder of why she was here and
of the ugliness that had erupted once again, threatening her life and her world. *'Tis no answer!* Brenna's
very soul screamed the protest. Yet what choice did
she have? He must be stopped.

Headlamps flashed past outside the window, sending
her eight centimeters off the floor. Her heart thundered into the hollow of her throat. The SAS captain,
come to search her rooms? Brenna caught her breath
on a ragged gasp and switched off the lamp before slipping over to her window to peer out through the murk
and the rain. She knew the car which rolled to a stop
at the cottage next to hers, knew the man who climbed
out into the raw night, who glanced toward her
abruptly darkened window before turning and heading toward the lab, crossing the road at an easy jog.
Damn, damn, damn! He was making his move and she
was out of position, wasn't ready . . . And there was no
time to call in the Provos team that was supposed to
make this hit . . .

She stuck the gun into her coat pocket, hands shaking, made sure of her own ID card to get through the
security door, headed into the wind and the downpour
at a run, slithering through puddles and mud and filth.
She had a longer way to run than he'd had, her cottage being farther than his. She fumbled the card at
the reader, had to grope through muck to find it, wiped
it against her skirt and got it, shaking, through the
reader. The door clicked and released and she yanked
it open, jerking the gun from her pocket and slipping
inside. She slid the Makarov's safety downward with
her thumb, ready to fire with a simple double-action,
first pull of the trigger. He had a good five-minute lead
on her . . .

She caught the sharp, coppery smell of death instants before his fist caught the side of her head. Brenna crumpled into blackness, knowing only the terror of defeat.

The telephone shrilled somewhere close to Stirling's ear, shattering sleep and jangling his nerves. He groped in the unfamiliar darkness, fumbling the receiver onto the floor with his wrist cast. He tried to read the time on the bedside clock as he searched along the cord to find the handset again. Bloody murder! *Two-thirty* A.M.?

"H'lo?"

"Captain Stirling!" He didn't recognize the voice.

"Who is this?" he demanded, coming slightly more awake as the panic in that voice hit home.

"It's Marc Blundell. Dear God, you have to come at once! We're sending a car for you, there's been a disaster at the lab."

That woke him up. *"What kind of disaster?"*

Blundell gulped, voice shaking. "It's . . . it's Dr. Beckett. Someone's killed him."

Oh, sweet Jesus . . . "Get that bloody car here yesterday!" Stirling was already out of bed and moving. "And for God's sake, *no one* leaves the building! No one in or out, except me."

"But—"

"But *what*?" He already had his uniform buttoned and was slinging on his gunbelt with the ease of long familiarity.

"The constables . . ." Blundell quavered. "We'll have to contact the police—"

"Like bloody hell you will! *Nobody!* Got that? Not even the local bobby, not until I've seen *everything* firsthand!"

The project liaison gulped audibly over the line. "Yes,

sir. Oh, God, *please* get here quickly! There's more—I daren't say what over an unsecured phone line."

Stirling snarled under his breath. *Worse* he did not need. "The car's just pulled up," he muttered as headlamps stabbed past the curtains in his cottage window, sending shadows swinging wildly. "I'll be there in five minutes."

He grabbed up his field kit, carefully prepared before leaving London, and ran, lurching on his bad knee. He snatched open the driver's side door. "Move. I'll drive."

Bad knee or not, he could outdrive any graduate student on the planet, and Miss Dearborne was shaking violently behind the wheel. She slid frantically into the other seat. Stirling gunned the engine and squealed out onto asphalt. He didn't even take time to fasten his safety belt. The road roared past in the wake of their passage, tearing great holes in the drizzle and mist. Water sheeted down across the roadbed. Ghostly trees skittered and jumped as he skidded the Land Rover through the turns.

He tried to recall who'd left the pub and in what order—and when. Significantly, Brenna McEgan had left first, pleading weariness. Cedric Banning had followed shortly thereafter, leading Stirling to wonder who might be sleeping with whom. A couple of computer techs had left early, as well, and Zenon Mylonas had called it quits a quarter of an hour after that. A whole laundry list of potential suspects.

He took the turning onto the access road on two wheels, drawing a sharp gasp from Miss Dearborne. They thumped back down and sent gravel flying. Lights blazed in most of the on-site cottages. Beckett's windows were a notable exception, dark as the night itself. *Poor bastard won't be needing them ever again, will he?*

He skidded to a halt in front of the door, having made the drive in three minutes flat. The main lab door stood open, held by an ashen Blundell. The man gestured frantically. A sharp babble of voices greeted Stirling. The senior scientists were clumped together, faces shocky and pale, voices shrill. Several of the grad students were crying. So was Indrani Bhaskar. Brenna McEgan was missing. So was Cedric Banning.

"Where?" Stirling asked tersely.

Blundell pointed, hand shaking violently, toward Beckett's office.

The death inside that room was nearly too terrible for such a small space to contain. Terrance Beckett had died hard. His equipment lay in smashed profusion, his files scattered across the floor where violent struggles had swept them off his desk. Blood had pooled beneath the body, with splashes across the files, the front of the desk, the broken document trays. Given the placement of the wreckage, Beckett had been tempted out from behind his desk before the attack was launched, taking him by surprise in the middle of a conversation. He'd been knifed repeatedly and his skull crushed for good measure. Stirling didn't have to use guesswork on the type of knife. It lay on the floor beside its victim, all twenty-two wicked centimeters of it. *Commando fighting knife*, he catalogued the weapon automatically. American-made, high quality, and even easier to smuggle than firearms.

Not a woman's choice of weapon.

Or was it? It wouldn't take much strength to inflict fatal damage with a knife like that, and a woman attacker might explain the prolonged struggle. Beckett could easily have fought his way from one side of his office to the other, if his attacker were female. Less upper-body strength, weaker grip, and the women members of the research group were decidedly petite, compared with Beckett. Might explain the crushed skull, afterwards, as well. *Hell hath no fury . . .*

"You said there was worse," he turned abruptly, nearly running Blundell over in the process.

"Yes." The project liaison had to swallow twice before his voice would hold steady. "There's—that is—"

Fairfax Dempsey, Beckett's grad student, snarled, "It's Brenna bloody *McEgan,* that's what! She's set up the equipment and transferred through time!"

Oh, dear God . . .

"Show me."

They led him into the transfer room, as they'd dubbed it. A row of padded tables, looking much like ordinary medical examination benches, lined one wall. Two of the five were occupied. *Two?* Brenna McEgan was closest to the far corner, a psychological choice indicating, possibly, subconscious fear of being caught. A bruise discolored her cheek, evidence of the struggle with poor Beckett. The other traveler was Cedric Banning. *His* table was the one closest to the door— the position of pursuer, or perhaps just plain haste. Both of them were soaking wet, from the storm or from attempts to remove blood from clothing or both. McEgan's clothing was badly bloodstained; so was Banning's. He must've come in and discovered Beckett, tried to reach the poor bugger, slipped and fallen in the gore . . .

"Banning left a note," Dempsey said, eyes reddened from the attempt to hold back tears. "She'd killed Beckett before he got here, set up the equipment to transfer herself. Banning plugged his headset into her coordinates and went in pursuit, to stop her . . ." Dempsey was clutching a crumpled sheet of graph paper, torn from a notebook.

Stirling smoothed it out, frowning over the hasty scrawl.

McEgan's done it, the bloody bitch, the note read, Banning's handwriting nearly illegible. *Must have known I was on to her, and the SAS showing up spooked her into jumping. Found out last week she's* Cumann Na Mbann, *although I couldn't prove it. Came in here to warn poor Beckett, slipped and fell in the blood, trying to get to him, but it was far too late. Have to stop her before she wrecks British history and kills off the whole bloody world. For God's sake, send through a backup to help me with this!*

Stirling lifted his gaze to find himself at the still-point center of an invisible, all-too-real sphere of terror. It radiated like a living heat source in the confines of the lab, pushing him up against invisible walls. With creditable calm, he asked, "Why don't we just pull the ruddy plug?"

"You can't!" Mylonas cried, pupils dilating in naked shock.

"Why not?"

"You'd kill them both instantly! Systemic shock, disrupted energy transfer lines, and God knows what the resulting flux in power would do to the fractural planes involved; the system's set on a timer, you see, to taper the power levels off gradually, so there's no possibility of an energy embolism! She's set the bloody timer for a *year,* and if we try to override it, I can't answer for the consequences! We can plug someone else into the system, send another traveler at the power level she's set, which is what poor Dr. Banning's done, but we can't possibly disengage the system in an emergency shutdown! If we could do so safely, Cedric Banning would have shut it down at once!"

"All right, I get the bleeding picture," Stirling muttered, mopping his face with one hand. Christ, he'd needed more sleep before facing this. *Cumann Na Mbann*, that was the last thing he'd wanted to hear. The women's arm of the IRA, the most secret part of the whole terrorist organization and the most efficient as well, damned near impossible to infiltrate. *Cumann Na Mbann* members had done everything from courier jobs, running guns and messages in their babies' prams, to blowing up Protestant social clubs and gunning down British dignitaries. A more ruthless, clever opponent, Stirling could not imagine.

Just his stinking luck . . .

"Right, then. I'll have to go after them."

"*You?*" Indrani Bhaskar gasped. "But you're not trained! You don't know the first thing about the time period—"

"And those two *do?*" Stirling shot back. The too-still bodies of McEgan and Banning lay shrouded beneath the wires of their time-transference headsets. "They're not exactly historians, Dr. Bhaskar. Although I suppose it wouldn't take a great deal of historical training to assassinate Henry II before he has the chance to invade Ireland."

The uneasy silence puzzled him. Then Dr. Bhaskar gave him the rest of the bad news. "They didn't go to the same time Dr. Beckett did. They're not at Henry II's court, not anywhere close to it, in fact."

"All right," Stirling grated out, "where *have* they gone?"

Her eyes, still wet from her shocked weeping, reflected a fear of not being taken seriously. "Well, Captain, you see . . . They've set the equipment for this region, right here in Scotland."

"This region?" Stirling echoed. Uneasiness stirred, worse than before, in the pit of his stomach. "Granted, Scotland's been the site of a number of historic battles, but major enough to upset all history? What could

McEgan possibly be after, *here*, that would benefit Northern Ireland?"

Indrani's lips worked. The answer came out as a ragged whisper. "King Arthur."

The unreality of it tried to crash down across him. Sleep-deprived, off balance, badly shaken by the possibilities for mass murder, that was the last answer he'd expected to hear. "King Arthur?" It came out flat, disbelieving. "Dux Bellorum Artorius? Sixth-century Briton war chieftain, fighting Saxons?"

"And Picts," Indrani whispered. "And Irish invaders. A very large number of Irish invaders, in fact. She's gone to the year 500 A.D. The height of Artorius' power. If the Irish were to kill him before his resounding victory over the Saxons at Mount Badon, the Irish clans could drive the Britons *and* the Saxons straight into the sea."

The whisper of air conditioning from the laboratory's vents raised a chill along Stirling's neck. Go back to the very beginning of the Irish invasions of western England and Scotland, rewrite history so the *Irish* took possession of the entire island, instead of the Saxons, so that later Anglo-Saxon kings would never exist, so that William of Normandy wouldn't be strong enough to wrest England from the weak Saxon monarchy, which meant Henry II would never exist to invade Ireland and murder its culture or set in motion Elizabeth I's centuries-long nightmare of colonizing Northern Ireland as a Protestant colony. And Brenna McEgan would destroy billions of lives in her own future, trying to give the Irish a victory over Artorius and his Saxon enemies.

It was exactly what he would expect of a *Cumann Na Mbann* agent. Subtle. Cunning. Utterly ruthless.

Cedric Banning, Aussie playboy scientist, had about as much chance of stopping a fanatical terrorist like

McEgan as the alley cats in Belfast's scarred neighborhoods had of stopping the bombings.

"I see." It came out ragged. "Very clearly, in fact. Which makes it absolutely imperative that I be the one to transfer after them."

"But—"

"I speak Welsh and Gaelic, Dr. Bhaskar."

"But do you speak Latin and Brythonic?"

"Latin, no. Brythonic, that's early Welsh, isn't it?"

"Yes. And as much like modern Welsh as the Old English of Beowulf is like the language you and I are speaking now!"

"Nevertheless, I'm still the best-qualified agent you have. I majored in military history at Edinburgh University. Cut my milk teeth on both my grandfathers' stories about the glorious King Arthur, and I'm familiar with all the legendary sites, in Scotland, England, *and* Wales. And I'm a trained counterterrorist officer. Frankly, you haven't *got* a better agent to send after them, not anywhere in Britain." He resolutely refused to think about the consequences to any mistakes he might make, that far back in history. He could easily destroy the future he was trying to protect, with one ill-timed blunder. He refused to consider it, because he'd spoken the simple, stark truth. There wasn't anyone better qualified to go. God help them all . . .

And a whole year to screw it up.

"I want an outside phone line," he said through clenched teeth.

"To phone the police?"

"No. To phone my commanding officer." Colonel Ogilvie was going to spit nails, when he heard, which certainly wouldn't do Stirling's own career much good. What the Home Office would do, once Ogilvie finished notifying the Minister, he genuinely did not want to contemplate. Pity was the overriding emotion he felt for the scientists left to face the authorities.

His conversation with Ogilvie was brutally short. "Stirling here. Beg leave to report full infiltration, sir, with casualties. Initiating pursuit, within the quarter hour."

"Geographical?" Ogilvie asked carefully, his voice a rasp through the telephone wires.

"No, sir."

"I see."

"Better run a complete security check on Brenna McEgan, Colonel, and Cedric Banning, as well. I'd like to know how Banning found out McEgan's *Cumann Na Mbann*."

"Bloody hell. Home Office won't like that."

"No, sir. They'll like what Dr. Mylonas has to say even less. Better get a full team up here, sir. I daren't say more over the telephone. I'll leave a complete situation report for you, before I go after them. Time is far more critical than you think."

An understatement, if ever he'd made one.

"Do what you must, Stirling."

"Yes, sir."

He was on his own. With all of history waiting.

Brenna woke slowly, through a dim and dreamlike confusion of images, sounds, and stenches. How long she'd been out, she had no way of measuring. She was quite sure she'd returned at least partway to consciousness at some point, for she retained memory of a throbbing pain in her jaw and cheekbone, of clothing plastered wetly to her body and the stink of blood from somewhere close by. She remembered terror at finding her coat and gun missing. She remembered, too, lying paralyzed on a padded surface, stretched out as though for sleep or a doctor's examination. And she remembered hearing him breathing, somewhere very close by, above the background of lab noises— computers and their cooling fans and the almost subliminal hum of expensive equipment brought to life.

Her final, fragmented memory was awareness of the electrical leads taped to her skin and a wavery image of his face, smiling merrily into her foggy eyes, the paisley scarf looking jaunty at his throat—a sick in-joke the other scientists had dismally failed to comprehend.

"Hello, love," he'd said with a laugh that froze her blood. "You've my undying gratitude for providing the perfect scapegoat. And don't worry, I'll be joining you shortly. Catch me if you can."

He'd thrown a switch—and her reality had shattered.

Leaving her . . . where? Or—more chilling—*when*? She was lying down, or at least her borrowed body was. When she struggled to focus her awareness, she felt a fluttering at the back of her mind, the frantic beating of a terrified bird trapped on the wrong side of a window glass. Thoughts not quite her own flickered like heat lightning, as though she had become someone else with a very different set of memories. The presence howling through her awareness was thinking in a language Brenna could not at first make out. It sounded a little like Gaelic. A very little. More like . . . Welsh? Not any Welsh she'd ever heard spoken. This had a very ancient sound to it. Why would Cedric Banning have chosen a time and place where archaic *Welsh* was spoken?

At first, she thought Banning might have marooned her in a time different from the one where he planned to attack, but a moment's further thought convinced her otherwise. Once the computers had locked onto a destination and activated the transfer, the system could not be reset. It was a simple matter of the computer's data storage capacity, processor speed, and power drain. Not even the grandson of the Cray supercomputer, an immensely fast and powerful machine used for the time-spanning jump, could have handled two temporal destinations at once.

She was unsure whether to feel relief or deeper alarm.

Gradually, meaning began to seep through the confused blur of unfamiliar words in her mind, giving her clues to the language, at least. The owner of her borrowed body was terrified nearly witless—but not completely so. She sensed a keen intelligence filtering through to her own mind, with overtones of religious—or perhaps superstitious—awe, triggered by the incomprehensible event which had befallen them. Brenna tried to relax into the flow of thoughts and churning emotions and finally succeeded in getting across her *own* fear and disorientation. The other mind, or rather, the mind they now shared, reflected startlement, followed by a guarded relaxation from the worst of its own frantic panic.

She gradually realized that the flow of memory images and thoughts ran both ways. Even as Brenna was inundated by a flood of images—a high cliff with a fortress of dark, rough stone at the summit, glinting in the slanted light of late afternoon above her horse's weary, forward-pricked ears; the smell of venison stew rising thick with savory herbs from a vast iron cauldron suspended over a hearth in a stone hall; a lingering, unpleasant impression of some deeply disturbing nightmare filled with blood and the screams of dying men—even as these images and impressions sank into Brenna's awareness, her host's mind was getting the gist of what had happened to *Brenna* in a twenty-first-century research laboratory at the base of a Scottish mountain.

And images of Northern Ireland's violence were

seeping through, as well, memories Brenna would have given half her soul to forget: her sister and niece lying on the pavement at broken, blasted angles; her father, dead and cold in his grave at the end of a prison hunger strike; the bloodied victims of IRA bombings and shootings; the whole, hideous patchwork of terror that was her homeland . . .

To Brenna's vast surprise, the mind she now shared space with did not recoil in horror and disgust. A moment later, she understood why, as memory images flooded into *her* awareness: villages burning in the snow, women and children butchered alongside the menfolk; the clash of steel and the scream of men and horses as battle raged while she struggled to lead a whimpering line of children to safety; her father lying cold and still, pierced in a dozen fatal places, her mother shrieking and tearing at her hair in a wild excess of grief . . .

They understood one another, even before they were aware of one another's names.

Brenna, she thought slowly and carefully, *Brenna McEgan is my name.*

Abrupt, flaring suspicion arrowed into her awareness. *Irish!* The word came as a snarl. Brenna was accustomed to such hatred, having grown up in Londonderry, but it jolted her badly all the same. Then she caught another undercurrent of memory, which showed her warships of a very ancient design against a backdrop of grey ocean and what looked suspiciously like the western coast of the Isle of Man, jutting like a sharp knife blade at the not-so-distant shore of Northern Ireland. Invasion, she realized, an invasion fleet, threatening the homeland of her host— or, rather, hostess.

Brenna tried to get across the idea that she was from the future, *far* in the future, and braced herself,

but met with much less incredulity than she'd expected.
After a moment's puzzlement, she understood why. As
strange as the ancient sailing ships had looked to her,
Brenna's memories of cars and lorries, electric lights,
telephones, and the explosive detonations of car bombs
were utterly alien to her hostess, alien and powerful
arguments that Brenna was, in fact, telling the truth.
She also began to get a sense that her hostess' religious beliefs somehow supported Brenna's claim. The
soul, being immortal and moving between this world
and the Otherworld, dying here to be born there, dying
there to be born here, was capable of crossing great
barriers, and was not time itself merely another form
of barrier which the soul transcended?

Brenna had to blink several times before that sank
in fully.

She had landed in the mind of a philosopher. . . .

I'm no threat to you or yours, Brenna tried to get
across, *but the one who attacked me and sent me here
is a very great threat. He's quite mad, utterly ruthless.
I don't know what he plans, but it will be a very great
disaster, whatever it is. I must stop him, whatever the
cost to myself.*

After a long moment of silence, a reply came
arrowing back. *Then we must find and kill this enemy
we share, Brenna McEgan of the Irish.* After a moment's
pause, the voice inside her head added, very formally,
*I am called Morgana, Queen of Galwyddel and Ynys
Manaw, Queen of Gododdin and the Northgales, stepsister to Artorius, the Dux Bellorum, and a healer born
to an ancient family of Druidic caste, trained by the
Nine Ladies of Ynys Manaw. You Irish call it by the
name Ablach, for it is a land rich in apples, symbol of
the soul and potent for use in healing medicines. You
will not find me an inconsiderable ally. Are you and
your enemy the only soul-travelers from your world?*

Brenna hardly took the question in, for the room had begun to spin as more and more clues fell sickeningly into place. Morgana of the Apple Isle, Artorius the Dux Bellorum of Britain, who was Morgana's stepbrother, war with invading Irish clans . . .

Cedric Banning, the devious, mad *bastard*! He'd brought her to the time of Arthur's cataclysmic war against Saxon, Pict, and Irish invasions. Banning had laughed at the notion of King Arthur, last night in the pub, with Indrani Bhaskar and the SAS captain comparing notes on the real Artorius. Banning had put everyone at ease with that laughter, pulling a monstrously successful cloak of misdirection across everyone's eyes. Her own included. She was furious with herself, for being so utterly, stupidly *blind*. Within two hours of publicly and carefully making fun of the notion, Banning had sent himself straight to Artorius' Britain—and Brenna with him, the perfect scapegoat, unable to testify on her own behalf with her mind trapped in the sixth century A.D. Banning was intent on destroying only God knew how much history. A vengeful blow at the most famous British commander in history, in retaliation for what the Orangeman saw as British betrayal of his entire culture . . .

And a chance to destroy the Irish utterly, by helping his own Anglo-Saxon ancestors smash and grab far more than they should have been able to, years too early and with who knew how many lives lost that should have been spared? The destruction of those lives would smash British and Irish cultures to flinders and fracture history to shards. How long had Banning been planning this moment? Long before the elections, certainly. She'd been activated by *Cumann Na Mbann* and put onto his trail months previously, which meant the Orangeman had realized well in advance that a Catholic majority population—the first such majority in centuries—would sweep Sinn Fein candidates into office across the breadth of Northern Ireland. Had known it, had laid his plans for retaliation, and set out to take the ultimate revenge, willing to sacrifice *everything* rather than see a Catholic state take away his power and his culture of hatred.

It was exactly what she had come to expect of the Orange terror machine.

And Brenna had not the faintest idea how to stop him.

Speaking very gently indeed, Morgana repeated her question, helping Brenna gather her scattered wits. *Are you and your enemy the only soul-travelers from your world, Brenna McEgan?*

Brenna struggled to answer that calm question. *I think not. One other will come, at the very least. A soldier who believes I am his enemy. Worse, he will believe that Cedric Banning, a murdering madman, is his ally.*

Morgana, calm and practical, said, *Tell me more of this soldier, Brenna McEgan.*

How to explain the British SAS? She took a deep, metaphorical breath. *He and many like him were sent to my homeland to keep the peace. It didn't work,* she added bitterly, *for the Irish have memories that stretch back centuries and we never forgive or forget a wrong. From what little I've seen of this man, he is honorable, intelligent, dedicated to his mission. He's an officer, used to command, a formidable ally and dangerous enemy.*

Morgana gave a slight nod, startling Brenna with the sensation of having someone else move her body without her conscious volition. *How is he called, this man we must ensure becomes our ally?*

Brenna's lips twitched into a fleeting smile, encouraged by the cool competence of that response. *Trevor Stirling, Captain in the SAS. Ah, Special Air Service is what that means.* When Morgana evinced an understandable confusion over the meaning of that name, she added, *They are an elite group of men with advanced training in the art of warfare.*

Ah. That is precisely what we shall need.

Brenna found herself grinning, despite the seriousness of her predicament. Then, curious about her surroundings—for the room was as black as the inside of a Paisleyite's heart—she tried to sit up, which took her three shaken attempts. A mass of long, unbound hair cascaded down her back, heavy and luxuriant, puddling like rainwater around her hips. She wore what felt like linen robes. A heavy band of cold metal circled her neck, the ends meeting in the hollow of her throat. She could see neither the outlines of windows nor the thin thread of light from a doorway. Brenna gulped hard. Was her hostess *blind*? A chuckle from Morgana rumbled through their shared mind, then a powerful urge to grope with both hands took control and sent her fingertips seeking across what must have been a low table. She found two small, hard objects, which her hands—clearly under Morgana's direction—picked up on their own.

She struck them together rapidly, with a scraping motion. Sparks danced in the blackness and momentary giddiness swept through her. She was not, at least, blind. She struck more sparks and, this time, some landed in a dry substance which crackled and briefly flared into brilliance. She blew gently and the flames took hold, revealing a small mound of dried moss in a pottery bowl, a sort of archaic tinderbox arrangement. She spotted an oil lamp of very ancient design, made of rough-fired ceramics and looking like it had recently been dug from the nearest archaeological treasure hunt. Brenna carefully lifted the burning moss and used the flame to catch the lamp's wick alight.

She then blew out the blazing moss to conserve it
for another night and sat for long moments, just gazing
at that disturbingly antiquated clay lamp, which cast
a soft light into the room. Other disturbing details
impinged upon her awareness. The room was small,
with plastered walls which had been decorated with
distinctive frescoes. The style was utterly and convincingly Roman—birds and gardens and architectural
forms, mysterious female figures performing some
religious ritual which involved wine and birds and
dancing. She could almost hear the music from the
painted pipes and lyres, while wisps of smoke rose from
painted braziers decorated with garlands of flowers.
The floor was a beautifully worked mosaic with a
mythological theme, Ceres and Proserpine, it looked
like. An incongruous and jarring note was struck when
she glimpsed a small crucifix mounted on the wall
amidst the riot of pagan celebration.

"Where *am* I?" she whispered aloud.

The whisper of an answer floated up from
Morgana's portion of their shared mind. *Caer-Iudeu,
of course . . .*

She was still puzzling it out when the door flew
open and a young man flung himself into the room.
"Aunt Morgana! Please, you must come at once!" The
boy's voice was ragged with distress. "It's Artorius and
Uncle Ancelotis—they've come with dreadful tidings.
Lot Luwddoc is dead from fighting Picts just across
the border and Ancelotis has collapsed, riding into
Caer-Iudeu!"

Blood drained from Morgana's face in a disastrous,
icy flood. "No . . ." The sound came out strangled,
a cry of protest and fear as Morgana swayed, dizzy
and nearly collapsing from shock. Brenna realized
with a flood of pity and sudden shared grief that Lot
Luwddoc was Morgana's *husband*. To give the boy

credit, Morgana's nephew splashed wine into a cup from an earthenware jug beside the oil lamp, and held it gently to her lips. Morgana leaned against the boy, fingers clenched around his arm, breath coming in shallow gasps that were not quite sobs, while she fought for control. She sipped at the wine, eyes streaming and hands trembling. Her next words astonished Brenna.

"The Saxons will take advantage of our disarray; dear God, Medraut, there could be no worse time to lose your uncle. We can afford to show no weakness to the Saxons, or they will strike like jackals in the night, grinding us between the hammer of their swords and the anvil of invading Picts."

To think first of her people, at a time like this . . .

Yet the pain of her loss burned in their shared heart, brought into even sharper focus by the helpless clench of her fingers around her nephew's arm. And somewhere farther down the worn stones of the road she and Medraut had been traveling—a Roman road, Brenna realized, cutting across the Scottish hills—Morgana had a son who would be king. Her fear for the young boy's safety, his and his younger brother's, burned nearly as brightly as the grief and twice as hot. Brenna's heart went out to her, along with a large dollop of respect for the grieving queen.

"Aunt," Medraut said quietly, but with a note of urgency, "Ancelotis is ill. He collapsed on the road into Caer-Iudeu, trying to bring the king's body home for burial. By luck, Covianna Nim is in the fortress—"

"Covianna Nim?" Morgana echoed, so shocked, she momentarily forgot the rest of the dire news. "What in Brigantia's name is *Covianna Nim* doing in Gododdin? Her home is Glastenning Tor, closer to Caer-Lundein than we are to the Firth of Forth! It must be well above four hundred miles from Caer-Iudeu to Glastenning Tor!"

Medraut nodded, still ash-pale in the light from the oil lamp. "Prince Creoda of Wessex asked the abbot of Glastenning Abbey to send a message to Artorius, bidding him meet Creoda and Prince Cutha of Sussex at Caerleul, to discuss matters critical to Britain's future. That's why Artorius rode for Gododdin a day ahead of us, trying to reach Lot and Ancelotis before Cutha and Creoda can arrive in Rheged. He's calling for a council of the kings of the north. Covianna Nim rode north to give Artorius the message. And she insisted on coming to Gododdin, as well. So," he added with a flush rising to his cheeks, "did Queen Ganhumara. They're *both* here."

And like to be scratching one another blind, I wouldn't wonder, Morgana snorted silently, apparently not wanting to share that opinion with her young nephew. "So, it's Covianna Nim's thought to treat Ancelotis' wounds?"

Medraut nodded. "She *has* studied, Aunt, at Glastenning Tor, even if she hasn't the training you had from the Nine Ladies of Ynys Manaw."

Morgana had swung her feet out of bed, was hunting for soft leather shoes. "A rat may train with the Nine Ladies of Ynys Manaw, dear nephew, but if it speaks not a human tongue in its little rat's mouth nor hears a human's sense with its little rat's ears, then its training consists of nine years of gibberish spouted in its presence and at the end of those nine long years, all you've to show for it is a very greatly talked-at, white-bearded, old and useless rat."

Medraut widened his eyes, gulped, and wisely, Brenna thought, considering her hostess' current mood, held his opinions to himself. Morgana drew on her outer robes against the frosty chill of the air. "Do not mistake me, lad. And fetch my satchel, please, Medraut, from the baggage there." She nodded toward a pile of cloth satchels and leather cases Brenna hadn't noticed before. "I do not hate the girl, nor even seriously dislike her, for all that she's copied the serpents themselves for the skill of weaving words with their tongues. It is only that the hour is late and the shock very dreadful, and the work that must be done this night may be worse, yet. I'll not sleep the night, as it is, and Covianna Nim simply hasn't the skills I do. She may pull the occasional splinter from some monk's holy backside—"

Medraut sputtered with barely repressed laughter.

Morgana smiled faintly. "And she is doubtless quite the expert on treating burns, those being the mainstay of a healer's work when she ministers to smithies who work gold and silver and forge the best weapons ever hammered against anvil. And she treats as well those who blow the glass as the Romans did, giving the Saxons' spies some innocent reason for that many forges to be running at one time on the Tor."

"Covianna Nim said the Saxons have taken to calling it Glastonbury Tor, the Isle of Glass."

Morgana said tartly, "Mark you, nephew, 'tis far better they mock our prettily colored glass than mark our finest steelmakers and ride across the marshes to the Tor, hacking down everything that moves to deprive us of the smithies. That threat alone," Morgana muttered as they hurried down a dark corridor toward a sound of men's voices not too far from Morgana's room, "would be enough to justify Covianna Nim scampering toward greater safety in the northern kingdoms. Doubtless, she will ingratiate herself with Artorius as much as she did with Emrys Myrddin during her last and seriously eventful visit to the northern kings."

Satchel of healing herbs in hand, Morgana and her nephew thrust themselves through a group of deeply agitated men at the end of the corridor and there was no more time for Morgana's intense personal grief, for the wounded man was in sight, needing Morgana more than the grieving queen needed her solitude and tears. Brenna, an unhappy passenger, had absolutely no idea what to say or do that could possibly help.

Chapter Four

Trevor Stirling's hands sweat against the plastic cushion of the transfer couch, while Cameron Blair, the medical technician whose supervisor had committed step one of the worst terrorist atrocity in the history of humankind, fitted the transfer headset to Stirling's skull. Blair was pale, eyes shell-shocked, jaw set in anger at what McEgan had done. The Irishwoman had inherited Blair, not brought him with her, but it was clear that the medico felt the suspicion radiating from his colleagues. He'd worked for the woman . . . Stirling had to quell a deeper flutter in his belly, letting the man fit him for a transfer he could not control, when he hadn't had a chance to thoroughly vet the man, himself.

No time, dammit, there's simply no time to do a proper job of this. He clenched his teeth, very much aware that his own arrival had triggered Beckett's murder and the terrorist's hasty flight into history. The only

81

other people in the transfer room with him were senior staffers. Zenon Mylonas sat in full symbiosis with his computer equipment, preparing to insert Trevor Stirling's consciousness into the same time stream Brenna McEgan and Cedric Banning had entered. Dr. Indrani Bhaskar was attempting to give Stirling a last-minute briefing on the historical situation he would emerge into, while Cameron Blair fastened more electronic leads to his scalp, his cheeks and brow and jaw.

He cut off Blair's attempted explanation of why the transfer equipment was attached only to his head, when the energy field of human consciousness existed throughout the body. It sounded like New Age psycho-babble about chakras and out-of-body soul transference, leaving Stirling's head whirling when he needed to focus as clearly as possible on what he was about to attempt.

"Only your consciousness will transfer," Dr. Bhaskar had taken over the explanation. "You will arrive inside a host mind. That is what Dr. Beckett described. The pattern of his consciousness entered another person's body and he shared awareness with that person for sixteen minutes."

"Shared awareness?" Stirling frowned. "You mean, he took over the other person's mind?"

"Not . . . precisely." She hesitated. "Terrance said it was more like a symbiosis of awareness. His host was terrified witless by the experience. Of course, when Dr. Beckett transferred, the power setting was lower."

"Lower? You mean, Brenna McEgan set it high enough to displace the host's mind?"

Indrani bit her lip. "I don't know. None of us do. *We* never transferred. And with only one short field test to judge by, we simply haven't the data to answer that. It's possible that the host mind is displaced."

"Killed, you mean," Stirling interrupted grimly.

"Or perhaps completely suppressed. Or not. There

may be a synthesis of minds, a bit like split personality, with a struggle ensuing for control of the body."

Lovely things to look forward to, Stirling groaned inwardly. Murdering an innocent bystander's personality—or driving the poor sod mad for control of the hijacked body—was not how Stirling had envisioned ending his career with the SAS. The very act of arriving might alter history in a catastrophic fashion, if a critical person's mind was the one's displaced.

"There's no way to determine who I'll take over when I arrive?"

Indrani shook her head. "I'm afraid not. We've theorized that you'll gravitate toward someone whose mind is very similar to yours, but there's no evidence to back it up, yet, of course. And there'll be very little to go by in identifying Dr. McEgan or Dr. Banning. Neither of them will be able to speak openly, or even act openly, for fear of giving themselves away. To one another, if not to the temporal natives."

Stirling closed his eyes briefly. McEgan could sit like a spider at the center of a web for months, doing and saying nothing, while her pursuers blundered about, giving themselves away in the very need to search her out. And if the natives grew too suspicious, they might well either confine or kill someone who had apparently gone mad or turned traitor. *Nobody ever said the SAS was an easy job.* When he got his hands on McEgan, or rather on her host . . .

What if she inhabited someone he couldn't safely kill?

For that matter, could he safely kill *anyone* without risking the whole future?

"Any last-minute instructions?" Stirling asked. "What's this transfer going to feel like? How do I get home again? What happens if my host's body is killed before I complete this mission?"

Marc Blundell, who sat at a computer console beside Dr. Mylonas, said over one shoulder, "Terrance Beckett said it was like being kicked in the head by a mule. As for the other, you'll return home when the timer begins shutting the transfer equipment's power down, a year from now."

"What if the power goes off?"

Blundell tried to smile. "We're operating on our own generators, Captain. Snap generators."

Nuclear power in a compact package. Bloody wonderful. At least a simple thunderstorm shouldn't be able to disrupt power to the equipment.

"We don't know what will happen if your host body is killed," Blundell added unhappily. "You might die from the mental shock. It could disrupt your own energy pattern of consciousness, when the host's pattern is disrupted. You might find yourself floating about, like a ghost, possibly a permanent state, or perhaps only until someone comes close enough for you to transfer into another host. We just don't know."

"But I wouldn't, say, return here?"

"No." Blundell hesitated. "What the shock might do to your body here, we don't know either. Dr. Beckett's heart was badly strained by the entire transfer process."

"But he wasn't young," Blair put in grimly. "Bloody lousy candidate for the procedure, but it was his project, his decision. *He* wanted to be the first to make history. Dr. McEgan and I barely got his heart restarted, when the timer brought him back." The savage tone implied, *And she killed him, afterwards, in cold blood.*

"How close will I arrive on their heels?" Stirling wanted to know, wiping sweat onto his trousers from damp hands.

"The method isn't precise," Blundell said quietly,

adjusting his equipment. "You should arrive after them, as they've been gone for more than an hour now, but it may be weeks or even months afterward. It might conceivably be *prior* to their arrival."

I've let these people strap me into a time-traveling shotgun and they can't even bloody well aim *it!*

Eventually, there was nothing anyone could add that wasn't sheer speculation. Dr. Mylonas detached himself from his computer long enough to say, "We're ready for the transfer, Captain. I've pinpointed it as closely as I can."

Trevor Stirling swallowed very hard. Tried to brace himself. "Right. Do it, then."

The last thing he heard was a chorus of good-luck wishes from the scientists.

Then a very large mule kicked him between the eyes.

Lailoken the minstrel, a dark man full of dark ambitions and angers, bitter from professional failures and personal losses, strode down the verge of the ancient Roman road which angled westward out of Gododdin, singing to an audience of bracken, cracked stones, and rainclouds. His harp and flute lay nestled at the bottom of the rucksack hitched over his shoulder, wrapped in waterproof sealskin bags which were, along with the instruments themselves, the most valuable things he owned. Without them, he would've been utterly penniless. But poverty didn't matter to him this morning, any more than his tattered and patched cloak mattered, or his worn boots, or his much-mended tunic and trousers, their plaids faded nearly to grey. None of it mattered, because he was the most blessed man in Britain.

Between sunset the previous night and dawn this morning, Lailoken had been chosen by the gods of old, the gods of thunder and blood sacrifice and revenge. They had singled him out as a worthy vessel and rode with him now, in his own mind. Banning, the god called himself, and promised wealth and fame beyond anything Lailoken could dream.

And they both hated the Irish with cold, murderous passion.

Who would not hate them? Banning had agreed the previous night, when Lailoken still sat reeling from the shock of being selected. *They rape and pillage, destroy everything that is good and holy and civilized. Drunken, vicious brutes, heathens who can't even worship God properly. They've destroyed my people and I will destroy them utterly. And you, Lailoken, will help me.*

Lailoken understood the need for vengeance. He had watched Irish invaders hack his little family to death before he could run across the fields from the plowing to fight for them. The Irish had struck him down as well, leaving him for dead after laying open his head to the bone, but God had seen fit to let him live—the better to take vengeance upon the people who had shattered his world at the end of Irish swords.

He had taken to the road, vowing never to farm or marry again. Lailoken had wandered from the Antonine Wall on the farthest northern border to Caer-Lundein in the south, a city almost abandoned now with the threat of Saxon invasion sending farmers and town-based traders alike scurrying toward the closest hill forts they could find, refurbishing the ancient walls and beating pruning forks and plowshares into swords and long, wicked spearpoints. From the dying city of Caer-Lundein, he had wandered west to Cerniw, where the Merry Maidens stood in a great circle, nineteen foolish girls turned to monolithic standing stones for daring to dance on a Sunday. He had loved Cerniw, where the Minack Theater lay dreaming in the summer twilight, its worn golden stones remembering the Roman engineers who had built it, centuries previously, flocking in to watch the ancient Greek dramas and the bawdy Roman comedies performed in it over a span of more than four centuries.

Lailoken had played his harp and flute for money at Minack, standing on the semicircular stone floor where even the whisper of the breeze carried with the clarity of bronze bells, and his music floated magically to the highest tier of stone seats and drifted above the sea, skimming out across the deep turquoise waters of the Purthcurno Bay, with its lacework fringe of breakers spilling across the shingle.

And from Cerniw, the long journey north again to Caerleul, along the Roman roads to Rheged and Strathclyde and up to Caer-Iudeu, nestled deep in Gododdin's mountain passes which guarded the way into Pictish country. Somewhere along the way, after months of starving as a desperately mediocre instrumentalist and singer, Lailoken had discovered a meager talent for composing poetry and a slightly greater one for making men laugh at the songs he sang.

He employed those talents well, hiding his rage and the black dreams of vengeance behind foolish smiles while drunken soldiers and celebrating sailors with more money than sense gathered in *tavernas* to spend their hard-earned pay on cheap wine, cheaper women, and Lailoken's raunchy comic bravado. They roared with laughter and tossed him coins by way of approval and gave him answers as freely as the wine flowed, when he asked about the Irish in the port towns and trading centers he was able to reach.

It was his dearest prayer to strike a blow that all of Ireland would bewail, leaving her screaming widows to rend their clothing in grief. *Oh, yes,* Banning

promised darkly. *We shall certainly send them to hell,
my very dearest friend. Thousands of them. Do as I
command and we will destroy the Irish race for all
time.*

Lailoken had never been happier in his life.

As they walked, Lailoken answered his new god's
questions about where he had been, and where he had
planned to go next. *I left the garrison of Caer-Iudeu
yesterday, when the King of Gododdin and his brother
left to strike across the northern border into Pictish
Fortriu. There's no money for a minstrel in a town with
no soldiers left in garrison to pay my bills. There is
talk of war again, rumors drifting north with every
southerly breeze. When I left Caer-Iudeu, I vowed to
journey to Caerleul, where the Dux Bellorum presides
over the high councils of the northern kings. They send
their* cataphracti *to him to do his bidding, defending
the kingdoms of the Britons. Men of the cavalry
enjoy the singing, the mead, and the women on the
eve of battle or after a long, chilly patrol of the borders. A city full of soldiers, that's the place for a
minstrel at such a time as this, if he wants to put food
in his belly.*

The Dux Bellorum? Banning mused. *Artorius, himself? Excellent, better than I could have planned. By
all means, we must journey to Caerleul. I can carry
out my plans there as easily as anywhere and it would
be amusing to meet the great man. But, Lailoken, we
cannot walk all the way to Caerleul. I have no intention
of taking weeks to get there, while my enemies entrench
themselves so completely I will never discover their
hiding places.*

Enemies? Lailoken asked, startled. *Have the Irish
infiltrated spies into Caerleul itself?*

*No, I speak of other enemies. Creatures of my own
kind, two of them, fools and criminals who would stop*

*me if they could. I must discover them, Lailoken,
discover who has sheltered them, as you have sheltered
me, and destroy them utterly. No matter who serves
them as host or hostess. Do you flinch from killing a
woman, Lailoken? Or a traitor?*

He considered the question. Lailoken knew he
would have had no more qualms about killing an Irish
woman than he would have had about squashing lice.
They had taken his woman and children away forever
and deserved to lose their own, in return. But a Briton
woman? That disturbed him. Still, if the woman
harbored an enemy who would betray the Briton
people . . . She would deserve a traitor's death, were
she born of royal blood.

Aye, Lailoken answered grimly. *I would kill such a
woman, or a man traitorous enough to harbor any
creature favorable to the Irish. With my own hands,
if necessary.*

In that case, Banning answered with a cold and
delightful calm, *I suggest we find and steal a horse.*

He was lying on the ground. At least, it felt like the
ground. Hard, lumpy, uneven beneath back and shins.
He could smell smoke and dirt and rank human sweat,
unpleasant odors that triggered a ballooning headache.
Or maybe the headache had been there first. Disorientation swept him every few seconds, while his
thoughts gibbered in a voice not quite his own.

It wasn't precisely like hearing voices inside his
head. It was more like some previously unfelt part
of himself was making its presence known, as though
a portion of his personality which had been submerged was now fighting to free itself from Stirling's
internal censors. The sensations reminded him, oddly,
of colliding air masses, which boiled up into storm
fronts before mixing into something that was neither

a cold front nor a warm front, neither high pressure nor low, a hybrid sort of weather that was wildly unpredictable.

The buried part of his eerie new personality was radiating abject terror, swamped with overtones of rage. Without conscious awareness of the process, he found himself thinking in a very archaic form of Welsh— Brythonic, Dr. Bhaskar had called it. Other voices were swimming into his awareness. Men's voices, rough with worry, a woman's shrill in tones of fear. One deep voice commanded instant respect from Stirling's fractured thoughts.

"Take him inside," that voice said, the meaning coming only after the flow of words had ended. "Thank God we were so close to Caer-Iudeu! With Lot's death, we can ill afford his brother's life in the crucible as well." The whole process of understanding what had been said was as fractured as Stirling's awareness, coming partly from a slow translation of the strangely accented Welsh and partly from the portion of his new and dual awareness, which gibbered in the same language as the unknown speaker.

He was abruptly overwhelmed by a frantic desire to cry out in terror. Stirling reacted violently and automatically—and bit his own tongue bloody in the effort to shut off the frantic plea for help. *Oh, God . . .* He wasn't entirely sure which portion of his dualized mind had thought it. Even as he clenched his teeth, he was struck by a critical need to know whose body he had invaded. Somehow, the struggling and terrified portion of his mind didn't sound female. And his senses were working well enough, at least, to recognize the familiar feel of male anatomy under his clothing.

He was thankful for that much, at least. . . .

He was lifted and carried by several men. Stirling caught a flash of chilly, star-dazzled sky circling in dizzy

arcs as he was ferried ignominiously toward "inside"—
wherever that would prove to be. His jaw already
ached from clamping his teeth over his host's screams.
Stirling caught a glimpse of dark stone walls, firelight,
a smoke-stained ceiling. Footsteps thudded with a
distinct, indoor sound. Then he was eased down onto
a horizontal surface and felt fur under his skin, a fur
sack stuffed with something that smelled organic. Straw
maybe. It made a lumpy mattress, although not as
lumpy as the ground had been, and a good deal softer.

A woman Stirling couldn't see snapped, "*Fetch
Covianna Nim!*"

Another voice said, "*Who* is here? Thunders and
damnations, man, fetch her at once!" And on the heels
of that, "We're fortunate, Ganhumara. Morgana's here,
on her way home from Ynys Manaw with Medraut.
They were told we'd ridden north toward the border
and followed to catch us up."

Who, Stirling wondered fuzzily, was Covianna Nim?
Who were Ganhumara and Medraut? And who, exactly,
was *he*? The strange new portion of himself radiated
surprise that he *didn't* know. How on earth had Cedric
Banning and Brenna McEgan adjusted to this disori-
enting sense of being divided into warring factions
inside one's own skull? A twinge of guilt struck at that
thought. Not *his* skull, at all. McEgan probably didn't
care that she'd crushed some innocent's personality.
And Cedric Banning? The Aussie raised in Manchester? Poor sod. Stirling wondered how many weeks it
would take them all just to adjust. And whether or not
any of their host minds went mad under the strain.
It'd be one way to track them, he supposed—look for
the unfortunates who'd lost their minds, apparently
between one moment and the next.

"Where is he?" a new voice, low and beautifully
female, demanded.

Stirling tried to get his bearings and managed to blink his eyes open. Steel-grey eyes met Stirling's with a forthright calm that spoke of a powerful personality held carefully in check. There was a quality of expression in those eyes that suggested she had recently received a dreadful shock of some kind and was keeping some terrible emotion at bay through the force of her will alone. She was in her late thirties, at a guess, dark haired and strikingly beautiful. She carried a brightly colored, woven cloth satchel. Her voice, when she spoke again, rippled like a waterfall deep in a sacred grove, full of mystery and compelling grace. "Lie quietly, Ancelotis, while I sound your pulse." She peered into his eyes as well, fingers light and gentle on his wrist and eyelids.

The other woman he'd first heard spoke again. "He collapsed without warning, Morgana, actually fell from the saddle on the road up to the fortress. It happened so quickly, Artorius wasn't able to break his fall, for all they were riding knee to knee."

Artorius? Stirling closed his eyes for a moment over dizzy relief. At least he'd arrived at the proper time and place. And he *hadn't* arrived in Arthur's body, which would have been utter disaster.

"Ancelotis," Morgana asked quietly, "can you tell me what happened? Was there pain anywhere before you fell?"

Both of them—Stirling and Ancelotis—tried to answer at once, each half of their dual personality determined to control shared mouth, tongue, and lips. The resulting sound came out part strangled groan and part choked wheeze, half in English and half in archaic Welsh, and all of it hopelessly garbled. As Stirling groaned and his host persona whimpered, Stirling wondered, *Who the bloody hell is Ancelotis? God in Heaven, don't let it be* Lancelot . . . *if that's whom I've invaded, we're* all *in serious trouble. Bloody hell, wasn't Lancelot something the flipping French made up?* His head throbbed fiercely, making it difficult to retrieve what he did know of Arthurian history, and his ignorance was making the headache worse—he could feel it thickening, like a summer thunderstorm building up behind the long black ridges of the Highlands.

I've changed my mind, he shouted uselessly at the scientists back in the lab, scientists who couldn't hear him anyway, and couldn't retrieve him for a whole year, no matter how badly he regretted his hasty decision to follow McEgan and Banning. He was stuck, well and truly stuck. And he had a terrorist to find. The room steadied down and he took a shuddering breath, then another. *All right. I've a terrorist to find and stop. That, I'm trained for.*

Morgana was frowning. "His armsmen saw nothing before he collapsed? No warning of illness?"

"None, stepsister." The male voice that had ordered him carried inside must belong to Artorius himself. Morgana was pouring something into a cup, holding it to his lips when a newcomer arrived. A slim woman in white robes swept into the room, doffing a heavy woolen cloak and striding toward them. "I'm dreadfully sorry, I was out collecting herbs under the full moon when the messenger traced me down. I came as quickly as I could. Does he rest quietly, Morgana?"

"Aye, Covianna Nim, more quietly than he deserves, I'm thinking."

Covianna Nim, whoever she might be, was striking, her long blonde hair unbound and flowing over her shoulders. She wore a very simple garment, which stood out against the sea of brightly colored reds and blues and yellows worn by the others, by virtue of being an unsullied white, only slightly dusty along the bottom hem which swept the ground. The robe, with a deep hood shrugged back over her shoulders like a cape, open down the front over an ice-pale gown of softest lamb's wool, was belted closed with a beautifully worked girdle of silver links, intricate with the loops and the interwoven animal shapes of Celtic knotwork. Stirling, lying dazed and confused, couldn't decide which healer he preferred bending over him, and finally decided he'd just as soon have neither of them.

"Drink this, Ancelotis."

Stirling had no idea what it was, but he didn't want it. Neither did Ancelotis. Unfortunately, Morgana was not to be denied. He swallowed the bitter stuff, which sent creeping lassitude through limbs and brain. Maybe, if Stirling got really lucky, he would wake up when the drug wore off and find this whole thing was only a nightmare.

Morgana sat close to the great hall's hearth, sipping a cup of mulled wine to which she had added soothing herbs, and listened in silence while her stepbrother outlined the size of the nightmare which had descended upon her. Upon them all, for that matter. Voices from the other side of the hall distracted her, officers of the garrison patrolling their northern borders, and the hastily summoned council of advisors for all of Gododdin, who had ridden hard half the night from the capital at Trapain Law. They had all gathered to speak quietly on the other side of the hall, making decisions for the kingdom's defenses in light of this latest disaster.

"It was the Picts," Artorius said quietly at Morgana's shoulder, resting a warm hand against her back. "If I'd known that Lot had taken most of his *cataphracti* from Trapain Law up to Caer-Iudeu, I might have arrived in time to change things. But I didn't find out until we were halfway to the capital. We stopped at one of the mile forts along the Antonine Wall, to rest the horses, let Ganhumara stretch her legs a bit. They told us he'd passed through with the bulk of his cavalry not twenty-four hours previously, heading for the border. That he was planning actually to cross into Pictish Fortriu, not just repel raiders. Lot meant to strike at their base of operations, prevent them from pillaging across the northern borders with such ease—"

"Yes," she interrupted harshly. "I am aware of the problem, stepbrother."

He moved around to grip her hand. "I know that, Morgana. God forgive me for having a blunt soldier's manner. Would that a learned Druid such as Emrys Myrddin had the telling of this, to soften it."

She managed a fleeting, watery smile. "I have no complaints in you, Artorius, and not even Emrys Myrddin could soften such news." The smile died away. "I, too, spoke with the officer of that mile-fort garrison, on my way home from Galwyddel. They told us you had passed not eight hours ahead of us." Her throat thickened. "I came north with news for him, news I thought shouldn't wait, and little thought I would never have the chance to tell him a word of it." Her voice shook and the wine in her cup sloshed dangerously up the sides. She sipped again to prevent spilling any across her lap.

Artorius found a square of linen tucked into a pouch at his waist and handed it to her, to dry her eyes, then soothed her arm with gentle fingers until she had herself under control again. Across the room, the councillors had either reached some decision or had a weighty question to ask, as their spokesman bowed his apologetic way into her awareness.

"Forgive the intrusion, Queen Morgana, but we must know . . . Will you insist on your eldest son inheriting immediately?"

She lifted her head sharply. "Put little Gwalchmai on Lot Luwddoc's throne, and the boy not above seven years of age yet? We would do just as well inviting in the Picts to take their choice of plunder!"

The councillor winced. "Yes, our thoughts precisely, but we had to ask. Will you then serve as queen of Gododdin until your son has reached manhood?"

Morgana gripped her wine cup until her fingers went white and cold, having dreaded this very question from the moment the council had arrived. Slowly, she shook her head. "No. Already I have Galwyddel and Ynys Manaw to govern, which I have done from Trapain Law since my marriage. To add Gododdin to this . . ." She shook her head once again. "It would be unfair to the people of Gododdin and to those of Galwyddel and Ynys Manaw."

The councillor paled. "Who then, Queen?"

Morgana glanced at her stepbrother, then sent a look toward the chamber where Ancelotis, her husband's younger brother, lay sleeping, having collapsed in the wake of his brother's death. Artorius followed her glance and nodded. "Yes, Morgana, you have the right of it. Ancelotis is exactly what Gododdin must have until Gwalchmai reaches his maturity."

Relief flooded visibly through the councillor. "Ancelotis. Yes, of course. You give your approval to this choice, Queen Morgana?"

"I do," she said softly, echo of other words, another time and place that seemed a lifetime ago, now. "Ancelotis is the best choice Gododdin could hope to have in this troubled time." After a moment's thought, she added quietly, "Indeed, Ancelotis may prove a better king than his brother." She winced to speak ill of the dead, but couldn't help remembering the fate of poor little Thaney, her husband's daughter and only child by his first wife. Disinherited and nearly drowned for failure to reveal the name of her lover . . .

His ire had not even been a Christian anger at the poor girl's immorality, for Lot held far more closely to the old ways than the new. A view she had shared, in fact, or her marriage would have been intolerable. No, there had been nothing of religion in his actions. He had simply been infuriated by Thaney's stubborn refusal to obey him. Lot's temper had, indeed, been a great failing of his character. But he had never quite dared strike Morgana during a rage, given her own pedigree and the strength of well-honed steel behind it, all the steel of Galwyddel and Ynys Manaw combined, her birthright as queen of those lands. Ancelotis, at least, was an even-tempered man, who would rule as a conscientious regent for Morgana's young son.

A short vote lasting less than two minutes confirmed it. When he woke, Ancelotis would be king. And Morgana would no longer be queen of Gododdin. The quiet presence which shared Morgana's inner awareness listened intently, trying to understand the nuances of what she heard. Poor refugee, to choose a place and time like this one as better than her own . . .

"Will you travel on to Trapain Law, Morgana," Artorius asked quietly, "to be with your sons, or return with us to Caerleul?"

She glanced up, gaze sharply focused on Artorius' worried eyes. "There will be a High Council of Kings, will there not, over this?"

"And over the renewed Saxon threat, yes."

"I am still a sovereign queen, Artorius, and must therefore join that council to speak for the people of Galwyddel and Ynys Manaw." She paused, then added,

"Perhaps my sons might be fetched from Trapain Law, to join us at Caerleul?"

Artorius nodded. "I will send a rider immediately. There are men-at-arms enough to defend Gododdin's borders and still provide escort for the boys. Lot brought a fair number of Gododdin's *cataphracti* with him from the capital, to meet the Pictish raiders. They will serve well at Ancelotis' back, to greet the Saxons with a show of strength."

Morgana sipped again at her doctored wine, but before she could speak, Covianna swept into the room and headed straight their way, having apparently stopped at her own room to put away her satchel of healing herbs. She moved with compelling grace and stopped to chat with most of the men in the room, by ones and threes and sevens, making the rounds with a charming smile for everyone and an avid eye for any conversation that might turn up interesting tidbits she might later use to her advantage. The men followed her with their eyes, like a pack of anxious puppies, tails wagging frantically in the hope of having those keen eyes and that flashing smile turned on *them*.

Even Morgana was affected by the woman's aura of mysterious sensuality. Lessons learned at her mother's knee, Morgana supposed, the need for secrecy about family business spilling into secrecy about everything, and all of it contributing to that aura of allurement. Her unseen guest, puzzled, asked understandably enough, *Who is this Covianna Nim, then? Is she someone we must watch?*

Oh, aye, Morgana agreed, *she'll bear watching, whether your madman or your soldier have anything to do with her business or not. Intrigue and secrecy are as necessary to her as feet are for me.*

But what's the secrecy about? If she's untrustworthy . . .

Morgana almost laughed aloud, converted it to a cough and sipped her wine again. *I should sooner trust the great Satan of the Christian church than trust Covianna Nim on any number of matters. But is she a traitor to the Britons? No.*

What is she, then? Brenna McEgan wanted to know.

Covianna Nim's family is part of a clan of metallurgists. Smiths who've been hiding their secrets on island smithies in an unbroken line stretching back to the days when Rome had not yet found the means to conquer Britannia. They make the finest weapons in all of Europe, better than the finest swords of the Franks and far superior to the few swords the Saxon lords carry.

Indeed, Covianna Nim herself made the sword Artorius wields in battle. None better exists. She is both healer and swordsmith, of high status in her clan and trusted with the secrets of her family's trade as well as those of the abbot of Glastenning Tor. She and all others at Glastenning, priests and monks included, know how to keep their secrets most effectively. And they've acres of surrounding marshland and treacherous bogs to protect them, and the annual springtime floods that overflow the River Brue. 'Tis not so easy a thing, to enter Glastenning Tor, if its inhabitants don't bid you welcome.

Morgana's guest didn't hold a high opinion of relying on the marshes and tidal lakes, should open warfare break out with the southern Saxons. *Is there any sort of army available to Glastenning?*

Morgana sighed. *None that would serve the purpose, no. The community, if one can call it that, has for centuries consisted of reclusive metallurgists and alchemists. They greeted Joseph of Arimethea sixty-three years after the Christ was born and helped him build his abbey, the first Christian church in Britain.*

*And then quietly went about their business, paying
open homage to the new God of the Abbey, while carrying on with the old ways at their iron forges, their
goldsmithies and glassmakers' furnaces. They're a bit
like my own family, in that regard,* Morgana admitted, *as we both hail from some of the greatest Druidic lines in Britain, craft masters and healers, poets
and artists. Both our families started calling things by
varying new names wherever and whenever expedient.*

Her guest was impressed. *As a survival strategy, it
sounds fiendishly effective,* Brenna murmured. *So the
local clergy and the metal smiths discourage casual visitors. Do Saxon merchants come under this heading?*

Morgana frowned. *Not as much as we should like.
The Saxons have an eye to snapping up the finest items
our British forges and glassworks and looms can provide, at the lowest possible cost—at the point of a
sword, when artisans have refused insulting offers made
for their wares.*

There was no further opportunity for discussion, as
Covianna Nim finished her rounds of the councillors
and officers, and undulated in their direction.

"Ancelotis is resting quietly?" she asked, voice a low
and sultry purr. It had not set well with her when
Morgana had made it clear Covianna's help was
neither necessary nor welcome.

"He is," Morgana nodded. "It was fortunate they
were so near Caer-Iudeu when the illness struck."

"Indeed," she smiled. "And fortunate to have such
skilled healers to look after him."

Morgana bristled silently, more at the tone and the
glance from under hooded lashes than the actual words
spoken. Covianna flicked the hem of her white robe
aside and drew a chair up to the hearth, settling herself
immovably into their conversation. She shrugged her
long, blonde tresses over one shoulder and began

plaiting them into a neat braid with nimble fingers. "I will, of course, journey with Ancelotis all the way to Trapain Law or Caerleul, whichever proves his destination," Covianna smiled, "to be sure he receives the best possible care."

Artorius stepped hurriedly into the conversation before Morgana could devise a rejoinder chilly enough to suit. "A gesture we all appreciate, Covianna Nim, and it looks to be Caerleul, rather than the capital of Gododdin. Your family is well?"

"They are, and thank you for the asking." She glanced briefly at Morgana. "I offer regrets for your sorrow on behalf of my entire family, Morgana. You will ride to Council at Caerleul?"

Morgana inclined her head. "I will. My sons will join me there."

Covianna nodded, apparently satisfied with the jibes she'd already delivered. "I regret your sorrow as well, and I am only too glad of other healers to look after Ancelotis on the journey." She added with a flash of gleaming white teeth, "As it happens, I have been longing for another opportunity to study with Emrys Myrddin, if he will have time for teaching me."

Considering the fool Emrys Myrddin had made of himself the last time Morgana had seen him in Covianna Nim's company, Morgana had no doubt that the Druidic councillor would *find* the time for such lessons, even if he had to forgo sleep to do so. Indeed, sleep was doubtless the last thing on a man's mind, in close and private company with Covianna Nim.

"I have not seen your nephew, Morgana," Covianna added, glancing around the hall where deadly serious conversations still held sway in every corner. "Is he not with you?"

"Medraut? Indeed, he is."

Artorius put in, "I sent him with instructions to the officers of the *cataphracti*, to send for Morgana's sons."

"And is the son of Marguase as well as the last time I saw him?"

Morgana stiffened, so utterly infuriated she could not even draw breath to answer.

Artorius had gone white to the lips. "*We will not speak of that poisoner in my presence!*"

Covianna's eyes widened in shocked alarm.

Artorius struggled visibly to control himself. "She was executed for good reason—and I am not a man given to speaking ill of kinfolk! I will not have her name uttered within my hearing, is that understood, Covianna Nim?"

Covianna returned his blistering gaze with a demure glance that hid more than it revealed. "Forgive me, Artorius," she purred with all the sweet civility of a Highlands wildcat with claws extended, "I intended neither insult nor challenge to your decrees as Dux Bellorum. Marguase was many things to many people. I meant only to ask after her son's health. The boy was young, the last time I saw him."

"He is young still," Morgana said coldly. "But not so young as you might imagine, nor half so arrogant as his mother. I will thank you never to speak to him of my unlamented half sister."

Covianna's blue eyes smoldered. "Of course not, Queen Morgana." She finished off the plait of thick, honey-bright hair and rose with a swirl of white robes. "I will take leave of you for the night. It is a long ride from Caer-Iudeu to Caerleul and we have all lost sleep we can ill afford."

She inclined her head to Artorius first, slighting Morgana with the gesture, then gathered up her skirts and strolled languidly through the doorway, once again drawing appreciative stares in her wake. Morgana held back a hiss of displeasure. Spend the whole, long ride to Caerleul in Covianna Nim's poisonous company? She tossed back the last of the wine in her cup with angry impatience, then rose from her own chair. "As much as I despise finding myself in agreement with that creature, she is right about the need for sleep. There is little anyone can do for Ancelotis that I have not already done, so I will take my leave, stepbrother."

Artorius laid a hand on her shoulder. "Don't let her nettle you so, Morgana. She is envious—and has much to envy where you are concerned. Still and all . . . You know that I will allow no harm to befall you and yours?"

Quick tears prickled behind her eyelids. "Yes. And I thank you for it."

She hurried away before he—or anyone else—could see those unshed tears fall.

Chapter Five

Stirling came awake slowly. The final thought he'd taken down into darkness with him was still reverberating through his mind. *Let it all have been some terrible nightmare . . .*

Unhappily, the scents and sounds and unfamiliar sensations coming from his immediate surroundings bore nothing in common with anything in the twenty-first century.

No such luck, then. It was entirely too real.

Stirling opened his eyes, to find that he lay sprawled across a fur bag of straw, which he vaguely remembered from a weltering confusion of images connected more or less solidly with his abrupt arrival in the sixth century. Someone had draped another fur across his body as a blanket. His dreams had been a hellish mixture of scenes: horseback combat, men in rough woolen tunics and padded leather armor dying from swords thrust through their bellies and throats; Belfast in flames, Orange terror squads shooting down women and children; the flash of heavy spears, a horde of blue-tattooed men swarming across a fallen rider, the crimson splash of blood across a muddy field, across a battered desktop, across pavements in Clonard . . .

He blinked away the disturbing images and studied the room, instead. It was well constructed and larger than he'd expected, some three by four meters. The ceiling was whitewashed plaster, stained with smoke and soot from pottery oil lamps, several of which hung from hooks in the corners of the room. The wicks had been trimmed low, sending a soft golden light through the room. The floor was utilitarian, made of simple stone flagging, although the stones had been shaped with skill and well mortared. The walls were plaster over stone, with murals of hunting scenes painted on them.

The style reminded him of Roman wall paintings, which surprised him. There were no Roman remains of this type anywhere near the Scottish Lowlands, not that Stirling had ever heard of, anyway. Plenty of small forts and watchtowers, in a line roughly paralleling Antonine's Wall and the Gask Ridge, with another line of them down along Hadrian's Wall in the border counties, but nothing like a villa with murals of this quality. Where exactly was he, then?

He was still puzzling it over when Ancelotis' part of his dual awareness woke up and tried to come to terms with the invader inside his skull. After one reflexive attempt to shout for help, Ancelotis and Stirling reached honorable compromise: they declared a truce in the interest of learning how to walk again. Trying to walk, with two fiercely competitive minds in the driver's seat—each of them utterly and ruthlessly determined to take charge of their shared body— landed them flat on the floor within two steps. They landed hard, jarring every bone against a floor that was startlingly warm under their shared skin.

Both of them swore aloud and creatively, with the curses breaking out in a mixture of Brythonic Welsh and modern English. Stirling rigidly ordered himself to stop thinking in his own native language. He couldn't afford to lapse into English when anyone else was around. Cedric Banning would find him faster, true, bringing him an ally, but Brenna McEgan would hear, as well. He'd certainly change history if Ancelotis *was,* in fact, the person Stirling's gibbering terror thought he *might* be, and McEgan and her unknown host slid a dagger through his ribs because of Stirling's carelessness.

I am in over my head, Stirling realized despairingly.

Explain why, Ancelotis' voice demanded abruptly, shocking Stirling half witless with the first clearly articulated words Stirling had been able to understand. *Why would this McEgan want to murder the brother of a dead king of Gododdin? McEgan, that's a foul, Irish clan name, is it not? Are you some Druid's soul from the Otherworld, sent to warn and guard me from the Irish threatening our western coast? You're too late for my brother's life, if you've come to warn of us against the Picts. They've had him under their knives and war clubs already, and nearly the Dux Bellorum and myself with him.*

Uh . . . Sprawled on a sixth-century stone floor, it seemed as good an explanation as any he might offer. *Close enough,* he thought carefully back at his host. *I'm afraid I don't know anything about Picts and I'm sorry about your brother. I've lost a great-uncle to war and most of my comrades-in-arms, as well.* The pain of his lost command, blown apart in Clonard, was a sickness in his gut.

It was not, perhaps, anything like losing one's brother, evidently right in front of his host's eyes, given the memory images bursting into Stirling's awareness, but it was enough to convey understanding of the loss—and a deep understanding of battle, as well. The images in Stirling's memory, of the entire city block in Clonard, Belfast, erupting into flame with whole buildings falling into ruin, was enough to stun Ancelotis silent, awed and horrified.

And this is the manner of war you fight? Enough flame and brimstone to cause even the bishop of Rome to flinch in dismay? May Afallach and his nine daughters of the Underworld preserve us, then, if Christ cannot, for we've nothing to stop that sort of death in our midst.

Stirling wanted to reassure his host that such death could not be reproduced in the sixth century by one man, working alone, but he could produce no such reassurance. It was a simple enough fact that he himself could have produced a crude but perfectly serviceable black powder, difficult to do if one didn't know the proper proportions, relative child's play if one did—and Sterling most assuredly did. And he would have bet several cases of Bibles that Brenna McEgan did, as well. And all it needed for a bomb was a containment vessel to hold the black powder.

A wooden keg or common crockery wine jug would suffice, since one didn't need to worry about building up sufficient pressure to launch a projectile, as one would need for a gun or a far simpler mortar or cannon. And the earliest of those, after all, had been made from church bells. Stirling was fairly certain that even Britain, as cut off from Rome as it must have been for the past hundred or so years, could supply a good-sized bronze bell.

I won't lie to you, he admitted. *There's a great deal of destruction she could wreak on you and yours. Brenna McEgan must be found and stopped. She's an*

Irish terrorist. That is, she murders for political gain. It's my job to find and stop her. I suspect, he added grimly, *that it's the Dux Bellorum she'll try to kill. I can't think of another reason for her to have chosen this particular time and place.*

After a long moment, during which Stirling could literally feel Ancelotis thinking rapidly, another carefully verbalized question came back. *And how will you find her?*

I don't know, Stirling was forced to admit. *She'll be hiding in someone's mind, just as I am borrowing yours. Dreadfully sorry, but I couldn't think of any other way to stop her.* After a moment's further consideration, he added, *There's another man who's come, a learned man who will help us, if we can identify him without risking your life. Unfortunately, I could easily do just that by accidentally exposing my presence in McEgan's company. Banning is his name, Cedric Banning. My own is Trevor Stirling. I was born not far from here,* he added hopefully. *Close to the city we call Stirling, where my ancestors have lived for generations.*

An unexpected chuckle startled him as Ancelotis took the memory images from Stirling's portion of their shared mind and recognized the landmarks. *Stirling, is it? There is truth in your mind, Stirling of Stirling. Truth is a powerful force, great enough to overcome even the barriers between worlds. It's Caer-Iudeu, we call it. Artorius was raised on that mountain I see in your memory, with that remarkable fortress you've built atop the cliff. We Britons should build half so well. Alas, the Romans departed with our finest engineers nearly a century ago. Artorius was, thank whichever God you prefer to worship, brought north for fostering, out of the short-lived kingdoms at the heart of the dragon lands of the south.*

Dragon lands of the south? Stirling echoed, confused. *Do you mean, actual dragons?* He had a brief, doubtless impossible vision of a surviving tyrannosaur or two stalking the southern coast of England, although come to think of it, weren't the tyrannosaurs American beasties?

Oh, aye, Ancelotis agreed. *The dragon lands. Old places of power, that's what the Druids have always said, even the ones who kissed the ring of the Roman bishop and turned their oaken groves into oaken churches and chaste nunneries and kept up the old teachings in the dead of night under a darkened moon.*

It's the dragon lines I mean, of course, that run from Cerniw—the name translated to Cornwall, in Stirling's mind—*and St. Michael's Mount, they call it now, up through Hurlers and Trethevy Quoit, twining their way along the northern route up through Brigit's Tor and Silbury Hill, Avebury, and Barbury, and along the southern route of Cerne Abbas and Stonehenge, meeting the northern line at the great white horse of Uffington that gallops its way toward Bury St. Edmund and the Norfolk coast.*

The sun sets the dragon lines afire each year at Lammas and at Beltane, rising poised atop the terminus at the coast northeast of Caer-Lundein, sets them ablaze with all its own wild energy that races from tor to mound to henge. The Druids say the fire runs along the old stone roads and the standing circles, that focus and feed the wild, splashing flood into the pools of rocky cairns and the wheels of the standing stones, to be stored up for the balance of the year.

Stirling blinked in surprise, superimposing a map of southern England over Ancelotis' description and coming up with a long, snaking line of prehistoric ruins under the national trust, a line that did, indeed, cut a path from Cornwall to Norfolk through some very interesting real estate, looking at it from the viewpoint of a sixth-century Druid.

Druid, I? Ancelotis chuckled. *I'm no teacher nor poet nor yet a prophet, although I've served often enough as judge when the disputes arise in Caer-Iudeu, which is my charge.*

All right, Stirling agreed, more than willing to accept his host's opinion on the matter. *So Emrys Myrddin brought Artorius north for safety's sake while the southern kingdoms went to hell in their own merry way? Leaving Artorius to rise to power in Ambrosius Aurelianus' footsteps?*

Aye, you've the right of it. It was Ambrosius Aurelianus, last of the Roman commanders in Britain, who taught even Uthyr Pendragon a thing or two about war. Had Artorius and Lot and I not learned the art of war from Aurelianus himself, chasing us up and down that mountain in your mind, there would be no Britain left for the Britons, save a shallow ditch to be buried in. How else think you we've held the Picts and Irish and Saxons at bay, along with the Jutland Danes and their Frisian Anglish cousins?

Even as Ancelotis spoke, a grim and empty hollowness opened up in his heart, as the man's grief and self-blame welled up. The memory image of a tall and heavy-muscled man being torn from a mortally wounded horse played out again and again behind Ancelotis' closed eyelids, along with the sudden, wounded scream of the horse, the long topple to the ground, the swarm of Picts like blue-painted carrion flies clubbing and stabbing until what remained little resembled a human form.

Ancelotis clenched his jaw so tightly, his molars ached. *They cut him down before my very eyes, before anyone could reach him or drive them back. I've a wild debt of blood to pay, Stirling of Caer-Iudeu, but once*

*I have avenged my brother and king, once I have
assured a safe transition of power for Lot Luwddoc's
throne, then will I help you. We will hunt your Irish
murderess together—and stop her.*

Stirling was so grateful for the unexpected offer of
alliance, he didn't know what to say. Ancelotis merely
chuckled and suggested they get on with the business
at hand—reaching the privy pot against the far wall.
Stirling grunted once, then dragged himself off the
floor and learned how to walk again, mostly by letting Ancelotis take over the driving, so to speak. It got
them to the pot, at any rate. And men of the sixth
century A.D. pissed in a pot the same way men of the
twenty-first century did, leaning with one hand against
the wall and taking reasonable care to aim. It was
vaguely reassuring that they *could* aim, under the
circumstances.

He wondered who'd stripped off his clothing, since
he was bare-arse naked, except for thick gold armbands
which circled his wrists and the ornate ends of a thin
gold torque, which rested in the hollow of his throat.
The room was surprisingly warm, the flooring actually
toasty beneath his feet. Ancelotis chuckled at his
puzzlement.

*Have you no central heating where you come from?
The whole fortress is heated, of course, with steam
pipes beneath the floors to carry the warmth from the
firepits. There's not a fortress or villa from Gododdin
to Strathclyde that hasn't a good central heating system. It's too cold here, of a winter, to build without
one. That much, at least, the Romans left for us when
they pulled out their legions and engineers.*

*The smaller camps and watchtowers aren't heated,
of course, which is one reason we rotate duty frequently, particularly during bad weather. Wouldn't be
fair subject the border guards to a whole winter in*

*unheated towers and fortlets. And those glen-blocking
forts are just as cold and unpleasant a duty station,
up in the passes through the Highlands.*

It made good sense, although Stirling could fore-
see trouble, if the enemy across the invisible border
with Pictland ever figured out the timing of the relief
columns. That was not, however, his concern and he'd
no business meddling in the internal military affairs
of the Briton commanders. So he stumbled back to
the bed, a wooden frame with ropes supporting the
fur bag he'd spent the night on, and sat down to drag
his clothes on. Stirling wanted a bath, but Ancelotis
conveyed a sense of considerable urgency in the journey which Stirling's arrival had interrupted. Getting
dressed involved learning what sixth-century garments
consisted of, and in what order he was meant to don
them.

He pulled on loose-fitting woolen trousers over a
linen undergarment more like a union suit than any
other modern equivalent. The trousers—secured at the
waist with a narrow leather belt which sported a
metalwork buckle of finely wrought silver in a looping, quintessentially Celtic style—were boldly woven
in a red-and-blue checkered pattern. Short lengths of
leather cordage puzzled him until Ancelotis explained
that they were meant to cinch the loose trouser cuffs
around his ankles, thus keeping anything unpleasant
from crawling up one's legs.

Before tying off the trouser cuffs, Stirling reached
for a close-fitting linen tunic dyed a rich blue, over
which went a long woolen tunic, in bright shades of
reds, oranges, greens, and blues, the garish precursors
of Scots tartan. The effect of plaid tunic and checked
trousers offended Stirling's admittedly Philistine aesthetic sense. The thought prompted a grin, however,
as mercifully there was no mirror in evidence to check

the gaudy result. The quality of the cloth was surprisingly high, considering the century of invasions Briton kingdoms had endured following the collapse of Roman government. He wondered what further surprises the sixth century would hold?

Light footsteps caught his attention as he picked up thick leather boots. A tap sounded at his door, which opened on silent leather hinges. Stirling wasn't sure whom he expected, but it wasn't the startlingly beautiful girl who slipped inside, at first glance no more than half grown, but at second glance perhaps as much as a very young seventeen or eighteen. Eyes the color of deep blue ice gazed at him in wide concern. Copper hair streamed over one shoulder in a cascade that stopped his breath.

Her gown, of a far more attractive style than he'd expected, clinging delightfully to her more than delightful curves, was cinched around an impossibly tiny waist by a belt apparently made from solid gold links. The woolen gown had been dyed a blue as striking as her eyes. Jewels glittered at her wrists and ears. A heavy woolen cloak, startling in shades of crimson-and-green plaid and lined with soft white fur, hung from her shoulders, held closed across her breasts by a jeweled chain.

"You're awake at last!" she breathed.

Belatedly, he noticed the golden circlet at her throat. Torque of royalty . . . Was this woman his—or rather, Ancelotis'—wife? Ancelotis' reply growled through his confusion. *She's no wife of mine, a fact she forgets far too frequently.* Her identity, reaching him from Ancelotis' memories, burst into Stirling's awareness with cold horror. *Ohshit, ohshit, ohshit . . .* He stood up hastily, which was a mistake, given his poor coordination. He stumbled off balance and the girl gasped, darting forward to steady him.

"I'm no child!" he snapped, pulling free and wondering for a bad moment if he'd spoken in Brythonic Welsh or English. She froze, eyes wide. The beginnings of fear—and anger—began to spark in those lovely pale eyes.

While Stirling scrubbed at his face, trying to dredge up some kind of response, Ancelotis simply muttered, "Forgive my short temper, it's that damned potion of Morgana's."

For a long, hazardous moment, she said nothing at all; then the danger passed and she relaxed, although she remained standing far too close for his peace of mind. "Aye," she nodded. "Belike. Druids' potions have left me dizzy a time or two."

He glanced curiously into her eyes, wondering about that. No sense in asking, however; that could be even more disastrous than snapping at her had been. "I *am* all right, truly," he tried to reassure her.

"What happened?"

He shook his head, neither of them able to come up with an explanation that sounded even remotely plausible. "It doesn't matter. I'm fine now."

Her glance remained wary, but she didn't press the issue. Just how much did a Briton woman argue with her menfolk? Ancelotis didn't answer him, instead speaking with a firmness that bordered on the grim.

"Thank you for making certain I'm all right, but you had better go."

She glared at the door with a flash of defiance, then her shoulders drooped, as though her cloak—or some other burden—were far too heavy. "Aye. It wouldn't do to stir trouble just now. The council met while you slept," she added, eyes flashing with some strong emotion Stirling couldn't interpret. "Summoned by Artorius from the capital."

"And did the councillors take a vote while I slept?"

he asked, voice on edge for a reason Stirling didn't quite understand.

Her ice-pale eyes glinted. "They did. You're wanted in the great hall."

"In that case," Ancelotis said coolly, "you had best not be here when they come to fetch me."

Her eyes flashed, rebellious again, but she subsided without further verbal protest. She did take one worried step forward—Stirling was pretty sure it was worry that prompted it—and checked abruptly at some tiny signal he hadn't realized he'd telegraphed until too late. She caught back a sob—of rage or frustration or grief, he had no idea. Then she whirled aside and snatched at the door, peering carefully into the corridor before slipping away with a rustle of woolen skirts. Stirling discovered an unmanly tremor in his knees and an even more disturbing response at his groin.

This was *worse* than riot duty in Clonard.

Ancelotis muttered, *A man may leave a city of his free will, if life there displeases him, but a woman like Ganhumara will plague a man to the grave, stirring trouble wherever she sets foot. And she but a girl scarce grown to womanhood.*

That, Stirling thought grimly, was doubtless the best reason for avoiding female entanglements he'd ever heard. He sat back down to tug on his boots, scrubbed his face for a long moment, and thought seriously of finding a very deep and icy lake to jump into. He was still wrapping ankle laces around his trouser cuffs when the door opened again, the knock so peremptory as to be nonexistent.

"Ancelotis! You're looking much better!"

Stirling found himself facing a man in his midthirties, perhaps a little older. His face had been deeply weathered by sun and worry and the harshness of battle. There was an odd, out-of-place look about his

features, better suited to the wilds of Persia than the
Lowlands of Scotland. He wasn't tall, but only a fool
would've made the mistake of calling him a small man.
Stocky, athletic under a tunic and loose trousers of cut
and quality comparable to the ones Stirling wore, his
hands were scarred and calloused. His nose had been
broken at least once and his stance communicated
instant readiness to fight. It was not belligerence.
Stirling had seen that look of hair-trigger readiness
before, in the faces of soldiers in a combat zone. This
was a man accustomed to war. And command. And
victory.

A golden torque, much smaller than the one Stirling
wore, narrower even than the copper-haired girl's,
glittered at the man's throat. High rank, then, but not
quite royalty. A red dragon, hand-embroidered by some
skilled needlewoman, blazed scarlet on the breast of
his tunic, giving Stirling the final clue he needed,
confirmed by Ancelotis.

Artorius.

Dux Bellorum of the People of the Red Dragon.

He didn't even know how to address this man. The
word "sire" froze in the back of his throat. Artorius
wasn't a king. That didn't stop Stirling from thinking
dazedly, *My God, it's King Arthur in person. . . .*

Artorius was staring at him rather oddly. "You *are*
all right, Ancelotis?"

He managed a nod. "Aye. It's that blasted potion."
He winced at using the same lame excuse, but Artorius
merely grunted.

"You'll need a clear head by week's end, man. The
council's voted. I sent for them the moment you collapsed. They're in full agreement and Queen Morgana
gives you her full backing."

Stirling had not the faintest idea what Artorius
was talking about, but his host's reaction gave him

an unpleasant clue. Ancelotis blanched, groping for the bed and sinking onto it before his knees gave way.

"She's refused it, hasn't she?"

"You cannot be surprised by that."

Ancelotis ran a distracted hand through his hair, a movement that startled Trevor Stirling, who still wasn't accustomed to having his body respond to commands he hadn't given. "No," Ancelotis agreed with a sigh. "It doesn't surprise me. If anything, I respect her the more for it. They've given it to me, have they? Until Gwalchmai is of age?"

"They have. I fear the formal ceremony must be kept far briefer than you might wish."

Ancelotis snorted. "I would wish for none at all to be needed. It was never my intent to rule Gododdin—or anything else, save my warhorse and a cavalry unit or two. That was Lot's desire, never my own."

Artorius' weathered face betrayed the depth of his concern in a whole series of deepened gullies through cheeks and brow. "This cannot be easy for you, old friend, nor is what I must ask now. I came to Caer-Iudeu because I had great need of both you and your brother in this matter of the Saxon challenge. This trouble has not diminished simply because the mantle of kingship has fallen onto your shoulders. I must ask it, Ancelotis, for the good of Britain. Don't return to Trapain Law yet."

"But—"

"Gododdin may be as far from the troubles of the south as it is possible to go in Briton territory, but if we allow Cutha and his machinations free reign while you look to Gododdin's internal affairs, you will wake one morning all too soon to find Cutha and his ilk massing on *your* border, not Glastenning's. Covianna Nim brought the demands from Cutha of Sussex and his puppet Creoda of Wessex, at the request of the abbot of Glastenning Tor. They are pushing, Ancelotis, and pushing hard. Glastenning is not yet theirs, yet already their eyes have turned north to Rheged—and if Rheged falls, my friend, there is no kingdom of the north that will be able to stand against them."

Ancelotis scrubbed his brow wearily with both hands, listening and cursing under his breath at every new piece of unpleasant news. "The kings of Dumnonia and Glastenning have asked your help?"

"They have. There must be a council of the kings of the north, to answer this Saxon challenge, to act in support of the kings of the south. Come with me to Caerleul, Ancelotis. Morgana rides with us to speak for Galwyddel and Ynys Manaw."

"And Ganhumara will speak for Caer-Guendoleu?"

Irritation flickered through Artorius' eyes. "She will. Would that God had granted her father another few years of life."

"And you wonder why I have never married?"

"No longer," Artorius shot back dryly. "Do yourself a favor, old friend, and marry a cowherd's daughter— queens of the blood have too much ambition and pride to make a man happy."

He held the Dux Bellorum's gaze for a long moment. "I grieve to hear you say it. Very well, Artorius, I will ride to Caerleul and speak for Gododdin in council. Does King Aelle of Sussex send his youngest son to us alone? Or does Cutha travel with company as pleasant and reasonable as that vile and odious mercenary he calls father? You had no real opportunity to give us details yesterday, with the fighting and Lot's death."

"No, Cutha of Sussex does not ride alone. God help us all, he's bringing Creoda with him. And it's Prince Creoda who's demanding a place in Rheged's council. You know only too well what *that* means."

Ancelotis swore with impressive Brythonic creativity.

Artorius grunted agreement. "King Aelle sits on his self-crowned throne and laughs at fools like Creoda, bootlicking dogs, he and his father both, styling themselves *Saxons* to hold onto lands they should have fought to protect. *Gewisse,* their own allies call them, and with good reason. His scheming grows ever bolder, Ancelotis, which is why I must speak to the kings of the north in council, without delay. Damn Creoda *and* his fool of a father, Cerdic, for selling their Saxon paymasters the rights they hold as Briton kings, to join our privy councils. 'They only wish to parlay,' was the message brought north by Covianna Nim."

Artorius growled, striking his open palm with a fist. "May the gods of our ancestors help us, for it is better—at least for now—that we talk when they offer it, than bleed for lack of trying." Artorius paced the room, an enraged dragon caged in far too small a space. "King Aelle is a crafty bastard, I'll give him that much, and Cutha is a right and proper twig off his branch. They supported Cerdic's bid for power and won him the thrones of Caer-Guinntguic and Caer-Celemion and Ynys Weith, and now they've turned that gain into a Saxon-controlled fiefdom with a stinking Saxon name. Wessex!"

Artorius spat disgustedly. "West Sussex, there's what that name really means, for you, and that name is our greatest danger, Ancelotis. Briton kings toppled by Briton traitors anxious for a taste of power for themselves and their by-blows of whores, too blinded by greed to see the price their Saxon masters will demand. Five *years*!" he snarled. "Five years, Creoda and his bastard of a father have strutted themselves under Saxon patronage, demanding treaties of alliance to secure guarantees they won't attack, and what have the kings of the south done about it? *Nothing!* While Aelle the mercenary grows fat and rich on land stolen from Briton widows and orphaned babes! God *curse* that fool, Vortigern, for hiring Saxon *foederati* fifty years ago!"

"Yes," Ancelotis agreed darkly, "Vortigern was as big a fool as Cerdic and Creoda, and the damned Saxons have been arriving by the shipload ever since." As Ancelotis spoke, Stirling was frantically casting back through his history lessons, trying to recall when the Kingdom of Wessex had been established, somewhere about the year 495, he thought. Which meant he'd landed more or less precisely on target. This ought to be the year of the historic battle of Mons Badonicus, Artorius' wildly famous twelfth battle.

Well, some scholars thought Mount Badon had been fought in the year A.D. 500, anyway. Others put it as many as twenty, thirty years later, and who in hell was to know, at this late remove, which piecemeal shattered records might hold the slightly larger grains of truth, never mind anything approaching genuine accuracy? All that could be said with certainty was that Artorius' victory at Badon Hill had driven the Saxons to their knees for nearly forty years, uniting Britons from the Scottish border to the southern tip of Cornwall.

Ensuring Artorius' defeat at Mount Badon could do a *lot* of damage. Enough to destroy a world. *His* world, Stirling's twenty-first-century one, with its billions of ordinary, innocent men, women, and kids, families watching the telly and taking a tea-time stroll through a world they naively believed to be safe.

The trouble was, no one, not even the scholars and archaeologists, knew where "Badon Hill" was supposed to be, which made Stirling's job trying to protect Artorius from being killed there a bit trickier. And Artorius was still pacing.

"We daren't show weakness before Cutha, old friend," he growled, pinning Ancelotis' eyes with a cold, hard look of anger. "Creoda may be a fool, but Cutha is another breed altogether. Aelle sends his son to us as spy, more than emissary, with Prince Creoda as means to a Saxon end." Steel-grey eyes glinted. "He'll challenge us to a test of arms, I have no doubt of that. Exhibition games with a darker purpose. Your brother's death will at least give us an excuse to stall them for a bit. We can declare traditional funerary games in his honor, even at Caerleul, to pay respect. King Meirchion Gul of Rheged will not stint Lot's memory, for Queen Thaney's sake, if for no other reason."

Ancelotis winced inwardly. "Thaney, surely, has not forgiven her father?"

Artorius grinned. "You know your niece better than anyone, Ancelotis. To my somewhat shaky knowledge, she has not forgotten any more than she's forgiven, but she remembers all too clearly the debt she owes you and Morgana, for helping her escape Lot's anger. Besides, the matter of paying proper tribute to her father's memory touches her honor as princess of Gododdin and queen of Rheged. And Thaney," Artorius chuckled a trifle grimly, "is a creature of honor, which you know only too well."

Ancelotis snorted. "That she is. All right, I won't worry about Thaney."

"Good. The funerary games will give us both the delaying tactic and excuse we'll need to gather all the kings of the north for council. It will also give us the opportunity to meet the challenge Cutha will inevitably deliver in the manner which best suits *us*. Fortunately," a nasty smile flashed into existence, "the Saxons are *infantrymen*. They ride horses only to *reach* the battle-field. They cannot match our heavy Roman cavalry, eh?"

Stirling bit back sudden panic.

He'd never been on a horse in his life.

Artorius frowned. "You're still pale, old friend. Would to God you could rest and recover your strength, but there simply isn't time. It's a long ride to Caerleul, if we hope to arrive before Cutha and his *gewissan* fool, Creoda. Damn, but it's a hellishly bad time for Lot to've gone riding after Pictish raiders! And the women, bless their good intentions, will slow us even further."

"Women?" Stirling blurted before Ancelotis could curb his tongue.

"Aye," Artorius nodded glumly. "Covianna Nim, who brought the news and insisted on riding with me to fetch Lot. Ganhumara, who would not hear of Covianna riding alone with me and demanded the right to accompany us. It's no fit time for Ganhumara to set foot outside the garrison at Caerleul, rail as she will about her status as battle queen in her own right. But she will throw her royal blood into the argument and, as queen of Guendoleu, I cannot ignore her demands, as I might a lesser wife's."

Artorius sighed, with the look of a man hard pressed to maintain peace on the home front, even as Stirling tried to take in the notion of that slender girl leading warriors into battle.

"And Morgana, of course," Artorius added, "will be riding with us. She must give her vote as queen of Galwyddel and Ynys Manaw." Stirling nodded, worried that the real delay wouldn't be the women and not daring to admit it out loud. Artorius rested a hand on his shoulder. "Can you ride, Ancelotis?"

"I'll manage," Stirling growled, tugging uneasily at the gold torque around his neck. It wouldn't do for not-yet-crowned King Ancelotis to develop a sudden nervousness of travel by horseback. He sighed. He'd have to work doubly hard to make sure King Ancelotis didn't sprawl onto his royal backside in the dust, trying.

The ceremony was a brief one, startling in its sixth-century simplicity. It took place in a large room that clearly served as the *principium,* or headquarters building, of the fortress atop Stirling Cliff. There were no murals, here, just cracked plaster over well-shaped stones roughly the size of bricks. The floors were simple stone flagging, once again joined with skill. Oil lamps burned bright, hanging from the soot-streaked ceiling, resting in iron lamp stands along the walls, cheering up the heartlessly plain room with flickers of golden light across ceiling and walls. The room was big enough to have served as officers' mess, war room, and dance hall, with large tables of rough-hewn wood and enough chairs to accommodate a meeting of a hundred, without any difficulty.

And there were enough men in the room to have filled every one of those chairs, all of them waiting for his arrival. Ancelotis was greeted informally by a rousing cheer from the men of his command and formally by one group of twelve, all of them older men with grey in their hair, who served Gododdin as a senior council of advisors. Among them was a Christian priest, distinguishable by his long, monkish robes, which were nevertheless of good quality, and by the cross he wore, an ornate and beautiful Celtic cross of exquisite workmanship. He was holding a gold torque that Ancelotis, at least, recognized as having been his older brother's.

"Ancelotis," the priest greeted him solemnly, "because time is of the essence, do you swear before Christ to uphold the laws of Gododdin and protect her from all threats until your nephew is of age to rule in your stead?"

"I swear it," Ancelotis replied, voice hushed with grief.

"Wear the royal torque of the kings of Gododdin then, and pass it on to Gwalchmai when the time is ready."

Ancelotis pulled off the torque he had worn all his adult life, then bent his head, for the priest was shorter than he. Lot Luwddoc's royal torque was far heavier around his neck, with a weight of more than poured and beaten gold. Queen Morgana, grey eyes brilliant with unshed tears, kissed each of his cheeks by turn and it was done. In a moment of brilliance or madness, Stirling wasn't sure which, Ancelotis turned to Morgana's nephew Medraut, who had watched the proceedings with shadowed, hurt eyes and a neck bare of any adornment.

His mother had been executed, leaving him with uncertain status in their carefully measured world. Ancelotis gave the boy his own, princely-rank torque. "I make you the holder of my honor, Medraut. Guard my own torque as you would guard the welfare of your family, and remind me that I am king only to save Gododdin for the sons of Morgana and Lot Luwddoc."

The boy's eyes widened, glowing with the shock of unexpected honor as Ancelotis placed the golden ring around the boy's neck. Morgana, watching from the side, allowed the tears to fall unheeded, as Medraut was transformed from an awkward boy, uncertain of his welcome and place, to a young man with purpose and the respect of his elders.

"I will not fail you, Ancelotis!" the boy swore, gripping Ancelotis' proffered hand and forearm in a tight grip.

The watching councillors of Gododdin, momentarily startled by the move, began to nod as they saw the wisdom of the thing, binding Morgana's nephew—until now an unknown factor in the politics of the north—firmly to the new king.

"Councillors of Gododdin," Ancelotis said quietly, "I thank you for the faith you've placed in my trust. Please take my brother's body home and see to it he is buried with all honors. Nothing but the safety of the realm could tear me away at such a time, but the Saxon threat must be met and countered."

The councillors bowed, murmuring assent and understanding. Then it was done and Ancelotis went striding across the hall, determined to leave as quickly as possible. The sun was just rising above the hills to the east, toward the distant Firth of Forth, when he and Stirling emerged from the Roman fortress of Caer-Iudeu with Artorius on their shared heels. Not that Ancelotis could actually *see* the sun. Heavy violet smudges of cloud, thick with unshed rain, raced overhead, casting a deep gloom over the fortress walls, the sprawling rooftops of the town below the cliff, and the forested mountains beyond.

Caer-Iudeu was larger than a fort, which generally covered a mere one to four hectares of ground, but was considerably smaller than a twenty-hectare fortress. The wall enclosing it ran along all four sides, studded with wooden watchtowers every few meters. Long, narrow stone barracks followed the classic Roman camp pattern, roofed in overlapping sandstone shingles, heavier and more permanent than clay tiles and the Romans' favorite roofing material for these northern forts. Workshops and granaries were visible, as well, along the neatly ordered streets inside the fortress walls. The fortress was a beautifully maintained symbol of organized military power, one that must have an ongoing, deep psychological impact on the Pictish tribes to the north.

Judging from the position of the sun, the chill in the

air, and the canopy of blazing crimson and gold amongst the trees down at the foot of the cliff—many of them already winter-bare—he'd arrived in late autumn, always a raw season in Scotland. The forests were a startling change from the bleak hillsides Stirling was used to seeing from this vantage point, high on the cliff of Stirling Castle—which would not exist for more than a full millennium. He curled his lips slightly at memory of the modern Scotsman's bitter, private joke about his wild, open hillsides, so popular with tourists.

The Scots lived in the wettest desert on the face of the earth, a landscape of low scrub and heather, kept deforested by high populations of sheep and large herds of deer. The sheep and the deer were carefully maintained by the landed nobility—many of them English—for their enjoyment in the kingly sport of hunting. Even native Scots landowners found it lucrative to maintain large deer herds, the better to earn money from enthusiastic tourists who came for the hunting. The dour hills weren't good for much else, really, besides growing timber, and money could be had far more quickly from sportsmen than from a stand of trees that took decades to mature.

Stirling had forgotten that the wilds of Scotland had once worn a thick mantle of virgin forest, filled with eerie shadows, drifting fog, and white-water cataracts roaring down through untamed glens. Early morning sunlight spilled through occasional rents in the clouds, striking the ancient trees with golden fanbursts. The forest had been cleared a good hundred yards from the outer stones of the Roman wall around the town, providing a wide perimeter of open ground across which an attacking army would have to charge, exposing themselves to fire from the defending fortress.

A full hundred horsemen of the Briton *cataphracti* waited, already mounted on massive animals that must have been the direct ancestors of medieval chargers. They greeted him with a great shout that sent the rooks flapping in alarm from nearby trees. The men were beating the flats of their swords against their shields. Ancelotis returned the salute even as Stirling's first real shock detonated behind their shared eyes. The faces of a startling number of those cavalrymen bore distinctly *Oriental* features—and the ones who weren't Asiatic still looked Middle Eastern, Iranian, perhaps. They looked for all the world like a band of the Great Khan's hordesmen—or refugees from Darius' Persian army—lifted out of Central Asia by a playful godling and dropped in the hills of Scotland.

He stared at the Asiatic horsemen, trying without much success to figure out where the devil they'd come from. Ancelotis' silent answer struck him with the strength of a thunderclap: *Sarmatians!* Memory stirred even as the impact of the word detonated. Sarmatian auxiliarymen . . . Thousands of the wild horsemen, Sarmatians and Alanians from the Hungarian plains to the steppes of Russia and even as far away as Central Asian Uzbekistan and Kazakhstan, had joined the Roman legions as auxiliary forces, mainly in the *cataphracti*—and the *cataphracti* was Artorius' strongest weapon, giving him a winning edge over Saxon invaders, an edge slated to last for more than fifty years, all told. There must have been *thousands* of Sarmatians stationed in Roman Britain, along Hadrian's and the Antonine Wall.

Aye, Ancelotis said with a hint of amusement in his thoughts, *fifteen thousand Sarmatians in all, the records say, were sent by Rome to patrol the border. A fair number of them decided Britain suited them better than Italy, so they stayed when the legions left a hundred years ago. Stayed and married the Briton girls who'd captured their wild hearts.*

Stirling was speechless. Among the best cavalrymen of the ancient world, the Sarmatians had held their own against Scythians, Persians, Germanic tribes, Gauls, Parthians in the deserts of the Middle East, and Carthaginians in Northern Africa. Over the millennium and a half separating Stirling's time from this one, the Sarmatian blood of the men who'd elected to remain in Britain must have been diluted until virtually no trace of Asiatic features remained in the gene pool.

But in A.D. 500, barely a century had passed since the departure of the legions—and a century was not nearly enough time to dilute the bloodlines of several thousand Asiatic warriors. He caught glimpses of battle pennons and shields bearing what must have been Sarmatian symbols, since only those men with Asian features carried them. Most of their spears were topped with bronze dragon heads, to which cloth banners had been tied, fluttering like windsocks, mouths wide open, with tails that ended in streamers flying wild as their Asiatic owners. And the symbols painted on their shields . . . A sword plunged into a stone was shocking in this context and left him wondering about the connection of that particular image with Arthurian lore.

Artorius, the Dux Bellorum who commanded the Sarmatian *cataphracti* . . .

Ancelotis said silently, *When Artorius was still a young lad, not yet turned seventeen, but already showing signs of promise as a shrewd and successful war leader, he persuaded the Sarmatians of Gododdin to finally give up their pagan gods and follow Christian ways. They began referring to him as the man who pulled the Sarmatian sword from its sacred stone, a true war leader who replaced their centuries-old tribal icon with a new god and new ways of worshiping. They also say he's the only mortal man ever born worthy to drain their sacred cup of heaven, like enough to Christ's grail, it wasn't so difficult for them to switch their allegiance to Artorius' new god. It didn't hurt, of course, that Uthyr Pendragon was one of their own . . .*

Stirling blinked. No wonder Artorius looked more Eurasian than Briton.

Oh, aye, Ancelotis agreed, *he's one of them, right enough, and they know it. They would dare things in battle under Artorius' direction they wouldn't even consider, when my brother, King Lot, was giving the orders. These men will follow Artorius anywhere and gladly die for him, if they must. In their eyes, he is more of a king than I will ever be, more than the Dux Bellorum of the Britons, far more than just their commander. They have given him their sacred souls for safekeeping. And he has never betrayed that trust.*

Nor would he ever betray it, Stirling realized numbly. Arthur, tribal "king" of the Sarmatian *cataphracti* of Britain . . . The far-reaching implications shook him, even while explaining the astonishing persistence of the sword-in-the-stone tale.

He shook himself slightly, focusing his attention on the men themselves. The cavalrymen wore an assortment of gear as widely varied as their genetic heritages. Most sported iron helmets, either of Roman design—looking something like a metallic baseball cap worn backwards, with protective metal cheekpieces— or a Celtic adaptation with conical iron points jutting upward and to the rear like metallic goats' horns. Many of the helmets, whatever style they might be, sported masses of feathers designed to make the wearer seem taller and more fierce.

All the men of the *cataphracti* wore close-fitting woolen trousers in wild checks and plaids, bloused and tied at the ankles over leather boots. Some wore wild-animal skins, others linen or leather tunics beneath Roman scale or ring-mail armor which glittered dangerously in the early sunlight, but most of them wore the scale armor that was a hallmark of Sarmatian heavy cavalry and had been for hundreds of years, going back several centuries before Christ even.

They were armed with a bewildering array of Saxon war axes, single- and triple-bladed spears with typically Celtic ironwork points, which were long and heavy, with concave edges. He also saw heavy Roman cavalry broadswords plus lances and javelins, even short Sarmatian bows and quivers full of bristling arrows. Iron-studded wooden shields—long, slightly dished ovals—were painted in bright colors, with a confusing mix of Christian and pagan symbols. Many of the weapons were heavily decorated with silver inlay, particularly sword and dagger hilts. The better a man's armor, he noted with a narrow-eyed glance, the more ornate his weaponry; but all of it was lethally functional. No ceremonial nonsense anywhere in sight.

Most of the horses wore at least minimally armored leather harnesses with circular metal bosses, which were spaced at regular intervals, wrought of iron and bronze. A fair number wore heavy coats of the same Sarmatian scale armor as their riders. Saddles were cinched tightly over fringed saddlecloths, many of them wildly patterned to match their owners' trousers. The saddles themselves were oddly horned affairs with four jutting projections that cradled a man's leg front and back. Weapons, water bags, and other equipment hung from leather cords slung around the saddles' four horns.

The detail that caught his eye almost instantly, however, was the presence of solid iron stirrups. Surprise caught him again—and Ancelotis chuckled once more. *A grand invention of our Sarmatian cataphracti, eh? The Saxons were as shocked as you to see stirrups the first time we rode them down.* He added with justifiable pride—and a dark sense of wasted lives and effort—*Had the Roman legionary commanders understood cavalry as well as we Britons, they might not have lost an empire.*

Stirling couldn't argue that. Roman generals had been notorious in their poor understanding of the proper uses of cavalry. Clearly, Artorius and Ancelotis and their Sarmatians had *not* made the same error.

Stirling was distracted by the sight of the beautiful copper-haired girl with the fur-lined cloak who had paid him a secret visit. She had already mounted a smaller horse, more suited to her petite frame than the massive horses of the armored *cataphracti.* Palfrey, they would call the smaller riding animal in later centuries. She sat easily in the saddle, however, clearly accustomed to riding astride. She looked very nearly as competent in the saddle as the armed warriors of their escort and she'd slung a smaller version of a war sword at her hip.

"Ganhumara." Artorius gave a curt nod to the lady as he accepted his own armor and helm, donning them with help from a standard bearer. Artorius' golden standard had clearly been modeled after the legionary eagles. For a legionary soldier, the eagle had been his personal "household" god and protector. The dragon standard was a brilliant ploy, echoing centuries of Roman military symbology, yet portraying a uniquely Briton symbol of nationhood.

A second rider carried another dragon standard, this one with distinctly Sarmatian alterations. The head of this second dragon was gold, as well, with silver throat and fangs. And fastened to it, exactly like those on the Sarmatian spears, was a blood-red dragon, its cloth body rippling like an angry, living beast in the stiff wind. The streamers of its tail would be visible even in the midst of battle, Stirling realized, providing a rallying point even easier to spot than the solid gold shape of the other standard.

Servants assisted Artorius into a Roman officer's burnished cuirass, ornate enough to have been worn by a victorious general during a triumph. Artorius settled onto his head a Celtic-style iron helm, covered with gold leaf and topped by a rampant dragon, clearly a Sarmatian symbol. He belted on sword and dagger and slung a crimson cloak of thick wool around his shoulders, pinning it with a heavy gold cloak pin of a style variously attributed to Celts and Vikings, then he vaulted easily into the saddle despite the weight of his armor.

His mount, a gleaming white stallion as big as a house, arched its neck and blew impatiently, pawing at the cold ground and rolling a wild, dark eye. Artorius checked the massive animal with a sharp word and a tightening of reins before accepting a long spear from the standard bearer. The bearer then mounted and took up position on Artorius' left flank, his gold-dragon standard glinting with burnished highlights in the cold sunlight.

Another servant brought up Ancelotis' armor, while others emerged from the fortress, carrying what must have been Artorius'—or Ancelotis'—personal baggage. Or maybe Ganhumara's. The heavy satchels and cases were strapped to pack animals while Stirling wrestled with unfamiliar fittings on Ancelotis' armor. The Briton king's personal armor was also of Roman design, nearly as ornate as Artorius', and must have been a well-preserved century old, at the very minimum. Unless there were still trade routes open to the Continent? Stirling didn't know enough to hazard a guess and Ancelotis wasn't saying.

Ancelotis' helm, unlike Artorius', followed the design of very late Roman cavalry. Burnished gold over the strong iron beneath, it formed a metal mask that completely enclosed his head, like an iron skullcap with cheekpieces that hinged around to cradle cheek and chin in metal. A thick blade of gold-covered iron projected above his brows, protecting eyes and to some extent nose from a glancing sword blow. He could smell dried sweat inside it, from many previous wearings as he settled it over his head.

His valet handed Stirling a thick woolen cloak of his own, dyed a brilliant scarlet-and-blue plaid, held closed across one shoulder with another circular cloak pin. His was decorated with chased dragon patterns and apparently made of solid silver. The artistry he'd already glimpsed in clothing and metalwork surprised Stirling—he'd expected such artifacts to be far more primitive. A modern man's prejudice, he realized, founded on nothing more than arrogance, when this culture was a direct heir of Roman civilization.

Morgana and Medraut appeared from the fortress a moment later, the latter carrying a heavy satchel of ornately decorated leather which he strapped to Morgana's saddle. Servants brought other satchels and bags, which they tied to pack animals. Morgana floated effortlessly into the saddle, despite the weight of a heavy, fur-lined cloak similar to Ganhumara's. Stirling gulped, realizing he would have to get onto his own horse before he could figure out how to ride it, and blessed the unknown Sarmatian who'd brought cavalry stirrups to the Scottish border country. Another woman Stirling vaguely recalled seeing from the night of his collapse appeared, blonde hair plaited neatly down her back, slim and beautiful in white woolen robes and a heavy cloak of dark fur. She, too, had a heavy satchel, which she strapped to her saddle.

The Dux Bellorum watched her mount, then spoke to Ganhumara, his voice nearly as cold as the wind. "We have a hard ride ahead, to reach Caerleul before Cutha and Creoda. We will ride by forced march, to the detriment of your comfort. I did warn you," he added. "It's no pleasure jaunt we're about, but preparation for war."

She lifted a shapely copper brow and said coolly, "I am as fine a rider as you, husband, and a battle queen in my own right, if not so skilled with a sword."

Steel-cold eyes glinted beneath glowering brows. "It is not your skill with saddle or sword which concerns me," Artorius growled. "Your stamina is *not* my equal, wife, and after the delay we've already had, to treat Ancelotis' illness, I will slow our pace for nothing and no one. If you cannot keep up, I will leave armsmen as an escort and ride on without you. Ancelotis, we dare delay no longer."

Only one beast remained riderless, clearly belonging to Ancelotis. Like Artorius' horse, his was a stallion, a dappled grey so massive, it must have been a direct ancestor of Percheron draft horses. He had to look up just to see the horse's back. Roman *heavy* cavalry was no joke. Stirling fumbled with his own sword belt and attempted to vault into the saddle, copying Artorius. Even with the assistance of the stirrup, his armor weighed so much, he stalled halfway up, lost his balance, and promptly landed in the dust, making a fine, disheveled heap under his horse's startled hooves. That damned Roman cuirass, solid armor plate formed of a single, thick slab of metal, skillfully forged to fit the human torso, gouged him in multiple, painful places.

He spat curses and glared at Morgana, trying rather desperately to shift blame to the potion she'd given him, while Ancelotis' scorn ricocheted off the insides of his skull. *It's not my fault,* Stirling growled at his host. *A man doesn't have to ride a horse to learn how to lay down suppressing fire with an MP5 submachine gun.* While Ancelotis tried to puzzle out his meaning,

Stirling regained his feet and straightened his cloak, tugging at his armor and trying to recover his dignity. Morgana, far from upset at the implied criticism, merely urged her horse alongside his and reached down to test his pulse.

"The lingering effects of the medicine will be gone in a few hours," she murmured.

Artorius glanced worriedly into her eyes. "He must needs make haste with the rest of us, sister. You know the danger from these Saxons as well as I. Do what you can for his illness, along the way."

"Of course."

Stirling tried again, face flaming. He blanked his mind this time and let Ancelotis' muscles do the work—and astonished himself by making it onto the horse's back in one try. The saddle made for an awkward seat. He gripped with both thighs, grateful for even the minimal security offered by those odd, projecting saddle horns, and shoved his feet more securely into the stirrups, doing his utmost not to slide off again. The Dux Bellorum put heels to his horse's gleaming flanks and the entire body of Romanized cavalry broke into a fast canter. The red dragon battle pennon crackled like living flames in the rising light of morning and the burnished golden dragon standard floated high above their heads.

Stirling jerked in the saddle, caught off guard when his horse followed the others without any apparent signal from him. He grabbed at the mane with one hand, nearly unseated by the abrupt start. He ignored stares from the other riders, particularly the men of the *cataphracti*, who cast worried glances at him every few moments.

Stirling set his teeth and set himself the task of learning how to ride.

Chapter Six

Colonel Hamish Ogilvie stepped out of the helicopter and headed for the laboratory's main entrance. His aide de camp scrambled out in his wake, while a detachment of troopers spread out around the site in a defensive cordon. A chap from Whitehall followed, one of the undersecretaries of the Home Office, a slightly rabbity and officious bureaucrat named Thornton Hargrove who had spent the entire journey up from London delineating the flaws, faults, and morally ambiguous antecedents of the SAS in general and Captain Stirling in particular. Ogilvie, weighing the pros and cons of tossing him out through the cargo doors, had finally snapped, "It's *your* chaps who vetted this terrorist and cleared her for top secret work. If you haven't the decency to admit your mistake, kindly refrain from blacking the reputation of the man trying to salvage this mess!"

Hargrove sputtered for several seconds, then clamped his lips shut and fell blessedly silent. Dawn had scarcely touched the Highland hills when Ogilvie stepped through the laboratory's main door, held open by a bleary-eyed, worried young man who introduced himself as Marc Blundell. "We haven't telephoned the constables, yet," Blundell said, "Captain Stirling told us not to until you'd arrived."

"Quite right," Ogilvie nodded. "Let's see it, then."

He went through the entire lab, examining everything, and had his aide photograph the entire facility. Hargrove stalked along in his wake, yammering more blithering idiocies about SAS incompetence. Ogilvie was more interested in Brenna McEgan's inert form, hooked into the time-controlling computers, than he was in the admittedly gory office where Terrance Beckett still lay where he'd fallen. And Ogilvie studied that crime scene with intense scrutiny, indeed, reconstructing the desperate fight in his mind, step by step.

The first, faint glimmerings of unease came when Ogilvie was examining Brenna McEgan's face, which was badly bruised and swollen from a terrific blow. Given her slight frame, Ogilvie wondered how in the world she'd been able to keep fighting a man taller and heavier than she after such a blow—and so effectively, she'd been able to kill him. Ogilvie would have laid a wager such a blow would have knocked her cold. The next stirring of worry came when he looked over Cedric Banning and found abrasions on his knuckles. Banning had hit someone or something very hard, and very recently. Brenna McEgan? In which case, how had she been able to fend him off long enough to set the computers, strap herself to the headset, and jump backwards through time?

The clincher came twenty minutes later, when one of Ogilvie's troopers, searching the perimeter of the site, came across a sodden bundle of cloth thrust under a rock at the bottom of a small stream which rushed past one corner of the property. "It's a woman's coat, sir," the man said, snapping out a salute. "No blood-stains on it, but there's a gun in the pocket."

Ogilvie fished the gun out using the barrel of an inkpen, never touching the weapon with his hand. There was, indeed, a gun in the coat, a wicked little Makarov 9 mm. "Now why the devil would Brenna McEgan walk into yon lab to kill a man and use a ruddy great knife—risking substantial injury to herself in the process—when she had this in her pocket?"

Thornton Hargrove had blundered up behind him, slipping in the treacherous mud and cursing in his high and irritating voice. Hargrove said, "A knife is a bet-ter weapon to send a message of terror with. I'm surprised you don't know that."

Ogilvie glanced around. "Really? Now the IRA is very good at sending messages with their weapons. Generally, they do so with car bombs and suchlike, trying to blow up the Queen Mother, taking out an entire street of British office buildings, leveling some Orangemen's favorite pub. Car bombs and AR-180s are their hallmarks. The one thing I have *not* seen them do is hack some man to pieces with a butcher's knife. Not when they've access to a perfectly serviceable firearm."

Hargrove sputtered again, turning red from the hairline down. Ogilvie studied the sopping coat, care-fully slipping the Makarov back into its pocket. "And why, for the love of Mary, would she bother to hike out here in a drenching downpour and bury this at the bottom of a streambed? There isn't a sign of blood anywhere on it—and there should be, if she stabbed Beckett to death. Nor can I imagine her taking it off and burying it, with gun in pocket, *before* killing him with the knife—yet there's no blood on this coat, and a great deal of it on her blouse and skirt, which were *under* the coat. It makes no sense."

Banning, on the other hand, had been stained in gore from shoulder to ankles. There was the note, of course, the claim that he'd slipped in the puddles of blood trying to reach Beckett, but something about that note and the little pieces of evidence mounting up rang hollow in Ogilvie's ears. He turned to his aide, his voice as full of gravel as the stream where *someone* had hidden Brenna McEgan's coat and gun.

"I want a background sweep on Cedric Banning, as well as Brenna McEgan. I want to know who pushed them in their prams and what they ate for dinner on their fifth birthdays. And I bloody well want it last week!"

His aide scrambled for the helicopter and its shielded radio equipment.

Ogilvie stalked back toward the lab while a cold fear grew in his heart that Trevor Stirling had gone into the past in pursuit of the wrong terrorist.

It is perhaps a hundred sixty kilometers, straight-line, from Stirling, Scotland, to the site of the Sixth Legion's ancient stronghold at Carlisle, in England's border country, which Trevor Stirling eventually deduced must be the fortress Artorius was heading toward. His use of kilometers confused his host, who had never heard of metrics, of course, and resisted thinking in meters and centimeters and kilometers. Stirling realized it would not only be easier for him, as a twenty-first-century man, to think in terms of miles and feet and inches—he'd at least *heard* of them and knew approximately what each measurement meant— it would also be far safer if he stopped thinking in metrics, even in the privacy of his own thoughts. One slip-up in Brenna McEgan's presence . . .

So he started the laborious process of allowing Ancelotis' way of measuring things to filter into his mind, recasting the distance from Stirling to Carlisle as a hundred miles, more or less, as the crow flies. Ancelotis and Artorius didn't call it Carlisle, of course, another difference Stirling had to get used to. They called it Caerleul. The Romans had called the winter-camp fortress Luguvalium, and later, Caer-Ligualid, names Stirling dredged up from rusty memory. Caer-Ligualid—eventually shortened in colloquial use to Caerleul—was close to the western terminus of Hadrian's Wall, down on the Scottish border. He cast back through everything he'd ever read or heard about Roman settlements in Scotland and the border counties, from public school and university courses, from tour guides, from family holidays to museums and ruins, from road signs and chance remarks made by shopkeepers and pub owners, and dredged up a few tidbits of his own to add to Ancelotis' memories.

There were two additional forts between Carlisle and the coast, far less important to the Romans than Luguvalium, itself, which had been winter headquarters of the Sixth Legion as far back as 127 A.D. or so. Three and a half centuries Artorius' stronghold had already existed, squarely astride the crossroads of the major Roman roads through western Scotland and England. Stirling was betting Luguvalium was just as important to the Briton defenses as it had been to the Roman ones, a notion Ancelotis confirmed.

Aye, the king of Gododdin agreed, *Caerleul is our greatest stronghold in the north. So long as we hold Caerleul, the Saxons will never take substantial ground from the northern Briton tribes. From Caerleul and Gododdin, we can thunder down on any army trying to enter from north, west, east or south, and meet them in force within a handful of days—and the Saxons well know it. As do the Irish and the Picts. Why else do you suppose Cutha wants alliance with Rheged? He hopes to probe our defenses at Caerleul and find a way to betray our fortress into his father's hands, which would give them free rein in the south and a great chunk of the north.*

It was, Stirling realized, a sound plan on Cutha's part, since the Saxons would never have a free hand in the north of England so long as the thirty-six forts along Hadrian's and the Antonine Wall remained in Briton hands. Those fortresses threatened any Saxon troop movements with a lightning attack from Briton strongholds between the Firth of Forth and the Firths of Solway and Clyde. Just how fast could a mounted troop of heavy cavalry move across country? Given their starting point from Stirling Castle Cliff, he estimated the journey to Carlisle would take a good three days, absolute minimum, by horseback. And given Artorius' steady course southwestward along the Romans' ancient but enduringly constructed military road, they would not be traveling the shortest route, either.

He had no idea how far west they would have to swing to find a road that cut south through the mountains. After a moment's thought, however, Stirling supposed the ancient road *couldn't* be too far from the modern roadway, given the same constraints faced by engineers at both ends of history. There were a limited number of options, when faced with the daunting and expensive task of pushing a road through mountains. In which case, they might well travel halfway to the Atlantic coast before swinging down through the natural pass in the Southern Uplands.

Three days might not be *enough* time, not if they had to follow that long, snaking route—and if his guess about the number of miles they could cover in one day was anywhere close to accurate. A very large "if" based mostly on the old cavalry song he'd heard a couple of slightly drunken American soldiers singing in a pub, once: *forty miles a day on beans and hay in the regular army-o* . . . The shift in thinking required to calculate travel time in terms of horseback, rather than car or even military lorry, was yet another rude awakening.

No wonder Artorius had been frantic to get under way.

Riding a horse was not as easy as it looked, either. Stirling discovered a few hours into the ordeal that if he blanked his mind and let Ancelotis' muscles take over, he was less likely to jar himself beyond endurance, but it was still a grueling ride. When the last light faded above the hills, they lit torches hacked from deadwood in the forest and kept riding. They needed the torches, too. Cloud cover lay so thick above the mountain peaks, blocking any hint of moonlight, the riders couldn't even see one another, much less the road. Stirling's respect for the Celtic *cataphracti* rose enormously during a night that stretched out beyond the edge of forever. The only good thing to come of the exhausting ordeal was as unexpected as it was welcome. The more fatigue took its toll, the easier it became to let Ancelotis' muscles take over on autopilot.

They slowed to a walk periodically to rest the horses and drank from skin pouches draped over the double front horns of their saddles. Stirling discovered trail rations—dried meat and leathery bread an unknown number of days old—in the oddly shaped saddlebags behind his rump, hung from the rear horns. He hadn't even noticed them until Ancelotis reached back, digging into them for a quick meal. The stuff wasn't remotely palatable, but he'd eaten worse field rations in the twenty-first century and he was hungry enough to eat shoe leather. It was still unsettling to have what felt like his own arm move under the direction of someone else's mind; Stirling decided he did not enjoy the sensation, but couldn't really complain, given the unpleasantness he'd inflicted on poor Ancelotis.

Ganhumara, as silent as the men of Artorius' cavalry, maintained the killing pace without complaint, although her face showed pale and strained in the flickering light from torches. Morgana and Covianna, too, rode like women carved of iron, rather than yielding and womanly flesh. It was positively humiliating, to be outmatched by women, one of whom was more than ten years his junior, maybe closer to *fifteen* years younger. What in God's name was he to do when the time came to fight the Saxons?

The dismal light of false dawn arrived with a cold dampness heavier than mist, not quite thick enough to call it drizzle. The wet air left him shivering beneath his woolen garments, deeply envious of the women's fur-lined cloaks. They flashed across the invisible border of Strathclyde—another Dark Ages kingdom from Stirling's history books—well before the sun could rise above the mountains at their backs. He wouldn't have recognized the border from any other bump of ground his horse had jolted across, if not for a brief murmur he overheard between Covianna and Ganhumara.

"Strathclyde at last," Covianna said quietly, catching the queen's glance in the oyster-grey light of predawn. "I have always loved this land."

"I would love it better without the constant wet and the God-cursed midges," Ganhumara shot back, voice bitter as the wind whipping down the mountainsides.

Stirling, who had grown up in the relatively dryer eastern half of the Scottish Lowlands, was inclined to agree with the young queen's assessment. The lowland reaches of western Scotland, far rainier than the eastern coast, were virtually uninhabitable during midge season, thanks to millions of aggressive gnats—a species apparently peculiar to the Scottish lowlands' marshes—which drove fisherman, farmers, and campers alike indoors from sheer desperation. Grown men, usually unwary foreign tourists, were occasionally reduced to gibbering lunacy by the stinging clouds. Stirling shuddered to imagine what the effect would be on a person unable to retreat indoors or—worse yet—without access to strong insect repellant. Maybe that was the origin of the Pictish practice of smearing themselves with blue-tinted mud?

Whether or not he'd hit on the answer, Ancelotis found his speculation enormously funny, which left him alternating between lunatic grins and scowls at each new jolt of his saddle against anatomy that Stirling, at least, was unused to having jolted. The whole concept of something that would repel insects captured the Scots king's fancy and he found himself attempting to explain the difficulties inherent in trying to produce from scratch something like DEET mosquito repellant, or even one of the widely available commercial brands, all of which required a fairly high-tech society with advanced knowledge of chemistry to produce. *Churlish sot,* Ancelotis complained at length. *You might at least pay for the privilege of showing up inside my skull by sharing your wizardry at keeping off the God-cursed insects.*

Stirling sighed. It was going to be a *long* year.

The distinctive scent of woodsmoke drifting on the early morning air tickled his nostrils before Stirling actually saw the source. As the road curved around the shoulder of a mountain, that source finally glimmered into view. Tiny fires dotted the grassy verges where the stone road stretched away through the predawn gloom. There was no village, which was what Stirling had expected to see, just hundreds of tiny cook fires where enough people to outfit a small army had camped beside the highway. *Was* it an army? More of Artorius' men? Or maybe warriors beholden to the king of Strathclyde, whoever that might be?

As dawnlight strengthened and they neared the first encampment, Stirling realized this was no army at all, but ragged bands of refugees, hundreds of them, mostly on foot. A few tired-looking ponies pricked ears at the approach of the *cataphracti*'s battle horses. More than a few women screamed and scattered for the forest, carrying small children, while their menfolk hunted for weapons. Who in the world *were* these people? The men were heavily tattooed, giving Stirling the answer even as Ancelotis snarled.

Picts!

The painted people.

Whole clans of them, driven southward by invading Irish. How the devil had they gotten past the line of watchtowers and mile forts along the border? Had they overwhelmed some isolated garrison, murdered the men on duty, and flooded across? Morgana, whose husband had just been murdered by Pictish invaders to Gododdin, went ashen in the grey dawnlight and young Medraut snarled out a string of oaths, gripping the pommel of his sword with a whitened hand. Covianna, riding close to Stirling's horse, followed his stare. Her glance softened into one of pity.

"With the *Scotti* invading from Ireland," she said quietly, the word *Scotti* translating into "brigand" in Stirling's mind, "the Irish are pouring more men and settlers into Dalriada, so these poor wretches have nowhere to go. Their Pictish kin in Fortriu won't give them land—Fortriu has enough trouble, holding its borders against the Irish. Strathclyde doesn't want them, any more than you do, in Gododdin." Covianna sighed. "Most of them want nothing more than passage to Galwyddel, I'll wager. We Britons have long since conquered the Galwyddellian Picts, of course, but it's a better destination for them than many I could name. Galwyddel has need of fighting men loyal to the Britons, if the queen of Galwyddel—and the Dux Bellorum—have the wisdom to gain that loyalty." Covianna glanced at Morgana, then back to Stirling. "If Artorius would grant these wretches safe passage, a place to settle, and a little training, he would gain several hundred infantry to defend the western coast against the Irish."

Her tone hinted most clearly that Artorius would do no such thing, particularly since his sister had just been widowed. At least, he wouldn't without a good deal of prompting from his allies—and Stirling realized abruptly that Covianna wanted *him* to argue the case to the Dux Bellorum. Her take on the situation made sense. A great deal of sense, both politically and from a military standpoint. Who better to throw into the breach against Irish invaders than desperate refugees who already hated the Irish bitterly? It would certainly save Briton lives. The trouble was, Stirling had no idea whether or not those lives were *supposed* to be saved. Anything he did out of the ordinary might change history, defeating his whole purpose in coming here. It was hellish, not knowing what he could and couldn't safely *do*, particularly when the soldier in him recognized a militarily sound solution to multiple problems. Ancelotis, whose brother lay in an early grave, also remained silent, for perfectly understandable reasons.

Covianna's eyes went as chilly as the morning wind off the distant Atlantic. Artorius was shouting commands to the *cataphracti* officers when a rumble of thunder rolled into their awareness, from further down the Roman road. A living thunder, Stirling realized abruptly, hundreds of horses at the gallop. An instant later, an immense body of heavily armed Celtic cavalry swept across the farthest visible Pictish camps, laying waste in a charge that struck the Picts like an earthquake. The newly arrived army drove the men back with brutal force, hacking down any who offered armed resistance, setting fire to ragged possessions, driving off weary ponies and scraggly herds of Highlands sheep.

Artorius shouted, "Attack! They're trapped between Strathclyde's men and ourselves! Cut them down where they stand!"

Stirling bit his tongue to keep from protesting. He had no right to protest—even if he'd dared risk changing history. Artorius led a second devastating charge that smashed into the desperate Picts, a hammer blow against the anvil of Strathclyde's forces. The Picts reeled, struck back desperately with pikes and arrows and spears, spitting the horses more often than the men, so that riders went crashing to the ground beneath their thrashing, pain-crazed mounts. Stirling had no choice but to follow Artorius' lead; for him to take any other action would amount to treason in the face of the enemy. The *cataphracti* of Gododdin roared into battle at his heels, even as Stirling struggled to free his heavy sword from its scabbard.

He managed to draw the sword and attempted a few ineptly clumsy swings with it, endangering nothing but his own horse. His mount clamped its ears back and went stiff-legged in a battle maneuver that nearly unseated him. In utter desperation, Stirling yielded to the fierce mind sharing brain space with his own. Ancelotis, clamoring for control of their actions, took over instantly, which left Stirling in the eerie position of passive observer while his body hacked and hewed and cut down men in a broad swath of destruction.

It was over within minutes. The *cataphracti* hunted down the last of the Pictish men through the forest and butchered them before herding the women and children across open fields toward the Roman road. Stirling found himself trembling with fatigue and shock. He clutched a filthy, gore-stained sword and blood dripped down his armor. He felt sick with the brutality of it, even after the combat and death he'd witnessed in Belfast. It was not at all the same, shooting a man or seeing someone blown to bits by a terrorist's bomb as it was gutting someone on swordpoint at arm's reach. Killing with a blade was far more personal, both for the man killed and the man doing the killing. He found no honor at all in riding down and slaughtering refugees who were all but helpless.

Ancelotis reacted to this with cold rage. *Look you there, Stirling of Caer-Iudeu, and tell me again that yon barbarians were helpless!* Men of the *cataphracti* were down by the dozens, wounded horses screaming, riders hacked to death by enraged, desperate men. Artorius himself had dismounted to kneel over one such fallen man. A boy in his mid teens, freckled and fair, with thick, copper-colored hair visible beneath the edges of his helmet, had crouched over the fallen man, as well, his distress so deep, it was clear the dead man could be no one but the boy's father. When Stirling caught a gleam of gold at the boy's neck—and at the fallen warrior's—he realized with a deep chill that a king had fallen in this battle. *Another* king, dead at the hands of Picts . . .

Ancelotis groaned aloud and spurred his horse closer, providing Stirling with a name. *Dumgual Hen of Strathclyde, may the saints help us. . . .* Stirling slid out of the saddle in time to hear the boy cry, " 'Tis *my* fault! Mother charged me to watch his back, and I failed him! Artorius, what am I to *do*?"

Artorius laid a hand on the boy's shoulder. "Take him home. Bury him with honors and give your mother what comfort and courage you can. No man could have guarded his back any better than you, lad. The pikemen took his horse down so fast, no one could have reached him before the bastards had cut his throat. You tried valiantly, lad, as did I."

The boy's tears tracked messily down his face, but Artorius' words had clearly eased at least some of his wild grief and guilt. The Dux Bellorum hesitated, then added heavily, "Strathclyde's council of elders must name a new ruler, lad, and quickly. Do not be distressed, Clinoch, whatever their decision, whether they confirm you now or name another to hold Strathclyde until you are ready. I will cast my vote in your favor, for I saw how well you fought this day, and I know you to be a steady and wise lad, with the nerve to do what must be done. But your councillors must act in the best interests of your people, just as the councillors of Gododdin have named Ancelotis to the throne until Gwalchmai is older. You must vow to aid them however you can."

The boy's head snapped up and his face washed white beneath its dusting of tan freckles. The full import of his father's death struck with devastating force as it came home that he might well be called upon to take his father's place as king—or, perhaps even worse, *not* be called.

Ancelotis slid to the ground and strode across to clasp Clinoch's arm in a grip of equals. "I grieve with you, Clinoch, and with all of Strathclyde. Your father will be sorely missed. But," and he, too, laid a hand on the boy's trembling shoulder, "your father has trained you well. My sword and men are at your call, should you need us. I pledge to defend Strathclyde if defense be needed in this time of confusion and grief. But you *will* avenge him, Clinoch, just as I will avenge my slain brother, this I swear by all that is holy."

Suppressed weeping shook the boy's young shoulders as he met Stirling's eyes, his own reddened and wet. "Yes," he said harshly. "I will have heads for this!" Then, visibly struggling to recall the courtesies, "Forgive me, I had not heard the news of Lot Luwddoc."

"Nor could you have, and him slain not two days since. We're bound for a council of the northern kings at Caerleul, a council I'm thinking you will attend as an equal, for I, too, will speak in your favor, Clinoch son of Dumgual Hen."

"I thank you for that," the boy said, bringing himself under steadier control.

Artorius said quietly, "Come, Clinoch, we must bear him home to your mother at Caer-Brithon, then ride for Caerleul as if all the demons of hell were at our heels, for the Saxons have challenged the sovereignty of Rheged itself."

Clinoch's breath caught as he stared into Artorius' angry grey eyes. "Challenged Rheged? Are they *mad*?"

"Only with greed. You're needed, heir of Strathclyde, as you have never been needed in your life."

"Then we will sing my father's funeral dirges in the saddle and leave him to be buried by my mother and younger brothers. Strathclyde can ill afford the number of orphans the Saxons would gift us with."

"Well spoken," Ancelotis nodded.

They lifted Dumgual Hen's body, placing him across the saddle of a riderless horse and bound him there securely for the king's final journey. Dumgual's own mount lay dead at Stirling's feet, chest and ribs pierced by long, broken pikes which had brought both animal and king down to destruction. Clinoch recovered his father's sword and cleaned the blood from it, then sheathed it in an ornate scabbard decorated with silver and strapped it to his own horse before vaulting into the saddle.

Soldiers of the *cataphracti* were recovering their dead, as well, while others stripped weaponry from the Pictish men they'd slain. So far as Stirling could see, the Picts had nothing else of value that would tempt the Briton cavalry to loot. The sight sickened him, however, worse than Belfast. Without food or supplies, the surviving women and children would starve. Surely Ancelotis and Artorius could see the risk posed by ravenous marauders desperate for food to put into their children's bellies? The Pictish refugees were heading disconsolately northward, not even permitted to bury their newly slain along the verges of the Roman road. Carrion crows were already circling overhead, waiting their chance.

As Stirling struggled back into his own saddle, he caught snatches of conversation from the Celtic cavalrymen, angry mutters about heathen Picts who refused to die properly on their own side of the border, who came in ravening bands to kill Celtic royalty. Covianna Nim, Queen Ganhumara, and Queen Morgana had remained well clear of the battle, although both queens clenched swords and Morgana's fingers were white from the strength of her grip. The women reined their horses nearer and Ganhumara edged her way over to Medraut, who had rushed into the battle with Artorius and Ancelotis and sat staring bleakly at the heir to Strathclyde. The boy's sword dripped with as much gore as any other Briton's.

Ganhumara spoke too quietly for Stirling to catch the words, but he found Morgana gazing narrowly at her nephew and Artorius' wife. Stirling realized with a start of surprise that Medraut and Ganhumara were almost exactly the same age. The look Medraut gave the young queen rang alarm bells at the back of Stirling's skull, a look of compounded misery, grief, and hopeless love.

The murky and complexly shifting political nightmare into which he'd been so abruptly thrust deepened another degree as the full import of that look sank in. Morgana's nephew, a potential heir surely, to *someone's* kingdom given his family history, was helplessly in love with Artorius' beautiful young queen. And the look—and touch—she gave in return were far more tender than any he'd seen her bestow on her husband. Deeper and deeper this disaster grew, and Stirling had no idea how to navigate his way through it.

They set out again, riding steadily south in a massive column, Gododdin in formation behind Ancelotis and Strathclyde in formation behind Prince Clinoch. The drizzle which had plagued them through the night thickened into an hours-long downpour which soaked through Stirling's wool cloak and ran in chilly runnels down the neck of his cuirass, soaking tunics and trousers to the skin. The wind blew mercurial sheets of rain across the road, slashing horses and riders alike. Stirling was used to patrols through the worst sorts of weather, but never on horseback and never after an exhausting and sickening battle from horseback, and certainly never faced with the prospect of no central heating and no tea—not even coffee—to warm him at the end of the grueling day.

During the long day, they passed small Briton settlements, mostly walled villages and small hill forts, and Roman fortlets, teacup-sized forts of less than a hectare, where auxiliary troops were quartered, along with the even smaller mile forts and fortified stone watchtowers with their circular wooden palisades, defensive ditches, and their boxlike wooden viewing platforms jutting out on all four sides. They sent riders to every fort and tower they passed, to spread the word of the kings lost in the fighting and exhort them to greater vigilance during this crisis.

Empty fields stood fallow, already stripped of their standing hay crop or grain, the bounty of harvest stored now in large stone barns to protect it from the rats and the rain. Ancelotis muttered, *Aye, and it's one of God's own miracles we got the crops in without disaster, for the weather's been foul, unseasonably wet and cold. We had men working in the fields by torchlight, in shifts with the women and the children, to get the harvest in before the rains left all in ruin. We lost a portion of the hay, as it was.*

Starvation, Stirling realized with a cold chill, was only one poor harvest away, when no international trade routes existed to ship food by air or sea. He was too accustomed to living in a world where one nation's bounty could be sent in a matter of hours to another's drought- or flood-starved thousands. Another surprise for Stirling was the number of Christian churches they passed, constructed of stone or wood, depending on the size and wealth of the village or town that had built it. His surprise, in turn, startled Ancelotis. *Are you not a Christian, then?* the Scots king demanded warily.

Well, yes, Stirling responded, *but I hadn't realized there would be so many churches, this early in history.*

Ancelotis snorted, a sound of mingled anger and disgust. *I may be descended from Druid judges and kings, but those Druids have been Christian for two centuries, Stirling of Caer-Iudeu. Mark you, there are those who follow the old ways, more now than when the Romans were still among us, but we follow the teachings of Christ closely enough. Not,* he added wryly, *that Rome is so very well pleased with us. Heresy, they call our notions of free will and the immortality of a*

*man's soul. It's been a century or more since they
declared our greatest Briton philosopher, Pelagius, a
heretic.*

Heretic? Stirling blinked, startled at the deadly
serious use of such a word. He'd forgotten, or perhaps
had never viscerally understood, how serious a matter heresy had been in the early Christian centuries.
That disturbed him, deeply. Ancelotis, undaunted,
continued to rail.

*Imagine, declaring a man heretic because he dared
stand up to that swine Augustine! And him with his
damnable notions of predetermination, giving a man no
moral reason not to sin! Why should a man follow truth
and righteousness, when his nature and fate are set in
stone before he's born, leading him to sin as God wills,
rather than as he chooses. Bah!* Ancelotis spat disgustedly to one side. *'Tis the knaves in Rome are guilty of
heresy. Any fool can see a man must have his choice,
whether to sin or no, or the notion of sin and redemp-
tion from it are nothing but a mockery. Let Rome rot
in her dissipation, I say. I would almost rather sit down
at table with these barbarians, Picts and Irish and
Saxons, pagan and godless though they be, than a priest
of Rome who calls us heretics for following the Christ
as He was meant to be followed.*

Clearly, the state of religion in the sixth-century
British Isles was every bit as explosive a matter as it was
in twenty-first-century Northern Ireland. Stirling vowed
never, ever to get into a philosophical debate over religion with *anyone* from the sixth century. Ancelotis'
vehemence reminded him all too unpleasantly of Belfast's raging argument over which version of Christianity
would be the accepted, right, and true one. Nominally
Christian or not, Stirling spotted occasional roadside
shrines, some of them obviously pagan. These were
often situated near groves of trees, wells, or natural

springs. He caught glimpses of women in several of the groves, doing what, he wasn't at all prepared to guess and Ancelotis wouldn't be baited into commenting.

Surrounding it all—hill forts, villages, churches, fortlets, and pagan shrines—were the stubbled fields, orchards stripped of their ripened fruit, their leaves having mellowed in shades of buttery gold and coppery fire against the dark, wet wood, and water meadows and common-land pastures where flocks of hardy sheep and sturdy cattle grazed. Peasant farmers and shepherds, busy at the tasks of slaughtering pigs and cattle for the winter's larder and the shearing of wool from those sheep marked out for mutton stew, shaded their eyes and shouted as the *cataphracti* passed, a glittering cavalcade of armor and sunburnished weapons.

Near sunset, the road they'd been following met up with another Roman highway running north-south through the mountains. A small fortification, larger than the mile forts they had passed with clockwork regularity, guarded the junction where two valleys met, each with their snaking road of stone looking like faded grey ribbons in the long shadows. Wooden towers jutted up against the darkening sky, while curls of smoke drifted toward the clouds from cookfires and—so Stirling hoped, at any rate—from the firepits that fueled the central heating system. The arched spans of a one-story aqueduct marched away toward whatever water source was nearest. Clearly, the Romans had considered this little crossroads fort critical enough to spend sufficient manpower, time, and money constructing a military aqueduct for it. A small village had sprung up in the shadows of the fort's walls, sending delicious smells wafting their way. Dogs broke into a furious clamor as they thundered into the village, heading for the fort's big wooden gates.

Artorius halted the combined cavalcade long enough to eat a hot meal, rest and feed the horses, and catch four hours' sleep. Stirling craved *that* more than anything else; more, even, than the thick stew and hot bread which their hosts at the little garrison served their royal guests. There wasn't even plaster on the walls here, just bare stones, squared off and mortared like brick. The lack of potatoes in the stew reminded Stirling with dull and admittedly selfish unhappiness of other deprivations he would face during the coming year. No fish and chips—at least, no thick-cut, deep-fried potato slices to eat with the fish—no ketchup to eat with the nonexistent potatoes, no corn, no coffee, no tea . . . not even a lowly chocolate bar. None of those items would be available anywhere in the British Isles for centuries.

The reality of sixth-century Britain crashed down across Stirling all over again, in all its appalling crudity, bringing home with brutal suddenness just how very trapped and alone he was. *Home* lay at least forty, maybe fifty miles behind him—and some *sixteen centuries* in his future. A whole millennium and more than half of another . . .

He held back a groan and sought the privy, a separate room with troughs engineered into the stone floors and wooden planks with holes cut through them topping stone retaining walls. The trickle of water could be heard, a steady stream of it entering from one side of each trough, washing the troughs clean through a drain hole in the other end, presumably into a communal cesspit. His privy business done, he staggered past several dark storage rooms piled high with weapons and spare lamps, jugs of oil and probably wine, judging from the smell, and stored foodstuffs, then reeled into the wet night air. He found the barracks where they were to be quartered by following the sound of Artorius' snoring.

Weary to his toe bones, Stirling collapsed on the camp bed reserved for his use, asleep before he finished falling down.

Lailoken had rarely been happier.

He'd ridden almost nonstop from Caer-Iudeu to Caerleul, in the process leaving behind two stolen farm horses, badly foundered by his ruthless determination to reach Caerleul ahead of the Dux Bellorum's *cataphracti* and its royal escort. Exhausting as it was, he reached the ancient Roman fortress on the Solway Firth well in advance of Artorius. He arrived just past sunset, riding a third sturdy draft horse liberated during the night from a farmer who had failed, foolishly, to brand his livestock. Banning, as pleased as Lailoken by the speed they had made, immediately gave him a deeply distressing order: *Sell the horse.*

Sell it? But—but, 'tis the most wealth I've had in years! It is one thing, surely, to ride an animal into the ground for good cause, but now we've made it safely here, you want me to just give it up?

Banning overrode his protest with ruthless logic. *If the farmer we borrowed this sorry nag from comes looking, he could make things difficult, even without the proof of a branding mark. I will not risk drawing attention in such a fashion! When we need another animal, we will buy it. And don't fret about money, I'll help you earn more cash than you've ever dreamed of owning. Just sell the damned beast and be quick about it!*

Within half an hour, he'd sold the horse for a good price, which left Lailoken's purse delightfully heavy with gold. At Banning's insistence, he scrubbed himself off at a horse trough behind a stable. *I can't bear the smell of your pits*, Banning growled, *and I'll not spend another moment with greasy hair and dirt three centimeters thick where you've not washed the filth off for a month, at least. And buy new clothing, the rags you're wearing now are fit for nothing but burning. Do you think we can win a place in the royal household, where the decisions will be made that affect our goals, stinking worse than a pigsty?*

Deeply chastened by the rebuke and mortified to his toes to be found wanting by his supernatural visitor—he didn't even dare to ask what a "centimeter" was—Lailoken bought a cake of soap, a new pair of boots and fine new clothing, even a warm woolen cloak to replace his tattered and much-mended one. Having cleansed himself in ritual appeasement, Lailoken emerged from the alley behind the stable as a man transformed, clad in the thickest woolen trousers he had ever owned, a beautiful yellow linen tunic worn under a crimson one of embroidered wool.

Strong leather lacings bound warm boots to his calves. He fastened the new cloak with a silver penannular cloak pin which his fingers kept drifting up to caress possessively. A new rucksack held his belongings—harp, flute, their protective sealskin cases, more new clothing—and he wore a long, heavy-bladed scramasax and sheath, hung from a thick and sturdy new belt with a silver buckle, its chased designs matching the cloak pin. The scramasax hilt and sheath might have been heartlessly plain by most standards, but Lailoken had never owned anything so fine.

He even bought a felted wool hat, a well-made Phrygian-style cap that he could pull down over his ears to keep them warm. His old clothing he gave to a one-legged old beggar sitting outside the gates of the massive legionary fortress, whose walls dominated the town.

Lailoken followed his nose to the nearest public

taverna to fill his empty belly and proceeded to polish off an entire roasted chicken, a heaping plateful of cooked parsnips and beans, half a loaf of bread, and a thick hunk of cheese, washed down with several mugs of mead. The *taverna* was crowded with off-duty soldiers from the fortress, whose voices roared like summer thunder and echoed off the ceiling beams. Laughter, ribald jokes, and stories of dubious veracity extolling the teller's great prowess in bed or in battle were shouted across the scarred wooden tables while cheap alcohol flowed like the tide.

A couple of women with brazen smiles and low-cut, tightly-cinched gowns, carried trenchers full of hot food and wooden pitchers full of mead, ale, and cheap wine, undulating their way between the tables, leaning over the customers' shoulders to fill plates and mugs, and laughing at the rough groping hands, lewd stares, and monetarily beneficial transactions proposed at least twice a minute. Lailoken had no desire to follow where doubtless several hundred men had plowed before, so he merely grunted at the suggestive postures and smiles, ordered more food, and watched narrowly as the occasional minstrel wandered in, broke into song, and was hooted, shouted, and drowned out by men who fancied themselves singers but could have claimed better kinship with a marshful of croaking frogs.

He found the tavern keeper and arranged to buy a room for the night, then sought out the other minstrels, pulling out his flute and joining in the lively jig that rollicked its way across the shouting, seething mass of drunken soldiers. Between songs, he asked after business and found, to both his and Banning's intense delight, that his newfound compatriots frequently provided music for Rheged's royal villa, playing not only for King Meirchion and Queen

Thaney, but also for Artorius, the Dux Bellorum, and
his favorite officers.

An hour's investment of flattery, of playing in a group
with flute and harp, and of half a dozen or so rounds
of mead paid for out of Lailoken's funds, won an invitation to play as a member of their troupe for as long
as he planned to remain at Caerleul. He accepted
graciously, paid for another round of drinks, and
launched into a comical series of songs that had the
nearest soldiers roaring and slapping the table in
appreciation. Lailoken tossed his new hat onto the floor
in front of him, brim up, and grinned as coins came
pelting his way, along with roared requests for bawdy
favorites.

It was nearly midnight before the last of the soldiers finally staggered out into the night, leaving the
tavern keeper to lock his shutters and the minstrels
to case their instruments and drift off to their rented
beds. Lailoken poured a surprising number of coins
from his hat, delighted at the jingle they made when
he added them to the balance of his horse-sale money.

All he had to do now was set in motion Banning's
plans.

*I shall want a large and private workroom somewhere
in the town,* Banning mused, *a place we can work
undisturbed.*

How am I to pay for such a room? Lailoken
frowned. *The gold from our stolen horse will not last
forever, and prices always rise when there is talk of
war. I cannot earn enough playing and singing to pay
for more than a few nights' lodging or a few meals.*

Banning chuckled. *Leave that to me. Britons enjoy
gambling, don't they?*

We're Britons, are we not? Lailoken responded with
stung pride. *Throwing the dice is a most popular sport,
has been ever since the legions brought the game from*

Rome. Lailoken's frown faded as he saw the possibilities. *A pair of dice and a board on which to properly toss them shouldn't cost too much, unless you've set your heart on some fancy thing inlaid with silver and fashioned from imported ivory from Africa or jade from Constantinople.*

A humble board will do, Banning mused, *but we must secure a good set of dice. Ivory would be best, as it's easier to make alterations that are less readily detected than with sets made of stone or wood.*

Alterations? Lailoken blinked. *What do you mean, alterations? Do you plan to cheat?*

Banning roared with laughter. *Oh, that is priceless, and you a man who's stolen three horses in as many days! You didn't think I would walk into a game and play fairly? Not when we require a large stockpile of money, as quickly as we can lay hands on it? Bah, what do I care if some wealthy Briton nobleman loses a portion of his fortune to us? Or a soldier, for that matter, when his gold is destined to help you and me destroy enemies he will therefore never have to fight with sword and spear? Think of it as a tax they don't know they're paying, to levy troops they don't realize they're supporting. Believe me, when the blow is struck, all of Britain will be in awe of what you and I accomplish.*

Lailoken couldn't imagine how cheating a few rich men at dice would enable him to destroy the Irish, but he had absolute faith in his personal god. Banning was a being of fire and awesome knowledge and knew so many secrets of power, the memories they shared left him dizzy and shaking with wondrous terror. If Banning said he needed ivory dice to destroy their enemies, then Lailoken would get them, whatever the cost.

Vengeance, after all, was worth no less.

Chapter Seven

Dragging himself into the saddle was harder than it had been the first time. They set out in total darkness, a clattering mass of heavy cavalry, and rode without stop through the night. It was well past sunup when a landmark Stirling would've known anywhere rose out of the smothering downpour: a long, cat's-claw glint of silvery-grey water and rising high above that, the immense volcanic plug known in his day as Dumbarton Rock. Mary Queen of Scots had taken refuge there as a child, before being smuggled to France at the age of five. He had no idea how many successive fortresses had been built atop that craggy high ground, but there was no question about where Artorius was headed: Caer-Brithon, home of the kings of Strathclyde, the latest of whom rode strapped to a pack horse, colder and stiffer than Stirling's aching body.

He would have given a great deal to bypass Caer-Brithon and the queen who did not know, yet, that she was a widow. Morgana caught his glance, her own pale and grim, and shame for his own cowardice touched his heart. Prince Clinoch, lips thinned, back ramrod straight, led the entire thundering cavalcade of Briton *cataphracti* up the muddied road toward the fortress atop Dumbarton Rock. The horses slipped and snorted protests at the steep, choppy climb, which Stirling would have dreaded making when snow and ice lay on the ground. Sentries saluted as they passed the outer walls, which did not look to Stirling like Roman construction, but which would certainly have sufficed to stand off most invaders for a good, long while.

Once past the wall, Stirling could see the royal hall of the kings of Strathclyde. The design echoed Roman construction, with outer walls of heartlessly plain stone and roof of overlapped stone shingles, but it was rougher than Roman buildings, the stone not as finely dressed, although certainly solid enough to withstand siege. It occupied the place where a Roman camp's *principium* would ordinarily stand, but the barracks buildings and workshops surrounding it were scattered haphazardly, taking advantage of the existing terrain features rather than altering that terrain to fit human notions of organization.

Lacking the neat, ruler-precise order of a Roman fortress, the settlement was a startling visual symbol of the Britons' slow slide toward darkness, a darkness settling rapidly across all of Europe. These people were clearly desperate to keep their Roman civilization running, without the highly skilled engineers, stonemasons, and architects to carry it off properly. Still, they'd done a good job building this fortress, large enough to shelter everyone in the town below, if necessary. A colonnaded entrance, its sandstone pillars drenched by the cold rain, was a suitably impressive entryway for visitors coming to call on Strathclyde's royalty. The doors opened as they clattered into the courtyard, a sea of mud with a border of chipped and shivering Romanesque sculpture, graceful nymphs and proud heroes half drowned in the stinging downpour, looking half frozen with filmy gowns and nude male torsos bare to the wind and rain.

A woman in her late thirties rushed into the muddy yard, taking in their grim faces and silence with a look of fright. Clinoch sat swallowing repeatedly, apparently unable to stir from the saddle. Morgana was the first to break out of the awkward paralysis that held them all as frozen and cold as the statuary watching from the fringes. She slid fluidly out of the saddle and crossed the muddy courtyard to grip the other woman's hands. "Braithna . . ." she said inadequately, voice breaking.

"He's dead, isn't he?" the queen of Strathclyde cried, voice shrill with terror. Her hair, streaming wild and wet down her face, lay in limp copper ribbons and her skin had run ashen beneath a dusting of freckles. Clinoch, deathly pale beneath his own scattering of freckles, sat watching in numbed silence from his saddle. The boy obviously had no idea how to comfort his grieving mother. Morgana lifted the wet hair back from the woman's trembling lips and brow so she could meet streaming blue eyes that did not want the worst confirmed.

"Braithna, I grieve with you, for my own husband is not yet in the ground, and my sons too young to safeguard the throne he has left empty. Your Clinoch fought as bravely as any man I have ever seen, Braithna. He will rule Strathclyde wisely and will take care that no harm comes to you or to any more of your family."

The other woman began to sob uncontrollably,

collapsing into Morgana's arms. The two queens clung together, their grief as raw as the rain pelting down with such pitiless fury. Stirling found himself on the ground without realizing he'd intended to move, and guided the women out of the rain, all but carrying Braithna. "See to the horses," he called over his shoulder, then they were inside and Clinoch was right behind them, paralysis broken, shouting for servants to see to his mother.

The royal reception hall was several degrees warmer than the raw outer air, clearly having been constructed by someone at least passingly familiar with Roman central heating, but all resemblance to Roman architecture ended there. Bare stone walls lacked plaster or murals, although someone had fastened animal skins as decorative insulation along most of the open wall space. Oil lamps rested in iron brackets riveted to the stones. One long wall boasted an open hearth, the most strikingly un-Roman feature of the large room, where a large fire blazed cheerfully. A bed of coals two meters long spilled additional heat into the room, while smoke escaped through a narrow opening in the roof.

A wide-eyed, red-haired boy of perhaps five stared at them from beside the hearth, sitting in the midst of toys he had clearly been playing with just a moment previously. He hung back, frightened and beginning to cry. A girl of perhaps ten, a slender, freckled version of her brothers, gathered the boy in, hushing and rocking him as Ancelotis guided their mother to the hearth.

Morgana retrieved her satchel of medicines, crushing a handful of leaves into a steaming kettle hanging over the fire and steeping them until the water turned a dark, mysterious shade that satisfied her. Someone brought blankets and wrapped them around the shuddering Braithna. Morgana dipped up her brew into a simple, wooden cup and got the entire cupful down Braithna's throat, coaxing her with apologies for the strong and bitter taste.

"Just a bit more, that's good, I've made it strong, to fight off the shock you've had."

Artorius, Stirling noticed, was quietly and efficiently giving orders to summon the council of Strathclyde while Clinoch sent riders to bear his father's body to the chapel. The boy retained enough presence of mind to order servants to bring food and hot, mulled wine for the weary and chilled soldiers who still waited in the rain outside. "Quarter the men of Gododdin with our own," Clinoch told an older man who clearly filled the role of that ageless and ever-present type of official who appears wherever courts of power come into existence, calm and colorless and competent. "Then send hot food for the men, hot bran mash for the horses, we've come a wicked long way and have a worse ride ahead. Artorius is calling for a full high council of the Briton kings at Caerleul. Bid the council of Strathclyde meet in this hall no later than one hour from now. Decisions cannot wait for time nor tide when the Saxons are on the march."

The colorless official bowed and departed in considerable haste.

Meanwhile, whatever Morgana had persuaded Braithna to swallow, it seemed to be helping. The harsh, uncontrollable weeping had tapered off to a few sodden hiccoughs now and again as she struggled to bring her wild grief into some manageable form of containment. More blankets put in a welcome appearance and Stirling wrapped himself in thick, woolen warmth, grateful as well for the mulled wine and fresh-baked, hot-from-the-oven barley cakes beginning to make the rounds.

Servants were bringing piles of dry clothing, as well,

and set up a heavy wooden screen near the fire, which allowed Morgana, Covianna Nim, and Ganhumara to doff heavy, wet gowns and capes that held the rainwater against the skin and added to the chill. The women soaked up the heat of the hearth on their side of the screen, even as the men changed clothing on the other side of the screen, equally grateful for the warmth. Servants took their wet garments away, presumably to hang near other hearth fires to dry them. The women emerged at length and began working on their drenched hair, while Queen Braithna had calmed enough to call her children to her and hold them close while *they* wept.

Grey-haired councillors began to arrive, full of apologetic horror at the news, hardly knowing whether to address their own grieving queen, their dead king's heir, Artorius the Dux Bellorum, Morgana who was also recently widowed, or Ancelotis, because he now sat on the throne Morgana had declined. They reminded Stirling of a flock of fluttering, uncertain pigeons, trying to decide which cat to placate first.

Artorius put them at their ease with few enough words, outlining the entire series of disasters in a handful of terse, to-the-point sentences, making it quite clear that he supported Clinoch ap Dumgual Hen. Morgana added her support, as did Ancelotis. Within a quarter of an hour, the decision was made and Clinoch was officially King of Strathclyde. His younger brothers and sisters looked on in confused awe as he was invested with the full power of the crown by the church, in a ceremony only slightly more formal and ornate that Ancelotis' own.

It was, however, just as brief.

The new king's first order was to see to his father's funeral arrangements in his absence, "for the Saxons are massing to the south," he explained to his councillors, "and maneuvering in the midlands, and if successful in both places, they could punch through to demolish the northern kingdoms within the year."

Braithna kissed her son's cheeks and murmured, "We will see to all proper ceremony. Ride like a sudden summer gale and do your part to keep the Saxons guessing and off guard."

They waited only long enough to shovel down hot stew and bread and stow more trail rations in their kit bags, then they were under way again, amidst a great flurry of trumpet calls. The brassy voices of the signal trumpets pursued them down the twisting, muddy road from the fortified heights down to the Clyde estuary. Narrow, cobbled streets echoed with the sound of unshod hooves on uneven stone. Then they were through the town's southern gate, clattering onto a well-paved stretch of Roman road leading south. Once past the cat's-claw hook of water that formed the very tip of the Firth of Clyde, they drove straight down through the Southern Uplands and the Tweedsmuir Hills toward the distant and meaningless—to anyone from the sixth century—border between modern Scotland and modern England.

After a grueling day Stirling hoped never to repeat in his life, the rain clouds finally broke up and let the sky show through, pale as ice and just as cold. The chilly sun dropped gradually behind the hills and left them riding into the faces of long, purple shadows. The sky blazed with the colors of blood and flame and faerie gold. Night slipped over them on silent cat's feet once more, toying with the vanishing sun until the fiery plaything fell over the edge of the world and left them riding by starlight. The heavens were far from dark, however. Stirling's first glance up left his mouth hanging open in astonishment. Stars blazed in such brilliant profusion, scattered like a carelessly overturned saltshaker on a velvet tablecloth, Stirling's breath caught.

He had never, not even during desert training, seen a night sky to equal it. The heavens were so thickly populated, it took him long moments just to spot familiar constellations and several moments more to understand why they were slightly skewed from true in their not-quite-changeless march across the night skies. Gooseflesh prickled beneath armor and sodden wool. Little wonder the ancients had revered the night sky as sacred, filled with the shining souls of departed heroes. Every man, woman, and child on Earth ought to see a sky like this at least once. The experience might instill perspective on the insignificance of squabbles like Belfast's, when weighed against the infinite reaches of the heavens.

Stirling held back a tired sigh.

The column entered the upper reaches of a land Stirling heard referred to as Caer-Guendoleu, passing a stone post which marked the border. Ganhumara, having ridden in silence for hours, beckoned to the nearest of Artorius' *cataphracti,* an officer if Stirling judged correctly the quality of his arms and the deference of the men who rode with him. The man reined closer to the queen's lighter mount.

"My lady?"

"Bear a message to my legate at fortress Caer-Guendoleu. Bid him sharpen my late father's sword."

The ominous words chilled Stirling, heavy reminder of the dead they'd already left behind, who were themselves mere tokens—or so Ancelotis feared—compared with those slated to die if this challenge weren't stopped in some bloodless and apparently impossible fashion. The officer bowed stiffly at the waist and reined around—but not to depart, as Stirling expected. He requested permission to leave the column from *his* commanding officer. A moment later, he vanished into the darkness with a muted drumming of hooves against wet earth.

Stirling watched him go, brows twitching in impressed surprise. Clearly, not even a royal command superseded military discipline. Artorius commanded well. Of course, he *must* command well, given the odds he fought against and his track record of victories. It occurred to Stirling for the first time that he could learn a thing or two about soldiering from the Dux Bellorum. The observation wrung another derisive snort from Ancelotis. Stirling sighed. He was not making a particularly good impression on his host.

It was well past midnight, with the constellations wheeling silently overhead in a bitterly cold sky and Stirling reeling in the saddle, when the bulky shadow of the Sixth Legion's stronghold appeared at last. An immense fortress of classic Roman design, it towered above the final stretch of road. The grey shadow of Hadrian's Wall, shocking Stirling with its height—a good five meters of it, when the only surviving remnants in the twenty-first century stood barely a meter high—vanished into the darkness on either side of the fortress, marching toward the sea in both directions. The moonlit waters of Solway Firth glittered in the distance, silver where an onshore wind pushed ripples across the black stretch of water. The estuary's farthest reaches vanished into the blackness of sky at the horizon line.

Torches burned at the entrance to the great Roman fortification. A sizable civilian settlement—which Ancelotis referred to by its Latin military term, the *canabae* of Caerleul fortress—had grown up around the Legion's winter camp. Houses and shops were an odd mixture of wattle-and-daub hovels, stave houses built of planked timber with twig-thatched roofs, and stone structures resembling miniature Roman villas, many of the latter in poor repair. No lights showed in the few windows Stirling could see, although a glance over his shoulder revealed sleepy inhabitants peering nervously from darkened doorways, roused by the thunder of Artorius' return to Carlisle.

The fortress, in sharp contrast to the *canabae*, had been maintained in excellent repair. Or, at least, had been repaired excellently. The circumvallation's outer layer consisted of a latticework of pits and potholes and trenches into which sharpened stakes had been sunk, pointed outward, with raised berms on either side of the trenches. Inside this defensive ring lay a series of five narrow trenches like the rings of a bull's-eye, filled with the bristling nastiness of thorny shrubbery, hawthorn boughs, from the looks of it. A good twenty-seven feet wide, when measured together as one massive unit, each of the five rings boasted a ramped earthen face, up which an attacker would have to toil before attempting to cross the thorns.

Inside the prickly circles lay two ditches, both of them nine feet wide and seven feet deep. And finally, the immense stretch of the fortress wall itself, made of blood-red sandstone which rose twelve feet above the bottom of the innermost ditch. More thorny branches had been embedded in the wall, which was topped by a tall stone palisade with twenty-foot stone towers every few yards. Each tower stood three stories high and provided three fighting platforms. The place had been built to last, since this fortress had been designed to serve as winter camp to the entire Sixth Legion.

Tired as he was and dark as the night was, Stirling still pinpointed the locations of a full guard contingent along those palisades. If he'd been an invader, he'd have thought twice—three times—before putting this fortress' defenses to the test. Maybe the Saxons counted on drawing Artorius' army into the open by laying waste to the dozens of little villages scattered throughout the region? It was the only sane tactic Stirling could see, without access to black powder and cannons, at the very least. Doubtless, the Saxons had already thought of it—or would very soon after Cutha's arrival. Artorius would have considered that, as well, if he was half the commander Stirling already suspected he was.

What Stirling hadn't expected was the prickle of awe which ran up his spine as they slowed to a walk and filed through the narrow, guarded entrance of Artorius' military stronghold. Stirling was, after all, accustomed to living and even shopping in buildings hundreds of years old. And he'd seen Stonehenge, which was considerably older than these fortifications—by several millennia, in fact. But he couldn't help feeling the strange, hushed wonderment that comes from entering a place of great antiquity, any more than he could help searching out what details he could see.

They entered by way of a traverse outside the fortress gate, a short arc of wall surmounted by an armed guard, which forced them to ride parallel to the fortress wall for a long way before entering the actual gate—then they had to ride back along the return of the long, S-shaped curve past an *inner* arc of traverse wall, doubling the distance and time a defender could shoot at them. It was nearly as effective as a medieval castle's murder room, which served the same purpose, come to think of it, allowing archers, javelin—or, in the Romans' case, *pilum*—throwers, or pikemen ample opportunity to wreak their lethal havoc.

Once through the convolutions of the gate, Stirling's gaze came to rest on a veritable small town of red sandstone barracks, stables, buildings for which he couldn't even hazard a guess as to their functions, tired as he was. A broad avenue at least a hundred and twenty feet wide ran along the inside perimeter, with stair-stepped terraces making access to the palisades and towers quick and easy. They followed this road to the left, riding nearly four hundred yards before reaching the corner—whereupon Stirling discovered that they'd entered through the *narrow* end of the fortress. The length of wall stretching out before Stirling's bleary eyes was half again longer than the length of the wall behind them.

They passed torches at regular intervals, their ruddy light flickering across neat lettering on the walls of buildings at the corners of the perimeter road and interior cross streets. Only half the width of the outer road, the street Artorius led them down was still a good sixty feet from side to side, with the intersection neatly labeled VIA QUINTANA in Roman lettering. Clearly, *someone* had been renewing the paint during the past century. The Britons were clinging to their Romanized roots with a typically Celtic passion.

Stirling was more than happy to turn his horse over to the boys assigned duty in the stables, which bordered the Via Quintana for many yards. He slid out of the saddle and had to grip the nearest saddle horns tightly to prevent himself sliding all the way to the ground. Horses whickered greetings, tired newcomers welcoming sleepy stablemates. One of the stable boys carried a water pail and dipper, which he gave first to Artorius, who passed it to Morgana, Ganhumara, and Covianna in turn before drinking his fill. Stirling got next crack at the water, which he needed rather desperately. He passed the dipper on to Medraut and the king of Strathclyde.

Stirling was pleased, at least, that he hadn't fallen down, although he had to speak sternly to Ancelotis' legs before they consented to carry him across the open courtyard. Artorius led them through the doorway of Caerleul's *principium,* clearly the largest building inside the fort, a long stone rectangle with its short end opening onto the Via Quintana. The men of Artorius' escort and the *cataphracti* of Gododdin and Strathclyde tended their horses before heading for other structures, presumably barracks, laid out with all the formal precision typical of a Roman encampment.

A young girl, a child no more than twelve or thirteen, with dark hair in braids and dark eyes too mature for her years, held the door as they passed the threshold. How much war had this child witnessed firsthand? Eleven victories Artorius had already won, driving back invaders from every direction. And how many children just like this girl had already died? Not as many as *would* die, if Brenna McEgan weren't stopped.

He saw the room through a haze of bleary-eyed exhaustion and the reddish gold, smoky light of torches flickering across the red sandstone of the walls. Torchlight was augmented by Roman-style oil lamps in both pottery and stone varieties. Sullen coals lay heaped in an immense hearth which sprawled across the very center of the room like a child's playbox full of sand, with marble border stones enclosing a space a good twelve inches deep and at least four feet on each side, sixteen square feet given over to the coals. The hearth had clearly been designed to augment the central heating beneath the floors, a double effort to keep out the chill of a Scottish border town's winter. The huge hearth simultaneously allowed a small army of women to prepare a wide variety of foodstuffs over a blazing sea of embers. A small forest of iron pothooks, support tripods, and roasting spits jutted up like stiff snakes. The huge firepit vented through a smoke hole in the ceiling, an opening that reminded Stirling of the atrium in Roman villas, only smaller and covered with some type of protective hood on the roof to keep rain from falling directly into the firepit during bad weather. Tables and benches surrounded the central hearth, forming a shape that was more a twelve-sided polygon than circular. Weary travelers collapsed onto the benches closest to the fire, huddling beside the coals for warmth.

Servants moved in shadowy anonymity, shapeless in woolen tunics and drab woolen dresses. Flames leaped higher in the huge firepit. Someone had added kindling to the coals. As firelight flared up, Stirling caught more details of the room. Most of the furniture had been crudely constructed from rough planking, underscoring the utilitarian, military function of the place, although he saw a group of massive wooden chairs along one wall, nearly hidden in shadow, which appeared to be more finely wrought. If this was supposed to be Camelot, it was a big disappointment in the aesthetic department.

Still, there was an indefinable air of mystery about the place, a sense that Stirling had stepped into a museum peopled with ghosts who'd forgotten they were dead. He rubbed his eyes and tried to clear his head, senses swimming. Thus distracted, he failed to notice the woman's appearance. At the sound of her voice, Ancelotis jerked his gaze up. Thaney, Ancelotis' niece and queen of Rheged, was not a beautiful girl, but there was a compelling intensity in the clear green eyes and if that mouth had ever uttered a cruel word, Stirling was no judge of human nature.

"Artorius!" she cried with glad welcome, while quietly gesturing for a servant who brought a pitcher of something that tasted strongly of alcohol and washed the fuzz out of Stirling's mouth when his turn came at the cups circulating round the tables. "We feared you would return too late. The Saxon emissaries are no more than a few hours' ride to the south. They will be here by dawn." Her gaze found Ancelotis and her eyes widened in considerable surprise. "Ancelotis? It's good to have you here, Uncle, but I don't understand why you've come."

Ancelotis moved quickly to take her hands in his much larger, calloused ones. "Your father is dead, child," he said softly. "Killed by Picts at the border, north of Caer-Iudeu. The council has given me the kingship until Gwalchmai is of age."

Thaney paled and her eyes widened, but she made no sound, although her fingers tightened almost convulsively around his. After several swallows, she finally whispered, "I will mourn him more than you know."

Stirling understood, even though Ancelotis was puzzled. She had desperately wanted her father's love and approval and had nearly been murdered by him instead, and now she had lost all hope of ever gaining what she had so understandably wanted and needed. As Stirling's insight burst through Ancelotis' awareness, he folded his niece into his arms and just held her while she trembled.

"What's wrong?" a man Ancelotis recognized as Thaney's husband asked urgently, having come into the room still buckling on his sword. Meirchion Gul was a tall and exceedingly lean man, with the incongruous look of an over-muscled scarecrow, too tall for grace, too physically fit for any real sense of awkwardness. Despite the lateness of the hour—it was the middle of the night, after all, and bad news had not traveled any faster than they had, bearing it—there was an alertness to his eyes that told Stirling this man missed very little, indeed. He moved swiftly to his wife, stroking her hair with a protective gesture. "What is it? What's happened?"

Ancelotis gave them the disastrous double dose of bad news quickly, neatly, and quietly. Meirchion Gul scowled like thunder and struck one fist against his other hand repeatedly. When the telling was done, King Meirchion greeted Morgana and young Clinoch in turn, murmuring the inadequacies one is reduced to mouthing when nothing can be said that will lessen the pain and shock of loss. "We will, of course, honor Lot Luwddoc and Dumgual Hen with all appropriate funerary rituals, given the short shrift you have each been forced to give your honored dead."

"My thought exactly," Artorius nodded, "and the very complexity of the rituals will buy us time with the Saxons."

Before Meirchion could respond, another voice interrupted, rising in irritation like a waterspout out of a storm-slashed sea. "The devil take you hindmost, imbecile! May Hades, Lord of Darkness, eat your ill-mannered cockles and spit out your soul for Manannan to bait his fishhook! Out of my way!"

The man who swept into the room was taller than anyone Stirling had yet seen, taller even than Meirchion Gul, certainly a distinction in a land peopled with compactly built Brythonic Celts. He was powerfully made, moving with the speed and single-minded purposefulness of a bull charging into a wolf pack. His chilly blue eyes missed nothing—and the moment Stirling looked into those eyes, he was utterly and irrevocably convinced that a great deal of what those eyes saw was invisible to mere mortals.

Whoever he was, he'd twisted iron-grey hair into long and intricate braids, reminding Stirling more of Vikings than Dark Age Britons. The man had counted at least fifty years, at a guess, and the robes he wore would have been monkish had they not been bleached the same snowy white as Covianna's and cut in exactly the same style, with the same long hood folded back over the shoulders. He wore no ornamentation, not even a cross, which Stirling certainly would have expected of a Christian priest.

"Emrys Myrddin," Artorius greeted the man drolly, "one day your wife will toss you into the nearest loch and where will the people of the dragon be then, eh?"

"Bad news travels swiftly, Artorius," the grey-haired man said coolly, ignoring the jibe, "and you have left it late, this time. Morgana, Clinoch, I grieve for your loss. Meirchion, summon the high council of Rheged and send messengers to all the kings of the Britons, north and south. Tell them to send their sons to vote their pleasure, if they cannot tear themselves away to meet in high council by week's end. Artorius, you did well to order the ancient hill forts of the south strengthened and refortified, where the old walls had crumbled to dust. With the deaths of two kings of the north, the Saxons will abandon guile and attack as soon as they hear the news. Ancelotis," he said with an abrupt shift of attention, "you are not well. Sit you down, before your knees collapse." The concern in his tone surprised Stirling, who was still trying blearily to follow the lightning-swift observations and predictions.

Stirling wiped cold sweat from his brow and stared, surprised, at his damp fingers. "Sorry," he mumbled, stumbling to the nearest wooden bench, where he sat down a trifle too heavily. Queen Thaney frowned and spoke sharply to the servants. They brought him another brimming mugful of the same alcoholic beverage he'd just drunk, which he decided must be mead as he gulped the stuff down like medicine. A joint of roasted meat arrived—he had no idea what kind—and hot soup rich with meat stock, vegetables, and barley.

A few mouthfuls later, he started feeling almost human again. Myrddin sounded his pulse while the others tore into their own meals.

As Stirling downed a third mugful of mead—probably a mistake in his exhausted condition—Morgana sat down across the table from him and consumed her own meal with the determined look of a soldier who is too keyed up to feel hunger, but knows he must eat, to retain his strength. Standing near the end of their table, Covianna told Myrddin succinctly everything she knew about Ancelotis' collapse, finishing with a description of the treatment Morgana had rendered that first night.

"Well thought," the older man nodded approvingly toward Morgana, who nodded back in appreciation, leaving Covianna's eyes glittering and her fingers curling into talons where she crushed the long skirt of her robes beneath her angry grip. By the time Emrys Myrddin glanced back at her, Covianna had herself under control again and presented him with a sweet smile.

"I would count it a great honor, Emrys Myrddin, if you could find just a few moments to teach me a bit more. I would have been all but helpless to assist Ancelotis, had Morgana not been present to see to his care. And with the Saxons massing on Glastenning's border, I would count it a great favor to learn all I can of healing, should the swine overrun Glastenning Tor and attack my kinsmen and the priests of the abbey."

Emrys Myrddin missed the piercing look Morgana shot his way, because he was gazing at Covianna Nim with such pleased infatuation, sharply at odds with his earlier, surgically precise manner, even Stirling felt a serious twinge of alarm. "My dear Covianna, I would be honored to continue your instruction." He lifted a hand to brush a wisp of honey-colored hair back from her brow, where it had escaped her long, single braid. She smiled radiantly and murmured, "I am all gratitude."

Emrys Myrddin gave her cheek a final caress, then dragged his attention back to the business at hand. "Ancelotis, you must be fit to meet those Saxon swine when they ride into Caerleul and you have a hollow, dazed look about you that I mislike."

"I'm here, aren't I?" Stirling mumbled around a mouthful. "And on time."

Myrddin favored him with a thin smile. "Indeed. And if you fall flat on the ground in front of Cutha, you might as well have stayed in Gododdin."

The barb struck home, mostly because it was true. Not that Stirling could have prevented the collapse, given the immense shock of transition through time. "I won't fall down in front of Cutha or anybody else," he muttered, washing down the mouthful of roast. "I'm fine. Or I will be, after I've had more sleep." He couldn't stifle the jaw-cracking yawn.

"We'll all fare better for some sleep," Artorius agreed, shoving back his empty bowl, scraped clean of every speck of stew. "Ganhumara." He rose, holding one hand out to his wife. "Morgana, Clinoch, Ancelotis, we'll speak again at first light." Artorius gave them a strangely formal salute, Roman-style, then took his leave.

The company was breaking up, servants scurrying to clear away wooden trenchers and mugs, Medraut escorting his aunt away while Thaney and Meirchion departed, and Covianna and Myrddin, still comparing notes on how best to treat Ancelotis' "ailment," abandoned him without a further glance. Sage and disciple, more interested in the intellectual puzzle than the patient—or perhaps merely self-absorbed in one another. If Emrys Myrddin had a wife, as Artorius had mentioned, Stirling wondered how *she* would feel about Covianna's presence. Clearly, Emrys Myrddin wasn't terribly concerned with a wife's opinion, as publicly besotted as he appeared to be over the hypnotically attractive Covianna Nim.

Whatever the case, Stirling wanted nothing more than to hit the nearest bed and sleep for about a year. Stirling staggered to his feet, then paused. He had no idea where Ancelotis was supposed to sleep, when in garrison. The king of Gododdin had no such difficulty, however, and steered a mostly steady path through the tables toward the doorway where everyone but the servants had already departed.

The narrow corridor in which Stirling found himself had the look of a covered portico which had later been closed in, the now-solid stone wall keeping out cold and rain and snow. Bricks, carefully mortared, filled in the spaces between heavy stone columns. These were not the fancier Roman variety—most of which were not solid marble, in any case, constructed rather of a thin facing of fluted marble over a rougher stone for interior support—but were simple, massive pillars of rough-dressed red sandstone, much like the stone used to build Carlisle's great castle and cathedral in later centuries.

It was entirely possible that the ancient Roman fortress had been dismantled to build that castle and cathedral, pre-dressed stone being easier to cannibalize from existing structures than undressed stone could be quarried raw from the earth and moved into place. And if Stirling's memory of his last visit to modern Carlisle was accurate, the castle and cathedral sat on the very site occupied by this stronghold.

Stirling stumbled into a little room Ancelotis had evidently used before, barked his shins on a wooden bed frame, and collapsed onto another fur-covered bag stuffed full of straw. He was asleep before he could even fumble his way out of his clothes.

Chapter Eight

~

Morgana rose at first light and made a surprising and welcome trip to the baths behind the *principium,* following a covered portico from the rear of the great headquarters building which was her stepbrother's command center. The bath was a somewhat lopsided structure, clearly having been enlarged at some later point, as the right half was built of stone and masonry that did not match the left half.

Aye, Morgana smiled at Brenna's puzzlement, *they say when the first Christian priests came to Caerleul— the Romans were still here, then, and called it Luguvalium in those days—they were scandalized by the low morals of the men and women who used the same bathhouse. Not together, but the temptation was there, so the commander of the fortress had his engineers build a second bath adjoining the first, for the wives and daughters of the officers stationed in the fortress.*

Given the amount of railing twenty-first-century

priests did against lax morals, Brenna was not surprised
in the least. When they stepped up into the bathhouse,
the floor of which was at least eighteen inches higher
than the ground, Brenna gasped in surprise. Frescoes
of garden scenes decorated the walls, with fruit trees
and flowers, fountains and birds, even butterflies recognizable as English Vanessas. A beautiful mosaic of
sea life covered the floor, with dolphins playing and
leaping above the waves, scattering turquoise and
aquamarine droplets into the tiled sunlight, while
fish glimmered in shades of blues and greens and
silvers. Light splashed down into the chamber from
a high, round window, glassed in to keep the heat from
escaping.

"It's beautiful," Brenna murmured aloud, since no
other bathers had gathered, yet. "I'd not realized how
beautiful such places could be." Or that anything in
the sixth century would be so finely wrought and
carefully maintained. She'd envisioned Arthurian
England as a realm of endless crudity and was startled
everywhere she went by the overwhelming evidence
of beautifully civilized culture.

Yes, it is lovely, isn't it? Morgana agreed, tactfully
not commenting on Brenna's unflattering illusions as
she used a dipper at a small, separate basin to wet her
skin. She soaped herself with a yellowish and slightly
greasy cake of soap that must have been extremely high
in fat and lye, given its texture, then rinsed the soap
off into a drain in the floor before sinking into the
deep, rectangular pool of the *calderium,* an Olympian-
sized hot tub with a marble bench submerged around
the outer edge for sitting on while soaking. *Ahh . . . We
had nothing so fine at Ynys Manaw when I was growing up, as the Romans never troubled themselves with
the island. It was better for Ynys Manaw that way,
for we kept our independence and our ways intact, but*

*the luxuries they brought would have been lovely to
enjoy, when I was still a girl. We traded for a few
things, but not even the kings of Ynys Manaw would
hire the engineers and artisans this required*—she
gestured at the walls, the floor—*not without risking
the Romans taking over the whole island, once invited
in. That was Vortigern's great folly with the Saxons.*

That particular folly, the Britons were still paying
for, in blood.

Morgana's worry about the Pictish and Irish troubles,
as well as the Saxon ones, led Brenna to commit an
error she wanted to snatch back, instantly. When
Morgana brooded, *We must devote so much of our
strength to defending our western coast from the Irish,
I fear we will not have enough strength to meet the
Saxons in the south,* Brenna couldn't help the thought
that came arrowing out: *You know, if we could persuade the Irish kings that the Saxons are a danger to
them, persuade them to alliance with Britain, we
wouldn't have to guard that coast at all.*

Morgana, deeply startled, sat up straight, sending
the hot water sloshing over her breasts. *A most intriguing notion, Brenna of Ireland.*

Oh, Lord, Brenna wailed silently, *what've I done?*
She couldn't help it, though. If the Irish and Britons
had managed to ally themselves against the Saxons and
Angles and Jutes, not only would the invaders have
found Britain a tougher nut to crack, the Anglo-Saxon
kings and their English descendants wouldn't have
existed to invade Ireland several hundred years later—
and Brenna found the idea of saving hundreds of thousands of lives by eliminating the centuries-old war
between Ireland and England *very* attractive. Too
attractive, in fact. The desire to meddle, to try and save
those hundreds of thousands of innocents—to save an
entire culture—was a temptation that Christ himself

would have found difficult to resist. That war, perpetuated in the conflicts of Northern Ireland, had damaged Brenna's life deeply, had led her to the mess she was currently in, trapped in the sixth century, trying to stop an Anglo-Saxon Orange terrorist. But if she acted to save those lives, she would be no better than Cedric Banning, putting the lives of billions at risk to save a few hundred thousand. It was a bitter situation, worthy of Irish history, that to act would destroy as surely as *not* acting.

Unfortunately, she had already done the damage, putting the notion into Morgana's mind.

I must consider this notion carefully, Brenna of the Irish. Very carefully.

There being nothing Brenna could do to stop her, and finding it utterly impossible to explain the danger inherent in trying to alter what would be Brenna's past and Morgana's future, she subsided unhappily and tried to recapture her enjoyment of the Roman bath. Morgana, however, atwitch with interest and restless to be dressed and waiting before Cutha arrived, stepped out of the bath, drying herself in a large linen bath sheet as other women arrived to bathe and ready themselves for the Saxons' visit. A few minutes later, gowned and jeweled, Morgana set out in search of her nephew.

It took her several minutes to locate Medraut, whom she expected to find haunting the street outside the royal villa of Strathclyde, which stood at a remove of several yards outside the fortress walls. A veritable horde of boys his age, sons of *cataphracti* officers and wheelwrights and stable boys, were waiting for first sight of Cutha's arrival, creating a colorful uproar in the village street. Medraut was not, however, anywhere in that street, nor was he inside the villa. A search of the command headquarters back inside the fortress walls also failed to yield him up.

She finally stepped out the back exit of the *principium,* where the portico led to the baths, and found him at last. Deep in conversation with Ganhumara, who clung to Medraut like a lover, clearly having met him on her way into the bathhouse. Icy rage blasted through Morgana, directed not so much at the lovesick boy as at Ganhumara. The girl used men for her own selfish purposes and discarded them when it suited her, a pattern Morgana had watched with narrow disapproval for several years, even prior to Ganhumara's marriage to Artorius.

"Medraut!"

They broke apart, startled and guilty at being caught. Ganhumara sent a look of utter venom at Morgana while Medraut's face alternately flushed and washed icy pale.

"Aunt?"

"Your place is in the royal villa, nephew, not trysting with"—she ran a wintry glance over Ganhumara—"other men's wives. You disappoint me severely. Go and prepare for Cutha's arrival at once."

He paused, torn between obedience and the desire to say a proper good-bye to Ganhumara. Morgana spat coldly, "*Now,* Medraut! Or would you prefer to tarry while Saxons butcher the whole of Britain?"

He bolted, visibly stricken. Morgana rounded on Artorius' young wife.

"Your manners and your morals are contemptible! Were your father alive, he would shorten your hair and disown you as a common slattern. Stay away from my nephew, Ganhumara. Seek for your royal heir elsewhere or know my full wrath."

Ganhumara's face washed white with shock. Not the shock of insult, but astonishment that her ploys had not only been correctly interpreted, they had been flung back into her face. Morgana left her gaping, with her fidelity and reputation in tatters, to wonder when the axe would fall on her neck in the form of full disclosure to Artorius. Morgana had no intention of handing her stepbrother such news, not now and perhaps not ever. She loved Artorius far too deeply to wound him with such tidings, particularly on the eve of war. Steps would have to be taken immediately to remove Medraut from further contact with Ganhumara and her wiles, else he would make a fool of himself and plunge them all into civil war with Artorius. The most logical course would be to marry the boy off at once, to a princess of royal blood as far from Ganhumara as could be arranged.

And without a kingdom to offer such a bride, not even a younger daughter with older sisters in line to marry kings would consent to marry the son of a woman executed as a poisoner, with no hope of ruling a kingdom of his own. Not while Morgana's younger son stood in line to inherit Galwyddel and Ynys Manaw, just as her elder son would inherit Gododdin. The only answer she could see to *that* was to give Medraut a portion of Galwyddel or Ynys Manaw and name him king. This was, of course, well within her rights as sovereign queen, a solution other Briton monarchs resorted to with fair frequency, to stop brothers and cousins from feuding.

Unfortunately, to give Medraut a kingship, even a small one, would make him doubly attractive to Ganhumara, who wanted an heir with royal blood in its veins, which Artorius could not provide. Cousin to kings and stepbrother to queens, he was not, himself, of royal descent—a fact Ganhumara had resented from the moment her father had announced the betrothal two years previously. Morgana suspected that poor King Carmelide, beset by seas of difficulties, had married the vixen off at fourteen simply to stop her from ruining both their good names with her skirt-flipping, hot-blooded passions.

That girl was a disaster poised to strike like the headsman's axe.

"Queen Morgana?"

The voice startled her from the shadows of a room just off the corridor which led from the baths back toward the main hall. A man she vaguely recognized as one of the minstrels stepped forward, hat literally in hand as he approached.

"Yes?" she asked, brows furrowed slightly at the interruption.

"I'm that sorry, I am, to have overheard you just now, but I'm thinking I might be able to help."

Morgana's blood ran cold. "And just how might you do that?"

He twisted his Phrygian cap and said softly, "Well, 'tis obvious young Medraut must marry, and soon, to prevent trouble breaking out. I'm thinking it would solve two problems, to seek a marriage of alliance to the north."

Morgana frowned. "Strathclyde? Clinoch has sisters, yes. All younger than he and not yet of age to marry."

The minstrel shook his head. "You mistake my meaning, Queen Morgana. It was farther north, I had in mind. A princess of Dalriada would give us the alliance we must have to secure our northern border while we deal with the Saxons in the south. And marriage alliance with the Irish *Scotti* clan would be of such political significance, Medraut would think several times before risking war by trysting with Artorius' wife."

Morgana narrowed her eyes while Brenna held her breath. It was a disturbingly attractive solution, one Brenna did not dare influence; she'd done enough damage already, priming the pump that would doubtless make Morgana far more receptive to the minstrel's idea. "And what would you expect by way of reward, minstrel?"

A fleeting smile touched the man's lips. "You need not buy my silence, Queen Morgana, for I have the interest of the Britons at heart. But a man must eat and a queen must have minstrels for her court. I am weary of walking from Strathclyde to Cerniw and back again, playing at every tavern along the way to earn my bread. I have spent this week with the royal minstrels of Rheged and I think they have found no fault with my performances, if you worry on that account. I'll not disgrace your court."

Something about the glitter of the man's eyes sent a chill of warning down Brenna's spine, but Morgana understood only too well that this man's silence would have to be assured. If he remained satisfied with an appointment as royal minstrel of Galwyddel, that was well and good. If not . . . Morgana was not averse to acting decisively for the protection of Briton interests. Galwyddel possessed many a cliff from which a traitor could be hurled. "You propose to act as go-between?"

The man bowed. "Of course. Who else could travel to Dalriada without raising suspicion? A minstrel is always welcome and comes and goes as he pleases without provoking comment."

"Your name, minstrel?"

"Lailoken, Queen Morgana."

"You will have to put your memory to the test, for I will commit nothing to writing."

Again, he bowed. "Your wisdom is well known."

"Meet me, then, after Cutha's arrival. I will wait for you on the road to Caer-Gretna, half-an-hour's ride by horse beyond the walls of Caerleul, as soon as we have dealt with Cutha and summoned the kings of Britain to council. I'll have no witnesses to any such discussion."

Lailoken's eyes glittered. "Your pleasure is my command." The minstrel turned and strode away, exiting the corridor past the baths and disappearing around the corner.

Brenna warned silently, *Trust that one at your peril.*

Morgana replied, *'Tis greater peril not to make use of him. Trust, however, will never enter the bargain. Of that, you may be sure.*

The queen of Galwyddel turned in search of her royal nephew. Morgana found him in his room this time, pulling on his boots, having already donned his best tunic and trousers. He tried to stammer out an apology, face and throat scarlet as he waited for further reprimand. Morgana reminded herself that he was very young and infatuated with a viper who presented herself as sweetness itself. She closed the door behind her, giving them complete privacy.

"As to your affair with Ganhumara," Morgana began quietly, "allow me to give you a word or two of warning. She covets an heir and scorns Artorius' common blood to give it to her. She has never forgiven her father for marrying her to the illegitimate son of a Sarmatian war leader and will not stop until she finds a fool credulous and smitten enough to give her an heir with royal blood in its veins—and you, Medraut, are a grandson of kings. If you show the common sense of which I know you to be capable, you may well rule as a king in your own right, far sooner than you might guess."

His eyes widened. "What do you mean?"

"Liaison with Ganhumara can bring you nothing but shame, disgrace, and outlawry, if your indiscretion or her adultery are discovered. I have in mind a far more advantageous union which would benefit you immediately and benefit all of Britain in the long run."

"What sort of union?" he asked curiously as the

shame and high color in his face began to fade.
"There's not a princess of blood royal anywhere in
Britain who would have the son of a condemned
murderess with no land to offer." The bitterness in his
voice was sadly understandable, as was the flare of
stubborn pride.

"Perhaps not in Britain, but there are other shores,
Medraut, and other alliances."

"Brittany?" He frowned. "The Celts of mainland
Gaul would draw a branding iron down their daughters' cheeks before consenting to marry them off to
a creature like me."

"No, Medraut, I do not speak of Brittany."

His brows drew even lower in confusion. "What
then?"

"Aside from the Saxons, where lies our greatest
danger?"

"The Picts."

"Ah, you see the immediate danger, yes, but not
the root cause. The Picts have become a deadly threat
only because they are forced south from their own
lands."

His eyes widened. "The Irish? Of Dalriada?"

"Indeed. And the enemy of my enemy is a potential friend. A potentially powerful friend. We must find
a way to convince this enemy that the Saxons are as
great a threat to Eire and Dalriada as they are to Britain. A people looking to expand their borders are generally far happier to marry into a throne and colonize
peaceably than to risk their sons' lives in war to drive
a native population out. And if they are not happier
to begin with, they often can be persuaded to see the
advantage of gentler intermarriage, particularly when
both groups have much to offer as concerns the safety
of the other."

"Do you really think you can persuade the Irish to

assist Britain without treachery such as the Saxon *foederati* used?"

"I do not speak of hiring mercenaries, Medraut. I speak of alliance through the marriage bed."

"But—"

"You will have a great deal more to offer a Dalriadan princess than you now imagine."

His eyes widened once more. "You'll *give* me a piece of land?"

"More than a piece, should this alliance work out. I have one son to inherit Gododdin and one to inherit Ynys Manaw. What I do with Galwyddel is my own affair."

Her nephew gasped. "*Galwyddel? All* of it?"

"Most of it, I should think."

He sat down hard on the edge of his bed. "Oh! Aunt, I—I hardly know what to say!"

She laid a finger across his lips. "Say nothing, nephew. I should not have to warn you about the need for discretion in such a proposed alliance."

He shook his head, then nodded vigorously. "I understand, yes."

"Good." She placed a kiss against his brow. "I have had so little time, Medraut, to attend to your needs and education as I ought. Marguase's crimes were none of your doing, but I fear you have been desperately hurt by them and I forget, sometimes, to tell you that you are much honored and beloved."

Tears sprang to his eyes and he turned his glance swiftly away to hide them. He groped with one hand and squeezed hers, able to make no other reply.

"I will see you, then, in the royal villa, when Cutha arrives at Caerleul."

Covianna Nim was still concealed in the shadows of her room, whose door she had just begun to open, when Medraut burst into view and slammed open the door to his own room, clearly in a state of extreme agitation. He was deeply aroused, flushed and erect beneath trousers and tunic, and desperately unhappy in his agitated state. Her curiosity piqued, Covianna started to step into the corridor only to melt back into the shadows when Morgana swept into view, in a state of cold-eyed anger. The queen of Galwyddel and Ynys Manaw, stepsister to a far better woman whose destruction Morgana had helped bring about, thrust open Medraut's door and closed it again behind her. For the first moment or two, she could hear Morgana's voice, too low to understand the words, then the voices in Medraut's room went even quieter. Deeply intrigued, now, Covianna waited patiently, hardly daring to hope that she had finally been presented with a way to strike back at Morgana and the stepbrother who had murdered Medraut's mother—a mistress of dark arts who had trained Covianna for a time at Glastenning Tor, a relationship Covianna was quite certain neither Morgana nor Artorius knew about and one she had been extremely careful to keep secret.

For years, Covianna had bided her time, had made Artorius a "wondrous" sword of Damascus steel that she herself had pounded on the anvil, after wheedling from Emrys Myrddin every tale he could recall of the fine Damascus blades produced by the smiths of far Constantinople. Her lips twitched in amusement as she recalled Myrddin's fond tales, whispered in the glistening aftermath of some of the finest lovemaking Covianna had ever enjoyed.

"They twist the soft and hard irons together," he had murmured, trailing fingertips across her breasts. "Fold them time and again, eight, sixteen folds per blade, but the finest smiths swore while deeply in their cups that the only proper way to temper such a blade was to lift it smoking and white from the forge and plunge it into the belly of a drunken slave."

"Barbaric," she had murmured, planning to put the notion to the test at the first possible opportunity. And she had done so, testing the procedure first on a sow tied to the anvil, then on a captive doe, a goat, every animal she could think to try it on, and with decent but far from satisfactory results. Determined to win the secret of Damascus for the smiths of her hereditary clan, she had procured a criminal at great difficulty and forged a blade in *his* belly, gagging him carefully beforehand to still the screams. Better results, but not the perfection she sought.

Then Myrddin's exact words had come back to her: the belly of a *drunken* slave.

Lips twitching with satanic delight, she had ridden out from Glastenning Tor to arrange an assignation with one of the princes of Dumnonia, a foolish and drunken young sot who would be entirely amenable to accompanying her in a bout of alcoholic and sexual revelry. That he was a cousin of Artorius only made the seduction all the more delightful. She lured him to Glastenning Tor, to her own private forge deep in the labyrinthine caves beneath the great hill, where water rushed through underground rivers, welling up as the sacred springs of the Tor, blood-red with iron in one place, white as milk from chalk deposits in another.

She seduced him with her body, with endless flasks of wine and sultry laughter, led him down into the caverns to show him a secret he would never forget, and allowed him to watch while she forged her greatest Damascus sword blade yet, smiled above the pounding of hammer against folded steel as he drank and exclaimed and drank some more, filling his belly full of liquid.

And then she plunged the sword into it and the young fool died with a terrible scream and a hiss of steam erupting from the wound. She laughed as he died, his blood pouring across Covianna's hands, then she tested the blade and found it perfect, a blade that sang in her hands and bit deeply to dismember the fool who had helped her forge it. The pieces of Artorius' young cousin she dropped down a sinkhole to vanish into the roaring water which boiled past beneath the stone, smiling as she did so.

This sword, she would gift to Artorius and laugh each time he praised it. One more gift did Covianna offer her great enemy: a scabbard of silver and precious wood imported from the shores of Africa, carefully lined with sheep's wool left in the grease to oil the blade and treated most carefully, indeed, with a concoction boiled down from the sap of the Druid's plant, mistletoe. After it had sat in the sheath for a few hours, she nicked a goat with the blade. It bled to death despite her considerable effort to stanch the wound.

Ten years it had been since she had gifted that blade to Artorius, and eleven battles had he won with it, eleven battles for which she had made very certain to renew the "magical" properties of sword and sheath— "for luck," as she laughingly assured him. The great Artorius, against whom no one could stand in battle, the magnificent Caliburn shining in the sunlight like living flame as he cut down foes who could not stand against the sword's power . . . And all that "magic" was nothing more than the boiled sap of a common plant found on nearly any oak tree in Britain. She planned, one day, to reveal the secret to Artorius, at the worst possible moment for his inconvenience and comeuppance. Preferably as he lay dying at her feet.

Until that time came, she would simply have to

content herself with stirring up trouble within his family. No one had ever guessed the fate of the poor princeling of Dumnonia, whose kin mourned him and puzzled over his mysterious disappearance. And now, it appeared that young Medraut and Morgana were about to hand her another golden opportunity at revenge. She waited patiently until Morgana swept from the room, then slipped across the corridor, tapped at the door, and stepped quickly inside.

Medraut started violently on seeing her, mouth working to try and form some coherent greeting while his face washed scarlet and his hands trembled.

"Have I come at a bad time?" Covianna purred, gliding across the room to rest a hand against his heart. It was pounding with some violent emotion, terror most likely.

The boy stammered and swallowed hard. "W-what did you want?"

"Poor lad, they treat you contemptibly." She smoothed back his ruffled hair and smiled up into his eyes. "How you remind me of your mother."

His eyes widened. "You knew my mother?"

Covianna laughed softly. "Oh, yes. Marguase was instrumental in my education. Did they never tell you, she taught healing at Glastenning Tor?"

He stared in open astonishment. Clearly, they had not.

"Not officially, of course," Covianna smiled, toying with Medraut's fine tunic and the muscle beneath it, "but Marguase learned the art from the Nine Ladies of Ynys Manaw, and when she came to Glastenning Tor as pupil, she took me under her wing for private tutelage."

Medraut seemed incapable of speaking. A terrible, burning look of longing had come into his eyes, a hunger for some snippet of news about his mother, whom he scarcely remembered, having been so young at her death.

"Sit with me, Medraut," she urged, drawing him to the bed and urging him to sit beside her. "Your mother was a beautiful, brilliant woman, a lady of much education and ambition. The others were always jealous of her achievements—so jealous, they began accusing her falsely."

A jolt ran through the boy, shocked surprise and a wounded look that amused her.

"Oh, yes," Covianna purred, "even then, there were false accusations about black arts and satanic rites. You must be wary of what others tell you, others who stood to gain by her disgrace and death."

Medraut shot an involuntary look toward the door. "You can't mean . . ."

"Morgana?" she said gently. "I do not accuse her, no. But Marguase was firstborn and half sister to Artorius, who preferred Morgana to her stepsister. Marguase knew her own mind even as a young girl and often was at odds with her half brother. Perhaps your mother was not, after all, suited so well to governance as Morgana. Whatever the truth of Artorius' preferences, you must realize, of course, that to Artorius, the security of Britain is an all-consuming passion. When the accusations of poisonings and black arts began in earnest, it certainly suited the Dux Bellorum to remove her and place Morgana on the throne of Ynys Manaw and Galwyddel."

Desperate hurt and confusion had swamped the boy's eyes. "Artorius has always been kind to me," he protested weakly.

"And why should he be anything else? He does, after all, carry the guilt of having persuaded your grandfather to execute his own child."

Medraut bit his lip. "It's true, then, that Marguase

was the child of Igraine and Gorlois? I have sometimes wondered if perhaps Uthyr Pendragon had sired her, as well as Artorius."

"No, she was Gorlois' true heiress. It broke your grandfather's heart to order her bound to the rocks and drowned by the tide. He died soon after, in the fighting when the Irish tried to invade Ynys Manaw, leaving the throne to Morgana. Poor Igraine was dead already, of course, had thrown herself into the sea in her shame at giving birth to Artorius, got on her by ravishment at Uthyr's hands. Morgana was daughter of Gorlois' *second* marriage, greatly favored by your grandfather in his dotage. As Artorius' stepsister—not *half* sister, as was your mother—Artorius was free to, shall we say, deepen his friendship with Morgana? Theirs is a close relationship, very close."

The doubt in the boy's eyes was delicious. Doubt and a growing, subtle fear of incestuous feelings for a man and woman who were, after all, not blood kin at all, but whose "deep friendship" would certainly have brought both their reputations down in ruins had Covianna been able to prove anything. Covianna had all but given up hope, but Medraut's current vulnerability presented tantalizing possibilities to explore.

Medraut sat frowning for long moments. "What are you trying to tell me, Covianna? I can't see that any of this changes my situation. My grandfather disinherited my mother, leaving the throne legally to Morgana, not to me. He had that right."

"Yes, perhaps he did," she said softly, reaching down to stroke his hand gently, a gesture which sent a shiver through him and an unmistakable surge through his loins. It was not difficult to guess what had caused his initial arousal and Morgana's ire. The looks between Medraut and Ganhumara had not been lost on her. His passions had been whetted and Morgana had clearly interrupted, leaving him unfulfilled and vulnerable. A situation she could make delightful use of, to be sure. "Yes, perhaps he had the right to disinherit Marguase and, thereby, you as well. But it is a pity, all the same. You have the makings of a fine king, lad."

The look he gave her burned with confusion.

She smiled up into his eyes, then leaned forward and kissed him, gently at first, trailing fingertips across his groin, then with more urgency as he hardened under her hand. The union was fast and furious, as she had fully expected, and cataclysmic for the boy, who apparently was still a virgin, given his awkward fumbling under her skirts and inexperienced thrusts, not to mention the swiftness of denouement. She bit his ear and dug her nails into his back, disappointed in the extreme but feigning excitement as he pumped away. "Ah, such a king you would make," she breathed into his ear. "Such a fine and virile king. You deserve no less."

"Perhaps," he gasped, "perhaps I will . . . and sooner than you guess."

She unfastened her bodice, drew his mouth down to her breast, reaching down to slow his frantic pace, then murmured between nibbling bites to his neck, "How so?"

"My aunt . . . she's . . . she's promised me Galwyddel . . . if I do her bidding. Unngh . . ."

The shaking began. Desperate to keep him talking, Covianna tightened down and hissed out, as though lost in the throes herself, "Dear God, lad, how shall this be?"

"D-Dal-Dalriada . . . alliance . . . God, oh, Christ . . ." He shuddered deeply, spending himself into her and collapsing on top, panting and trembling violently.

Covianna exulted, petting him and making him quiver until he slid out and off. She kissed him deeply and hard, bringing him to swift arousal again in order to exhaust him, so that he would be less likely to blurt out his indiscretion, later, in divulging Morgana's plans, then rode him to another frantic release. After which, he collapsed utterly, all but asleep. She left him lying in the ruin of his clothing, trousers disarranged around his knees, not even having bothered to remove them. Covianna pulled her bodice closed, flicked her skirts to order, and murmured, "Come south to Glastenning Tor as soon as you are able, Medraut. I have much, indeed, to teach you, before you wed your Irish princess."

She smiled all the way back to her room, where she retrieved a small packet from her satchel of medicines and brewed herself a cup of tea from the contents, ensuring that any seed Medraut had planted would not germinate in her womb. She had far more important fish to catch than the spewing of a milk-brat who would never be king of anything. Not after Artorius learned of the proposed treason he and his aunt had concocted between them.

During the next week, when the kings of all Britain would be summoned to High Council, to discuss the threat of Saxons in the south, Covianna would have ample time and opportunity to bring her plans to delightful fruition. And to renew her liaison with Emrys Myrddin, as well, who was a far more skillful lover than that little idiot Medraut could ever hope to be, and capable of bringing her even more of what she wanted most from life. She cleansed herself from her basin and laughed all the way to the royal villa of the kings of Rheged, just beyond the fortress walls, to wait for Cutha and his Saxon dogs.

Morning came too soon for Trevor Stirling.
With it came the Saxons.
Much to his surprise, Stirling met them in a sprawling

villa situated just outside the fortress walls. He had
been shaken awake well before first light by the manservant who had followed him all the way from Caer-
Iudeu, serving as combination valet and batman.
Stirling gulped down a steaming breakfast of oatmeal
sweetened with honey and donned the finest clothing
his servant had brought from Gododdin, heavily
embroidered layered tunics of crimson and royal blue
wool, soft leather trousers as supple as velvet, dyed
a deep, pine green, and a hip-length black cloak
trimmed with dazzling white ermine fur and held
closed with an immense penannular cloak pin of heavy
gold that must have weighed a quarter of a pound. He
shoved his feet into thick leather boots, strapping them
around the leather trousers, raked back damp hair, and
pronounced himself as ready as he would ever be.

Outside, Ancelotis' horse waited patiently, chewing
at the bit and blowing steam in the chill air of morning.
The sun had not yet cleared the horizon when Stirling
laid his reins along the big grey stallion's neck, turning him with a touch, and jogged through the fortress'
wide streets with a rattle of hooves on paving stones.
He noted with approval the heavy guard mounted
along walls and watchtowers. In the daylight, the
immense fortress was even more impressive than it had
been in total darkness. Red sandstone walls stood
impenetrably thick, immune to virtually anything but
artillery fire—and Europeans wouldn't discover the
secrets of gunpowder for several more centuries. As
Ancelotis clattered through the snaking turns of the
fortress' main gates, Stirling stared in rapt fascination
at the sixth-century town which spread out in every
direction.

Seabirds drifted high above, crying their raucous
and mournful loneliness to the wide horizons, while
sunlight flashed in tones of pink and honey on the

undersides of white wings and high grey clouds. The waters of Solway Firth glinted in the distance, where the tip of the bay narrowed down into a thin finger of water. That fingertip curved inland toward Carlisle like a giant, hooked claw, raking deep into the coast-line's flank. Hadrian's Wall marched steadily westward out of town, paralleling that long claw of water for several miles, before finally dead-ending at the Atlantic Coast. A tall aqueduct completely unknown in the twenty-first century carried water to the fortress, while feeder lines supplied the whole town.

Despite the early hour, the town was already awake. Caerleul's inhabitants filled the morning with the ring-ing slam of blacksmiths' hammers on iron, the scrape of saws and rasps on wood, the deep lowing of cattle and the sharper protest of sheep and chickens being driven to market. Fresh-baked bread sent tendrils of deliciousness through the muddy lanes, while merch-ants threw back shutters on their shop windows. Stirling couldn't help staring at glass panes set into several shop-window frames, a sight that shocked him speechless.

He knew, of course, that the Romans had used glass extensively and that glazed windows had not been all that uncommon. Shards of glass from wide windows overlooking the sea had been discovered during excavations of Herculaneum's public baths, he remem-bered reading an article about that, but somehow Stirling hadn't expected to find glass windows in a shopkeeper's storefront at the extreme edge of Rome's one-time empire, a full century after the Roman pull-out from Britain. The merchants eyed him hopefully as he passed, calling their wares to any and all inter-ested customers.

Stirling's first impression of the town was of calm and ordinary urban bustle, but closer inspection

revealed strain and the shadows of uncertainty and fear.
It didn't do his jitters much good when Ancelotis
commented, *Aye, they're afraid, and with good reason. Two kings newly slain and the Saxons knocking
at their doors. Think you we Britons are immune to
such emotions, for all that we're certain of the Afterlife? A man may accept a promissory note from a
debtor to collect payment in the Afterlife, but that
hardly means we welcome the transition with arms
thrown wide.*

Stirling couldn't find a single response to that
astonishing piece of information and decided it was
probably best if he didn't try. Their destination, a large
villa which lay perhaps a dozen meters beyond the
fortress and its multi-layered rings of defensive barriers, had doubtless served as residence for the commander of the Sixth Legion and his family, if not as
the main residence of the client kings of Rheged. The
inhabitants had probably evacuated to the fort for
safety—along with the rest of the town—during times
of trouble. Whether the villa had been kept up by the
kings of Rheged or refurbished by Ambrosius Aurelianus and his protege Artorius was difficult to decide,
just by looking at the outside.

For the most part, it was as plain and utilitarian as
any other Roman house in the sprawling, once-great
Roman empire, its coat of whitewash faded from
exposure to years of Scottish weather. The sandstone
roof had been maintained in excellent repair, greeting the strengthening light of morning with a rosy red
glow, the cheeriest sight Stirling had yet seen. The
entrance, invisible during the night, was its most stunning feature, with a triangular pediment resting on no
fewer than six immense sandstone columns, fluted
gracefully. The entrance lay at the end of a flagstone
path bordered by statuary and formal flower beds,

which separated the villa from the commonplace bustle
and mud of the street.

A servant, one of the burliest roustabouts Stirling
had ever seen, who fairly bristled with weaponry and
stiff-necked military pride, held the door. Stirling
expected to find the interior as faded as the outside,
perhaps because every Roman villa he'd ever seen, in
pictures or on the telly, wore a melancholy air of
ancient glory gone dim, a ghost dissolving into the light
of dawn. But when he stepped into the vestibule, his
jaw dropped.

Frescoes in a beautiful, deep red covered the walls,
highlighted with golden birds frolicking amongst
painted fountains. Beyond the vestibule lay an atrium,
with its marble basin for catching rainwater, its frescoes bright and fresh, depicting deities, pastoral scenes,
and architectural elements. And beyond the atrium,
through open doors that could, at the owners' whim,
be closed for privacy, was a stunning colonnaded
reception hall, reminding him strikingly of the
Fishbourne Roman Palace, but on a smaller scale.

The entire villa was an archeological treasure trove.
These two rooms alone were. He moved forward
through the atrium and reception hall with a sense of
awe, glad of his soft-soled boots, for even a clicking
footfall would have been sacrilegious in such rooms.
The marble basin of the atrium pool glinted like quicksilver where sunlight struck the grey stone through a
shimmer of clear water. The colonnaded hall was the
backdrop for bronze statues on marble pedestals and
a breathtaking fountain in the center of the floor. Water
splashed softly in the hush, catching sunlight in brilliant sparkles, obviously fed by the aqueduct outside.

The villa's mosaic floors might have been laid yesterday, they were so immaculately maintained; they
caught the eye with complex patterns, depicting the

wildlife of the Scottish border counties—deer with liquid eyes, hares and songbirds, snarling Scottish wildcats, blood-red foxes, and leaping silver fish, in groups of three paying homage to a divine huntress and a horned god at the very center. Celtic triskelions, sunwheels, and intricate knotwork borders ran along the edges. The fusion of Celtic sacred images with the Roman medium of expression—thousands of tiny, colored tiles laid with loving precision—created a breathtaking hybrid art form.

Ancelotis asked irritably, *What is it you're staring at, man? 'Tis nothing but a floor and we've just as fine at Trapain Law! Even at Caer-Iudeu!* It took enormous effort to tear his attention away from what Ancelotis must have seen dozens, if not hundreds, of times. Voices further along drew his footsteps through the hall and out into a peristyle garden, where more fountains danced in the sunlight and beautifully shaped hedges marked the borders of winding pathways. Again, Stirling was reminded of Fishbourne, with its formal gardens that led awed visitors into the private sanctum of Britain's ruling elite. A barbarian seeking an audience with the king and queen of Rheged would be forced to run this whole, immaculately civilized gauntlet of rooms, altered landscapes, and engineering which shrieked of organized power.

Beyond the garden lay an open, airy chamber that clearly served the kings of Rheged as throne hall, given the presence of two immense chairs, beautifully carved from oak and decorated with writhing, animal-form Celtic knotwork. Silver and gold leaf on the carvings glittered in the sunlight, which fell like a golden river through the open doors leading from the peristyle garden to the throne room. It was here the leading citizens of Caerleul and most of the northern kings and queens had gathered to wait for Cutha and his Saxon escort. The Britons made a colorful splash of movement against the cool elegance of the Roman room.

Queen Morgana stepped into view from the shadows of an adjoining chamber, a slim and pale figure in black, her hair as glossy as a raven's wing, her eyes shadowed with grief and worry. Gold glinted at her throat and wrists, even her hips, where a delicate girdle of golden links circled her waist. She stood unmoving for a long moment, as icy and silent as a figure carved from basalt. Stirling wished he could find something comforting to say. Ancelotis cleared his throat, also feeling awkward in the face of her grief and the dire political disaster they all faced.

"You bear no ill will, Morgana?"

One corner of her lips twitched. "Ill will, brother of my husband? How should I, when I refused the throne outright when it was offered me? No, you are my first and best choice for Gododdin." She held out a slim hand and he crossed the mosaics quickly, taking the offered hand and kissing her cheek. "You slept well?" she asked worriedly, gazing into his eyes while her fingers sought the pulse at his wrist.

He quirked his own lips in a faint smile of response. "I did. Perhaps better than I should have done."

"Exhaustion," she agreed, "has a way of assisting in such matters."

A sound of voices reached them and Thaney swept into the room, greeting them both with genuine warmth. "Morgana, Ancelotis, there was so little time last night to greet you properly." She gave Morgana a hug that spoke eloquently of the younger woman's feelings. "Please forgive me if I cannot be overly distressed by my father's death," she added, peering anxiously into Morgana's eyes.

"Of course not, child," Morgana smiled, brushing a wisp of hair back from Thaney's brow. "Did you think

I would not understand? He tried to murder you. Your son is well?"

Thaney broke into a radiant smile. "He is. And you will be so proud of him, Uncle," she added, turning her attention to Ancelotis. "He rides like the wind and has never taken a fall, although my heart bids fair to choke me when I see him set his mount at some obstacle he is determined to leap."

Ancelotis chuckled. "As I recall, a certain young girl used to do the same, terrifying the wits out of her uncle when she set her mind to something a strong man would have thought twice of attempting."

"Fond uncle," she laughed. "I have missed you."

"And your laughter has been too long absent from Trapain Law. You will be welcome there, as from now."

She touched his cheek with a gentle hand. "As from now, I accept the invitation. But first," and the smile died from her eyes, "we must deal with the Saxons. My husband has gone with Artorius to brief the officers they will dispatch as escort to bring the Saxons into town. They've commanded half-a-hundred *cataphracti* to greet them, to prevent any mischief Cutha might have planned for their arrival."

"A wise precaution." Morgana nodded gravely.

Artorius, wearing chain-mail armor over a fine tunic and gripping the hilt of his sword, strode into the throne room at that very moment, arriving from the peristyle gardens. His choice of armor, Stirling realized abruptly, was a calculated insult to the Saxons: *Your visit is supremely unimportant,* was the message that ordinary mail conveyed. *So unimportant, I won't even bother to wear my cuirass and battle-dress armor.* He paced restively across the mosaics, looking like he hadn't slept for even five minutes, and said tersely, "They're in sight at the edge of town. Meirchion will join us momentarily, for it would not do to give Cutha the impression that we will ride placatingly to meet him, like some trembling virgin bride awaiting her doom."

Ancelotis nodded agreement at the wisdom of that decision.

Young King Clinoch of Strathclyde, pale and silent in his finery, entered the hall, fingers white on the pommel of his own sword, which he gripped the way a younger child might have clutched at a stuffed toy. The boy wore the look of the exhaustion which comes from prolonged stress and chronic lack of sleep. Emrys Myrddin strode into view, querulous blue eyes raking the room with a narrow gaze. He stalked over to Clinoch, speaking to him in a low voice that did not carry. A group of minstrels drifted into the room, touching fingertips to harps and lips to flutes, playing a soft melody that helped soothe Stirling's on-edge nerves. Ancelotis frowned slightly, however, catching sight of one of them.

What? Stirling asked, puzzled.

That fellow in the corner there.

Stirling frowned until he'd spotted the man Ancelotis meant, an eerie experience as Ancelotis moved his eyeballs without Stirling's consenting volition, to center their shared gaze on the individual in question. *What about him?* Stirling asked.

I had not thought to see him in Caerleul. He was in Caer-Iudeu the day my brother died. He wandered into town a couple of weeks ago, made himself popular with the men of the cataphracti. *He made excellent time, to arrive here at the same time as we did, moving by forced march.*

Who is he? Stirling asked curiously.

Lailoken, he's called. A minstrel of modest fame, travels from kingdom to kingdom. Has rather a flair for the comical, although I dare say there's little enough to laugh at, these days, and even less, this past week. I wonder how long he's been in Caerleul?

Stirling frowned. *If he was in Stirling—er, Caer-Iudeu—the day your brother died, he made damned good time on the road. He must have a fast horse.*

If he does, Ancelotis replied, *he won it gambling with the soldiers, for he came to Caer-Iudeu on foot. 'Tis the reason I was so surprised to see him here.*

Before Stirling could respond, Ganhumara swept into the room. Arrayed in all her finery, which included a flame-colored silk overdress and a great deal of gold, she looked like a well-fed vixen, with her coppery tresses swept up into an elegant, patrician style full of ringlets and wispy tendrils. Her stunning beauty hit Stirling like a fist in the gut, but the opulence of her appearance on this particular morning jarred with a deep sense of impropriety. At the very least, her blazing finery betrayed a certain callous disregard of Morgana and Clinoch's grief.

Ganhumara darted occasional glances toward Morgana, secretive little glances Stirling couldn't interpret, but she looked more frequently toward the young king of Strathclyde. She and Clinoch were nearly matched in age. Doubtless she and the young men of Clinoch's generation shared more in common with one another than with anyone else in their immediate society or this room. Stirling found himself wondering whom Clinoch would marry. For that matter, he wondered whom Medraut would marry and fell to wondering where the lad was, surprised he had not yet put in an appearance. Covianna Nim slipped quietly into the room and swayed her way across the atrium floor to murmur something low in Emrys Myrddin's ear, laughing softly and slipping her arm through his.

Old men will be fools, Ancelotis snorted silently, observing the interchange between Myrddin and his much younger acolyte. *And there's another trouble we could have done without,* Ancelotis added sourly, watching Ganhumara insinuate herself into Clinoch's company. *The matter of Clinoch's betrothal and marriage. Clan chieftains and kings from Dalriada to Cornwall will try to foist their awkward daughters on the lad. The Saxons and the Irish would both pay handsomely for the opportunity to marry into the royal house of Strathclyde and claim its throne legitimately. And Ganhumara will be even more trouble, for all that she's married to Artorius.*

A young boy dressed as a servant burst through the doors from the peristyle garden, gasping, "They're here! The Saxons are here!"

Clinoch went another shade whiter, which Stirling wouldn't have believed possible, then the boy crossed the mosaics quickly to stand beside Rheged's queen. Morgana moved to Clinoch's side, giving Ganhumara a hard, cold look until the younger queen moved away, clearly piqued and not caring to instigate a public scene. Thaney seated herself in the throne farthest from the door as Stirling wondered silently, *Where's Rheged's king?* He was unsure where he should stand and opted to stay where he was, near the entryway from the garden.

Meirchion is doubtless up to his usual tricks, I should imagine, Ancelotis replied. *Thaney picked a crafty one, when she defied Lot Luwddoc's will.* Ancelotis didn't dispute Stirling's choice of vantage points near the door, either, although the king of Gododdin did wrap one hand around the pommel of his sword, a seemingly casual stance betrayed by the tension Stirling could feel in their shared grip. A moment later, the Saxons brushed arrogantly past the servants who held the doors leading from the colonnaded hall out to the peristyle garden.

It didn't take much guesswork to spot Cutha. He was younger than the men of his escort, a cocksure mid-twenties at most, heavy boned and taller than anyone save Emrys Myrddin. Young Clinoch looked like the child he was, by comparison. Long blond hair and a square-cut, Germanic face marked Cutha as the Teutonic prince he claimed to be. Cold blue eyes glittered like chips of ice. Muscles bunched along his jaw spoke of a certain level of discomfort. A barbarian's response, no doubt, to that long walk through rooms calculated to flaunt wealth and power, all the while under the watchful, hostile eyes of servants, courtiers, soldiers, even the Roman statues that stood like sentinels, glaring blindly in his direction. Stirling had felt the effect himself, and he was far less susceptible than an illiterate Saxon soldier would be. Particularly one whose father had won a throne at the point of a sword, rising from obscurity in a land where civilization was something other people possessed and penniless warriors longed to steal for themselves.

Cutha's dismissive glance at Ancelotis as the Saxon strode through the doorway into the throne room sent the hairs on the nape of Stirling's neck bristling. *Aye,* Ancelotis growled silently, *a mannerless heathen, well schooled in testing a man's temper with calculated and subtle insults. The Saxons have made an art form of discourtesy.*

Unlike the men of his bodyguard, who wore leather tunics to which iron rings or overlapping metal plates had been sewn, Cutha wore a heavy chain-mail shirt which fell just short of his waist. Cutha's conical helmet bore a rim of iron around the bottom edge, and two arches of iron met at the crown. The spaces in between sported thick horn plates. An iron boar covered with gold leaf had been welded at the top, strengthening the helmet as well as decorating it. An iron noseguard added to the young man's fierce appearance. Bindings made from linen sewn to leather wrapped his calves from ankle to knee, fairly useless as greaves, but effective at keeping the bottoms of his trousers from catching on things that might snag or trip him up.

In his wake came another young man, thickset and short and flushed from exertion or nerves or both. Like Cutha, he wore sword and ornately inlaid wooden scabbard through a slit in the side of a mail shirt. Unlike Cutha, who carried a war axe with a surprisingly narrow cutting surface, this second young man wore no other weaponry. The men of their bodyguard wore axes, but not swords, and carried long thrusting spears with ash-wood hafts a good five feet long. The spears ended in bristling iron points. Circular wooden shields with iron-bound rims and cone-shaped bosses at the center, brightly painted in pagan designs, made for a glittering, barbaric display. Cutha's guards were staring, goggle-eyed, at the display of wealth on every side.

Cutha stalked toward Thaney and the empty throne beside her, allowing a contemptuous glance to slide across Clinoch's beardless face without even acknowledging the boy's presence. Clinoch stiffened, but he did not say anything, neither in anger nor in nervous fear. He simply glared at his enemy with a look that promised blood. If Cutha noticed, he gave no outward sign.

"Queen Thaney," the Saxon said as he halted several paces short of the twin thrones. He sketched a perfunctory bow which was nearly as insulting as his tone. "I would speak with your husband on important matters that touch your kingdom."

Thaney, cool as a winter sky, didn't even bother to return the insulting bow, not even inclining her head in greeting. "You will speak your business with me, if you seek to discuss Rheged's business. Unlike your Saxon sows, Briton queens are fully capable of ruling. Particularly when mere Saxons come calling."

Cutha flushed a dull red against the blond hair which stirred in the cold breeze drifting in through the peristyle garden's open doors. Behind him, Prince Creoda of Wessex, a Briton traitor Ancelotis would have spat on were they in Gododdin, paled so disastrously, Stirling wondered that he didn't keel over on the spot.

Thaney, eyes cold and voice chilly, asked, "What is your business in our kingdom, Saxon? Why have you demanded a place in Rheged's council, as though you were Briton born, not an invader with pretensions to royal blood?" Her glance raked Creoda, tarring him with the same brush. The insult scored blood with Creoda, at least, whose face darkened in a flush of anger and embarrassment.

Cutha's mouth twitched in feigned—or perhaps real—amusement. "Alliance, Queen Thaney. Profitable alliance against mutual enemies."

What mutual enemies? Stirling wanted to ask.

Echoing Stirling's thoughts, a new voice asked in a slow, amused drawl, "What mutual enemies might those be, Saxon?"

Cutha slewed around and Prince Creoda actually stumbled in his haste to take himself out of Cutha's way. King Meirchion Gul had appeared from the garden, balanced lightly on the balls of both feet, eyes glittering as he swept a contemptuous glance across Cutha's men. Cutha regained his composure with difficulty as Meirchion Gul sauntered lazily forward, nodding toward Artorius as he took the high-backed throne next to his wife. "What enemies?" he repeated, crossing his legs at the ankles and giving Cutha a slow, infuriatingly dismissive smile.

The Saxon narrowed his eyes. "Angles," he spat out. "Angles from Frisia, and Jutland Danes. They land by the shipload between our Saxon kingdoms of Sussex, Kent, and Wessex, and your strongholds of the midlands and the north, challenging and harassing our power, laying waste to farms and villages alike, killing and plundering. If we do not act to crush these brigands, they will grow so bold, there will be no stopping them." Cutha's smile deepened nastily. "But alliance between the Saxon kings and the kings of the Britons would crush our enemies between two strong armies and give further raiders pause when looking to these shores for plunder."

And leave the Britons understrength, Stirling thought darkly. It would also put Saxon armies deep in the heart of Briton territory, able to strike at will in any direction, catching off guard any Britons fool enough to make alliance. It had almost worked for Hitler, making a pact with the Soviet Union long enough to rape Eastern Europe, then striking at the Russian heartland in a surprise betrayal.

Only the bitter Russian winter had stopped Hitler's plan, as harsh winter weather had stopped Napoleon a century previously—and there was not a finger's length of ground anywhere in the British Isles with winters bitter enough to do the same for the Britons. With the interposing Angles and Jutes out of harm's way, there would be little to stop Wessex and Sussex from expanding to fill the entire island.

King Meirchion answered Cutha with a scornful drawl, gazing up from under hooded eyes. "We will, of course, give your offer the full consideration it deserves. But we will make no such decisions for the next seven-day. Mayhap you have not heard, but we Britons honor royal dead this day. The kings of Gododdin and Strathclyde have joined their ancestors and we will spend the coming week honoring their memory. The heirs of Gododdin and Strathclyde have joined us this morning," he added, "as have the queens of Galwyddel, Ynys Manaw, and Caer-Guendoleu, by chance here on other business. You are welcome, of course, to participate in the funerary games while you wait for our holy observances to end."

Funerary games? Stirling wondered, even as Cutha's eyes widened in a moment of unguarded shock. Prince Creoda's mouth dropped open. He stared wildly around the room while tugging at Cutha's sleeve in agitation. When Creoda saw Artorius in the shadows, saw the Dux Bellorum's smile of grim pleasure, the traitorous young Briton gave a start of pure horror, realizing too late the true nature of what the Saxons had blundered into here. Cutha ignored Creoda utterly, narrowing his eyes in swift recognition that the boundaries of his game had just shifted, perhaps dramatically. "My sorrow for your sorrows, King of Rheged."

"We thank you for your concern," Meirchion Gul replied with fine irony.

Cutha bowed slightly. "I am not familiar with your customs. What funerary games are these you speak of?"

Morgana stepped forward with quiet authority. "They do honor to my husband's departed spirit, and to King Dumgual Hen's, as well," she said with a chilly look, "and give their spirits a glimpse of the pleasures awaiting them in the Otherworld. They will dwell in the Otherworld with the Christ as warriors in God's army and will fight against the Great Deceiver and all the powers of darkness. We will honor their bravery in this world, as well as the battles they will fight at God's side. We celebrate their birth into the Otherworld with feasting and contests of strength and skill and speed, wrestling and races on foot and horseback, prowess with weapons. Warriors will fight to the glory of their memories, and horses and dogs will be sacrificed to journey with them to the Christ's eternal kingdom."

"Games well worthy of any king," Cutha murmured. "Where are these heirs you speak of, Meirchion of Rheged?" he asked, glancing away from Morgana as though she had ceased to exist.

Clinoch stepped forward, flushed with anger. "I am Strathclyde's heir, Saxon! King Clinoch ap Dumgual Hen." The boy shot a lethal stare at Creoda, who gulped nervously, then snapped at Cutha, "Why do you ask?"

"Why, to discover who my new allies will be." His glance slid unpleasantly across Clinoch's slim, boyish frame. "I would honor your father, as well, Clinoch ap Dumgual Hen. Many times have I matched swords with a man in ritual combat. It would please me to match strength and skills with Strathclyde's new king."

Even as Stirling snarled under his breath, Ancelotis tightened his grip on the pommel of the sword under their shared hand and strode forward. "With all apologies to King Clinoch and no insult intended to his good name," Ancelotis growled, "I would prefer that Gododdin gave you the opportunity you seek." Cutha slewed around, taken off guard a second time and clearly infuriated by it. Ancelotis added, with an apologetic glance toward Clinoch, "Gododdin's king died before Dumgual Hen was killed, giving Gododdin the right of first challenge and response. I would gladly show Saxons how we honor a fallen Briton king."

Cutha glared at Stirling. "And who are *you*, to issue such a challenge?"

"Ancelotis, King of Gododdin. I'll meet you on the field, Saxon. Unless, of course, it is the habit in Sussex to fight only beardless boys and women?"

Creoda gasped. King Meirchion toyed almost idly with the hilt of his dagger while watching Cutha through narrowed eyes. Young Clinoch gulped, looking both insulted and relieved to have escaped the challenge.

Cutha snarled, "I will meet you on any field you choose! Name the time and place."

"On the final day of the funerary games, Cutha of Sussex. I will meet you then with sword and lance on horseback and finish you on foot when I've unhorsed you. Match me, if you can."

Cutha's mouth twitched. "Talk is cheap. I accept your challenge with pleasure."

"Done."

Emrys Myrddin stepped forward from the shadows. "Until then, you would do well to remember that this villa is in mourning, for King Lot Luwddoc of Gododdin was Queen Thaney's father. Take your men and retire until summoned to the field, if you have any respect for civilized customs. An escort will show you the way to your quarters. And take the dregs of Wessex with you. Traitors are not welcome in the councils of Briton kings."

Creoda flushed and gulped nervously and would not meet Emrys Myrddin's eye. As the Saxons stalked out into the clear sunlight of early morning, Stirling resisted the urge to wipe sweat off his brow, mostly because his trembling hand would have betrayed him. What in God's name had he signed up for, fighting a sixth-century duel with weapons he scarcely knew how to use? Oh, for one lowly handgun and a bottomless supply of cartridges . . .

Artorius broke the tense silence. "We have bought a little time, at least," he said quietly. "We must watch him day and night, lest he send a courier to Sussex with word to strike while we are in disarray. If such an attempt is made," he added in a voice like a steel rasp, "we kill the courier. No warning, no mercy. Cutha will *not* get a message out to his father."

Ruthless, thoroughly dangerous . . .

Exactly what the Britons needed.

Stirling thanked God *he* did not face Artorius as enemy.

Lailoken hummed contentedly under his breath as he strolled through the crowded, muddy streets of Caerleul, carrying a heavy sailcloth bag over one shoulder and jostling elbows with the largest group of people he had ever seen in one place. Soldiers in armor haggled over the prices of knives made by the secretive island smiths of Ynys Manaw and Glastenning Tor, which lay many days' journey to the south. Shrieking children darted nimbly through the crowds with the quicksilver lightning of schooling fish.

Gold-torqued royalty strolled in their silks and long woolen robes with ermine trim, with exquisite cloaks stitched from wild mink pelts or ruinously expensive, imported black sable—the coveted favorite of northern queens during the harsh northern winters. Other cloaks had been made from shining silver fox furs that caught the light like a full moon over snow. Kings and queens, arrogant young princelings and their elegant, fine-boned sisters strolled serenely along in self-absorbed groupings of two and three, even as many as five at once, a sight Lailoken had never seen in his life.

He had never before been able to reach Caerleul in time for the councils of kings held in the ancient Sixth Legionary Fortress. The influx of royalty summoned to Caerleul by the Dux Bellorum and the soldiers and tradesmen who followed them, had jammed into every available inn, *taverna*, private house, barracks room, stable, privy, and hog lot within half an hour's ride of Caerleul's walls. It was a rare thing, indeed, to celebrate the rebirths into the Otherworld of *two* Briton kings at once and the merchants were making the best of it.

Native townspeople hawked fine needlework and hand-dipped beeswax candles scented with herbs stirred into the heated wax—far cleaner to burn than smoky, smouldering tallow and a far steadier light, for those who wished to sew or read by candlelight. There were beautifully carved chairs, platters, and bowls with a knobbly, gnarled texture, cut from the burls that disfigured many a tree in the forested hills. Jewelers displayed cloak pins, ear bobs, necklaces and bracelets and animal-motif brooches, their patterns twisting and curling back on themselves. Belt buckles as ornate as the brooches were displayed next to ladies' waist-clasping girdles with delicate links of silver or shining, sunny gold.

Farmers in from the countryside, having culled their herds in preparation for the long northern winter, sold their surplus of newly slaughtered smoked and salted meats, alongside freshly plucked and roasted chickens and ducks, all of which sent mouth-watering aromas spilling into the streets. The farmers jockeyed for the best positions at the open-air markets, squeezing in cheek-by-jowl next to fishermen with their reeking barrows and baskets crammed full of gleaming, silvery blind-eyed fish, mussels and cockles, scallops, shrimp, and freshwater oysters and eels, just pulled from the sea or scoured from every lake bottom for miles around.

The fish drew appreciative and thieving attention from the town's population of half-feral cats and hungry dogs, as well, looking for a free meal while the tantalizing smells of fresh-baked breads, jellied fruits, slabs of cheese coated with thin layers of protective beeswax, and wreaths of dried onions and garlic cloves mingled with the other scents of abundance Lailoken mourned the inability to share.

Tradesmen's daughters in pretty lace caps, their

dainty white stockings peeping out from under tucked-up skirts, laughed and chatted gaily, calling out to townsmen they knew and attracting everything male within ogling range. The girls set out finely made wares, some of them imported at great cost and danger and all of them to be had at premium prices—but made to seem a bargain when sold by those dewy-eyed, well-endowed maidens. Lailoken returned a few sinful smiles without stopping, ducked into a narrow side street where small boys were playing a tag and fetch game with enthusiastic puppies, and unlocked the door to the room he had rented just a few hours before Artorius had summoned the bedlam through which he and his secret companion, Banning, had just walked.

Lailoken shifted the heavy sailcloth bag to the floor, loosened the neck, and lifted out bottle after bottle to be set in rows on his new worktable. He had acquired the table cheaply from an inn which had suffered the effects of several hundred cavalrymen arriving from kingdoms scattered all across the British Isles, acting as guard escorts for the royalty. He made sure the firewood he used to prop up the broken table leg was securely in place, leveling the surface, then started setting out glass and rough-fired clay bottles and jugs. He'd been forced to scour the surrounding villages and several trash middens, just to find as many as Banning wanted, but this morning's trip had finally garnered enough to do a proper job of it and the work was well under way.

Into each bottle or jug, he spooned chunks of boiled beef, stewed vegetables, and several spoonfuls of dirt, mixing the earth liberally with the food. He capped them with a stopper of wax, which he further secured against expansion of gasses—something invisible which Banning insisted would be created by some alchemical process Lailoken didn't understand in the slightest—by tying thin cords around them, mouths to bottoms, several snug twists each. He didn't understand *why* he was to do all of this, other than it would somehow magically produce a potent poison, their means of vengeance against the Irish. More potent, Banning assured him, than even witch's bane, which had been used to poison wells in the face of advancing armies.

Filling Banning's bottles took relatively little of his time each day, so Lailoken carried out a number of other tasks as well, borrowing a horse from one of his new minstrel companions and riding out to meet Queen Morgana at the time they had arranged. On the day of Cutha's arrival, they met near dusk in a grove of crimson oaks along the Roman road leading north. The grove sheltered a little stone shrine that was doubtless older than Christ, from the look of its carvings. The wind had lifted his new cloak and Morgana's long, unbound hair, fine tendrils of which blew across her face like strands of silk. She had not dismounted from her saddle, waiting for him on horseback, along with a young boy who could scarcely claim manhood, he was still so young.

"Lailoken," she greeted him quietly, "my nephew, Medraut. Nephew, this minstrel proposes to help you to a wife."

Medraut gazed at him with guileless, curious eyes. "Then we are well met."

"It is my pleasure to serve Britain. When shall I leave, Queen Morgana, for the north?"

She considered for a moment. "Not until the High Council of Kings has met at week's end. I will be traveling home to Galwyddel then, and will take Medraut with me, to meet our proposed allies to discuss terms of marriage."

"And what token might I give the king of Dalriada as evidence of good faith?"

She lifted one hand, on which glittered a large gold ring. "My signet, with Galwyddel's royal seal. I will loan it to you the day you travel north to arrange the meeting, along with the precise message you are to carry."

He nodded, satisfied. "And where, precisely, shall I bid the king of Dalriada to meet you?"

"Along the coast, at the Lochmaben Stone Circle. Do you know the place? On the northern shore of Solway Firth, not far south of Caer-Gretna."

"Yes, I know it," Banning said smoothly when Lailoken hesitated. "A fitting trysting place for a marriage of alliance," he added with a smile. Indeed, as an ancient shrine dedicated to Maponos, god of youth and music, Lochmaben was still famous in the twenty-first century for hastily concluded marriages between runaway lovers. And if Banning's memory served, it had also served—for several centuries running—as the spot where border disputes were settled. "I cannot imagine a more perfect spot."

She lifted a brow. "Indeed? So long as you can find it without difficulty, I will be satisfied. Do this quietly and you will never lack for a home or money. Cross me," she added, eyes glittering like ice chips struck from a glacier, "and you will discover just how intense my displeasure can be."

His borrowed mount, picking up Lailoken's abrupt surge of nervousness, shook its head and mouthed the bit. When the animal pawed restively at the ground, Lailoken booted him under the shoulder with a toe, eliciting a snort and an unhappy shifting of weight. Banning, speaking smoothly over Lailoken's discomfort, assured her, "I have only the interests of Britain at heart."

"See to it that remains so. Meet me here again the morning after the High Council of Kings. We'll ride together to Caer-Birrenswark, for there is safety in numbers. From there, you will continue on to the coast and travel north by water."

Medraut glanced curiously at his aunt. "Why by water?"

Her glanced softened. "Because," she said gently, "a man riding north by horseback must pass the Antonine Wall. Our border guards allow no Briton north of the mile forts, just as they allow no Pict or Irishman south. Not without meeting heavy resistance." She pursed her lips, studying Lailoken. "You should pose as a trader. Yes, I think that would be best, to reduce Dalriadan suspicions. A British bard might think twice about sailing into Dalriadan waters, but traders eager for profit will sell to anyone with the coinage— including an Irish clan chieftain who has proclaimed himself king. Return by water, as well, when you bring our proposed allies to Lochmaben."

"When shall we meet?"

She considered the question for a moment. "On the night of the next full moon, I think. That will give you time enough to travel both ways. Find me there at moonrise. Take this now," she pulled a small leather bag from under her cloak. "You will have expenses to bear before leaving Caerleul, for a man who poses as a trader must have something to trade—and a pack animal to carry it. I leave the details—and much else— to your discretion."

Lailoken accepted a small purse heavy with gold, exulting in his good fortune. Once back in town, he bought a fine riding horse, two sturdy pack horses, a variety of baubles such as women coveted for their necks and wrists, fine woolen gowns and kidskin slippers for delicate feet, several bottles of excellent wine imported from Rome itself, and a bale of hay to cinch down over the sets of panniers he bought for the pack animals, baskets which would carry the trade goods near the top, as a screen for the more lethal cargo carefully cushioned beneath.

With Morgana's gold, he had no need to gamble for money, as Banning had originally intended. He still picked up the odd coin playing as a minstrel, of course, and spent many pleasant hours at the town's sandstone racing and gladiatorial arena, watching the games and cheering the crowd's favorites to victory. Banning, in particular, was fascinated with the arena and the games.

'Tis a grand arena, Banning said the first time they entered the immense structure which stood like a red sandstone battleship at the edge of town. *It's completely unknown in my own time. Doubtless the poor dismantled it for building materials, over the centuries,* Banning mused, *more's the pity.* It boasted an outer, one-story colonnade of the same red sandstone as the legionary fortress. One end was gracefully rounded, typical of raceways from one end of history to the other, but the opposite end had been squared off, giving the outer portico a truncated, clumsy look, like an elongated horseshoe with a blunt, square wall closing off the opening.

This puzzled Banning until they passed through one of the arched entrances cut into the portico. Sandstone starting gates had been built right through the squared-off end, a series of wide arches which formed stone chambers giving access to the track. A red sandstone balcony capped the starting boxes, roofed over to shelter officials who moved with a colorful flutter of woolen plaids stirred by the wind. A wooden machine something like the wheel of a sailing ship evidently controlled the heavy wooden doors of each racing stall. At the moment, these doors stood open, giving

Lailoken and Banning a clear view of the open space beyond the back of the starting boxes. Runners and wrestlers stood waiting for the end of the foot race currently under way.

What startled Banning most of all was the seating. Unlike other Roman-era arenas he'd seen, which boasted tiers of stone seats, Caerleul's outer colonnade enclosed multiple ranks of tall wooden bleachers, the highest tiers of which rose some twenty feet above the sandstone parapet. The bleachers gave the arena an incongruous look, reminiscent of a small-town cricket or soccer field—games Lailoken didn't understand, even when Banning attempted to explain the rules.

Cricket's a bloody marvelous game, if you'd brains enough to learn it, Banning finally said in peevish ill temper. *Now shut up and let me watch your idea of sport.* Fortunately for Lailoken, who was coming to dread Banning's anger, his unseen guest enjoyed the barbaric splendor of the funerary games even more than Lailoken did. And so the week passed, very pleasantly indeed, with money in his pouch, games to entertain him, and lively music each night, with plenty of good wine to wet his throat. Even better, as one of the minstrels favored by the royal house of Rheged, he had access to the royal villa and the Dux Bellorum's councils virtually any time he wanted it. For the first time in his life, Lailoken had every luxury he wanted or needed within reach.

All that remained now was the waiting.

Chapter Nine

The morning of Stirling's fight with Cutha dawned as dismally as his spirits: overcast and cold, with a wet wind whipping across Solway Firth from the distant, slate-grey Atlantic. Ragged, racing clouds were a low-scudding promise of more rain before midmorning or Stirling was no judge of late autumn weather in the border counties. Ancelotis merely grunted agreement after their mutual, quick look at the sky. Stirling, with a twenty-first-century soldier's appreciation of the need for cleanliness, nevertheless muttered under his breath about the tepid bathwater his servant Gilroy brought in a pitcher and basin, shivering in the cold air as the rapidly cooling water sluiced down his chest and back.

Ancelotis, growing impatient with his bellyaching, finally said, *The villa's baths are kept fired, you know. Meirchion and Thaney would hardly begrudge you a long, hot soak. Or if you're reluctant to trespass on Thaney's charity, the officers' baths at the fortress are kept heated, as well. We're hardly barbarians,* the Briton king growled in an irritable tone, due more to pre-combat nerves than Stirling's naivety about the Britons' civilized manners. *It's the Saxons who don't bathe or comb their hair more than once or so a month,* he added peevishly.

Stirling blinked, taken completely by surprise. The Roman baths were still operational? A delighted grin chased its way across his face. *Jolly well fabulous!* He'd arrange for a very long and very hot soak, at the earliest possible moment—say, right after his bout with Cutha. He couldn't think of a better way to soothe the inevitable crop of bruises and cuts he would pick up.

Stirling had no sooner finished pulling on clean clothing and his armor, assisted by Gilroy, than Emrys Myrddin arrived. "An excellent morning to you, Ancelotis. One might have wished the weather to grant us more favorable conditions, but I have every faith you will prevail."

"May your faith in my sword arm be justified," Ancelotis responded as they strode briskly outside to their waiting horses. Gilroy followed, carrying Ancelotis' spare weapons and shields.

They rode through the town at a bracing trot, past cheering Britons who closed ranks behind them and followed eagerly toward the field. Little girls along the side of the road waved branches of greenery cut from pines and spruces before joining the throng at their heels and small boys darted in front of Ancelotis' immense charger, shouting gleefully as they dared each other to dash past the war-horse's enormous hooves. The horse snorted and tossed his head and pranced almost sideways down the road, proudly flicking the white feathers which hid his feet, slinging mud every which way and having a marvelous time with all the attention directed at him.

Ancelotis let the animal dance, commenting laconically, *He mirrors my feelings, belike.*

Stirling muttered, *If all you feel is nervous tension, you're a better man than I am, Gunga Din.*

Gunga Din? Ancelotis frowned. *Who or what is a Gunga Din? And why do you call me by the name?*

Stirling's ill-advised quotation left him trying to explain Kipling. *Ah, yes, well, Gunga Din was a water boy, not a boy at all really, that's just a name given to natives who carried water to the wounded during battle. A rude name, I'm afraid, demeaning and given to a grown man who was both a native of India and a servant. Two things guaranteed to earn such a man scorn from the British soldiers who had gone to India to win an empire—*

British soldiers, fighting a war in India? Ancelotis interrupted excitedly. *Building such an empire as exceeded Roman might? Emrys Myrddin has a piece of ivory taken from the tusk of an elephant that came from India, stolen, he says, while he was still a slave in Constantinople. Traders still ply the route from the city astride the Bosporus and the fabled realm of eastern spices and mysterious, veiled women. So far as I know, not one Briton has ever been there. This Kipling, then, was he a British soldier in India?*

Stirling tried frantically to recall details of Kipling's career. *Not a soldier, exactly. Well, maybe he was, I don't remember that part of it, and I ought to. In my opnion, he was the greatest poet Britain ever produced, should've been Poet Laureate, the way he understood people and the military—*

Poet Laureate? Ancelotis interrupted again, his thoughts both excited and dreamy, this time. *Now that's a grand idea, so it is, to give a laurel crown of victory to the greatest poet of the Britons . . .*

Stirling kicked himself mentally and tried to convince

himself that nothing critical would be altered, surely, if the Britons decided to name a Poet Laureate a millennium or so before they were supposed to? Before Ancelotis could ask for the rest of Gunga Din's story, which put the British in a rather seriously unpleasant light, full of bigotry and pride and arrogance to a man who had given his life bringing water to wounded men who despised him, Emrys Myrddin interrupted.

"Cutha," the one-time slave leaned in his saddle to speak above the crowd noise, "has spent the week carousing, an activity we have encouraged with plenty of wine and ale and a ghastly excess of mead, which they have drunk by the hogshead. That will give you at least some advantage, since we made very certain that the Saxons were up late last night." Myrddin smiled a crook-mouthed, conspiratorial little smile. "They're already celebrating Cutha's victory, in fact. Drank themselves into a stupor recounting the glorious blows he plans to strike against you. When we roused them at cockcrow, they could barely stand, much less offer anyone serious threat."

Stirling nodded his appreciation. "While I've gone to bed early every night and have taken care to sleep well. It certainly ought to help. After all, 'Early to bed and early to rise makes a man healthy, wealthy, and wise.'" That quintessentially American tidbit of wisdom didn't come out with quite the same poetic impact, translated into Brythonic Welsh, but the idea came across well enough.

Nicely enough that Myrddin shot a startled stare his way.

Ah, bugger all, Stirling swore under his breath, *if Brenna McEgan's taken shelter with Emrys Myrddin, I've just cocked it up as badly as a fool could manage.*

"Yes," the Druid said thoughtfully, his keen glance revealing his thoughts only too clearly. Ancelotis might be respected as a warrior and man of honor, but quite obviously he was *not* noted for the glib turning of a phrase. "A lesson worthy of an ancient Druidic master," Myrddin mused, "if somewhat awkwardly phrased," he added with a faint smile, "and lacking the proper meter and alliterations of a teaching epigram. The thought, however, is sound enough. Let us hope it bears the fruit we seek."

"Right."

Stirling vowed to keep his conversations with Emrys Myrddin as laconic as possible, during the eleven months, three weeks and one or two odd days he had left to stay in the sixth century. As they neared the arena, the cheering crowd which had followed them through town abruptly broke away, spilling through arched entryways that led to the arena's wooden seats, everyone scrambling eagerly for places not already taken. Emrys Myrddin ignored the pedestrian entrances and reined around toward the circus' farthest end. When they turned the corner, Stirling peered curiously through the starting boxes into the arena floor. He'd been to the arena several times during the week, but hadn't come down to look through the starting boxes.

Ten racers clad in linen trousers were pelting down the long straight stretch toward the far turn. Sweat pouring down their bare backs suggested a multi-lap event nearing its conclusion, since the day was chilly and full of blustery cold wind. A wildly cheering crowd encouraged the runners to greater efforts. The thing that surprised Stirling the most was the large number of empty bleachers. There didn't seem to be enough people in Caerleul or even the surrounding country-side to fill so much as a quarter of the viewing stands. No wonder the Dux Bellorum worried about Saxon incursions, when apparently there weren't enough Britons left to do the fighting.

Too bloody right, Ancelotis muttered, picking up one of Stirling's favorite swearwords. *We cannot breed ourselves fast enough to replace men lost in battle. Meanwhile, our enemies arrive by the endless shipload from lands far larger than our own, all of them eager to plunder and seize ground that isn't already overcrowded with their uncles and brothers and cousins and their nagging wives and children.*

It was, God help the Britons, the classic predicament of civilized nations who found themselves under siege by migrating peoples or by cultures who bred themselves faster for any of a variety of reasons. The runners rounded the end of a low central spine, little more than a meter in height and not much wider, that divided the two straightways of the racetrack. Some of them skidded in the sand as they raced back toward the starting gates once more. Regular and deep holes in the long central spine, digging into its pitted surface like badger holes, suggested missing monuments which had once crowned the low dividing wall. Stirling wondered what had become of them, since the rest of the arena had been maintained well.

To Stirling's irritation, Ancelotis didn't know, nor was the Scots king particularly interested in statues and monuments that had vanished more than a century previously. Doubtless any statue depicting a pagan deity had ignited the full and blazing wrath of Caerleul's Christian priesthood—and anything bronze had doubtless been melted down long since to recover the valuable metal. Britain had been providing the ancient world's supply of tin for centuries, but it was much easier to melt down existing bronze than create new batches of the alloy from its constituent metals. Bronze hadn't been required for weapons in centuries, of course, but many a luxury item was fashioned of it.

It was rather sad, however, that the grand arena had

been stripped of what had doubtless been its greatest finery, since what was left was heartlessly plain and utilitarian. The one luxurious note stood halfway down the homestretch, shading the only section of stone seating in the entire arena: an awning of purple-bordered white wool, which protected Briton royalty from inclement weather. A wise precaution, given the threat from ragged, rain-heavy clouds racing low across the sky, in tattered banners caught in the crosscurrents of unpredictable winds.

Kings from most of the kingdoms of Britain shared the pavilion, along with their queens, councillors, and a few princes of royal blood from distant Briton neighbors, representing their fathers and voting proxy in the council to be held tonight, after the last of the weeklong funerary games. It had taken this long for some of the visiting princes and kings to *reach* Caerleul. Stirling couldn't help wondering what the outcome of the council would be, and how it might affect his mission.

He puzzled for a moment over why the royal pavilion hadn't been set up on the balcony above the starting boxes, which would have offered better shelter from the weather, then decided the view would be better from mid-track. Stirling picked out Morgana under the awning, seated next to her nephew and her two very young sons, Gwalchmai and Walgabedius, names that had startled him when they'd first translated in his mind into their English equivalents: Gawain and Galahad, aged six and four, respectively. The boys had arrived from Trapain Law only the previous day, unable to travel any faster. Stirling's throat closed, or perhaps Ancelotis' did, seeing those two small figures huddled close to their mother. Both children had clung to her since their arrival, eyes wide and bereft. Little Gwalchmai, not quite seven years old yet, had gazed up at his uncle with a brave attempt at manliness in his little face. Ancelotis had crouched down in front of the child and very gently removed the heavy golden torque from his own neck.

"You see this, lad?"

The boy had nodded, wordless and hurt.

"Well, my king, 'tisn't mine at all. It's yours." He placed the heavy torque around the boy's neck, where it flopped down his chest in a forlorn fashion.

"It doesn't fit very well," Gwalchmai said uncertainly.

"No, not yet. But it will, my king. Give it time and it will fit you very well, indeed. I'm only borrowing it until then. So that I can protect your mother and your brother and all the people of Gododdin until you're a man grown and well able to do that, yourself."

"Will you teach me?" the boy asked plaintively, fear in his eyes. "Better than Father?"

His throat closed. "Better than your father? How is that possible, lad?"

Gwalchmai wiped tears with one fist. "Father let the Picts kill him."

"Oh, no, lad, never think that," Ancelotis murmured, drawing the boy close. "Your father was a great warrior. Why, he and Artorius trained together as boys, taught by Ambrosius Aurelianus, himself. In war, lad, it isn't a matter of *letting* someone kill you, sometimes it just happens that the other side is a bit stronger that day. Sometimes, it's nothing more than bad luck. A man does his best, Gwalchmai, learns all that he can about his trade, and does his very best, and no one can ask any more than that of a man. I've never seen any warrior fight harder or more bravely than your father did, the day the Picts killed him. And even though they killed him, lad, we defeated them, because his battle plan was a good one. The Picts won't be crossing our borders again for a bit because of that."

Gwalchmai leaned against his shoulder for long moments, thinking about that, then finally said, "Uncle, I don't know how to make a battle plan."

He kissed the child's hair. "Not yet, Gwalchmai. But I will teach you. That's part of my sacred charge from the council of advisors, to teach you all the things your father would have done, had he lived long enough. It will be a great honor to teach you, my young king."

When the boy met his eyes again, some of the deep hurt had gone. "Like you taught me to saddle my pony and take him across the jumps and care for him after?"

"Exactly like."

His lower lip quivered for a moment, then he put his small hands around the torque and pulled it off. "It's too heavy, Uncle."

He had never heard a better summation of kingship in his life.

"When the day comes, Gwalchmai, you'll be strong enough to lift and carry it. This, I vow before God."

The child who would be king put the torque into his uncle's hands and he slipped it back around his own neck. "Thank you, Gwalchmai. I will wear it in your honor until you are ready to receive it back again, as a man fully grown."

The boy hugged him spontaneously. The slight little body was trembling. "Don't die, too!"

He kissed the boy's hair again. "That, my little king, is in God's hands. But I will take great care, this I promise."

When Ancelotis glanced up, he found Morgana watching with tears streaming down her face, holding her younger son in her arms and rocking him gently. "Gwalchmai," he said gently, "your mother needs you, lad."

The boy looked around, saw his mother's tears, and ran to her. "Don't cry, Mamma, I'll protect you!"

A strangled sound escaped her, then she was on her knees, clutching her older son close and weeping against his neck. Ancelotis left silently, allowing them the privacy their grief demanded. Now, seated in the arena, preparing to watch the ritual combat about to transpire, Gwalchmai all but glued himself to his mother's side, face a pale blur in the distance. The boy was doubtless terrified that he would lose an uncle, this day, right before his eyes.

And there wasn't a thing he could have done to disabuse the child of that notion, since he knew in his bones that was precisely what Cutha intended. He would have liked to have spared the child the sight of this combat, but he would do the boy no favors by sheltering him—nor would such a course serve Gododdin's best interests. It was brutal, the harsh reality that a king must learn from his very childhood, if he were to govern wisely. That ugly reality didn't stop Ancelotis from wishing, rather desperately, that little Gwalchmai didn't have to learn it quite so soon.

Ancelotis clenched his jaw even tighter when he realized Ganhumara sat on the boy's other side, offering neither comfort nor even acknowledgment of the child's presence. Artorius' wife blazed in a shimmer of copper hair and flame-colored woolen gown, a startling contrast beside Morgana's black mourning attire. Ganhumara seemed to flicker around the edges against the slate-colored sky, wildfire against the looming threat of thunder. Ancelotis wasn't proud of the thought, but couldn't help thinking it, either: *Pray God that one never has children. She'd let them starve for affection among the dogs of her kennels, while she flipped her skirts at whatever had caught her fancy for the moment.*

Stirling, watching through Ancelotis' eyes, agreed darkly.

A burst of raucous laughter from behind brought

Ancelotis and Stirling around in the saddle. Cutha and his personal guard contingent were making their way across a broad meadow beyond the racing arena, through a substantial herd of horses and ponies left to graze by visitors in from the countryside. Cutha's men were accompanied by a contingent of stone-faced soldiers wearing the colors and insignia of Rheged's *cataphracti*.

Whatever the Saxons had been up to, at least they'd done it under the scrutiny of Briton military might. Cutha gestured toward Emrys Myrddin and Ancelotis, then said something that drew howls of laughter from his companions. Most of Cutha's men swayed in the terminal stages of drunkenness, clearly having indulged in an extended celebration which had continued right through until morning and apparently had no intention of ending until Cutha had actually defeated his opponent on the field.

"Overconfident windbags," Ancelotis muttered, drawing a chuckle from Emrys Myrddin.

Stirling, however, had noted quite narrowly that Cutha neither swayed in his saddle nor appeared to be even the slightest bit drunk. Creoda, riding in his wake, had gone from looking like a scared rabbit to resembling a potted one, badly drunk and too terrified in his drunkenness to put so much as a toe wrong in Cutha's presence.

"Looks to *me*," Stirling muttered under his breath, "like he holds his liquor better than his pals do. Jolly wonderful."

A shout went up from the arena and signal trumpets blared as the footrace competitors, having made one more complete circuit of the track, shot past a finish line marked with white chalk. They slowed to a halt, many of them gasping deeply for breath. The winner jubilantly retraced his route, jogging a victory lap before halting at the royal pavilion halfway down the homestretch. The panting victor climbed sandstone steps up from the track and bowed low to Thaney and Meirchion. The king of Rheged made some sort of speech, which Stirling couldn't hear, then Thaney laid an honest-to-god laurel wreath on the winner's head. It had been made from actual leaves, rather than the more opulent golden versions which competitors in the Eternal City had aspired to win although at second glance, they looked more like oak leaves than laurel. As the crowned victor accepted a money purse and turned to bow to the crowd, the arena exploded once more into cheers.

They don't realize they're not Romans any more, Stirling thought sadly. *They've maintained the trappings, but Rome has long since gone from their lives.*

Ancelotis' response surprised him. *We never believed ourselves Romans, Stirling of Caer-Iudeu. But we are a civilized people, as civilized as Rome ever was. We teach our sons and daughters Latin and Greek and bring them up on Plato and Aristotle and Julius Caesar and Cicero. We pass on to our children, and their children in turn, the skilled trades which the Roman legions and colonists brought among us, adding to our own skills in metallurgy and healing and the arts and suchlike. And we are just as determined as Rome to preserve our way of life when barbarians threaten our borders. This is all that really matters, is it not? To safeguard the beliefs and learned arts which Britons share, from the Wall to the southern tip of Cerniw, no matter which tribe or kingdom is at immediate risk? Artorius lives for this purpose only: to protect Britons from marauding savages. It is a good purpose. It is enough.*

It *was* a good purpose—the same purpose which had sent Stirling plunging through time itself. He realized with a chill that it would be all too easy to be seduced by the desire to *help* these people; to interfere in beneficial ways he couldn't afford, given the danger to humanity's entire future. Ancelotis, distracted by instructions Emrys Myrddin was giving him, fortunately didn't hear that last thought. The Scots king would doubtless consider Stirling's failure to assist whenever and however possible as base treason.

At some unexplored level he didn't want to probe too closely, perhaps it was.

Weary runners exited through the starting gates, stepping past Stirling and Emrys Myrddin on their way out of the arena. Following Myrddin's instructions, Stirling reined his charger into the nearest starting stall. Cutha, red-eyed but sitting straight in his saddle—a much inferior type of saddle, possessing neither the Celtic style's supportive horns nor its innovative stirrups—grinned at Stirling and gave a mocking salute before entering another of the starting gates.

Behind him, Myrddin said, "May God and your ancestors look favorably upon you, Ancelotis."

Stirling nodded. Gilroy appeared like a silent shadow, handing Stirling a long thrusting spear reminiscent of Swiss pikes, a slimmer Roman-style *pilum,* with its javelinlike haft and long-necked soft iron barb, and an iron-rimmed shield of heavy oak. The shield had been built up from multiple layers laid crosswise one above the other for strength, as modern marine plyboard was made, sawn into an oval shape that was slightly curved toward the edges. An iron boss jutted up from the center, topped with a nasty spike that gave Stirling all sorts of darkly intriguing ideas.

He slid his left hand through leather-wrapped iron braces on the back, then slid the pike and the *pilum* into rawhide holders strapped to his saddle horns. He wondered uneasily how Ancelotis would manage shield, weapons, and reins all at the same time and received a snort of derision in response. Clearly, Ancelotis knew what he was doing.

Glad one of us does, Stirling muttered to himself.

Directly overhead, a man on the officials' balustrade, invisible on the parapet from Stirling's perspective inside the starting gate, began shouting out a speech that Stirling finally realized was a benediction, rather than instructions to the combatants. The exhortations to abide by the rules of conduct laid down by God, to strive with all one's might to find the truth and live by it, to strike no wicked blows, etc. *ad infinitum,* were an odd blend of early Christian dogma and lingering pagan values. Cutha, a confirmed pagan, was struggling not to howl with laughter—the sound of snorted and ill-mannered mirth drifted from Cutha's chosen starting stall, two gates down.

The moment the sermon or benediction or whatever it was came to an end, Stirling's valet fled, scrambling out the front of the starting box, loaded down with extra shields and weapons. Gilroy ran hell-for-leather toward a spot along the sandstone wall that separated the arena floor from the lowest circuit of seats. The wall was just slightly too high for a man to jump and reach the top. Gilroy stacked the shields against the base of the wall and piled a fistful of *pila* beside them, along with a second thrusting pike, even a spare *spatha*—a long, heavy-bladed, two-edged Roman cavalry sword with its characteristically blunt, rounded tip.

Curiously, one of Cutha's thanes, busy at the same task on the opposite side of the arena, laid out nothing but spare shields, and only two of those. A psychological ploy, perhaps, demonstrating supreme confidence that he would need nothing more? Or sheer, blind arrogance, incapable of imagining defeat? Stirling didn't care for the implications, either way.

Men with wide-tined wooden rakes worked in gangs to smooth the sandy track surface, removing animal dung from previous horse races, a shoe some unfortunate runner had lost, and dozens of colorful little twists of plaid woolen scraps. Ancelotis, sensing Stirling's curiosity, commented, *Even a poor man can afford to shower a favorite who wins a laurel, if he bundles up the tailings from his wife's loom. In the days of the Romans, they say people threw coins more often than flowers, so a man could grow rich at the games. If,* Ancelotis added with a dour laugh, *he survived the arena.*

A fairly substantial "if."

Signal trumpets rang out again from somewhere above Stirling's head, a shimmer of brassy notes defying the sullen pewter of the sky. His pulse picked up at the sound, thudding in his eardrums and beating at his throat, a heady mixture of anticipation, pre-combat jitters, cold anger at Brenna McEgan for having forced him to come after her, and a healthy dollop of sheer, schoolboy excitement. He was about to participate in an honest-to-God sixth-century duel, with *King Arthur* as the ruddy field judge. For a boy raised in broody grey hills steeped in Arthurian lore, it just didn't get much better than this.

If he lived to see the end of it.

The trumpets sang out again and the men raking the arena floor rushed toward arched exits at track level, swinging shut heavy iron gates as they gained whichever access tunnel was closest. A series of muffled booms like distant cracks of thunder rolled across the arena as the massive grillwork gates slammed shut. These, clearly, were leftovers from the era of gladiatorial games and bestiary fights, which would have produced a fine and grisly abundance of corpses to be dragged off the field between successive bouts. The

arena was, Stirling had to admit, beautifully engineered
for its bloody purpose. He was thankful this was *not*
a genuine gladiatorial death match, even if Cutha
harbored intentions of making it one.

On the balustrade overhead, an official shouted:
"Upon the trumpets' next signal, you will leave the
starting gates and ride a countersunwise circle around
the full distance of the arena. Cutha will then return
to the far end of the course and turn to face the starting gates. The trumpets will signal the beginning of
your charge with lances. If your lance strikes anywhere
but an opponent's shield, you will be instantly disquali-
fied and your opponent named victor. The aim of this
combat is to exhibit skill at arms in honor of King Lot
Luwddoc and King Dumgual Hen, not to maim or kill
your opponent. Combat will end the moment a man
has been deprived of all his weapons and shields,
including those held in reserve, or when he formally
yields. A man rendered unconscious will be judged
to have yielded, granting his opponent victory. May
Almighty God, slayer of heathens, who smites the sin-
ner with His flaming sword, strengthen your sword arm
and lend you the cunning to achieve victory. Amen."

If that so-called benediction was meant to include
Cutha, Stirling would eat his horse, hooves and all.
Ancelotis gave a snort of laughter. *It's perceptive you
are, that's certain.* Then the trumpets sang out and it
was time. Ancelotis put heels to his charger's flanks
and the horse shot from the gate at a thunderous pace.
The stallion required a firm hand on the reins and several stern verbal commands before Ancelotis could collect the animal's stride and hold him to the decorous
pace demanded by a formal lap around the arena. The
immense war-horse seemed almost to levitate across
the long straight stretch of sand, so smooth was the
action of that effortless floating trot.

Stirling had been to Vienna once, to see the Lipizzaners dance, gliding more like great white birds than stallions of solid flesh and bone, descendants of Europe's finest war-horses, capable of killing a man with those ancient battlefield maneuvers they performed so gracefully. Here, under the sullen rain-bruised sky, there was no chandeliered ballroom, no raked tanbark ring beneath marble balustrades, no portraits done by Europe's finest master painters, no loudspeakers, no great classical scores penned by Vienna's most gifted composers. The comparison began and ended with Ancelotis' war-horse, which had clearly been schooled by similar methods in similar maneuvers and doubtlessly at nearly as great a cost.

Sterling's presence made Ancelotis' grip with thighs and calves less certain than normal, sending the animal mixed signals and causing it to fret and sweat down its neck and flank. Cutha's horse, not nearly as massive as Ancelotis', had also broken from the starting stall at a canter, sweeping down the long stretch of straightway less than a sword-length's distance from Ancelotis. Neither man so much as looked at the other, which was intensely irritating to Stirling, who wanted to learn as much detail of the Saxon's equipage as he possibly could before coming to blows with any of it.

They rounded the great curve at the far end of the central spine, cantering around and down the home-stretch, past cheering Britons, a handful of sneering Saxons, and the royal pavilion where Morgana and the flower of Briton royalty sat, the former, at least, as still and white as an ancient marble masterpiece. Her fear, Stirling realized, was as much for Ancelotis, her brother-in-law, as it was for a necessary show of strength before the Saxons. They flashed past the terminus of the central spine and Ancelotis reined around to face the far curve once more, moving his dancing charger sideways until the animal stood more or less in place at the right-hand side of the low spine. Cutha had reined around as well, heading at a gallop for the far curve, where he took up a similar position.

It was to be a joust in fine medieval style, but with critical differences. Both men readied lances, shafts of seasoned ash a full five feet long with wicked iron points that added another seven inches to the weapon's length. But unlike medieval lances of later centuries, these featured no hand guards, no bell-like flare to help brace one's grip. Ancelotis tucked the butt end under one arm, securing it as snugly as possible while using hand and wrist to point the tip toward Cutha— no easy feat, given the weight of the weapon. Neither he nor Cutha wore armor that would even begin to deflect such a lance's point, driven at full power by a charging war-horse. It was abruptly all too clear why men had died at this sport, even when protected by the heavy plate armor of "classical" tournaments of knights. In A.D. 500, the very concept of "knights" had yet to be invented.

The Scots king lifted his shield to protect his torso, draping the reins loosely across the front of his saddle. With a skill that bespoke years of practice, he guided the massive war-horse with knees, legs, and feet alone. They were in position now, weapons at the ready. Stirling tensed, waiting for the signal. The bruised sky flickered with lighting, like bubbling pots and cauldrons in the sky. Wind blasted through the arena and hurled cold droplets against his face, the first spatter of what promised to be a deluge very soon.

Trumpets screamed at Stirling's back.

Ancelotis and Cutha kicked their horses into a thundering gallop. The central spine whipped past, a blurred red snake in Stirling's peripheral vision. They crouched low behind shields, lances held like battering rams. Closer . . . closer still . . .

The shock of concussion nearly unseated Stirling. He came several inches out of the saddle, both arms almost numb. Without stirrups, he'd have landed flat on the ground. Cutha's lance had struck his shield a glancing blow, failing to bite solidly into the wood. His own spear had smashed into Cutha's shield with such force the collision slammed the young Saxon nearly a foot backwards. Lacking stirrups, Cutha toppled right off his horse's backside, dragging Ancelotis' spear with him. With its point deeply embedded in Cutha's shield, the long shaft dragged at his arm, hindering him as Cutha staggered to his feet on the arena floor.

Stirling's surge of confidence was short-lived, however. Even as the Briton crowd roared approval, delighted at the Saxon's early downfall, Cutha tossed the encumbered shield aside, scrambled to recapture his horse, and vaulted back into the saddle. The man detailed to assist him raced forward with a second shield, then put booted foot on the other one and yanked out Ancelotis' spear, handing it up to Cutha. Ancelotis snarled under his breath, but his own man, Gilroy, had already reached his side, handing up two Roman-style *pila* to add to the one he still carried. The javelinlike weapon was not as useful for cavalry work as the long, heavy lance, but Stirling was quite happy to postpone hand-to-hand fighting as long as possible, given the state of sixth-century medical care.

They made a second thunderous charge.

Ancelotis leaned low over his horse's flying mane, one *pilum* in his right hand, the other two resting in the socket on the saddle that had held the lance now in Cutha's grip. They were still several meters apart when Ancelotis hurled the first *pilum*. Stirling was about to shout *you bloody idiot!*—and other, less civilized epithets—when Cutha's shield jerked abruptly down. The *pilum*'s long, soft-iron neck had bent downward, dragging at the shield just as heavily as the lance had. Distracted, Cutha's lance point wobbled slightly off course—and completely prevented him from seeing Ancelotis' next move.

Using knees and thighs, the Scots king urged his charger slightly to the right, in a shallow swing out of range of the unsteady lance point, which passed harmlessly by Ancelotis' shoulder. The clean miss upset Cutha's balance, braced as he was for the shock of collision. The lance was considerably longer than the *pilum,* which meant that Cutha's missed blow, due to arrive at Ancelotis' shield at least a full horse's length before the two horses drew even, left plenty of time for the Scots king to hurl both his second and third *pila* into the Saxon's shield, dragging Cutha even further off balance.

The Saxon prince sprawled in the dust a second time.

His lance shaft snapped under the impact.

The Britons in the stands went wild.

With both lances—Cutha's own and Ancelotis'—shattered and two shields damaged, Cutha was left on foot with one remaining shield, his sword, and a fighting axe. Ancelotis turned his mount and thundered down the track in a long, outward swing toward the stands while Cutha was still on the ground, staggering and trying to reach his horse. Ancelotis then swept across in a sharp one-eighty-degree turn and urged his massive war-horse to jump the central spine. The stallion's quarters bunched, then they were airborne, momentum and the animal's powerful muscles driving them straight across the sandstone barrier and—not coincidentally—straight into Cutha's still riderless mount.

The Saxon horse screamed in alarm and shied violently to one side, thus preventing collision by a matter of centimeters. Cutha, in the act of vaulting into the saddle from the other side, went down with a smashing blow from his own horse's shoulder. He rolled frantically out from under thrashing hooves, blistering the air with Saxon curses. The Scots king brought his charger around in a spinning turn worthy of an American cowhand, drawing his sword in the same instant. They plunged toward Cutha's already-shaken mount. Ancelotis shouted a blood-curdling string of Briton curses and swung his sword in a circle around his head. Cutha's poor horse gave another scream and kicked at his infuriated owner in sheer terror, then bolted and ran, leaving the enraged Saxon prince on foot and spitting curses of his own. The glare he turned on Ancelotis made Stirling's blood freeze.

The Saxon drew sword and war axe, gripping the latter in his shield hand. Cutha's assistant was frantically dragging iron points out of Cutha's shield, lunging and tossing the shield to the Saxon prince like a frisbee. Cutha clutched his axe in his teeth and caught the shield in a movement that would've broken Stirling's wrist, if he'd tried it. Lightning split the sky as Cutha thrust his axe into his belt and banged the flat of his sword against his shield, an invitation to mayhem. Thunder rolled across the arena, slapping up against the sandstone walls and reverberating back into Stirling's face, an avalanche of sound, with him buried at the bottom.

Ancelotis charged before the last echoing peals had died away. He swung mightily at Cutha's shield. Cutha dodged the blow, leaving Ancelotis out of position. The Saxon whirled around, faster on his feet than the Briton king's war-horse, which was already trying to pivot and strike. Out of position, neither Stirling nor Ancelotis saw it coming. One moment, the Briton king was turning his charger with knees and thighs—and the next, Cutha was underfoot, hooking the edge of his shield under Ancelotis' leg and wrenching upward.

The Scots king lost his stirrup, his balance, and his horse.

The bloody horse's back was taller than Stirling was. It was a long, *long* way to the ground.

The landing jarred him so badly, Stirling couldn't draw breath for several critical seconds. Ancelotis' sword went flying from a numbed elbow, the abused joint having been driven into the ground with terrific force. The only thing that saved him from Cutha's sword at his throat was Ancelotis' Briton-bred warhorse. Trained for battle, the massive horse screamed a warning at the Saxon, biting and rearing threateningly, hooves the size of dinner plates lashing out like pile drivers.

Cutha was forced to scramble backwards, unable to get past those hooves and teeth without a lance or even a javelin and unable to maneuver fast enough to strike with his sword. The Saxon retreated, which gave Ancelotis time to drag himself to his feet. He hunted for his sword, couldn't see it anywhere in the sand, wondered with a chill if Cutha had snatched it up, then spotted it. The weapon had clattered onto the raised sandstone of the central spine.

Spitting curses, Ancelotis faced down the Saxon, who retained shield, sword, and axe, while Ancelotis was shieldless and weaponless. A frisson of real fear skittered through Ancelotis' gut, an eerie and unpleasant echo of the lightning overhead, which seethed like volcanic vents amongst the clouds. When Stirling looked into Cutha's eyes, he saw death leering back at him. Breathing heavily but grinning in supreme confidence now, Cutha charged, forcing Ancelotis backward, toward the sandstone barrier. He ducked the swing of Cutha's sword and scrambled away from the central spine, which lay at his back like a sandstone trap. Ancelotis danced out into the open, where he had more room to maneuver, and faced the Saxon again.

Cutha's second charge was a feint that lured Ancelotis off guard, but only for an instant; the Scots king was as agile as a wildcat, turning and skidding to get his feet under him again while avoiding the lethal reach of the Saxon's sword. A bone-deep ache stung one shoulder from a nasty blow from the edge of Cutha's shield. When Cutha drove straight toward him again, sword point thrusting straight for his throat and the killing blow, Ancelotis hesitated for a fraction of a second—

—and Stirling's close-combat reflexes took over.

He dove forward in a snap-roll that took Cutha completely by surprise and carried Stirling under the Saxon's swing. On the way past, he swept Cutha's ankles out from under him, knocking him flat even as Stirling came to his feet again. The Saxon, astonished by the move, rolled over and surged upwards, face flushing an angry red. Stirling not only sidestepped Cutha's off-balance blow, he applied just the slightest amount of leverage to that outstretched arm.

The aikido move, practiced hundreds of times in SAS training sessions, sent the Saxon airborne, careening out of control toward the arena's wall. Cutha lost his sword in the process and the edge of his shield dug into the sand, flipping him onto his back, like a stunned beetle. Ancelotis crushed the Saxon's shield wrist under one foot, scooped the sword up from the dirt, laid the point at Cutha's throat, and said softly, "It looks as though you must yield or die, Saxon."

Completing the Saxon's ignominious defeat, the sky chose that moment to crack wide open. Icy rain drenched them to the skin. Mud spattered Cutha's face where he sprawled under Ancelotis' foot. The defeated prince snarled at him, a truly hideous curse, but made no effort to rise. The Briton crowd had gone wild, rivaling the thunder with their roars of delight. Cutha's humiliation inspired a veritable hailstorm of coins, headgear, colorful snippets of plaid, even muddy shoes, which rained down onto the arena track.

Stirling slipped Cutha's war axe from his belt, then stepped back, allowing Cutha to rise. He smiled tightly. "I believe I'll keep this"—he hefted the axe—"for remembrance. You're welcome to your sword and shields. I've no use for weapons of inferior quality." He tossed the sword aside, where it landed in the mud with a splat.

Cutha's already crimson face went deadly purple. The veins in his neck stood out in stark relief, pulsing with the man's fury. *"Filthy cur!"* the Saxon snarled as he came to his feet. "Insult *me* with your open hand, will you? By Woden's spear, *you will regret this day!*"

"I seriously doubt it," Stirling replied with a lazy drawl.

Only then did Stirling belatedly notice Ancelotis' shock at the swiftness and arcane mystery of Cutha's defeat, when Ancelotis had actually expected to be spitted on the end of Cutha's sword. Clearly, nobody in the sixth century had ever seen the relatively simple close-combat and martial-arts moves he'd just used. *How did you* do *that, man?* Ancelotis demanded in childlike delight. *You must teach me more of this fighting style, Stirling of Caer-Iudeu!*

Stirling groaned, realizing too late just how seriously he'd screwed up—again. If Brenna McEgan sat somewhere in that howling crowd of ecstatic, rain-drenched spectators—and he couldn't imagine that she *wasn't*—then he'd just given himself away in the stupidest, most boneheaded *public* display of twenty-first-century origins imaginable. Of course, it had seemed rather more important at the time to avoid having Cutha's sword jabbed through his intimate anatomy. . . .

Perhaps there would be a silver lining to this mess? The only one he could remotely imagine was that Cedric Banning might come forward, giving Stirling an ally. All in all, it had been a bloody stupid thing to do, an attitude which puzzled Ancelotis no end. Cutha gave him a stiff, formal bow and stalked away, limping visibly. He collected his horse, leading it out of the arena by way of the starting gates. He plucked his sword from the mud on his way.

Stirling was left wondering what to do next, so Ancelotis retrieved his own sword, thrust the Saxon's beautifully inlaid war axe through his belt, then rounded up his charger and mounted, moving somewhat stiffly, as bruises were already making themselves felt in a variety of places. Climbing the rain-slick steps to the royal pavilion required careful concentration to avoid falling flat and bouncing all the way down. The awning had kept the worst of the rain off, although Ganhumara wore a sullen look that boded ill for the laundress or fuller given the task of repairing rain damage to the silk he could see layered beneath her flame-colored wool.

Ancelotis bowed formally to his fellow kings and queens. The Dux Bellorum was grinning fit to crack his face and Medraut's glance mirrored hero worship. Gwalchmai's eyes shone like lanterns as he danced in place, ignoring the icy downpour as he celebrated his uncle's victory. Little Walgabedius, confused and too young to understand, nevertheless looked excited as he gazed up at his uncle. Even the young king of Strathclyde wore a stunned and reverent expression. Emrys Myrddin, however, gave him a long, slow frown and Morgana's gaze was as icy as the rain pouring down his back.

She said coldly, "Congratulations on your victory, Ancelotis. It will doubtless speed Cutha on his way to planning vengeance, when we can ill afford invasion. Wear your crown with pride—it may be the last victory we win against the Saxons!"

Lips compressed in white fury, she crowned him with the traditional wreath, which *was* made of oak leaves. The moment the victor's wreath touched his wet hair, a fresh roar rose from the celebrating crowd who could not, happily for most of them, hear what she'd said. Artorius gave him a wink that said, *She'll get over it, man, and it was worth the risk to see that lout put in his place!*

Unsure which reaction was the correct—or safest—one, Stirling simply bowed, refused the traditional money pouch, tossing the coins into the ecstatic crowd instead, and descended the steps to mount his horse. He made one victory lap around the arena, accompanied by the tumult of celebration, then exited through the stone starting boxes. He had only one desire, now that the bout was behind him. Stirling wanted that very long, very hot soak in the deepest Roman bath available.

Ancelotis agreed wholeheartedly.

Chapter Ten

Brenna was thoroughly chilled by the time she and Morgana made their way from the rain-swept sand-stone arena back to the fortress where Morgana and the other visiting royalty of Britain had been staying. The largest building inside Caerleul's fortress walls, the great hall possessed no fewer than twenty rooms along its outer corridors, where high-ranking guests could be accommodated for lengthy visits. "Medraut," she said, turning to her nephew, "take the boys into the baths and warm them up, they're half frozen from that rain."

Still grinning, Medraut hooked a gesture at the boys, who ran excitedly at his heels, yipping in their delight at the Saxon prince's defeat. Morgana watched silently, heart aching, for her sons simply didn't understand, yet, the price the Britons would doubtless pay for Cutha's comeuppance. Brenna McEgan said firmly, *Take a hot bath yourself, Morgana. We'll both feel better for it.* So they made a hasty trip to the baths and within half an hour, warmed up by the steaming water of the *calderium*—which had grown crowded as more women returned from the arena, chilled and in need of the heated water—Morgana dressed her sons in their best and sent them on with Medraut, then donned the finest linen chemise and woolen gown from her trunk, a rich crimson with a long, trailing skirt, neckline and sleeves edged with ermine fur and caught at the waist with a golden-link girdle. Brenna delighted in the feel of the long, heavy skirts and luxurious fur trim, guiltily pleased there would be no crazed Green environmentalists lurking anywhere about to toss paint across the dead animal skins. She slipped on heavy gold jewelry and warm, fur-lined shoes and caught her hair back with carved ivory combs, then swept out into the main hall, where the kings and queens of Britain were gathering.

Emrys Myrddin and Artorius were there already and young King Clinoch of Strathclyde stood near the central hearth, where a blazing fire warmed the room. Morgana's sons raced to her side, eyes wide at the glittering array of Britain's gathered royal houses. A fine drift of mist occasionally fell through the opening immediately above, where the rainstorm had finally abated outside, dwindling away to an occasional drift of dampness. A cover had been tilted over the opening, anyway, channeling the rain away from the open roof while allowing the smoke to escape. A few wind-blown droplets hissed against the coals every now and again. The light slanting through the opening in the ceiling fell at a long oblique as the sun westered down the lower quarter of the sky overhead.

Clinoch was trying valiantly to look nonchalant and succeeded only in underscoring his youth and inexperience as he swallowed nervously and warmed his hands like a cold child. Morgana noticed Gwalchmai staring at the young king of Strathclyde, eyes dark and pensive, and squeezed her son's hand. The boy leaned against her leg, sighing and holding tight to her fingers. Voices hushed in worried tones washed across the room, while a group of minstrels gathering in one corner produced harps and flutes and began to play softly, dulling the worst edge of tension in the room. Lailoken was among them, glancing boldly into Morgana's eyes and smiling at their planned assignation on the road to Caer-Gretna at this council's end.

Twelve massive tables had been drawn into a rough circle surrounding the central hearth, an arrangement Emrys Myrddin was overseeing, directing servants to place the tables end to end with cushioned benches for the royal gathering. Other servants were laying out cups and wine flasks and pitchers filled with mead, while still others hung an immense oxhide against one wall, onto which had been drawn the outlines of every kingdom in Britain.

Brenna stared in fascination at the familiar coastline, drawn with surprising accuracy, and gazed intently at the unfamiliar shapes and names of the kingdoms, a few of which she could decipher as later English regions. Several bore names which had survived right into the twenty-first century as "counties" in modern Wales, even the spellings having been retained intact through the centuries. Brenna had actually visited Powys as a girl, on holiday with her mother, a wonderful walking tour of the region. Areas overrun by Saxons had been colored a lurid red. Brenna was still studying the map when Emrys Myrddin, who must have been paying close attention to arrivals, or perhaps to a Roman-style water clock in one corner, murmured something to Artorius, who nodded and rang a bronze bell for attention.

"The High Council is now commenced!" Artorius

called out strongly. "Kings and Queens, Princes and Princesses of the Britons, take your places at the Tables of Council."

Morgana stepped to her place in the general shuffle and sorting out, leading her sons with her. An expectant hush fell across the room as a priest raised one hand in a benediction, his dark robes and simple wooden cross marking him as a member of the ancient Briton Church. "Our Father, we pray Thy guidance for this great council of kings, that Britain may defend herself and defend Thy faith against the incursions of the pagan hordes. Amen."

The murmured response ran around the room, then the priest retired and Artorius, who stood between the kings of Gododdin and Strathclyde, said formally, "We will read the roster of the Britons. I, Artorius, was elected by you to serve as Dux Bellorum in this time of trouble, a post I have gladly served for these ten years past. I speak for the greater good of all the tribes and cities of the Britons." He seated himself and Emrys Myrddin inclined his head next. "I, Emrys Myrddin, speak as advisor to the Dux Bellorum."

After Emrys Myrddin, the roll call ran sunwise around the collection of tables. Brenna was quite startled when she realized they had sorted themselves out into alphabetical order, without the need to consult any master seating chart.

"I, King Rigenew ap Rhein, speak for the Kingdom of Brycheiniog."

A very old man beside Rigenew spoke next. "I, King Gorbanian, speak for the Kingdom of Bryneich."

As the white-haired king took his seat on the long, cushioned bench, the next speaker, a young man not yet twenty, who had a narrow weasel's face and eyes like glittering blades of obsidian, met Artorius' gaze with an insolent stare. "I, King Idnerth ap Briagad ap

Pasgen ap Vortigern, speak for the Kingdoms of Buelt and Gwerthrynion."

Morgana bristled silently. When Brenna wondered why, Morgana said, *He claims descent from Vortigern with pride, when the dog brought the Saxons among us during his tenure as Dux Bellorum. Vortigern's own sons turned against him and supported Uthyr Pendragon and Ambrosius Aurelianus, but the spawn of Vortigern would be high kings, if they could manage it.*

A man to be watched, then.

The king of Caer-Baddan had spoken already; King Einion of Caer-Celemion named himself next, adding, "Not a week passes that the Saxons and the dogs of Wessex do not test our borders. I have ordered every hill fort in Caer-Celemion to be refortified."

He was followed by King Cyndyddan of Caer-Ceri, the kings of Caer-Colun and Caer-Durnac and Caer-Gloui, all heavily threatened by Wessex and Sussex and all visibly worried as they took their seats. Brenna glanced at the great map on the wall as each man spoke, tracing out the borders and their relative positions to Saxon-held lands. These men were right to worry about the threat to their borders.

Brenna's attention was wrenched back as Artorius' young wife, hair shining like flame, spoke languidly. "I, Queen Ganhumara, heiress of King Carmelide and wife of the Dux Bellorum, speak for Caer-Guendoleu." Every male eye in the room locked on her, doomed moths drawn to her fire and shimmering beauty. A young man Morgana identified as Melwas of Glastenning stared at Ganhumara so longingly, even Brenna was disturbed. Ganhumara smiled sinfully into the poor young man's eyes as she flicked her long skirts aside and took her seat.

King Elafius, who ruled three kingdoms, Caer-Gwinntguic, Caer-Lundein, and Caer-Mincip, in the midlands, had to clear his throat before he could even speak clearly and the kings of Caer-Lerion, Caeston, and Calchfynedd had nearly as much difficulty tearing their gazes away. Artorius brooded silently, darting black looks at his wife from time to time.

"I, King Ceredig, speak for Ceredigion," the next man in line nodded to his peers, then introduced the young man beside him. "My son, Prince Sandde."

Brenna did not like the way Sandde looked at every woman within range; something about the young prince left her skin crawling, a sentiment Morgana shared. *His reputation is a poor one. Ceredig is a fine man, but has shown too lax a hand in raising his son. That one will cause trouble. And trouble, we do not need.*

The next man spoke slowly, with a deeply troubled air. "I, King Mar, son of Ceneu, King of Ebrauc, speak for the Kingdom of Dent." He stepped to the oxhide map and used a stick of charcoal to sketch out a chunk of land between modern Yorkshire and the Humber River. "When Vortigern was Dux Bellorum, he forced us to accept Saxon *foederati*. When the Saxons rose in the south, we of Ebrauc and Dent were forced to a compromise, to keep the Saxons from overrunning the entire countryside. This territory, all of Dewyr, we have been forced to give the Saxons to buy them off long enough to protect the rest of our kingdoms."

Exclamations of dismay rose like startled birds.

"My God," one man gasped, "with a toehold like that, they can strike Dunoting, Elmet, Lindsey, even the Pennines!"

The king of Lindsey growled out his agreement. "We have been forced to shift our heavy cavalry to our northern border, to keep the Saxons bottled up in Dewyr."

As the uproar died down, a stocky man who shared the same coloration as Artorius spoke out strongly. "I,

Cadorius, King of Dumnonia and Earl of Cerniw," Brenna glanced at the map, locating Dumnonia and Cerniw as the modern Cornwall, "have news nearly as grave as this. Cousin," he spoke directly to Artorius, "Wessex looks to expand its borders through Caer-Durnac straight into Glastenning sometime in the next few months, which threatens not only Dumnonia and Glastenning, but the entire Briton southwest. As a sub-kingdom under Dumnonia, Glastenning is the strongest ally we have between us and the Saxons."

Cadorius turned to introduce a younger man with him. "At my request, Sub-King Melwas of Glastenning has undertaken the refortification of Caer-Badonicus at the border with Caer-Durnac, for if Wessex should take Caer-Badonicus, there is no force in all of Britain strong enough to dislodge them. Anyone who holds Caer-Badonicus would be able to field a fighting force that could ravage the countryside for miles around and provide a strong point to attack kingdoms further north and west. The work to strengthen the fortifications has begun, but will require more men than we can readily spare. The summit is a full eighteen acres of land, five hundred feet above the Salisbury Plain. This is too much land for Glastenning and Dumnonia working alone to fortify as quickly as the work must be done, not if we are to safeguard the gateway to the kingdoms of the southwest. I must ask for help from the other kings of Britain to refortify Caer-Badonicus."

King Idnerth, the weasel-faced descendant of Vortigern, asked in a tone just shy of insolence, "What other work have you undertaken, that men cannot be spared to repair Caer-Badonicus?"

Cadorius flushed. "Our crops are not yet safely in, for the season is more advanced here in the north than it is in the south, where the harvesting has just reached its peak. The weather is bad as well, unseasonably bad.

The hay is already lost, rotting in wet fields, and the rye is thick with ergot from the rain, a total loss. If we don't salvage what we can from the wheat and barley fields and the orchards, the entire south will risk starvation this winter, leaving us weak and unable to defend ourselves at precisely the time the Saxons are threatening our borders. If we hope to keep our people at fighting strength, to hold the Saxons out over the long winter ahead, we *must* get what remains of the harvest in, leaving precious little in the way of manpower to work on fortifications. Even the toddling children are in the fields.

"My own brothers, Prince Justanus and Prince Solomanus, are strengthening every hill fort in Dumnonia, using women and half-grown lads where necessary to carry out the work, and Meliau, Prince of Cerniw, is rebuilding the walls of our coastal defenses from St. Michael's Mount north to Tintagel, where our cousin Artorius was born." He inclined his head to Artorius, who was frowning, deeply unhappy with the grim picture King Cadorius was painting. "Meliau has been charged with holding the Irish coast," he swept his hand across the oxhide map, indicating the entire western coast of Cornwall, "to prevent the Irish high kings from striking from the west while we are preoccupied with the Saxons to the east."

It was as good an arrangement as could be managed, under the circumstances. Even Idnerth could not find anything further to complain or needle Cadorius about and fell silent, darting dark and dangerous looks at his fellow kings and queens as King Dingad ap Einion of Dunoting named himself and his son, Prince Meuring ap Dingad, followed by King Aricol Lawhir and Prince Vortepor ap Aricol of Dyfed. The king of Ebrauc—modern York and, in several centuries to come, the heart of the Viking Danelaw—rose next.

"I, King Gergust Letlum ap Ceneu ap Coel Hen, and my son Prince Eliffer ap Gergust, will gladly field as large a force as Ebrauc can muster, for the Angles harry our seaports in growing numbers and already the Angles speak of alliance with King Aelle of Sussex, to strike in a pincer movement. Cutha may have mouthed pretty words about a Saxon-Briton alliance against the Angles, but that is all it ever was: pretty words.

"We have intercepted dispatches between them, giving us written proof of their planned cooperative ventures against Briton kingdoms of the eastern coast. Ebrauc will answer Dumnonia's plea for men to help with the fortification of Caer-Badonicus. And Ebrauc will send as many of its lads not yet old enough to fight as can be spared, to help bring in the southern harvest, our own being safely in the barns and granaries. Ebrauc will help and gladly, for if we fail to act together in this crisis, the Saxons and Angles and Jutland Danes will peck us to death like carrion crows, one at a time."

"I, King Masguic Clop ap Gergust of Elmet," the young man next to Gergust spoke up at once, "will also send men with those my father will raise from Ebrauc."

"As will I," the king of Ergyng agreed.

Every gaze in the room rested on Morgana. Brenna gulped nervously as Morgana composed herself to speak. "I, Morgana, daughter of King Gorlois, speak as sovereign queen of Galwyddel and Ynys Manaw. My sons, Prince Gwalchmai ap Lot Luwddoc and Prince Walgabedius ap Lot Luwddoc. With the death of my husband and the election of Ancelotis to the throne of Gododdin until my son Gwalchmai is of age, my responsibility lies with Galwyddel and Ynys Manaw.

"There are serious threats besides the Saxons, which must be considered by this council. Ynys Manaw is an island, very small and vulnerable to Irish invasion.

Galwyddel's coast is but twenty miles from the coast of Eire and only a narrow portion of Strathclyde lies between Galwyddel's border and the Irish kingdom of Dalriada, another land which will certainly seek to spread its influence before long.

"Already, Irish raiders have struck the entire western coast of Britain, emboldened by the Irish *Scotti* clan's successes in Pictish territory. The Picts driven south have killed two of our kings in one week. And now we have insulted Cutha of Sussex, perhaps without meaning such a profound insult," she inclined her head toward Ancelotis in apology, "but the insult will be avenged, do not doubt this for one moment.

"But in our rush to strengthen defenses in the south, we must not forget the threats from the north and the west, as well. If we do not seek alliances to buy time, we will find ourselves fighting all-out war on three fronts, against three enemies, not even counting the raiders from Jutland and Frisia. With that threat added to the others, we find ourselves facing war from every cardinal point on the compass, with battles for survival on all four sides of this great island. I offer apologies to Cadorius, but Galwyddel and Ynys Manaw cannot spare the manpower to fortify Caer-Badonicus, when our own towns are in gravest danger of destruction. Not without seeking treaties of alliance to delay open hostilities long enough to deal with the Saxon threat."

The man next to Morgana spoke with deep bitterness. "I, Meurig ap Caradog, King of Glywssing, know the folly of alliance with pagan outsiders more than most. I rule the kingdom that Vortigern and his son Vortimer after him once ruled, a kingdom they held so cheaply they treated with Saxon swine and called them *foederati*, rather than the bandits and killers they are. I, for one, will tolerate no talk of alliance with

godless heathens who look to our borders with greedy
and bloodthirsty eyes. Glywssing faces threats from the
Irish harassing our coast and from the Saxons, trying
to push past our neighbors to the south. Which devil
does Morgana ask that I crawl into bed with, to form
this insane alliance of which she speaks?"

A roar of angry mutters, many of them directed at
Meurig for the crudity of his question, erupted around
the tables, throwing the council into chaos. Morgana
turned to glare at Meurig ap Caradog. "I would sooner
crawl into bed with a godless Irishman than some
Britons in this room!"

The angry mutters exploded into violent arguments,
women's shrill voices battling men's deeper ones. The
thud of fists on wooden tabletops rattled like thunder in a canyon. Gwalchmai and Walgabedius huddled
fearfully against Morgana's skirts, the younger boy
whimpering aloud before she pulled them close.
Artorius surged to his feet, drawing his sword to pound
the tabletop with its hilt and shouted down the lot of
them. "*Silence! By God, silence I say and silence I
mean! I'll have the ears of the next man to say a bloody
word!*"

The shouts died away, replaced by a shuffling of feet
as Artorius glared from one table to the next. He
growled, "Queen Morgana's fears are justified. I say
this not as her stepbrother but as the Dux Bellorum
who had to bring word of her husband's murder at the
hands of Pictish bandits! Think you it was easy for
Morgana to look into her sons' eyes and tell them why
their father died? And in this same room stands a lad
barely a man, who watched his royal father hacked to
death by *another* lot of heathenish Picts. If Cutha and
Aelle of Sussex and their minions of Wessex were the
only threat we face, I would not have called a council of all the kings and queens of Britain! Morgana is

right to say we face war on four fronts—for that is *exactly* what we face. If we do not exercise extreme care in the judgments we make this evening, all of Britain could bleed for our folly."

A few hangdog expressions replaced anger and strident rebelliousness. Ganhumara, delighting in the turmoil, looked like a well-fed kitten savoring the cream on her whiskers. Two seats down, Morgana's brother-in-law spoke into the momentary silence.

"I, Ancelotis of Gododdin, king until Prince Gwalchmai reaches his majority, speak for the people of Gododdin. We know only too painfully how serious the threat is from Pictish and Irish invaders along our northern borders. It was not my intention to draw the ire of the Saxons so quickly, but I am not convinced that anything would have prevented them from finding insult from some one of us, an insult that would give them an excuse to strike openly. What remains is for us to find a way to defend *all* our borders against *all* comers, when we have but limited numbers of men to do the fighting and run the patrols, not to mention bringing in the southern harvest. It might be less onerous than it first appears, to at least open negotiations with one of our northern enemies. We could then use those negotiations to buy the time we need, allowing us to shift resources without actually promising full alliance, since invasion on four fronts must be avoided at all cost."

Artorius did not appear pleased by Ancelotis' speech, but spoke no word of anger. He merely inclined his head slightly and said, "The Dux Bellorum thanks Gododdin for its concern over the severity of the problem before us."

A white-haired man whose deeply lined face betrayed years of worry and struggle said quietly, "I, King Ynwyl Gwent, speak for the people of Gwent.

My son, Prince Caradog Freichfras, joins my worry that any alliance or even *talk* of such would weaken us in the eyes of the men we seek alliance with, making invasion more certain, not less. The Irish raid and the Picts strike in war bands, but the Saxons move in great armies, under the concerted direction of one powerful king. Aelle of Sussex is the most dangerous man in Britain and Cerdic of Wessex is the instrument he will use to strike at us.

"If we are to preserve Britain, we must deal with the Saxons *now,* and worry about Picts and Irish pirates at some later date. For those kingdoms under direct assault from the north and the west, I would not expect men or arms to be diverted from current emergencies, but for those of us whose kingdoms are not yet seriously threatened, we must provide men-at-arms and the swords and armor they will require, to stop the Saxons before they can march any great distance. To this end, I pledge every third fighting man of Gwent."

"And I, King Cadwallon Longhand of Gwynedd," the man beside him spoke immediately, "pledge the same. My son, Prince Gwyddno Garahnhir, will guard the borders of Gwynedd and organize the refortification of the hill forts. How speak the sub-kings of Gwynedd?" He turned to the men seated beside his son.

"I, King Elnaw ap Dogfael pledge a third of Dogfeiling's fighting strength."

"As do I, King Gwrin Farfdwch ap Cadwaladr of Meirionydd."

The next man spoke quietly. "I, King Owein White Tooth and my son Prince Cuneglasus speak for the Sub-Kingdom of Rhos. We plead hardship, for illness has struck hard in Rhos this harvest season, spread, I fear, by the same damp and moldering rot that has destroyed the southern hay and rye fields. Too many deaths have left our defenses ragged. I will send Cuneglasus with what men Rhos can spare, but that will be fewer than would please me."

Artorius, who had sheathed his sword once more, gave Owein a nod of understanding. "I cannot ask more than any kingdom is able to give. Send what you can and we must all be content with the best we can manage."

"I, King Aidon ap Mor of Rhufonios, can send aid to my brother sub-king of Rhos. We have many younger sons eager for work and too little land to subdivide it further amongst the heirs, as is the custom. Whether you need hands for the harvesting or the building of stone walls round your heights, Rhufonios can assist and still send seasoned warriors to the Dux Bellorum."

Owein clasped his neighbor's hand in gratitude. "We have many an orphaned heiress who will welcome young men of Rhufonios to work the land and take them to wife. Both our kingdoms will benefit."

"Well spoken," Emrys Myrddin gave the agreement a Druidic nod of approval.

The king of Lindsey pledged a third of his men to the cause of strengthening the southern borders, as did King Arthwys ap Mor of the Pennines, offering to send his son Prince Pabius in command of the sizeable force. The next man to speak, whose grey hair and deeply lined face spoke of age and strain, shared the same narrow, weasel-eyed face as King Idnerth, great-grandson of Vortigern. "I, King Concennus ap Vortimer and my son Prince Brochfael Ysgythrog speak for Powys and the kingdoms of the midlands. Powys has no borders that are threatened and will not contribute young men needed for the harvesting and the fishing to drive invaders from someone else's land."

A shocked and angry roar erupted as the aging king

and his buck-toothed son took their seats. King Meirchion of Rheged snarled, *"I would expect no less than treason from a spawn of Vortigern!"*

"Treason, is it?" Concennus shot back. "There's no treason in protecting one's own interests! Powys is not threatened. Why should Powys bleed and die for the errors in judgement committed by fools in Glastenning or Strathclyde?"

Young Clinoch went ice pale and gripped the hilt of his dagger. "You will not insult my father's memory within the same week as his death, Concennus! Meet me steel to steel, like a man, if you intend slander!"

Another thunderous round of shouting erupted. Artorius was slamming the hilt of his sword against the tabletop again, roaring for order. Clinoch, shaking with rage, stood glaring at Concennus, who measured him lazily with a dismissive eye, compounding the insult. His buck-toothed son grinned at the young king, while paring his nails with his own knife, insulting everyone in the council chamber. Emrys Myrddin strode between the tables, passing the central hearth in a billow of white robes, and slammed an immense oaken staff between Clinoch and Meirchion on one side and Concennus and Brochfael on the other. The young prince of Powys had the grace to jump in startlement at the crash.

"This is a council of kings," Myrddin hissed coldly, *"not a brawl between milk-brats!* Brochfael, you shame your father's name with your insolence. Put up that knife or leave this council under the geas of excommunication and end your days an outlaw cast out of Britain!"

The young prince glared at Myrddin, but quickly realized the threat was serious and that Myrddin would brook no refusal. He resheathed his knife with a sullen look.

"Concennus, you have the sovereign right to refuse succor to your brother kings. No one denies this. If you stand by that right, know that the geas will be laid upon you and all of Powys, as well. Expect no aid, no comfort, no assistance should *any* disaster befall you, whether it be famine, flood, plague, or invasion. A man who stands selfishly alone bleating of his rights when his brothers are dying can expect no aid when he, himself, is mortally wounded."

Concennus, older than Emrys Myrddin by at least twenty years, if not thirty, glared coldly at the Druidic councillor. "Powys is a large kingdom, advisor, and controls Caer-Gurican, Caer-Magnis, and Caer-Luit-Coyt as well, a stretch of land as great as Rheged. Famine or plague in one portion of the kingdom hardly threatens the whole. Your threats do not impress me."

Emrys Myrddin said softly, "Only a fool will permit wolves to ravage one flock simply because the other flocks are not yet threatened. Your kingship shames the Britons. Leave our meeting hall and do not darken Rheged's hospitality again with your reckless disregard of civilized manners and your failure to abide by prudent conduct in affairs touching the survival of every Briton man, woman, and squalling babe on this island!"

As Concennus jerked to his feet, anger crackling in his insolent and rheumy eyes, Clinoch muttered, "And may the Saxons rape you as you so richly deserve!"

Myrddin held out an imperious hand, forestalling further outbursts from the young king. Concennus had locked gazes with Myrddin, who stood immovable as a monolithic standing stone—and very nearly as tall—and gave back Concennus' curled lip of insolence as a withering, blue-eyed stare. At length, Concennus looked away and muttered, "Powys will send a hundred archers to the Dux Bellorum."

"Our thanks," Myrddin said scathingly, then retrieved his oaken staff and strode back to his place.

Brenna discovered that she was shaking. Even Morgana was shaken by the confrontation. Meirchion of Rheged straightened his tunic with a jerk and said, "Rheged sends half its fighting force south to the aid of Glastenning and Dumnonia."

Clinoch, whose turn was next, swallowed before he could find voice. "Strathclyde has troubles along its northern and western borders, beset as we are from the north by Picts and Irish from Dalriada and from the west by Irish pirates, across the Irish Sea. But Strathclyde is a large kingdom, greater in size even than Gododdin. Strathclyde will help Gododdin reinforce the northern boundary forts along the Antonine Wall and mount increased patrols along our borders with Dalriada. In addition to this, Strathclyde will send five hundred men-at-arms south, from the region bordering Galwyddel and Caer-Guendoleu and Bryneich, whose borders are secure, so there will be no danger to their farmholds and families if they are absent."

Brenna felt like cheering. The boy's concern for his people, in contrast to Concennus' utter disregard, was a well-deserved slap in the face which left Concennus flushed and angry. As Morgana had already spoken on behalf of Ynys Manaw, she did not rise to speak again. Artorius said quietly, "There is no one to speak for Ynys Weith, for the Saxons and their pawns of Wessex have overrun the island, murdering the entire royal family, and now control its harbors and its men.

"All the kingdoms of the Britons having been spoken for, I will now speak as Dux Bellorum. As you have heard, we face grave troubles from many directions and have lost two of our number to what most of us consider the least threat of all those facing us. With apologies to Strathclyde and Gododdin, who bear the brunt of Pictish hostilities, I must however agree that the greatest threat to the Britons as a whole people comes from King Aelle of Sussex and Cerdic of Wessex. Cutha came to us determined to provoke incident and succeeded. Meirchion, look well to your people, for I predict Cutha will take vengeance in blood on his return journey south."

King Meirchion of Rheged nodded, his expression grim. "I have sent men in every direction to warn the farmholds and towns, and pray that I am not already too late with the warning." Cutha had already been gone nearly two hours.

Artorius lifted a long, slim wand and used it as a pointer, stepping to the great map nailed to the wall. "The area of greatest danger lies here"—he pointed to the border where Glastenning and Caer-Durnac touched the border of Wessex—"north along the line of Caer-Baddan, Caer-Celemion, Caer-Mincip, and Caer-Lundein." The pointer swept from the Bristol Channel along a wide arc through Somerset, Dorset, and the Salisbury Plain, across through Wiltshire and Berkshire, and east to Surrey and the city of London.

"The so-called king of Wessex, Cerdic, sent his son Creoda with Cutha to demand a place in Rheged's council. If Creoda had been successful, the Saxons could have established a base of operations right here in Caerleul. From the borders of Rheged"—the pointer swept across an immense stretch of land beginning at the modern Scottish border and stretching all the way south to Wales and across to Yorkshire, fully half of the northern-midlands territory—"Saxons could have swept across in any direction they chose. This is the audacity we are faced with, the strength of Saxon greed."

Low murmurs buzzed like angry hornets. Even Concennus betrayed discomfort.

"The hill forts along this whole line must be refortified and quickly. Emrys Myrddin, I would ask you to ride south to Caer-Badonicus to oversee the defenses. The experience you garnered in Constantinople may well prove invaluable to us, erecting defenses at the summit of the hill."

"How can we be certain the Saxons will meet us there?" Concennus demanded.

Artorius favored him with more courtesy than Brenna would have shown under similar circumstances. "Because we will harry his flanks and slash his supply lines, forcing him to march west along his existing northern border, rather than north as he would prefer. We will shift northward as much of the grain and livestock as we can along the route of that march and torch what we cannot shift, to prevent Briton supplies from victualing Saxon invaders. The kingdoms of the north and the midlands must make up any shortfalls suffered by the areas put to the torch, to prevent suffering amongst those deprived of stock and food stores.

"By cutting their supply lines here and here"—the pointer flicked across the map—"we force the Saxons to scavenge off the land, and by moving and destroying supplies where they wish to go, we force them to scavenge in their own territory. And with all due apologies to Caer-Lundein," he added, "there simply isn't a great deal in Caer-Lundein to interest Aelle, not when Caer-Badonicus sits like a knife poised above Wessex, denying Cerdic the expansion he and his Saxon masters desire. They want the rich trading centers of Dumnonia and Cerniw. They want more than land, they want the ports that trade with Constantinople and Africa, they want Italian wines and silks from the east to cloak and gown their women."

Most of the men in the room glanced involuntarily

toward Ganhumara, resplendent in her own silks. She smiled, preening under the attention. Artorius scowled and cleared his throat.

"Aye, the Saxons want silk, and they want amber and furs from the north, as well. They've already struck at ports along our eastern shores which can provide them control over that northern trade. They want the tin mines of Cerniw, to control the smelting of bronze which we sell as far away as Constantinople itself. And they will try with great desperation to take the iron mines of Rheged, Galwyddel, and Dunoting, which I am certain is the reason they tried to force our hand over Rheged's council. The Saxons need iron for weapons and the great iron mines of our northern kingdoms are rich plunder for them."

He glanced at Covianna Nim, who sat in one corner, not part of the high council, but present as representative of her own powerful clan. "I look also toward the safety of our master smiths, not only in the north, but especially those closer to Saxon-held lands. Glastenning Tor, whose smiths fashion fine Damascus steel such as my Caliburn, is a rich prize for men like Aelle." He drew his sword, letting the light glint off the sworls of Damascene pattern-welding in the blade. "Saxons have few swords at all and none so fine as those carried by the most common of British soldiers. Saxons give such blades as this mystical powers, having no smithies capable of producing such weapons and precious little gold with which to buy them."

He slid Caliburn home with a ring of steel.

"We know their strategic targets and why they must take them. What remains to be done is to bottle them up in the south and to do that, we must stop them at Caer-Badonicus. You have pledged your fighting strength, your sons, and yourselves. Return to your homes as quickly as you may ride and send your men to me. I will write out a plan of rendezvous and send it with each of you, that we may waste no time in forming up the march south. Emrys Myrddin, will you ride with the kings of Glastenning and Dumnonia to assist with construction of Caer-Badonicus' defenses?"

"Gladly."

"Then if there is no further business before this council, I suggest we move immediately to put our plans and resolutions into action. Cutha certainly will."

The priest who had opened the council hastily stepped forward to offer a final benediction, then the high council split into groups, neighboring kings meeting to discuss mutual assistance and movement of troops through their roads, while servants scurried like stirred-up ants to fetch baggage and alert the grooms-men that riding horses would be wanted within the hour.

Morgana remained seated, having made her own decisions about Galwyddel and Ynys Manaw, and simply held her young sons close. Brenna watched in silence, torn by conflicting emotions as the Britons prepared for war.

Chapter Eleven

The first report of disaster came before Ancelotis' manservant, Gilroy, had even finished packing for the journey back to Gododdin. Stirling, helplessly along for the ride in the unfolding political and military affairs of Britain, jerked around in startled surprise when a great bronze bell began to toll a clangorous alarm. An armed soldier appeared at the entrance to the council hall, moving at a dead run and escorting a boy of no more than thirteen, a runner who staggered with every stride. Mud plastered his clothes and ran in rivulets from sweat-soaked hair. "Attack," the lad gasped out, "attack by raiders near Long Meg and Her Daughters! They've burnt every farm within five miles of the standing stones!"

"The heart of Penrith!" King Meirchion snarled. "We should have hanged that Saxon bastard from the nearest oak! More's the pity you didn't cut his throat, Ancelotis, when you had him at your mercy, and host laws be

damned. The Saxons certainly don't abide by them." He
strode away, bellowing orders as the alarm bell continued to send its warning reverberating through the late
afternoon air, the sound dropping through the open
ceiling above the hearth like hailstones.

Artorius met and held Ancelotis' gaze. "I must stay
here and prepare the campaign in the south. Meirchion
could use your judgement and skill."

Stirling most emphatically did *not* want to leave
Artorius unguarded, convinced as he was that the Dux
Bellorum was the IRA's main target, but he didn't have
much choice, since Ancelotis agreed at once.

"Aye," his host nodded, "I'll send riders to Gododdin
to spread the word, to strengthen the forts and raise
an army to send south. I'll take most of the *cataphracti*
who rode with me from Gododdin and try to catch
that Saxon bastard before he does more damage.
Meirchion was right. I *should* have killed him."

Within minutes, Stirling found himself in the saddle
once more, shouting orders to the narrow-lipped
Sarmatian cavalrymen who had ridden with him from
Caer-Iudeu. The combined *cataphracti* of Gododdin,
Strathclyde, and Rheged thundered through the great
fortress gates and left Carlisle behind in a sea of
churned-up mud flung on house walls by nearly three
hundred heavily armored horses. Stirling couldn't help
the thrill of adrenaline through his veins, caught up
as he was in the glittering midst of sun-struck armor,
helmets, and spearpoints.

They followed the Roman highway south toward
Penrith, a town deep in the heart of Cumbria, which
Stirling had driven through on many a holiday. The
Cumbrian mountains rose as a massive barrier to the
west, lifting their craggy heads from the lowlands
around Carlisle and marching straight south through
the Lake District. It was less than twenty miles to

Penrith from Caerleul's sandstone walls. At a gallop for much of the way, they covered the distance in just a few hours.

Smoke and ruin rose on every side as they neared Penrith. Farms lay scorched, with wildfires still spreading beyond villages that were nothing but smoking rubble. Livestock—cattle, goats, sheep, horses, and barnyard fowl—lay slaughtered in every direction while carrion crows flocked in such numbers, the sky blackened when they took wing, deafening the armored column with their raucous protests. Far worse than the livestock were the other bodies lying twisted in the late-slanting sunlight. Farmers cut down with cane knives or spears in their hands, women butchered in their kitchen gardens, skirts disarranged in violation inflicted before the killing blow. Children, rosy-cheeked boys and fair-skinned girls with their hair in long braids, had been hacked to pieces, gobbets of flesh scattered in ghastly splashes of blood.

The deeper they rode into the zone of devastation, the harder Stirling ground his teeth over rage. The Saxons, like the Vikings who would sweep down from the north in later centuries, were not averse to using the blood eagle, where a victim's rib cage was hacked open and his lungs yanked out across his back like hideous wings. Rage swept the length of the *cataphracti's* column. Everywhere the stench of blood and death permeated the air, thick with coppery blood, sickly sweet. The only sound was the massive clatter of horses' hooves on the stone road and the calls of the crows, interrupted in their grisly feast.

The village of Penrith still smouldered, embers flaring beneath the top layer of white ash, adding to the general stench a sickening smell of cooked flesh. At the head of the column, King Meirchion halted his horse and sat staring at the destruction for long moments, jaw muscles working and fingers knotted around his reins. Ancelotis joined him.

"You know the land better than I," Ancelotis murmured. "Where will the bastard strike next?"

Meirchion spat to one side, as though trying to spit out the taste of death itself. "He may follow the Roman road south out of Penrith, but I suspect not, as he's fired every farmhold between here and the great stone circle on the River Eden. If he cuts east between Long Meg and the Caldron Snow rapids, he could strike as far north as Wall's End, then follow the coast south to Sussex. If he fired the villages near Long Meg first, destroying Penrith last, he may have ridden south already, toward Merecambe Bay and the road that drives through south Rheged, into the Pennines, and south through Calchrynned and Caer-Lundein to Sussex."

Stirling superimposed Ancelotis' knowledge of the region and the oxhide map of the great council over his own mental map of England. "Whichever route he takes, he'll have to move fast, for he knows the *cataphracti* will ride hard to catch him. The borders of Wessex are closer than those of Sussex and Creoda rides with him. He could also reach Dewyr, south of Ebrauc, which would give him a Saxon haven far closer at hand and ships to return south without risking the long ride through Briton-held territory."

"We must split our forces then," Meirchion decided. "I'll take my own cavalry south, following the possible route through south Rheged. Take your own *cataphracti* and Strathclyde's to the east, toward Long Meg and Her Daughters. If he's raiding in that direction, you'll find evidence of it soon enough. If it's Dewyr he's heading toward, you'll have a hellish ride trying to catch him up."

On that point, both Stirling and Ancelotis agreed. The column split, with Meirchion heading south out of the smouldering ruins of Penrith and Ancelotis riding hard east, with young Clinoch leading the men of Strathclyde behind him. Cutha and Creoda had clearly passed this way, for Ancelotis' path followed a swath of devastation sickening in its barbarity. It was nearly nightfall before they reached the headwaters of the Eden and the great standing stones of the megalithic circle known as Long Meg and Her Daughters. Smoke hung on the air, turning the sunset at their backs a lurid, blood-smeared red. The immense stones stood eerie watch above the countryside, with its squabbling, black-winged clouds of scavenging crows rising in drifts like charcoal mist in the long, slanting light. In the distance, they could hear the roar of water as the Eden gathered herself to tumble her way to the sea and the Caldron Snow rapids in the other direction snarled their way toward the lowlands of the south.

Beyond the sound of falling water, dark against the smudge of approaching night on the far horizon, smoke bellied up into the evening, clear evidence that Cutha was, indeed, riding east for Dewyr as hard as he could push his horses. The villages and farmholds in his path would have no warning before death burst in amongst them. Stirling ground his molars over the deepest and most savage anger he had ever felt in his life. Desperate as he was not to alter history, he could not witness such butchery and not hate the man responsible with a cold and knife-edged passion. Stirling found it difficult to bear, that by his failure to kill Cutha when he'd had the chance, Stirling himself had condemned these people to the ghastly butchery Cutha had gifted them with. The thought that he might already have changed history with an irrevocable failure to act haunted Trevor Stirling long after sunset, as they guided their horses deep into the smoke and shadows looming ahead.

✧   ✧   ✧

Morgana waited for the first shocked hubbub to die
down, then sent her sons with Medraut to begin packing for the journey home, and quietly took aside the
young runner who'd brought the news. She poured a
cup of wine for him with her own hands and guided
him to a bench near the fire, gesturing for servants
to bring hot food. The lad gulped almost convulsively
at the wine, with a stark look in his eyes that Brenna
McEgan had seen all too often, in the eyes of survivors after a bomb blast or a spray of bullets or a bottle
of flaming petrol had set a block of flats alight. Both
she and Morgana waited patiently for the lad to calm
himself, to recover his strength and his wind, waited
for him to begin eating the thick venison stew in his
steaming bowl. At length, Morgana spoke, very gently.
"When you are able, lad, I must know what you've
seen."

He jerked a frightened gaze up to meet hers. "Isn't
seemly t'tell a lady such things," he said, voice cracking
with distress.

"I understand your concern. But I am a sovereign
queen, Morgana of Galwyddel and Ynys Manaw, and
my lands and people are also threatened. I must know
the scope and depth of what our Saxon adversary is
willing to inflict, before I can make decisions on how
best to protect my people."

The boy thought for a moment, tears battling a
hardened, old man's anger in his eyes, then he nodded.
"'Tis vile, Queen Morgana. They left alive not even
one downy yellow chick in the farmyards. Burnt the
fields and forests for miles, it was, and left the dead
hacked into pieces. Men, women, infants in their
cradles. 'Twas unnatural savage, what they did, and to
every living thing that came in their way. I'd gone to
the marshes to cut withies for me mother, when they

came. Burnt the house and killed her and all my sisters, and me with nothing but a three-inch knife on me belt."

Tears welled up, impatiently knuckled aside. "I wanted to kill them, and would have tried, but if they were killing everyone the way they killed me mother and sisters, there would've been no one left to sound the alarm at Caerleul. So I lay in the mud with the marsh grass all round me 'til they'd gone, and ran from Long Meg to Penrith, to reach the Roman road, and everywhere I ran, there was nothing left alive save the crows." He hesitated, then asked in a voice breaking with youth and stress, "Did I do wrong, to lie in the grasses while me own family lay dying?"

Morgana smoothed the boy's lank, sweat-soaked hair back from his brow and placed a gentle kiss there. "No, lad. Hundreds of others may well be saved, because you hid in the grass to warn Caerleul. Thousands, perhaps, for once the *cataphracti* of the northern kingdoms begin the hunt, Cutha will be forced to fly ahead of our chargers, without taking the time to butcher every Briton whose path crosses his. 'Tis certain, God guided you to the wisest course, there in the marsh, and sent you with wings on your feet to speed the warning. Finish your stew, then, and I'll have a servant show you where to wash and sleep tonight. Were your father's people freeholders?"

The boy nodded.

" 'Tis good, then. I'll ask King Meirchion to look after you properly. If ever you need or want a place to start again, remember my name and come to Caer-Birrenswark at Galwyddel. I'll see that you receive a fine freehold."

The tears spilled over as the boy's eyes lost at least some of the starkness which had aged him so traumatically. "I'm that grateful, I am.".

"And so am I." Morgana left him to finish his meal and found Queen Thaney, who was busy organizing an army of servants to help the kings and queens of Britain make haste for departure. Morgana passed along her request that the boy's courage and quick wits be rewarded suitably. Her stepdaughter's eyes misted. "Of course we'll take care of the lad, Morgana. Thank you for letting me know."

"I'll be riding for Caer-Birrenswark as soon as the horses can be saddled."

Thaney gave her a swift embrace and Morgana kissed the younger woman's cheek, then left her to her work. It was the task of only a few moments to ready her own things, find Medraut and her sons busy stuffing clothing into leather satchels, and arrange for her retainers, who rode as armed escort everywhere Morgana traveled, to prepare for the journey north. As she was looking for a servant to help carry their baggage out to the stable for tying to the packhorses, the minstrel Lailoken brushed past, murmuring, "Half an hour's ride north along the road to Caer-Gretna?"

She nodded, moving on without speaking.

When someone behind her began whistling a shockingly familiar tune, Brenna whipped around, startling Morgana with the force of her reaction. She peered into the throng of men and women jammed in the hall, unable to see who had been whistling that particular song.

What is it? Morgana wanted to know, understandably perplexed at having her body hijacked in so public a fashion.

Realizing that she might well have given herself away by her own reaction, Brenna turned quickly and headed for the door, fighting hard to disguise her distress. That particular song was engraved in her memory, sung each July during the Orangemen's parades, commemorating a battle in the bloody seventeenth century. Bloody, indeed, as Irish Catholics had been slaughtered like pigs, hunted down in the fields for sport by the conquering English Protestants, with bounties offered on Irish heads, the same hideous sort of bounty the huntsmen collected for bringing in wolf pelts . . .

More than four hundred *years* of gloating later, the Orangemen still celebrated their victory in their "marching season" with parades through Catholic neighborhoods—parades received with much the same welcome as American Ku Klux Klan marches were received in the Jewish neighborhoods they swaggered through, exercising their right to free speech and assembly to rub salt in the wounds of their favorite victims. Every marching season, violence erupted between hotheaded Catholics who refused to take it any longer and hotheaded Protestants who had not yet tired of dishing it out.

No, Brenna McEgan was not likely to forget *that* song.

Morgana, realizing the full horror of Brenna's associations with Cedric Banning's favorite tune, not only sent her a great wave of sympathy, she also stopped the next servant she spotted, asking softly, "Can you tell me, has anyone been singing this tune?" She hummed the melodic line in a near whisper, to keep the sound from carrying to anyone else's ears.

The woman gave her a curious stare, then nodded. "Oh, aye, that they have, Queen Morgana, all the minstrels have been singing it of late. It is a catching little tune, isn't it? I've caught meself many a day now, humming it while I work. It does make the day go a bit faster."

"Yes, I can see that it would. I was just curious, since I hadn't heard it before this week. I'd like my

minstrels at Caer-Birrenswark to learn it. Thank you,
I'll ask Rheged's court musicians about it."

One of the minstrels . . .

Lailoken himself?

'Tis possible, Morgana mused, *but with so many
visitors in Caerleul, who can guess where the tune was
first heard and from whom? Minstrels have a quick
ear for such things and it does have a way of sticking
in the mind.*

It certainly does, Brenna agreed darkly.

Morgana pursed her lips in thought. *Would your
mad Banning have needed a host somewhere close to
Caer-Iudeu, as I was for your arrival?*

Brenna hadn't thought about that. *It's likely, yes.
But I can't tell how far the range might be. We'd had
no chance to field test that, before Banning murdered
poor Dr. Beckett.*

It would be interesting, Morgana mused, *to discover
who has recently been in Caer-Iudeu, and compare
those names with the men and women who've been in
Caerleul this week past.*

Brenna held back a groan. *Beginning with Artorius
and your brother-in-law Ancelotis and Medraut. And
Covianna Nim. There's nothing to indicate that a host's
body must match the traveler's gender. Banning could
have taken over any man or woman within several miles
of Caer-Iudeu. Lord, and there's every servant who
came south with us, not to mention the soldiers of the
cataphracti,* Brenna rattled off the list in some despair.

True, Morgana nodded, making her way back to the
stable to collect her palfrey, *but we can look for other
clues. I'm thinking Ancelotis' collapse is a matter to
consider most carefully. If someone arrived in his head
the way you appeared in mine, like a thunderclap out
of hell, I would've been astonished if he hadn't fallen
from his horse, struck senseless.*

In one sudden and blinding flash, Brenna put together all the odd little discrepancies about Ancelotis' recent behavior. A frequently distracted air, as though in conversation with himself, focused inward. Clumsiness on horseback, when Ancelotis must surely have grown up in the saddle. And that display of martial arts in the arena, when he'd defeated Cutha with his bare hands. That was a twenty-first-century fighting technique.

But is it something your terrorist, Banning, would have learned? Morgana wanted to know. *Or is it likely the other traveler, the soldier who is mistakenly hunting you?*

Brenna wasn't sure. *I don't know what Banning will or won't have studied, learning his trade. Martial arts are popular enough with all sorts of men; with women, as well, come to that. But the SAS most certainly does train its soldiers in unarmed combat techniques. Just like the ones Ancelotis used.*

Morgana frowned. *If your life depended upon a guess, which would you choose? Terrorist or misguided enemy?*

Huh. Brenna grimaced, unhappy with the choices offered and well aware that a mistake could cost her life—and the lives of innocent billions. Weighing all the factors at hand, she finally decided. *Misguided enemy, I think. Somehow, Ancelotis' behavior strikes me as confused but honorable. And if there's one thing I learned, working with Cedric Banning day after day, it's his love for games of deception. Hiding his true identity while flaunting little hints like his paisley scarf. I haven't seen any such quirks in Ancelotis' personality.*

What is this paisley scarf, what does it mean? I don't understand its significance.

It's a nasty little visual pun. Paisley is a pattern

woven into cloth. It's also a name given to Orangemen who advocate violence. Banning's a Paisleyite, Brenna explained grimly. *The group is named after a Protestant minister of the late twentieth century, an icon of Orange culture. He preached Orange supremacy from his pulpit in Belfast, to the shame of many other Protestant ministers—most of whom deplore the killing as much as the Catholic priests do. But Paisley was so caught up in the fight to save Orange culture from the Catholic menace, he behaved like a man under siege, fighting for survival.*

Brenna sighed. *He gave many a questionable organization his public approval, while never quite staining his own hands. Wearing the Paisley scarf was Banning's way of laughing at me, flaunting his beliefs under my nose when I'd no way to prove who and what he was. And I'd not act to kill a man unless I were absolutely sure of his guilt.* For the first time since finding the inner strength to leave *Cumann Na Mbann,* Brenna regretted—bitterly—her decision to wait until she had more evidence. If only she'd called in the IRA hit squad sooner . . .

Morgana said gently, her thoughts full of grief and understanding, *Never castigate yourself, Brenna of Clan McEgan for trying to spare the lives of innocents before moving to strike the guilty. To do otherwise is to become as he is, mad with hatred and the desire for vengeance. There are many great injustices in life— that, at least, has not changed over the centuries. We shall simply do our best to see that your world's injustices do not add to mine.*

Brenna could not ask for anything more.

Covianna Nim watched in deep satisfaction as Morgana rode out the gates of the Sixth Legion's fortress of Caerleul, on her way to commit treason—

a circumstance that Covianna found utterly delicious. Once certain that Morgana and her fool of a nephew were truly gone, she returned to her own room, where her clothing and satchels of herbs and other substances—poisons with far darker uses than mere healing—sat waiting for her own departure.

She pulled from her baggage a small, flat packet in which she kept a precious supply of thin-scraped vellum, calfskin as pale as the skin of a white onion, with a far smoother surface. She chose a smallish piece, trimmed from a larger vellum she had written while in Caer-Iudeu, and set it on the table beside her borrowed bed. Mixing a small amount of ink from a powdered base, using a few splashes of white wine— the best liquid for producing a fine writing ink— Covianna trimmed her goose-quill pen, tapped her lips with the feathered end of the shaft, then dipped and began to write.

Artorius, she began, using the beautifully scripted, cursive Latin she had learned as a girl from her dearly beloved Marguase—*it pains me enormously to be the bearer of ill tidings, but my concern for the safety of Britain impels me to send you this warning. It is, perhaps, a symptom of some inherited madness, but Morgana has lost all reason. She has made secret arrangements to betray Galwyddel to the Irish of Dalriada.*

I heard her, with my own ears, plotting to secure for Medraut the throne of Galwyddel, which he will earn by betraying you and all of Britain. It is the form of this betrayal which distresses me so deeply. He is to marry a princess of Irish blood, a marriage Morgana is negotiating to bring about. As soon as the marriage is consummated, he will invite in her Dalriadan kinsmen as foederati.

My heart grieves that this is so, for I believe

Morgana truly thinks this insanity to be the right thing to do. It is clear to me, at least, that the Dalriadans will take full advantage of our distraction in the south and invade at full strength the moment she has concluded this mad treaty. Please, for the sake of Britain, ride to Caer-Birrenswark and stop her before she commits this act of desperate folly.

I will ask a minstrel to deliver this into your hand, as I must ride south with all haste to help my own kinsmen at Glastenning Tor prepare for defense—for if the Saxons break through our lines at Caer-Badonicus, they will surely strike next at the Tor. I pray that you do not blame Morgana too deeply, for I believe the shock of her husband's death has left her so deeply shaken, she is not in her right mind. Treat her gently, I beg of you, but halt this madness before it is too late for Galwyddel and all of Britain. I am, humbly, your obedient servant, Covianna Nim of Glastenning Tor.

She carefully blew the final lines of ink dry, disposed of the excess ink by pouring it into the chamber pot, and rinsed the little glass inkwell with water from her basin before carefully storing it away again in her baggage, along with the quill in its pen case and the penknife in a second case tucked inside the first. She lit a taper of beeswax from an oil lamp, then creased the vellum into a small square, so that all sides were sealed by folds.

Covianna dripped melted wax onto the final, open edge and pressed her ring into it, leaving an impression of Glastenning Tor's heraldic symbol: a labyrinth with a sword at the center. Blowing out the candle flame, she sat back and surveyed her handiwork. A small, satisfied smile chased its way across her lips. She laughed softly, a low and sultry sound, then tucked the note into the sleeve of her gown and went in search of a minstrel who could be trusted to do exactly what he was instructed to do, no more and no less. She had made use of him before, a time or two, and had found him to be quite reliable. His eyes lit like bonfires at Beltane when he saw her.

"Covianna Nim!"

She allowed him to kiss her fingertips.

"Bricriu, I would have you deliver this note to Artorius after I have gone. But do *not* take it straight to him. I must try and verify the matters written herein. If I do not contact you by the next full moon, then the matter is true and Artorius must know of it."

She handed the small, folded vellum over—and with it a coin glittering golden in the late and slanting light of afternoon. A gold *aureus* of Rome, it bore the portrait of the last emperor of the west, Romulus Augustulus. Twenty-five years after their last minting, the golden Augustulus coins still circulated amongst the peoples of the vanishing empire, even as far afield as Britain, which still managed a lively trade with her former imperial masters despite unrest, civil war, and invasion that seemed to sweeping across the entire known world.

Covianna, brought up in a tribe of artisans who were also shrewd traders, had learned the value of such coins almost before she could walk. She had acquired a goodly collection of the *aureus* coins over the years, which she made excellent use of from time to time. When she held up the glittering golden disc, worth a hundred silver *sestertii* and twice the value of Constantine the Great's gold *solidus,* and caught the answering glint in the minstrel's eye, she knew she had him.

"Agree to follow my instructions to the letter," she purred, "and this will be yours immediately. Breathe not one single word of this to anyone, not even to your fellow minstrels or bedmate, but give it straight into Artorius' hand, and I will provide others. Multiple others. Once you have given it to Artorius, bring his response to me at Glastenning Tor—and ride like wildfire, for time will be critical by then." As she spoke, Covianna turned the coin over and over in her fingers, toying with it, watching in amusement the way the minstrel's eyes followed the glitter of light. She flipped it to him without warning.

He caught it with a snatch like a starving dog, turning it over and staring at it while babbling, "I swear by Afallach and Christ, I will put your letter into the Dux Bellorum's own hand and no other's, even if I must ride to Avalonis across the waves and back again." He slipped the coin into his belt pouch, then held out his hand for the note. "Provided I have not heard otherwise from you, come the full moon, the task will be done."

Satisfied, Covianna slipped the letter into his palm and it vanished up his sleeve. "Do this for me quietly and you will be rewarded accordingly."

"Your servant," he bowed.

Covianna left him whistling merrily and retrieved her satchels, carrying them across the road and giving them to a stable hand to pack behind her saddle. Emrys Myrddin appeared in the doorway as she was making her way back to the street.

"Covianna," Myrddin smiled, eyes brightening when his gaze rested on her. "Where will you go, in all this turmoil and confusion? Back to Gododdin?"

"No," she said in a low voice, giving him a look of grave concern. "With war brewing in the south and my kinsmen at Glastenning Tor considered one of the most lucrative targets on the Saxons' list, I will be needed there far more than at Gododdin."

"You need not risk yourself," he protested, twisting a strand of her golden hair around his fingertips.

"I don't fear death, Emrys Myrddin, any more than you. You must understand, surely, that my place is working at the forges with my kinsmen? Making swords and doing what I can to doctor injuries."

He frowned. "Do you think so little of our chances that you must be on hand to treat the wounded if the Saxons break through and lay siege to the Tor?"

Covianna laughed softly. "Oh, no, you mistake me entirely. I have every confidence in our fighting strength. But when kings demand hundreds of new weapons in a very short time, to prepare for war, smiths must make many more blades, spearpoints, and *pilum* heads in one month than they might ordinarily make in half a year. Such a heavy demand means long hours at the forge, with little time for food or even sleep.

"Even the apprentices are run into exhaustion, keeping the forge fires hotly stoked and the bellows in good working order, turning out simpler pieces on their own anvils, or heating the iron bars the master smiths and journeymen will forge into weapons. Work done at that pace causes fatigue and accidents—and if the work goes on long enough at that pace, exhaustion can cause crippling injuries, even death. Master healers are desperately needed when the forges are kept running day and night before battle."

Myrddin blinked in surprise, much to her delight. It wasn't often *anyone* was able to startle the aging Druid. Then he gave her a rueful smile.

"Forgive me, my dear, for being so obtuse. At least"—he caressed her cheek fondly—"I will have the pleasure of your company on the road south."

Covianna let her gaze smoulder. "I cannot think of anyone I would rather travel with, Myrddin."

He cupped her chin, lifting her face to meet his lips. He then breathed against her ear, "It is, alas, a long journey in the company of others."

Covianna whispered back, "Even an overcrowded *taverna* has a stable, and stables have hay lofts and not even the stableboys stand guard on a dark and empty hay loft."

He laughed aloud. "I haven't been in a hay loft in . . ." he paused to consider " . . . it must be twenty years, if it's a day. It wasn't until after I'd tumbled her that I decided to marry her."

Covianna, who disliked—intensely—any reference to Emrys Myrddin's wife, swatted him in seemingly mock ferocity. In truth, Covianna hated Myrddin's wife, who was not only alive and likely to outlive God himself, but was an intensely suspicious bitch, nosing around in Covianna's affairs whenever both women happened to be in the same city. Which was as infrequently as possible, making it difficult to find time to pump Emrys Myrddin for everything he could teach her—including how to apply one's own ambition and make it look like another's idea, or how to salve the affronted intellect of the British kings who were, in Covianna's opinion, among the dullest, stupidest men on the earth.

Myrddin grimaced. "My apologies, Covianna, I will forget and mention her. I will make it up to you on the road south to Caer-Badonicus."

You'd better believe you will! Covianna snarled under her breath, while smiling with the fondness of a mildly irritated mistress. Men, even those with Druidic training or Emrys Myrddin's keenly incisive mind, were by and large a stupid lot, driven by their gonads more than their brains. Aloud, she murmured, "I must go and see that my medicines are properly packed and stored."

"We will meet, then, on the road out of Caerleul."

Covianna slipped back into the great hall and spotted Artorius deep in conversation with a group of grey-haired kings and their younger sons. The Dux Bellorum had removed his sword and sheath, neither of which were in evidence. A swift search of the hall found no trace of the weapon, so she slipped away to the room Artorius and Ganhumara had shared.

The young queen was not in the room, although an appalling amount of clothing and jewelry was scattered carelessly like peacock feathers thrown down in the barnyard mud. From beneath one of Ganhumara's exquisite silk gowns Covianna spotted the tip of Artorius' scabbard. Covianna slipped the lovingly forged blade from the scabbard, letting Caliburn itself drop to the bed again amidst the riot of silks, furs, and kashmir wool imported from far Constantinople.

The sword, she left behind, leaving Artorius with nothing but naked steel between him and a ruined reputation. The power of Caliburn was not in the Damascus pattern-welding so coveted by wealthy, high-ranking officers, but in the sheath—and Covianna intended to remain in possession of that for a long time to come. Laughing softly, she hid the scabbard in the folds of her skirt and slipped away to her own room to hide it amongst her remaining baggage.

Intrigue, she sighed happily, was nearly as delicious a sport as murder. Particularly since those she planned to embroil in her nasty little web would—if all went well—end up deliciously dead.

Caer-Gretna wasn't much of a village, Brenna thought sourly as their horses plodded through the gate in the town wall, taking them toward a fortress that might have been better dubbed a mud hovel. It was smaller, even, than the mile forts along the Roman roads through Gododdin and Strathclyde, and boasted a garrison of ten soldiers, their plump wives, and a gaggle of scrawny hens and equally scrawny children vying for the same patches of dirt to scratch in. The town wall overlooked a long, low slope to the sea, where Solway Firth, its waters turned luridly crimson by the slanting light of the setting sun, lapped against tidal mud flats and a short stretch of sandy beach where fishing nets had been strung up to dry overnight. The tidal flats and beach stank of mud, dead fish, and human waste.

You want us to sleep here? Brenna asked with a note of dismay she could not hide.

Morgana sighed. *It is safer inside the walls than it would be further along the road, where there are no forts at all to protect us should an Irish raider and his crew decide to strike. I enjoy the smell no more than you, but I prefer my sons and I to wake tomorrow still among the living.*

There being no argument to counter that, Brenna tried to breathe shallowly until her nostrils accustomed themselves to the pervasive stink. The little garrison was, at least, kept scrupulously clean inside by the commander's wife, whose reaction to royal visitors was to fly into a frenzied state of agitation that soon had the entire town in an uproar, bringing in foodstuffs to be cooked, properly comfortable beds from the hamlet's wealthiest residents, even a keg of ale from the *taverna*, into which Lailoken happily disappeared with his harp and flute uncased and ready for the evening's merriment.

Morgana wisely suggested they allow Caer-Gretna's women time to work uninterrupted on their evening meal and guest quarters. Medraut followed Lailoken into the little *taverna*, smiling and eager for a bit of fun after the strain of the week at Caerleul, while Morgana's sons, carefully chaperoned by their guards, joined the village boys in a game involving wooden hoops, sticks to keep them rolling, and at least a dozen eager, panting puppies which kept darting underfoot as the boys ran and shouted. Morgana, feeling a need for more solitude than the *taverna*, the garrison, or the children could offer, sought out the little village church, a rough-hewn structure of planks and logs cut from the surrounding forest.

She stepped into the chilly, dim interior, where a low table to one side supported a few flickering candles. There were no pews, no chairs, just a long, flat floor made of smooth-worn sandstone, an altar of finely carved wood, and a riot of paintings on the wooden walls, half Christian saints, half pagan symbols left over from earlier beliefs that could not and would not be set aside in a mere handful of centuries. Morgana observed the proper form, going to one knee in genuflection, crossing herself while facing the altar, then pulled her fur-lined cloak more closely about herself for warmth and walked slowly toward the front of the little church, needing the balm of silence it offered. So much had happened in such a rushed blur of days, she had not yet been granted the luxury of simple grieving for her husband.

When the tears began to well up, Morgana sank to the floor, leaning against the carved wooden rail separating the altar from the rest of the church, and cried in deep, gasping grief. She wanted Lot Luwddoc's arms around her, a foolish desire, since even his arms would not have kept the threat of war at bay, but she had felt so very much safer when lying beside him. The decisions she had made for Galwyddel and Ynys Manaw had been so much easier when her husband still lived.

She'd felt secure in the knowledge that she could always turn to someone as familiar as she with the heavy responsibility of command, and with the sometimes desperate necessities one had to force upon one's people, to protect them from greater harm. With Lot Luwddoc dead and Artorius riding south into war, Ancelotis at his side, Morgana had no one left to share the burden of decision with, no one left to calm her fears in the night, no one to whisper, "It will all come right, you'll see it will."

Was she wrong to pursue alliance with Dalriada?

The Irish invaders had already struck at Galwyddel repeatedly, landing on her shores by the hundreds, eager for conquest and rich farmland, until Morgana's *cataphracti* had managed to drive them northward, toward easier conquest against the Picts. Was she signing the death warrant of Galwyddel, giving it to Medraut to rule with Irish *foederati* as kinsmen? She had not yet found an answer when the village priest, who lived in a small hut behind the church, stepped into view through the rear entrance, halting in surprise when he saw her leaning against the railing, lost in helpless weeping.

"Oh, my child," he murmured, hurrying forward, "how long have you been here, alone and crying in the dark?"

She shook her head, too choked to answer.

He knelt beside her, stroked wet hair back from her face, gathered her into his arms and simply rocked her like a child, allowing her to weep out her grief against his shoulder. At length, with the worst of the emotional storm spent, she simply leaned against him, breathing quietly and feeling absurdly safe once more. He murmured, "We heard the news, these seven days past, of Lot Luwddoc's death and the call to council. Know that we grieve with you, Queen Morgana."

She managed to dry her cheeks with one hand. "I am grateful for it."

"How can we of Caer-Gretna help?"

She managed a smile, surprising even herself. "You have already." She sighed and sat up, pulling herself together again. "It is a poor time of year for the necessity, but we must look to refortify every fortress in Galwyddel. It is our task to hold the northern and western borders secure, as war is breaking out in the south."

"The Saxons again."

"Aye. Sussex and Wessex, both. You've heard the news of Penrith?"

"We have," the priest growled. "Godless bastards, they are, Queen Morgana. They'll not take Caer-Gretna by such surprise."

"Nor any other village of the Britons," she agreed. "Word has gone out in every direction to leave the harvesting and the fishing to the smallest children, for the men and women of Britain are needed for the heavier work of rebuilding stone walls and forging weapons."

"Troubled times, indeed. There is little here to protect, but even a humble priest knows from Caer-Gretna a band of raiders could strike deep into Briton land, doing enormous damage."

"Yes. You must organize the people to do whatever the commander of the garrison needs done. I will speak with him before the night is out."

"The tithes to the church, small as they are, will help buy iron for the forge. We've a good smith in Caer-Gretna, with three strong sons and a good, strapping daughter, as well, all learning the trade from him."

"Put some of that coinage aside to buy grain, in case of siege. With the armies of the Britons riding south to war, our coastal towns will be at greater risk of raid than ever before."

"It shall be done."

"There is little more I can ask than that." She sighed and pushed herself to her feet, grateful for the priest's steadying hand. "I thank you for the comfort rendered."

"It is harder to bear grief when frightened people look to you for strength and guidance. But you descend from kings and queens of iron strength and the well-tempered will to survive. Galwyddel rests easier, knowing the daughter of Gorlois has the task of leading us when war looms on the horizon."

The comment struck unexpectedly deep, hurting her heart with the knowledge that she was preparing to hand the Galwyddellians to an untried youth, in a risky gamble for safety. "I will do what I believe best for Galwyddel. Whatever comes, try to remember that."

"A promise I will gladly keep. Here, you're shivering, pull that cloak tighter round yourself." He tucked the edges firmly together and warmed her hands in his own, rubbing them briskly while she battled to blink back more tears. "There. Go now, go and find a warm fire and eat a good supper with your sons beside you. Drink a mug or two of ale, it will help you sleep."

Her lips twitched in a faint smile. Advice from a novice to a master healer—but welcome, nonetheless, for its gentle concern. "I'll do that. Thank you."

She left him to tend his guttering candles and found her way back to the garrison, where the mouth-watering scents of a major feast wafted through the evening air. Shortly, she and her children were served up a good, hot meal, insisting that the garrison officers and their families share the repast, and spoke of Britain's danger and Caer-Gretna's need to arm and defend itself. In that odd way men have of greeting trouble with a certain inexplicable air of excited anticipation, the garrison commander and his men launched into a voluble, animated discussion of precisely what was needed, where it could be obtained, and who was available to procure it.

She left them to their happy plottings and retired for the night, exhausted and bruised in body and spirit. The dawn and another day's grim reality would come all too soon, as it was.

Chapter Twelve

Trevor Stirling hadn't visited the Yorkshire Dales in years. He'd come with a school group long ago and remembered being deeply impressed by the broken country of towering limestone cliffs, deep and mysterious caverns, glacier-cut gorges, and rugged karst topography. When Stirling and the *cataphracti* following Cutha's trail thundered down into Ebrauc, he was deeply dismayed when the mud-churned trail led straight into the wild tangle of broken, eroding rock that comprised the roughest country to navigate by horseback anywhere in England. The stony soil did wonders for hiding the bastard's tracks—doubtless why he'd chosen the longer, more snaking route toward Dewyr. Every time they came to a feeder stream or intersecting gorge, they had to pause and waste valuable time searching for signs of Cutha's party—a muddy hoofprint on a streambank, horse dung, broken branches in the scrub.

In contrast to his earlier lightning assaults on villages and farmholds, Cutha's tracks now assiduously avoided what few settlements there were tucked away into the Dales, bypassing even tiny hamlets like Malham. He followed, instead, the Pennine Way down to the River Aire, which eventually burst out of the broken country in a froth of rain-swollen whitewater and spilled down into a gentler countryside that would one day see the cities of Halifax and Leeds rise to prominence. The river roared along, spilling over into wide water meadows where thousands of waterfowl clamored for food and mates.

The marshes bred mosquitoes and midges, as well, which plagued them by night, whether they stopped for an hour or two of sleep or pressed doggedly onward. What sounded like—and might well have been—several million frogs turned the marshes into a drum-roll chorus of territorial challenges and peeping, bellowing, bell-throated calls for females of their own particular kind. Stirling, unused to the countryside in any case and certainly unused to a countryside not yet denuded by pesticides, urban runoff, and heavy-metal pollutants, had never heard so many frogs in his entire life. It sounded at times like the night would crack wide open under the onslaught of so much raw, primeval sound.

After a race of nearly two hundred kilometers, they arrived at the mouth of the River Ouse, where it dumped flood-stage debris—swirling brown water, snags of deadwood, uprooted trees—into the Humber. They stopped on the muddy bank, staring in dismay at the barrier, for the river was clearly impassable without a ferry—and the ferry lines had been cut, from the far side. Cutha, reaching the far banks of the Ouse at least a day, perhaps two days, ahead of them, had left the ferry boat stranded on the eastern riverbank, along with what looked sickeningly like a dead ferry-man sprawled in a puddle of black blood. Carrion crows were once again in abundant evidence, a sight which still had the power to turn Stirling's stomach.

Ancelotis cursed long and loud.

Young Clinoch muttered, "Surely we can cobble together another ferry?"

Before Ancelotis could answer, a Saxon patrol appeared on the far bank, marking the line where Ebrauc gave way to Saxon territory in Dewyr. The appearance of that patrol forced them to admit defeat. Cutha had outrun them. To attempt further chase would be to precipitate immediate war with the Saxons of Dewyr, which the Britons could not yet risk. The bitterness of it tasted like poison in the back of Ancelotis' throat. Clinoch snarled a few choice oaths himself, before turning back. "I've defenses to build," the boy said in a harsh, weary voice, "and men to send south with the Dux Bellorum."

"Aye." Ancelotis spat to one side. "We're both of us a long way from home. I'll take word to Artorius, my-self, that Cutha reached Dewyr ahead of us." That decision, at least, brightened Stirling's mood consider-ably. Any number of fatal "accidents" could have befallen Artorius by now, with Brenna McEgan watch-ing for the chance to complete her mission. And the chaos of preparing for war would present her with many excellent opportunities to strike, with Artorius distracted and not expecting treachery from a Briton. Stirling's sense of urgency had begun to affect Ancelotis.

"I'll ride by forced march back to Caerleul," he told the others, "traveling light and fast. Half my *cataphracti* I'll send home to Gododdin to strengthen the hill forts along the northern borders. The other half, I'll send on to Caer-Badonicus, for Cadorius and Melwas will need every sword arm and strong back they can beg or borrow. You can bet whatever you care to wager that Sussex will mobilize for invasion the instant Cutha arrives home, and it won't take him long, by sea. Spread the word northward, as you ride, that Cutha has made good his escape."

"That I will," Clinoch muttered. "Beginning with King Gergust of Ebrauc, should yon bastards"—he nodded toward the distant shore of Dewyr and its armed Saxon patrol—"decide to launch an attack across his border to distract us from the greater threat to the south."

Stirling, impressed by the lad's grasp of tactics, was immediately informed by Ancelotis—somewhat peevishly, since they were both tired—that Briton royalty learned such things from infancy. *Princes and their heiress sisters study Greek histories of Alexander the Great and they read Julius Caesar, both the* Gallic Commentaries *and his* Civil War, *to learn the art of winning battles from warfare's greatest masters. How else do you suppose Artorius learned his trade as Dux Bellorum? Emrys Myrddin and Ambrosius Aurelianus spent years teaching Artorius, alongside my brother Lot Luwddoc and myself, drilling into us the tactics and strategies that lead to victory, even against greater numbers than your own.*

I meant no insult, Stirling apologized, even as a fierce glow of pride in his ancestors had begun to suffuse itself through his conscious awareness. A dangerous glow of pride, as he found himself identifying ever more strongly with the Briton cause, his loyalties shifting like quicksand between the future he was trying to save and the past he was beginning to identify as something worth defending against all comers. He had joined the SAS from a sense of patriotic honor, after all, determined to defend "king and country" to the best of his ability. The longer he stayed in Artorius'

Britain, the shakier his definition of "king and country" grew.

In the twenty-first century, such notions were diluted by other distractions, by larger loyalties as a subject of the British Empire and a member of a world community that had set itself in opposition to tribal violence and terrorism. In the sixth century, Stirling's larger loyalties were fading away, increasingly insubstantial, half-remembered dreams, while the raw immediacy of his new reality—where a man's honor and personal courage were often all that stood between loved ones and brutal death—tugged at him with almost irresistible strength.

As miserable as the trek from Carlisle to Humberside had been, the journey back was infinitely worse, with nothing but saddle galls and shaken loyalties and defeat to carry back with him.

Emrys Myrddin and the kings of the south sped rapidly along the dragon's spine, rousing the men to arms as they passed town, village, and farmhold. And as they rode, day by miserable, rain-swept day, Myrddin began to develop his plan for defending Caer-Badonicus. He had been to the hill fort only once, but his was an excellent memory and he had been watching men wage war for more than fifty years. He knew how leaders thought, had studied the histories, understood very well indeed, why Alexander of Macedonia and Julius Caesar had won victory after victory. By comparison, the Saxons they were soon to face were little more than yelling apes, baboons with swords and thrusting spears and no concept of strategy other than overwhelming an opponent with sheer numbers.

That, of course, was Britain's chief problem: the sheer *number* of the barbaric creatures. Still, Saxon ignorance was an advantage to be used and Myrddin had a fair idea how to go about exploiting it. Hard riding took them deep into the southlands, where unseasonal autumn rains were even heavier than they had been in the north, destroying crops and threatening the countryside with starvation over the winter. Little wonder King Cadorius and Sub-King Melwas were all but frantic, facing such a winter with such neighbors about to come calling at their borders.

Emrys Myrddin and the kings of the south skirted the eastern end of the Cotswold Hills to enter a countryside thick with ancient monuments, places like the monolithic barrow dubbed West Kennet, with its mass graves hidden deep within the mound, and the mysterious Silburis Hill, a man-made tower of white chalk blocks rising more than a hundred thirty feet into the air. By riding cross-country from one great monument to the next, a man could follow the ancient ley lines Myrddin's Druidic instructors had named the "dragon lines," conduits of energy that wound, braidlike, through the region, touching such places as Caer-Aveburis and Stonehenge, where immense circles of standing stones had sat since the beginning of time, erected by a people so ancient, not even the Druids could recall their names.

The dragon lines snaked through more than a dozen such ancient monuments left by the old ones. Emrys Myrddin might not know who had built these holy places, but he understood very well, indeed, their deep impact on the minds of those who lived near to them. He and Uthyr Pendragon and Ambrosius Aurelianus before him had used that awe to forge ties of alliance between widely scattered tribes of southern Britons. It had worked so well, Emrys Myrddin had spread the concept north and east and west, throughout the whole of Britain, literally creating one people united by a commonly held identity.

It was, Myrddin knew, his greatest legacy to the people of Britain. And now he must fight to save that legacy from foreign destruction.

There was no mistaking Caer-Badonicus for any other hill in Britain. Even Silburis Hill was a mere child's toy, compared with Caer-Badonicus. Its wind-swept summit, a broad, flat stretch of land fully eighteen acres in area, towered five hundred feet above the Salisbury Plain. Broodingly immense against the stormy grey rainclouds scudding past its flanks, Caer-Badonicus was a natural fortress, crowned with ancient and crumbling walls, an earthwork fortification so old, not even Emrys Myrddin had ever heard its original name. During the long centuries of peaceful Roman rule, hill forts like Badonicus had fallen into ruins, no longer necessary to safeguard the people of the surrounding plain. The wheel of time had turned, however, and walls were needed once again. Emrys Myrddin was here to ensure that the walls they built were the strongest, most protective walls ever built by Briton hands.

The future of an entire people depended upon it.

And upon him.

Keenly aware of the pain Atlas had felt of old, Myrddin squinted against the downpour to study the profile of the hill rising up from the flatlands. The wind whipped through the crowns of mature trees at the summit, lashing them with brutal fury. As they drew closer, he spotted several white-water cataracts where rainwater poured off the hillcrest, surging and spilling its way down the steep, bramble-covered slopes.

It gave him an idea.

"I want to get right to the top," he said over the sound of rain and wind.

King Cadorius of Dumnonia grimaced, while the younger Melwas of Glastenning, in whose territory

Caer-Badonicus actually lay, turned to him in visible dismay. "*Now?* In this driving downpour?"

"Aye, now. We'll be fighting the Saxons up there in conditions just as bad."

Covianna Nim, as bedraggled and mud-splashed as the rest of them, frowned. "I doubt we'll get the horses up that, not in this muck. That's a good thirty- or forty-degree slope and if ever there was a road to the summit, it's long since grown over and vanished."

Myrddin chuckled, which startled Cadorius and Melwas into staring. Accustomed to the limitations of most men's minds—and particularly those of kings, several of whom he had tutored personally—he explained with the same patience a mother reserves for her child: "The fact that there is no road works in our favor, for the Saxons will have just as hard a time reaching the crest as we will. Even *without* the nasty surprises I have in mind."

They did, indeed, have to leave the horses behind. Slogging their way through mud, through freshets of runoff that cut eroding gullies into the hillside, past wild brambles and outcroppings of native bedrock that scraped the hands and left the footing slick and treacherous beneath their feet, they climbed steadily toward the storm-lashed clouds. Panting, pausing to rest now and again, they finally scaled the summit, standing beneath a towering oak for protection from the wind-whipped gusts of rain.

Clumps of mistletoe, the "Druids' weed," had shaken loose from the oak's boughs, littering the ground with dark green leaves and clusters of tiny white berries, along with larger limbs snapped off by the storm. Blocks of stone lay piled haphazardly where work had already begun on the refortification, work interrupted by the rain. That, alone, would have to change. They didn't have time to wait on niceties like cooperative weather.

The view from the summit was impressive. Myrddin squinted against the rain, shielding his eyes with one hand while absently pulling his sodden cloak tighter around his shivering frame. Pacing off the distances, he walked the ancient walls, surveying the entire hilltop, while the king of Dumnonia and Melwas trailed along in his wake. Covianna remained huddled beneath the oaks, shivering and trying to stay out of the wind.

"We'll want circumvallations," Myrddin said at length, "several layers of them, right around the summit." He pointed, then knelt to retrieve a small branch, sketching what he intended in the mud, using his cloak to protect the muddy drawing as best he could. "My suggestion is five walls, at a minimum, arrayed like this, and we'll need shelters for a good-sized armed force to hold out against siege. Barracks, arms rooms, privies, stables for horses and livestock, pens for chickens and goats, shelters for womenfolk and children, for they'll need shelter behind strong walls when the Saxons come marching from the southeast, else they'll repeat Penrith on a grander scale."

"We'll need to dig wells," Cadorius muttered, "to support that number of people."

"Aye, and cisterns for rainwater, as well."

"There won't be room for cisterns," Melwas protested, squatting beside Myrddin's mud map and using a finger to sketch in the outlines of the buildings Myrddin had just enumerated.

Myrddin chuckled. "Ah, you're thinking in terms only of the summit. There'll be plenty of room. It's why I want five walls, not just the one or two you generally find with hill forts like this one. Look you, now, we'll build the five circumvallations like the labyrinth of Glastenning Tor, a maze of walls, with stone-lined cisterns between and gutters cut across the entire eighteen acres of the summit, feeding the rainwater into them, so none is wasted."

Melwas gaped. "You can't be serious? No one could build such a complicated structure in the time we have!"

"Nonsense," Myrddin snorted. "Haven't you read your *Gallic Commentaries*? Caesar's legions could have done it in a week, if not less."

The young king of Glastenning tried to find his voice, mouth working like a fish drowning in air. "But—"

"He's right," Cadorius cut in. "Remember, we'll have more than the farmers of Glastenning to help with the quarrying and the digging. Half the fighting strength of Britain is on its way here, with a fair percentage of them close enough to Badonicus, we should have a sizeable work force by tomorrow's sunset. We may not have the equal of Roman engineers, but we've plenty of strong backs and this is a brilliant defense plan." He tapped the muddy sketch, which rainwater was spattering into oblivion. "We could hold this hill for weeks, if need be, provided we can lay in the foodstuffs as quickly as we lay in the walls and cisterns and put up the shelters."

Myrddin nodded. "That, too, will be critical. The *cataphracti* and infantry due to join us will be certain to bring their own baggage trains with them, as even the greenest commanding officer knows an army of the size needed here cannot scavenge off the surrounding countryside as their only source of victuals. They'll have a sizeable store of grain and smoked meats with them, never doubt that. It's our job to be sure we've places to store it before the Saxons reach us.

"It's certain as sunrise the Saxons will cut any supply lines to Caer-Badonicus, the moment they arrive. It's a holding action we'll be fighting, distracting and keeping the Saxons bottled up here, goading them into trying to take this fortress, while the armies of the midlands and the north rush southward to join us. Without that fighting strength of the north, we'll never drive them back, so we must take great care to hold out until they can reach us—and make damned sure the Saxons don't scatter and ravage the countryside the way Cutha ravaged Penrith."

Melwas was still frowning down at the disintegrating mud map. "Why so many cisterns, though? With eighteen acres to provide runoff, surely so many won't be necessary? That's a lot of wall you're talking about, a lot of water, thousands of hogsheads, I'd say."

Emrys Myrddin grinned. "Indeed, you show a fine grasp of the mathematics. It's fortunate for us that the season's been one of the rainiest in memory. Come, let me show you something," Myrddin said, leading them back to the edge of the hill, where workmen had begun repairs to the old fortress wall. They had to squint into the teeth of the wind and shelter their eyes with upraised hands against the slashing rain. "If you were going to besiege this hill, would you put your tents here?" he gestured at the steep, rain-slashed slope. "In the brunt of the wind and rain? Or"—he led them across the summit to the opposite slope, where the wind and rain pummeled their backs— "would you pitch your tents here, in the lee of the hill?"

The lee side of Caer-Badonicus still suffered the effects of wind and rain, but the storm did not rattle so fiercely through the scrub here, nor did the rain fall with such brutal, wind-flung force. Myrddin spoke above the howl of the wind at their backs. "With this kind of weather to contend with—and it shows no sign of clearing up—the Saxons will have to cope with the same conditions we're fighting right now. They'll throw up a ring of men all the way around Caer-Badonicus, don't mistake that, but for any lengthy siege, even a day or two's worth of attacks, they'll want the bulk of their army out of the wind, particularly their sleeping tents. And that slope is the only place they can get it." He pointed downward. "So we prepare a little surprise for them."

Cadorius shot him a startled look. "With the cisterns between the walls?"

Myrddin chuckled. "Indeed. I'll draw up detailed plans to work from tonight. Work can begin at dawn, with more men being added to the effort as they arrive from the other kingdoms."

"I almost pity the Saxons," Cadorius grinned. "Wherever did you come up with such a notion?"

Emrys Myrddin laughed, clapping him across the shoulder. "After you next visit Constantinople, come and ask me again. Now, let's get down off this godforsaken summit, get some hot food into our bellies, and get to work."

Lailoken discovered very quickly that the North Channel is a nightmare to sail across when October's gales sweep in off the North Atlantic with the scream of storm wind in the rigging. The sickening roll and pitch of the ship's hull twisting clear of the wave crests, only to smash down into the black-water troughs, leprous with grey foam, left Lailoken groaning in acute misery. Stinging white spray blasted his face every few moments. Lailoken's entire experience of boats totaled perhaps five or six rides on the occasional flat-bottomed scow of a river ferry, poled across a long, low, relatively shallow stretch of water under civil if not quite genteel conditions. The sailors manning the fishing sloop held very little sympathy for a man whose chief interest was lying in his hammock and wishing the world would hold still long enough for him to quietly die without throwing up his guts one last time.

The bad weather held for two solid days, all the way up the coast past the Mull of Kintyre, the longest peninsula in Scotland. It dogged their heels past Islay Island, where they turned inland to parallel the long Kintyre coast. Irish ships, at least, were nowhere in evidence, their captains and crews doubtless too intelligent to set sail in weather so rough. The way Lailoken felt, he would almost have welcomed the thrust of an honest Irish sword through his gut—at least it would end this Godforsaken, spinning nausea that turned his whole existence unbearable.

Banning was none too pleased about Lailoken's seasickness either, and his guest's scathing, angry disgust added to his utter misery. They lurched and rolled past Jora Island, that long, low strip of land lying opposite the great Irish fort of Dunadd, where the *Scotti* kings had crowned themselves lords over all the sub-kings of the Irish clans pouring into Dalriada.

Across the heaving, pitching deck of the fishing sloop, Morgana's nephew Medraut stood with wide-braced legs, eagerly watching the coastline slip past as they approached the harbor below Fortress Dunadd. Medraut, disgustingly, had not spent even five minutes seasick, to the hearty approval of the fishermen— who had been well paid with Morgana's gold to run the risk of sailing into Irish waters during bad weather.

"Speak you any Gael?" the captain asked, threading his way across the cluttered deck to Medraut's side.

The boy glanced around. "Nay, not a word, I'm afraid. I've been wondering since we left Galwyddel last night how I'm to communicate with them."

The captain grinned. "The very act of sailing into Dunadd Harbor is communication of a bold sort, lad. They'll respect you, if nothing else."

Aye, Lailoken thought uncharitably, *they'll respect us all the way to the gallows. Or do the Irish lop off heads with an axe?* Lailoken had very few words of Gael and when he'd asked Banning shortly after setting foot on the trawler, his guest had responded with outrage. *Irish Gael? That barbaric tongue? I would sooner have my tongue ripped out and nailed to a wall than ever speak Irish Gael!*

Lailoken hoped very fervently, indeed, that the Irish didn't grant Banning his wish.

The sail rattled and shook as the tillerman turned them inland toward the harbor entrance. The boat rolled broadside on to the heavy seas and Lailoken swallowed hard, managing to stuff the nausea back down before thoroughly humiliating himself again. He clutched the edges of the hammock—which the sailors had rigged so he wouldn't, at least, fall overboard while ill—and literally held on during the long, miserable stretch of time it took to round the headland and reach calmer, protected water.

The coastline here was rugged, with a slope of rocky beach above which rose an outcropping of rock. It was there the Irish had built an immense stone fortress, with a commanding view of the harbor and the sea beyond it. The town which huddled at the fortress' feet was a substantial settlement, housing several thousand people, at least, with smoke curling black as peat from the chimneys of low, solidly built cottages. Thatched roofs rustled in the wind, held down with nets of rope weighted in place with heavy rocks at the end of every single strand of rope netting. The heavy grey stones hung down nearly to the ground along the cottage walls, one for every twelve inches or so of roofline, swaying in the storm winds like beads on a rosary. It was a technique the Britons would do well to copy, Lailoken had to admit, earning a derisive snort from Banning.

By the time the fishing boat had crossed Dunadd Harbor, Lailoken managed to drag himself out of the hammock and reach the boat's rail, tottering but on his feet. Medraut glanced briefly his way, then turned his attention back to the shore, where a group of men had begun to gather, fisherfolk, from the look of them, curious about the foolhardy sailors out in the storm. Certainly they weren't armed soldiers, although movement on the road from the fortress suggested that someone had noticed theirs was not an Irish boat and was taking steps to determine just what the boat was and what its crew wanted. Lailoken was still too seasick to be overly alarmed and Medraut merely seemed excited by the whole grand adventure.

They dropped anchor where the water shoaled and when the sail came rattling down, wet and heavy and ponderous as a sow's belly, the sailors threw a rope ladder across the gunwale, down which Medraut skinned, landing in hip-deep water and holding the bottom of the ladder for Lailoken. He swallowed back nausea, muttered to the captain, "Send someone ashore with the gifts, eh?" and limbered himself awkwardly over the side. The seawater was cold, soaking him to the skin as he waded grimly for shore.

"You'd think they'd build a pier, at least," he growled under his breath, prompting a nervous chuckle from Medraut.

The knot of fishermen on the beach had grown to a lively crowd of curious men and boys. A few women had put in an appearance as well, but stayed back from the water's edge, watching from a safe distance. A babble of voices speaking incomprehensible Irish Gaelic deepened Lailoken's uneasiness, but no one had drawn weapons, which was a mercy, particularly since they'd been recognized for what they were. Several voices sent the word racing outward through the crowd: *Britons!*

A moment later, the crowd parted for new arrivals from the hill fort above the harbor. The newcomers were armed with long swords and shorter, wicked belt knives, but for the moment the blades remained sheathed, their owners more curious than threatened by a handful of Britons very far, indeed, from their home waters. The man in the lead, a stocky fellow with the characteristic blue-black hair and ice-blue eyes of the dark variety of Irishman, looked them up and down, then spat out a question in language that left Lailoken's tongue aching, just hearing it spoken.

Lailoken, as the designated messenger, spread his hands in a gesture of incomprehension and said very slowly and clearly, "We speak no Gael. Have you anyone that speaks Brythonic?"

The man frowned, rubbed his heavy black beard thoughtfully for a moment, then turned to a lad at his elbow and issued some sort of instructions that sounded like a cat swallowing its tongue. The boy raced across the beach, pelting up the road toward the fortress. While they waited, everyone on edge and uncertain what would happen next, one of the women came down to the water's edge, handing them thick, dry cloaks to wrap around their sodden clothing. Medraut flashed her a smile of intense, crimson-cheeked thanks, which prompted giggles among the younger girls watching from behind their mothers' skirts.

"They're more like us than I'd ever believed possible," Medraut said in quiet astonishment. "I'd not expected them to make such an offer." The loan was deeply generous and very welcome, as the wind whipping across the harbor drew a foul bit of shivering from both of them.

"Aye," Lailoken was getting his stomach back under some reasonable semblance of control again, "it's rare that an offer to trade goes sour at the beginning. It's what you're offered for your goods—and what you think of their offer—that causes war to break out in little sheltered bays like this one. Pride is a fine thing, so long as it doesn't plunge a man into trouble by the refusal to bend his head. A trader's job is never an easy one."

"Nor a matchmaker's."

"Hah!" Lailoken wiped his mouth with the back of one hand and wished mightily for that drinking skin he'd sampled just before coming aboard. "That's the bloody truth."

Another delegation was descending from the hill fort, headed by a woman this time, who was surrounded by a group of older women and a few men with white in their beards. The younger woman's eyes were a soft blue-green shade, like deep waters of a steepy loch in summer's haze, eyes that were violently alive and intelligent. Her copper-flame hair, caught back in one long plait and held neatly in place by a tubular hair net that glinted with threads of gold, hung down her back like a thick and immensely expensive jeweled serpent from some pagan god's pleasure garden. As she approached, several of the fisherfolk whispered, *"Riona the Damhnait!"* passing the astonishment back amongst themselves.

Lailoken stared, having picked up just enough Gael at waterfront *tavernas* to comprehend that much of the conversation out of the general babble of speculating voices. *Riona the Bard? The king's own councillor?*

Lailoken studied her intently as she approached, wondering whether the king's own councillor might be a good omen, or a sign of trouble. She halted before them and saluted them with a gesture of greeting, which Lailoken and Medraut gave back again, taking care to mimic the formal flourish.

"You are Britons, I see," she said, studying them with long and slow curiosity.

Her Brythonic was not, perhaps, astonishing in its quality, for her command of the language was obviously strained. But it was astonishing, nonetheless, that she spoke it at all. "I am Riona the *Damhnait*, Druidess to King Dallan mac Dalriada, the *Scotti*, and tutor for Keelin, Dallan mac Dalriada's daughter and heiress, who will one day be queen of the Scots. Why have you come into Dunadd Harbor? Do you seek shelter from yon storm?" She lifted a graceful hand to indicate the low-scudding rainclouds and the squall line even now pouring its way across the long reach of the harbor. The wind picked up as she spoke, rattling sails and flapping cloaks and long-skirted gowns against their owners' knees.

"Aye," Lailoken nodded, "but there are more storms than those which fly above men's heads on the wind and more ways than one of meeting them."

"Speak your meaning, then, and plainly, for I do not know your tongue well enough to translate niceties of phrase."

Medraut, foolishly in Lailoken's opinion, blurted out, "Where did you learn Brythonic so well?"

She measured him with a glance that seemed to find him well-intentioned, if not overly tactful or bright. She favored him with a slight smile. "Britons have visited Irish towns and royal courts a time or two, lengthy visits, for the most part, and often ending unhappily for at least one of the parties involved. It pleased me to learn their language, for one never knows when knowledge of an enemy may help create a friend in time of critical need."

Medraut brightened, since that was precisely what his aunt was hoping to accomplish with Irish alliance, even as Lailoken's stomached knotted painfully.

Slaves . . . Poor British bastards taken off their fishing sloops, dragged from coastal villages and put to work in Irish fields, in Irish workshops as millers and coopers and smiths, all the trades it was cheaper to steal a slave to perform than to pay wages to a craftmaster to produce the same work.

"So," she smiled to remove the worst of the threat from her reminder that they were on very shaky ground, indeed, "what brings you to Dunadd?"

He cleared his throat, summoning his best official voice. "I, Lailoken the Minstrel, bard to the Queen and King of Rheged, bard to the Queen of Galwyddel and Ynys Manaw, come bearing a private message for the King of Dalriada." He produced Morgana's signet. "I bear the seal of Galwyddel and Ynys Manaw, given me from the hand of Queen Morgana herself, whose sons will rule Ynys Manaw and Gododdin and whose nephew will soon, if things work out as may be hoped, rule Galwyddel." He turned to the boy and introduced him. "Medraut, nephew of Morgana, Queen of Ynys Manaw, Queen of Galwyddel, who has come to Dalriada seeking alliance."

Despite what must have been excellent training in political affairs, Riona's brows rose in astonishment. "Alliance?" she repeated blankly. "What sort of alliance?"

"Ah," Lailoken smiled, "that is for the king of Dalriada to hear. I am certain he would be pleased to have you translate our generous offer. We bring gifts, as well." He gestured to the fishing sloop. "With permission, they can be brought ashore."

Riona turned to her companions, clearly the Irish equivalent of the Britons' councils of advisors, and spoke rapidly, voice low to prevent it carrying to the curious crowd. A ripple of surprise washed across their faces, then they answered in brief. Riona turned back to Lailoken and Medraut. "We would be pleased to see your gifts and hear your message."

Lailoken turned to call across the water, "Captain, have your men bring the gifts ashore! And our baggage as well, I think?" A swift glance at Riona gave him the hoped-for nod of welcome, since the storm showed no sign of letting up and night was not many minutes away.

A few moments later, several dripping sailors had wrestled ashore a heavy chest, a hogshead of fine wine imported from Rome, a variety of misshapen leather bags containing Medraut's personal effects and gifts for his prospective bride, and a heavy trunk that was Lailoken's personal baggage, in which several bottles of death were layered beneath clothing and a generous amount of ordinary hay, to keep the bottles from shifting or breaking in the rough seas. Banning smiled secretly as the sailors staggered across the beach with their fine gifts, following Riona Damhnait and her retinue across the stony beach and up the access road to Fortress Dunadd.

The fortification had been solidly built, with respectably thick stone walls, although it was nothing compared to the fine Roman forts like Caerleul—doubtless, Banning supposed, the reason the *Scotti* would never manage to invade further south than Hadrian's Wall. The interior was gloomy, damp, and cold, the walls hung with furs and the floors strewn with rushes cut from the coastal marshlands. Light filtered in from narrow, archer-slit windows and flickered from torches set into brackets, long tapers of wood wrapped with more of the marsh-cut rushes, soaked in oil to burn longer.

The place smelled of cold, damp stone, marsh grass, and rancid fat. An immense hearth along one wall sent heat pouring into one end of the room, supplied by what must have been half a tree blazing cheerfully away. It was near this hearth that a large chair had been placed, hewn from stone and lined with cushions and furs. Beneath the occupant's feet was a curiously carved flagstone in which Lailoken made out the hollowed-out shape of a human footprint.

Ah, he smiled to himself, having been told by Banning—who had, as a young man, visited the ruins of Fortress Dunadd—what he would find beneath the king of Dalriada's foot. *The Stone of Destiny, as you called it.* The king was gazing at them in considerable curiosity, understandable given their bedraggled, sea-soaked appearance and the sailors at their heels, sweating under their burdens.

Riona Damhnait gave the king a small bow and began to speak. Lailoken composed himself to recall Morgana's offer word for word. King Dallan mac Dalriada, the *Scotti*, listened in attentive silence. Medraut's attention wandered between King Dallan and the girl who stood a little way behind the throne. It was clear that she was Dallan mac Dalriada's daughter, for the likeness was striking—and so was she.

Perhaps sixteen, with an air of innocence about her, oddly paired with an expression in her eyes that spoke of steely strength of will, she was a slender and comely girl, her hair falling in long, chestnut ringlets and waves, most of it caught back in the same kind of jeweled netting Riona Damhnait wore; the ends of the girl's hair swept her knees, while her skin was a fine, clear shade of cream with the faintest blush of roses beneath the surface. Her eyes sparkled like sun-struck water. Medraut couldn't stop staring at her, utterly entranced. Even Lailoken felt the magnetic pull of her beauty.

The king made his answer and Riona turned back to Lailoken and Medraut.

"King Dallan mac Dalriada, the *Scotti,* would hear the message you bear from Queen Morgana of Galwyddel and Ynys Manaw."

Formalities thus successfully launched, Lailoken began his rendition of Morgana's message. "From Queen Morgana to her brother king of Dalriada," he began as Riona's eyes widened over that startling, opening phrase, "I send offers of alliance, of mutually beneficial trade, of protection from common enemies, of joining our two peoples as one through an alliance of marriage between the heiress of Dalriada and the heir of Galwyddel, my nephew Medraut, son of Marguase, Princess of Galwyddel, now deceased. Galwyddel is my sovereign right to rule or to give to an heir of my choice. I have two sons by Lot Luwddoc of Gododdin, who will inherit Gododdin and Ynys Manaw. Medraut, who has been more son than nephew, I will give Galwyddel to rule as sovereign king, should the treaty of alliance be fairly met by both our councils and serve both kingdoms as greatly as I believe it will."

"This is a custom amongst Britons? To hand kingdoms to whomever they please?" Riona asked, interjecting the question before he could finish reciting the message. It was, he supposed, a fair question to have answered, but he disliked losing the rhythm, once well begun on a recitation. He was a fair minstrel, with his gift of comic bawdiness, but he was not in the same league as this Irish Druidess Riona Damhnait or the greatest Briton Druid ever to live, Artorius' own Emrys Myrddin. He needed all the assistance he could muster, dealing with alliances at this level, and fervently hoped his knees were not shaking.

He cleared his throat, looking longingly at a wine flask, so that the girl behind her father's throne spoke to a servant. Wine was poured and carried to them

on a carved wooden platter, rough stuff in ordinary clay
cups, but it served wonderfully well for all its metallic burr on the tongue, to wet his throat and warm
his quaking innards.

"Aye, it's a grand custom that, keeps the peace in
families with proud sons and nephews and daughters
looking to be battle queens in their own right, as is
Morgana of Galwyddel and Ynys Manaw."

"You do not name her queen of Gododdin, yet her
sons will rule there." Riona waited patiently for the
explanation. Medraut started to answer, flushed, and
glanced at Lailoken, the properly designated spokesman. He gestured at the lad to continue, for the
alliance would sink or swim on how Medraut disported
himself in this hall, not on any eloquence Lailoken
might muster. If the king's daughter found him repul-
sive, if the king found him a doltish colt with no hope
of ruling much of anything save a household of ill-
mannered brats, nothing that Lailoken said would alter
the reality—or King Dallan's decision. They'd best
know straightaway what sort of lad they would be
marrying their heiress to, the sooner the better.

Medraut, catching at least some of Lailoken's train
of thought in his rapidly shifting expression, nodded
and took a moment to compose himself.

"I, Medraut, nephew to Queen Morgana of Galwyddel and Ynys Manaw, will explain, if it is permitted?"
The boy's voice only quavered on a couple of the
words. It was a gallant effort, one not lost on Dallan
mac Dalriada's daughter, who smiled and blushed
prettily in understanding, a smile so radiant Medraut
blossomed under her approving regard. He bowed to
her father and then to her, then launched into his
portion of the explanation.

"My aunt is sovereign queen of two Briton lands,
Ynys Manaw from her father Gorlois and Galwyddel

from her mother. Her sister Morguase was my mother. When she died, Aunt Morgana raised me with gentle and loving concern for my education and my place in the royal affairs of my family. Morgana married the king of Gododdin and bore him two fine sons, my cousins Gwalchmai and Walgabedius. Gwalchmai is but six years of age and Walgabedius younger still.

"This is critical, for their father, Lot Luwddoc of Gododdin, was killed not yet a fortnight ago fighting Pictish raiders at the northern border with Fortriu. Gwalchmai and Walgabedius are too young to rule the kingdoms they have inherited. Lot Luwddoc's brother Ancelotis has been named king by Gododdin's council until Gwalchmai is of age to rule in his own right. The throne was offered to Morgana, as his widow and mother of his heirs, but she has strong responsibilities in Ynys Manaw and Galwyddel and these are uncertain times. So she has left her sons' inheritance in excellent and capable hands and has turned her attention to her borders on the western coast of Britain."

Riona nodded. "Where Dalriadan Irish have invaded through Galwyddel, albeit striking immediately north." She smiled to acknowledge the high price Irish fighting men had been made to pay at the hands of Briton military strength along that particular border. "I am told the Irish traders sailing the waters between fair Eireland and Dalriada are not above piracy. And the Picts are barbaric trouble for us all."

Medraut bowed. "You grasp our situation well."

Too well, perhaps, given the speculative look in her eyes. Lailoken hastened to interject his own spin on the situation and take the conversation back to Morgana's official offer. "It has occurred to Morgana that catching the Picts between two allied forces would help put an end to this particular blue-tattooed irritant. But there is much more to this offer of alliance, much that is of very great importance to both our peoples, of Britain and of Dalriada—and even of great importance to Eire, as well."

Riona translated all of this to King Dallan, who gazed at them for a long moment through narrowed eyes, then gestured for them to continue the tale they were spinning.

Here it goes, Lailoken took a deep breath, *the most important bloody speech of your life . . .* Then he launched once more into Morgana's message.

"You have perhaps heard that the Germanic barbarians of Saxony and Jutland are leaving the continent by the shipload, intent on carving out kingdoms for themselves? Younger sons who have no hope of inheriting a throne, not with the Germanic people's right of firstborn sons to inherit title, throne, land, and the wealth their peasants hand over to the king's keeping. Where, then, do younger sons look for wealth and land and throne? To others' borders.

"Britain's shores are both close and wealthy. With the Romans gone, they believed the Britons to be an easy conquest. Our war leader, Artorius the Dux Bellorum, has proven to them that Briton wolves still have fangs. We have kept them bottled up in the far southeastern corner of our large island. Morgana sees with very clear eyes where the Saxons of Sussex and Wessex will turn for easier plunder, when we next defeat them in war—and that war looms large on our horizon, a matter of only weeks, perhaps.

"When the Saxons are driven back—and we *will* drive them back, never mistake that outcome—where will these self-anointed Saxon kinglets turn their sword blades? To Eire, King Dallan mac Dalriada, to Eire and her young but already wealthy colony of Dalriada. Morgana would not have war between the Saxons and the Dalriadan Irish with her borders so dangerously close to the war zone, not when alliance between us now can stop such disasters before they have a chance to befall us.

"Why should Morgana send these enemies of Galwyddel north to make war on a people who are, after all, as Celtic as we Britons, sharing in common many things, while the Saxons are alien in their ways, Germanic and barbaric? When their bid to force entrance into Rheged's high council failed, Prince Cutha of Sussex left the royal villa in a state of rage and burned the farmholds and villages for a terrible swath of miles, butchering every man, woman, and infant in his path. To have seen little children"—he glanced at a girl of perhaps five seated cross-legged near the princess' feet—"literally cut into pieces and flung about the kitchen yard like so much spoiled meat for the hogs . . ."

He shuddered, quite convincingly. "When we Britons drive these bastards into the sea, they will come at Irish coasts, butcher Irish girls and lads barely old enough to toddle across a floor. This, too, Queen Morgana refuses to allow. Should Britain sit back on its laurels and do nothing when Saxons rip apart the Irish coastal villages and farmholds? Should Britain do nothing at all when Saxons strike Dalriada, stirring up so much trouble with the Picts that Irish men-at-arms will find themselves struggling to survive on two fronts, against Saxons and Pictish insurrection?

"Alliance will give Galwyddel and Dalriada strong partners to keep the Saxons out of northern Britain and *Scotti*-land. Alliance will give Dalriada access to much more than mutual protection from this new enemy. We have brought gifts, tokens of the trade Dalriada may secure for herself with the far-flung lands of the Roman Empire. British crews can teach Irish

captains the trading routes and the languages in which
to do the bargaining. Here," he had one of the sailors
open the heavy chest, "are tokens of what treasures
may be found in the ports British ships enter every
year."

He took out a section of elephant tusk, raw ivory
cut from an African beast's jaws, and several items
fashioned from another length of that same tusk:
delicately carved bracelets and boxes with pierced-work
patterns in Celtic scrollwork design, combs for a lady's
hair, amber from the far north, raw pieces and a
necklace of matched amber beads wrapped round with
gold wire. Black sable furs caught and cured by trap-
pers deep in the land that Banning said would one day
be called Russia, the rich pelts sewn into supple,
beautiful cloaks and muffs to warm the hands, with
sable hoods lined in ermine, the stark white trim off-
setting the black beautifully.

Deeper in the chest, he lifted out a ladies' gown
in a delicate, porcelain-thin shade of lavender and
ornamented with Celtic embroidery, with tiny freshwater seed pearls sewn to the embroidered bodice.
Well worthy of adorning the wealthiest of queens, the
gown had been commissioned by Ganhumara, the
seamstress had explained, but it had ended up in
Morgana's basket, with the donation of a very heavy
purse and the suggestion that Ganhumara be told the
gown had been ruined during the sewing.

When Medraut's new Irish queen appeared wearing it, there would be trouble, all right, trouble that
Morgana, at least, seemed quite able to take in stride.
If Lailoken had read the situation correctly, the pur-
loined gown was Morgana's way of saying, "Interfere
in my nephew's life and my business again and I shall
gladly see you ruined, as easily I plucked this bauble
out of your grasp."

Lailoken thought the joke enormously funny.

So did Banning.

The princess, forgetting the formal protocols of court business, came around her father's throne like a bow shot, exclaiming over the gown, its iridescent sheen of color, its texture and the soft, sensual feel of the silk under her fingers. "What *is* it?" she asked in an awed voice, her Brythonic as fluent as Riona's. "I have never seen its like!"

The other women had gathered to feel the softness and exclaim over it.

Medraut rose gallantly to the occasion. "It is called silk. The people of a country far, far to the east spin it, they say, from the cocoons of special caterpillars. We traded for the silk from Constantinople, which trades with lands as far as can be imagined. The master seamstress of Caerleul, who sews the gowns for Queen Thaney of Rheged and Queen Ganhumara of Caer-Guendoleu, turns raw silk into artwork for the finest ladies to wear."

The girl was enchanted with the gown, holding it up to herself and swirling about to see how it moved, eyes sparkling like liquid sunlight at the result. The pale lavender hue had been a fortuitous choice, complementing the girl's coloring divinely. And Ganhumara and the Irish heiress were of close enough size that the gown should fit strikingly well. Even her father unbent enough to smile a little at her open delight. Lailoken decided the moment was auspicious to complete Morgana's message.

"These gifts are yours, whatever you decide in the matter of alliance, but Queen Morgana hopes they will serve as a token of the bride fortune Galwyddel offers for the Dalriadan heiress' marriage to Medraut. Queen Morgana has proposed that she meet the King of Dalriada and his lovely daughter in person, along the shore of Galwyddel, at the standing stone circle of Lochmaben, on the next full moon night. The king is invited to bring his councillors and armed retainers, if that is his pleasure, but for her part, Queen Morgana has faith in the open-handed offer she has made and will wait at the Lochmaben Stones without resorting to armed escort at her back.

"She trusts, as well, that you will understand any mischief which might befall her would be repaid by her brother, Artorius, the Dux Bellorum of all the Britons, who has led British armies to victory in eleven battles against the Saxons. This is the double message she sends, offerings of gentle alliance, backed with the might of Briton military strength, a strength which can assist allies as readily as it can threaten enemies. Thus speaks Queen Morgana of Galwyddel and Ynys Manaw, to her brother king of Dalriada and his lovely heiress."

He gave them a formal bow, then waited.

Riona Damhnait translated the long speech, speaking with great care to choose the correct nuances of meaning, that much was obvious in both her expression and the lovely princess', as well, since she, too, had understood every word Lailoken had uttered. He wondered briefly why the girl had learned Brythonic, but her father had not. Ah, well, who could explain the oddities of Irish custom?

King Dallan mac Dalriada listened with hooded eyes, although the occasional quirk of brow or lips betrayed surprise. When the translation ended, he glanced curiously at Medraut and Lailoken, then gave a lengthy response. Riona Damhnait gave them both a smile and said, "King Dallan will consider very carefully your offer of alliance and thanks you for the honor to his royal house and to his heiress. He offers his hospitality in return for the duration of this storm and suggests that you must be cold and miserable in your wet clothing. Servants will take you to guest quarters, where you may change into warm and dry garments and unpack your things from your wet baggage.

"King Dallan will order a great feast tonight, to honor your presence and your generous offer. The sailors will be shown every courtesy, as well, in the servants' quarters, with dry clothing, a warm fire, and plenty to eat. If the others from the ship wish to warm themselves, as well, they are welcome at the fortress or at any cottage in the village." Her lips quirked briefly. "King Dallan understands that yon captain may be wary of leaving his boat unmanned in an Irish harbor, reluctant to place his entire crew in reach of Irish prisons, so he offers a trade in hostages, if that would please your captain?"

She gestured to the young girl sitting at the princess' feet. "Princess Keelin's little cousin, Fineena, is much beloved by King Dallan, and would enjoy, I think, a chance to see a Briton boat, for she loves the sea already and delights in the little boat she and Keelin keep at the harbor."

The beautiful Keelin's eyes widened in alarm, but she made no sound, clearly not wishing to frighten her cousin with a display of her own fear. It was an effective offer, the safety of the child for the safety of the crew. Lailoken bowed. "I am sure the captain would be delighted to show Princess Fineena his beautiful fishing sloop. After all, should this alliance be cemented in marriage, the child would be welcome on any boat in British waters, at her disposal to visit her cousin in Galwyddel's lovely capital."

Keelin relaxed a trifle, darting glances at Medraut, who was smiling down at the little girl in a friendly fashion. Fineena, aware of the sudden interest in her, toddled to her feet and slipped her hand into Keelin's, clutching a little doll to her chest with the other. She glanced up at her cousin, who murmured reassuringly in Gael, evidently translating the offer, since Fineena brightened at once and replied in a clear little voice, obviously excited. The child, all innocence, had no inkling of her abrupt new status as hostage. Lailoken sent the child a smile, as well, but the smile behind his eyes was for the image of little Fineena lying in a puddle of blood, a gift to repay the Dalriadans for Lailoken's own little girl, butchered by Irish bastards off a Dalriadan ship.

He was still smiling as servants escorted them out of the grand hall.

Chapter Thirteen

Trevor Stirling and King Ancelotis were exhausted by the time Caerleul's great sandstone walls appeared on the road in front of them. Both guest and host looked forward to a long, hot soak in the Roman baths, a good hot meal, and undisturbed sleep in a soft bed. But the moment they entered the town, they discovered something badly amiss. The townspeople were frightened, deeply agitated, and sent unreadable looks after them.

I mislike this, Ancelotis muttered silently to his guest.

Bloody right, Stirling agreed, deeply uneasy over the mood of these people.

The moment they approached the royal villa, Queen Thaney rushed out to greet them.

"Ancelotis!" she cried, flinging herself into her uncle's arms. "Oh, thank God you've come!"

"What is it?" Ancelotis asked urgently, drying tears

that had begun to spill down her cheeks. "Meirchion isn't . . ." he began, sudden dread striking him.

"No, no, it isn't that, it's Artorius!"

Ancelotis went deadly still. "What news of Artorius?"

"Come inside, please, I don't wish the whole town to hear."

Dreading what he would hear, Ancelotis followed his niece into the royal villa, to a private little room off the atrium and closed the door. She stilled shaking hands against her skirts and said, "He's gone. Rode out of Caerleul in the worst rage I have ever seen come over him. Didn't even take the *cataphracti* with him."

"But—" Ancelotis protested, then shut up at the look in his niece's eyes. "Tell me the rest."

"It isn't Ganhumara, I know that much. She was as mystified as Meirchion and I when he went tearing out of the city. She's gone home to Caer-Guendoleu to raise troops for Caer-Badonicus. I . . ." She bit her lip, hesitating, then plunged on. "I asked the servants to tell me anything that might explain what had happened, and one of the serving women said a minstrel had been seen giving him a letter. When I questioned the minstrel, he said he didn't know what was in the letter, only that Covianna Nim had charged him to hold it until the next full moon, then deliver it to Artorius, which he did.

"He said Artorius went white as ice when he read it, then strode away shouting for his horse. The minstrel left Caerleul immediately after, riding south. I am sure he's taking some horrid message to Covianna Nim; I can't prove it, but I *know* it, I feel it here." She touched her heart.

"Which direction did Artorius ride?" Ancelotis asked quietly, already dreading the answer.

"Toward Caer-Birrenswark," Thaney whispered.

"Ancelotis, Covianna Nim hates Morgana! I've seen it in her eyes when she thought no one was watching her. I don't know what she's told Artorius with her dirty little letter, but I don't trust that witch from Glastenning Tor, I never have. Artorius trusts you, Uncle, can't you ride after him and *do* something? I owe Morgana my life! I can't—*won't*—believe evil or treachery of her!" Tears were rolling down her cheeks and her shoulders shook with suppressed sobs.

Ancelotis gathered his niece into his arms and let her weep against his shoulder, stroking her hair soothingly. His mind, however, was racing, and so was Stirling's. What could Morgana possibly have done, to upset Artorius so greatly? At the High Council of Kings, she had spoken strongly in favor of alliance with the Irish at Dalriada, as a way to buy time and secure at least one border while Briton forces raced south to meet the Saxon threat. It was entirely possible that Morgana, strong-willed and shrewd as she was, could have engineered an alliance on her own, without informing Artorius.

And if Brenna McEgan were involved, if she were, in fact, a guest in Morgana's mind, an alliance with the Irish would be the first thing she considered, possibly talking Morgana into it with glib Irish persuasion. Certainly, it would be the simplest way to open the northern border to Irish armies the moment Artorius went south with the combined military strength of the northern kingdoms. It was a perfect opportunity for an IRA terrorist to smash the British kingdoms and change history in favor of the Irish. Where his potential ally, Banning, might be, Stirling had not an inkling, but he was very much afraid he'd just located Brenna McEgan. How, he wondered, would Morgana arrange such an alliance? What could she offer that would interest Dalriada?

"Where," Ancelotis asked abruptly, "is Medraut?"

Thaney looked up, startled. "Medraut? Why, he's with Morgana, of course. They rode together for Caer-Birrenswark."

"Alone?"

"No, they rode with armed retainers, of course. Her sons rode with her, but I heard her telling their guards that she would turn west for Caer-Birrenswark while her sons would ride north and turn east for Trapain Law and home." She frowned slightly. "And one of the minstrels went with her. Lailoken, I think he's called. Spent a lot of money buying jewelry and gowns and wine and pack animals to carry them."

If Morgana were sending her sons home to Trapain Law, chances were good she was up to something she didn't want the children embroiled in, which deepened the cold in his belly. It was just possible he'd found Banning, as well. Lailoken had been in the environs of Caer-Iudeu, after all, and so was a good candidate for hosting someone's mind, and he couldn't think of any other reason a simple minstrel would buy up a lot of trade goods with money he hadn't possessed two weeks previously. He must be involved, somehow, in Morgana's plan to arrange an Irish alliance. If Banning were a guest in Lailoken's mind, he might be well placed to foil McEgan's schemes. Stirling couldn't bank on it, however. There was only one response possible. Ride after them and do whatever was necessary to stop McEgan from changing history.

It was a measure of how greatly he had changed, these past few days, that the thought of harming Morgana sickened him, and the desire to protect her, to protect Artorius, to keep these people from being destroyed by Saxons or Irish or even by one another, burned fiercely in his heart. He had found more to admire and respect in the sixth century than he had in the twenty-first, which he was sworn to protect. His duty was to king and country. The trouble was, he was no longer entirely sure *which* king commanded his loyalty.

Or which country.

He had not yet found an answer to that dilemma when he mounted his horse again and headed grimly north, to try and stop disaster.

The storm lasted a full week, howling across the distant shores of Jora Island to smash into Fortress Dunadd, perched stolidly above its grey-water harbor. It was a merry week, considering. King Dallan was a congenial host, delighted by the gift of fine Roman wine and eager to show his own kingdom's wealth to best advantage. Princess Keelin was a vision in the lavender silk gown, distracting everything male within viewing distance of her. She and Medraut spent carefully chaperoned afternoons playing silly games and talking of everything from inconsequentials to privately held dreams for the future.

Lailoken watched and listened, nodded and smiled to himself, assigned the role of male chaperone, just as Riona Damhnait had been given the role of female chaperone: part companion, part tutor, part servant. Only in Riona's case, the servant was a royal Druid and a very shrewd judge of character. Lailoken was exceedingly careful in her presence, lest he betray his own and Banning's seething hatred of everything Irish.

The young potential couple, aided by Keelin's grasp of the Brythonic language, got on famously, boding well for the future of the alliance. At least, it would have if alliance had also been on Lailoken's agenda. He made it a point to become friendly with the soldiers who patrolled the fortress walls and village streets at night, playing his harp and flute and plying them with good Roman wine and more ordinary Celtic mead and ale, which solved many a problem of translation—alcohol, music, and laughter being universals of human expression. He got to know the soldiers well and, more importantly, got to know the timing of their rounds, down to the minute. He located the wells which supplied the fortress and the town, noted their positions and when the patrols of the soldiers took them close to those wells and when they didn't.

And every night, Lailoken broke open one of his foul bottles, mouth and nose carefully masked, hands carefully gloved, and poured a bit of the filth from it over a bit of fish or boiled beef, which he gave to one of the many dogs that roamed the fortress and the town, always a different dog, to be certain that he wasn't witnessing the effects of cumulative poisoning, but rather the effects of accumulating potency. It took the full week they spent in Dunadd before he got the results he had been waiting so patiently to witness. A brindle bitch he had singled out some twelve hours previously died near noon their seventh day in the town, vomiting, wracked with convulsions, and progressively paralyzed.

The moment he noticed the animal's illness, he made his apologies to Medraut, hinted that he wished to spend a bit of time with an Irish lass he'd met, and slipped away into the forest that crowded the edge of town, carrying the dog with him. It took the beast several hours to die, in agony. Lailoken watched in rising delight, amazed at the potency of Banning's bottled poison. *'Tis wondrous powerful!* he crowed. Banning chuckled. *Tonight, we'll drop one bottle down each well in town and press Dallan mac Dalriada for his answer. If he and Keelin come with us, grand. They'll return from Lochmaben to a town filled with death. If they decline the offer, I fear our lovely little princess will not have much time to enjoy her silks.*

It was almost a pity to destroy a creature so lovely and innocent.

Almost.

His wife had been just as lovely, and the Irish had gutted her without mercy.

Once the dog had finally died, Lailoken kicked the corpse into a fast-flowing stream, washed his hands in the icy water, and made his way back into town, whistling merrily despite the continuing squalls of rain and wind. As he emerged near the harbor, he caught a glimpse of blue sky far to the west. The storm was breaking up. Better and better. They would leave on the morrow's dawn, whatever answer Dallan mac Dalriada made. He hunted up the captain of the fishing sloop, which still rode proudly at anchor where the water shoaled, and suggested that this would probably be their last night in town, given the break in the weather.

"Aye," the captain nodded, tankard of Irish ale in one hand, a hunk of black Irish bread in the other, "I'd noticed it myself. We'll be ready, come the dawn."

Well pleased, Lailoken made his way up the wind-swept road to the fortress, where he found Medraut fairly dancing with impatience. The boy rushed forward to greet him.

"You've been gone for hours!"

"That I have," Lailoken nodded, winking. "What is it, lad? You're fairly trembling."

"King Dallan has said he will give us his decision tonight! Lailoken, she's lovely! Sweet and intelligent and full of laughter and curiosity."

"Does she like you, lad?"

His eyes shone. "She does. She whispered to me not three hours ago, she'll tell her father so, before the feast tonight. Riona Damhnait supports her in this, I'm sure she does!"

"Well, then, your worries are over, are they not? You're a fine catch for any maiden."

Medraut sighed happily, then exclaimed, "Oh, whatever am I to wear? My best things are wrinkled and musty!" He clapped a hand to his forehead, then plunged away through the fortress gates, hurrying to repair the damage to his wardrobe before appearing in front of the girl's father. Lailoken chuckled aloud, then headed for his own rooms. He had preparations to make as well.

The sun was sinking into the western sea, an immense ball of orange flame balanced on the water, when Lailoken entered the grand hall, where great trestle tables had been set up for the night's feast. As well fed as they'd been on previous nights, this evening's banquet outdid the rest of the week's feasts combined. Lailoken couldn't even put names to most of the dishes offered, with costly sweetmeats vying for space with venison roasts and great haunches of ham from wild boars, roasted ducklings, pastries of mouth-watering variety, and an abundance of ale. So much food, Dallan mac Dalriada must have emptied the fortress larders.

He smiled. The townsfolk wouldn't live long enough to miss the food consumed here tonight. The king's table had been set with shining silver cups and finely carved wooden trenchers. Fresh rushes on the floor added a tang of salt air to the mouth-watering scents rising from the tables. Irish musicians had already begun to play, down in one corner of the hall, since the fortress had no minstrels' gallery—an architectural feature that Banning had halfway expected to find and one that Lailoken had never even heard of, although the notion intrigued him.

Medraut appeared, nervous and resplendent in his finest—and freshly pressed—woolen tunics, plaid trousers, and golden torque of rank, the one given him by Ancelotis to wear while that worthy served as regent king of Gododdin. "Is she here yet?" he asked anxiously, peering through the crowd of Irish nobles which had begun to gather.

"Nay, lad, I've not yet seen her. But then, the king her father isn't here, either, so hold your patience and wait."

He nodded, tugging absently at the hem of his tunic, fidgeting with his belt, fingering the hilt of his sword, worn ceremonially in a silver-inlaid scabbard. He was every inch the wealthy and cultured Briton princeling, about to inherit a kingdom and help himself to a wealthy wife. It amused Lailoken that Medraut had evidently forgotten Ganhumara even existed. Lailoken smiled, toying absently with the strap of the satchel he carried over one shoulder, a satchel carefully filled with ordinary dirt taken from the shore of Galwyddel. Banning had warned him that should the Dalriadan king agree to this alliance, he would be likely to insist upon a certain ceremony for which the Dalriadan kings had become famous. That being so, Lailoken had carefully scooped up the dirt before their departure from Galwyddel's western shore, and carried with it a well-made Briton shoe, to be used at the right moment.

A hush fell across the hall, warning them of Dallan mac Dalriada's appearance. He strolled easily into the room, nodding to the lords and ladies of the nobility, some of whom had evidently journeyed here from other towns, as Lailoken had not seen them before— a sign which boded well for Medraut's hopes and dreams. Somehow, Lailoken could not imagine Dallan summoning the nobility of Dalriada to the fortress, simply to have the Britons imprisoned or enslaved. No, the mood tonight was one of celebration. Medraut's breath caught at the sight of Keelin, strolling with her hand on her father's arm. She wore the silk gown, with her hair netted in jewels, a radiant creature with happiness sparkling in her eyes. She was a girl who saw herself soon to be wed and crowned queen of Galwyddel, or Lailoken was no judge of character.

When the king held up his hand, instantaneous silence fell, even the musicians laying aside their harps and flutes and drums. Dallan mac Dalriada gestured for Medraut and Lailoken to join him at the front of the hall, where he stood with his daughter. Medraut's knees were trembling as they set out, but King Dallan was smiling and Keelin's look of welcome was breathtaking. When they had joined him, bowing slightly to both king and princess, who returned the gesture in kind, Riona Damhnait appeared at Medraut's elbow, to translate as Dallan spoke to the assembly.

"Welcome this night to Dunadd, capital of Dalriada, to join in a celebration of our present joy. You have heard that Britons have come among us, in a gesture of friendship, to offer alliance. We have listened to their offer and considered it most carefully. We are honored by the offer brought to our shores by Prince Medraut, soon to be King of Galwyddel." A buzz ran through the room, since the Dalriadan Irish had learned a very stern lesson about the fighting strength of Galwyddellian Britons. King Dallan mac Dalriada smiled, clearly pleased by that reaction. It was no shabby alliance the Britons offered; Irish fighting men valued the strength of arms in those against whom they had fought and lost. Medraut's offer would give the Irish all of Galwyddel, without another drop of Irish blood spilled. Or so they thought.

"For the past seven-day, we have hosted our Briton guests and have found them courteous, generous, and pleasing in every way. They are, after all, Celts as we are, however different may be our private customs. And they bring word of serious threat to Irish interests, from the shores of Saxony. Even in Dalriada, we have heard the tales of Saxons marauding the eastern and southern shores of our neighbors, the Britons, even harrying our enemies the Picts, to the east of our borders, driving bands of the painted barbarians westward into our farms and forests. The Britons have warned us, very fairly, of Saxon treachery and greedy Saxon eyes looking toward Irish shores and Irish shipping. They think us easy conquest, by comparison to the Britons with their Roman military might and skills at weapons-making."

The buzz that ran through the great hall this time was shocked and angry. It was an excellent tactic, Lailoken nodded approvingly, hitting the Irish nobility with an insult to their honor. Riona's eyes glittered as the Druidess caught his look and agreed with it.

"The Britons, well aware of the dangers these Saxons pose, have offered alliance against our enemies, both Saxon and Pict. With Britons as allies, we can smash the painted peoples and take the whole of the Highlands, not just the Lowlands we have already wrested from them, and with Britons as allies, our brothers and cousins in Eire will certainly join us when we urge them to make our shores inhospitable to the Saxon scourge.

"It is no meager alliance they offer. Prince Medraut is nephew to Queen Morgana of Galwyddel and Ynys Manaw, lands we have never defeated in war, and she is, herself, sister to the Dux Bellorum, as they call their high king, who conducts their battles and trains their warriors. Morgana's brother is a shrewd man, of whom we have heard much since coming to these shores. All the kings of the Britons send soldiers to him and he leads the Britons to victory after victory.

"Should such a man be our enemy, when he and

his sister offer alliance of marriage? They honor us with sending their nephew to us, heir to Galwyddel. I say the time is ripe for bridging the differences with our neighbors to the south. Prince Medraut seeks the hand of Princess Keelin in honorable marriage. I, King Dallan mac Dalriada, the *Scotti*, do formally give my daughter and heiress to Galwyddel's future king, as betrothed bride."

A shout went up, shock and delight and the shrill congratulations of the women. Medraut clasped Dallan's arm in the greeting of equals. Lailoken stepped forward and bowed, saying, "We have heard much of the customs of Dalriada and offer this token of our esteem, in honor of your traditions." He produced the shoe, holding it high for the crowd to see, then carefully poured it full of dirt from the shores of Galwyddel. "If I may be so bold, might it not be fitting to join to this, the earth of Galwyddel, the earth of Dalriada, that you each might set foot upon the commingled lands?"

Another shout went up as Riona translated, although the mere gesture of producing shoe and dirt had signaled exactly what Lailoken intended. Dallan mac Dalriada beamed at them, ordering another shoe to be brought. They carried the shoes of earth to the throne of Dalriada, which sat on the curiously carved flagstone of which Banning had spoken. On it were carvings of a boar, the hollowed-out shape of a human footprint, and lines of Irish ogham script.

Riona and Lailoken handed the earth-filled shoes to Medraut and Keelin, who smiled foolishly at one another, then moved as one to sprinkle dirt into the footprint. First she, then he, placed foot upon the mixed earth, then the king did likewise, joining his daughter's hand with Medraut's. The shout that went up this time rattled the groaning tables, with their load of nuptial feast. It was lovely symbolism, worthy of a bard's saga. Two kingdoms, one land, one people.

Until Artorius found out.

And Lailoken's poison took effect.

He smiled and smiled, and no one but Banning knew why.

The Lochmaben Stones were eerie by moonlight. Only one of the stones still stood in the twenty-first century, a ten-ton giant famous throughout modern Galloway. In the sixth century, the entire circle was still complete, eleven massive standing stones, shadows in a moon-bright ring of light. The storms of the previous week had left Morgana worried, having sent her nephew into double danger, but the weather had cleared and this was the first night of the full moon, full of hope and promise and dread. Would they come this night? Had the Irish butchered the lad and his minstrel companion, who might or might not be the Orange terrorist Banning? Would the Irish land in force on the shore below the standing stones and murder her, as well, or carry her into slavery, or sweep across Galwyddel like a scythe?

Was she an utter fool, to have set this in motion?

She had not come alone to the clearing, having ridden out of Caer-Birrenswark in the late afternoon accompanied by Father Auliffe, abbot of Caer-Birrenswark, and his young assistant, the abbey's most capable scribe, telling them only that an important messenger was to come to Lochmaben this night and she might well need their services, did all go according to plan. She had sent them down to the beach to wait, preferring to be alone with her thoughts and worries. One of the few pleasing thoughts that had come to her during the long afternoon and evening was that the harvest had been safely gotten in before the storms

descended. A few days sooner with the rains, and
Galwyddel would have faced the same disaster striking
the south, with crops rotting in the sodden fields. She
shivered absently and folded her cloak more firmly
about her shoulders, walking the perimeter of the stones
to keep herself warm.

An almost superstitious dread filled her as she moved
among the ancient stones. Older than Rome, they were,
older even than the Britons; they had been standing
here beside the sea when her ancestors had first come
to these shores. A place of power, this light-filled ring,
where echoes of sacred rites eddied across the centuries, vibrating through her bones as she passed each
hulking, ancient monolith. She laid a hand against one
cold surface and snatched it back again as though
burned, almost willing to swear she had felt the cold
dead stone buzzing with eerie power beneath her palm.

Brenna McEgan, jittery and uncertain as well, did
not argue the point.

It *had* felt like the stone was buzzing.

"What was this place used for?" Brenna whispered
aloud, needing to hear a human voice in this deep well
of silence and secure in the knowledge that her whisper would not carry down to the beach, as the wind
was blowing steadily in the other direction.

Morgana's answer was also whispered aloud, for the
queen shared her jitters. "It is said," she murmured,
"that this was a place of worship for the god of youth.
Marriages have been held here since Briton Celts first
came to these shores, centuries before the Romans.
It is also said in my family, all of us Druids in a long,
unbroken line, that kings were made in this circle,
border disputes settled, and queens betrothed, as well."

"Were you betrothed here?" Brenna asked.

A wave of grief ran through Morgana, prompting
Brenna to offer an abject apology.

"Nay, there is no need. In my way, I loved Lot Luwddoc very well, but I am certain of his comfort in the Otherworld. He was a fine father, an excellent king, and an honorable husband. His temper was his greatest failing, but he could be gentle and kind, as well. Yes, I was betrothed to Lot Luwddoc in this circle of standing stones. I was very much younger, then," she added wistfully.

A deeper grief told Brenna that Morgana had borne the king of Gododdin several more children, besides the two sons still living, sons and daughters lost to the fevers and the childhood illnesses that had claimed the lives of as many as half the children born, before the advent of antibiotics and aspirin and other miraculous drugs taken for granted in Brenna's time. Marriage and motherhood had been difficult for Morgana of Galwyddel and Ynys Manaw. Brenna, who had not yet married, grieved with her.

They had lost count of the number of turns they'd walked around the circle when a glint of moonlight on sail caught Morgana's attention. An instant later, the priest shouted up to her, "Queen Morgana! A ship is rounding the headland!" She picked up her skirts and ran toward the shore for a better look. Yes, it was a sail, the familiar sail of a Briton fishing sloop. And there was another ship with it, a low-slung Irish warship, with moonlight glittering on the shroud lines as they rounded the headland and made sail for the Lochmaben shore. Her heart had begun to pound very hard and her palms were wet against the folds of her cloak. *Dear God,* she breathed silently, *they've come, they've really come with him . . .* But did they come in friendship? Or was Medraut a prisoner aboard the fishing sloop, perhaps forced by an Irish crew to lead them to this trysting place?

We'll know soon enough, Brenna retorted prosaically,

even as the priest waiting on the shingle, the elderly abbot who had officiated at Morgana's own betrothal, stared in astonishment. "Queen Morgana, that's an Irish ship! What is the meaning of this?"

"The salvation of Britain, I fervently pray."

The old man's eyes widened and his acolyte's jaw dropped. The abbot sputtered, "You've—you've offered alliance? With the *Irish*?"

She placed a gentle hand on his arm. "Think you there is a better way to guard our western and northern borders in this time of trouble? Yes, I have offered alliance with Dalriada. The alliance of marriage between the royal house of Dalriada and my nephew, to whom I will give Galwyddel. Father Auliffe, alliance now buys us time, precious time to meet the Saxon threat, and ensures that our borders will not be raided by those who are tied to us through the marriage bed. And what better way to send the word of Christ amongst them, than to convert their heiress and send priests north into Dalriada with the holy word of God?"

Abbot Auliffe stared at her a long moment more, then began to laugh, very quietly. "Oh, Morgana, you are ever the shrewd one. Your father would be that proud, he would. What Artorius will say, I shudder to think, but I feel you have the right of it, this time. What better way, indeed? Very well, I will perform the marriage, which is clearly why you asked me here, this night."

She smiled, in a wave of tremendous relief. With the church behind her decision, even Artorius would think twice, protesting it. "Thank you, Father Auliffe. We will have need of your wisdom and the skill of your scribe, for we must also arrange the details of alliance, no small matter."

He patted her shoulder. "I am honored you have

entrusted this matter to me, child. Cleary, lad, you'd best prepare your ink and parchments. Take your things up to the circle, we'll join you there shortly."

The scribe swallowed nervously and nodded, then gathered up his satchel and ran for the Lochmaben Stones, to be ready to record what was about to transpire. Morgana peered seaward, watching the approach of the ships. There was no pier at Lochmaben, only wild and empty shoreline. Both ships bellied their way across the breakers, dropping anchor with a rattle and splash, while sails came snaking down in the moonlight.

A moment later, the rope ladders had gone down the sides and men began tumbling to the shore, men who clutched no weapons in their hands, surely a good sign. And there was a woman with the Irishmen, no, two women, then a third, climbing gingerly down and carried ashore by strapping men, so their long skirts would not become soaked in brine. Morgana held her breath, hardly aware that she'd stopped breathing. Then Medraut came striding across the shingle, greeting her with a glad cry.

"Aunt! You're here!"

He embraced her roughly, eyes shining in the moonlight.

"You are well, Medraut?" she managed.

"Aye, well and happy. Aunt, she's a lovely girl, and her father has agreed to the marriage of alliance!"

"Then you had better introduce me properly, nephew."

A tall, bearded man with a proud bearing was approaching from down the beach. With him were the three women, one Morgana's age, one older woman dressed as a servant, and one a lovely young girl whose eyes shone as brightly as Medraut's. The men who crewed the Irish warship did not approach, but remained on the beach, as the Briton sailors did. Lailoken joined them, grinning in triumph. He swept her a low and elegant bow.

"Queen of Galwyddel, I bring you alliance with the king of Dalriada."

"You have served Britain well then, minstrel. You will be amply rewarded."

His teeth flashed white. "I am all gratitude."

Medraut greeted the newcomers in halting Gael, then said formally, "Aunt, I present King Dallan mac Dalriada, the *Scotti,* and his daughter Keelin. Riona Damhnait serves the king as Druidess and translator. King Dallan, my aunt, Queen Morgana daughter, widow, and mother of kings."

Dallan offered his bare hand. Morgana accepted the greeting and they clasped forearms. The king spoke in a deep and pleasant voice, his eyes easy and smiling. His Druidess translated. "My king greets you with honor and thanks you for this gesture of friendship. We are pleased to unite our heiress with your heir in holy marriage."

"Greetings to you, King of Dalriada," Morgana said formally, "and welcome to Galwyddel, now the home of your child, who is soon to be sovereign queen. We are happy to welcome her to our family. I have brought with me a priest of our faith, to finalize the vows according to our customs." She turned to greet the Druidic counselor with him. "I am pleased that you have come with our future daughter, Riona Damhnait, for I would be a poor hostess did I not permit the vows to be solemnized by your customs, as well. My own family line descends from Druids of the Brythonic Celts."

"I am pleased to hear it," Riona nodded gravely, returning her welcome with a handclasp.

Keelin smiled and said in delightfully good

Brythonic, "I thank you, Queen Morgana, for your welcome. I am honored to be chosen as the means of bringing our peoples together."

Morgana, surprised by the girl's fluency, gave her a warm embrace, smiling at the nervous tremors shaking the girl's shoulders and knees. Morgana, too, had trembled on the night of her betrothal and marriage at the standing stones. "You are lovely, child. Welcome." She turned, then, to Dallan mac Dalriada. "Let us go to the standing stones, where treaties are made and marriages arranged, and draw up the details of alliance."

The king glanced up the hill, then spoke quietly. Riona Damhnait said, "Dallan mac Dalriada wonders where the wedding party is? Surely your illustrious brother, war leader of the Britons, would wish to see his nephew wed? Is it possible he does not approve of this alliance?"

Morgana had been expecting the question, or one like it. "He is not here because he does not know of the wedding or the alliance plans. Artorius ap Uthyr Pendragon is at Caerleul, busy preparing for battle in the south. When he is presented with news of this marriage, he will have little choice but to accept it, for I am sovereign queen of Galwyddel and no man, not even my brother, has the right to refute my decisions."

When Riona translated, the king's eyes widened, then he began to chuckle.

"Dallan mac Dalriada appreciates your courage, Queen Morgana, and salutes your wisdom. He, too, has secrets to keep from kin in Ireland, who may be just as shocked to learn of Keelin's marriage."

"We are agreed, then, that this union is best done privately, then presented to the world as a *fait accompli*?"

"Oh, yes," the answer came back, "we are quite agreed." He said something further to his daughter which Riona did not translate, but the girl blushed prettily in the moonlight and smiled shyly at her betrothed.

Morgana had never seen Medraut so radiantly happy and thanked God—and Brenna McEgan, whose idea it had been—for it. "In that case, let us draw up the marriage agreement and seal this handfasting."

They climbed the long slope of land to the stone circle, where Cleary had set out his parchments, pens, and ink, the thin-scraped vellum gleaming white in the bright moonlight. He had lit oil lamps, as well, sheltered in the lee of the standing stones, the better to see his work. Dallan mac Dalriada nodded his approval of the arrangement, speaking quietly to his Druidess, who turned to Morgana and said, "I would be grateful for a copy of the agreed-upon details, that I might translate it into Gaelic ogham script."

"Of course."

That settled, they settled down to business.

Chapter Fourteen

The fortifications at Caer-Badonicus went up with astonishing speed. Covianna Nim had never seen so many men in one place, hundreds of them, with more arriving every day from the kingdoms of the midlands, bringing arms and armor, long pack trains of supplies to be cached in the summit's new granaries, groaning wagonloads of rough-dressed stone blocks, ripped hastily from quarries for miles around and ferried by the hundred-weight per horse, thousands of stones to build walls and barracks on the high hill.

Nor had she seen so many labor for so many hours without stopping, day and night, working in shifts to haul the stones laboriously to the top of the five-hundred-foot hill. Five layers deep, the walls went up, mazelike, the outermost layer studded with whole forests of thorny hawthorne branches, hacked down by women and children and carried on mules, on ponies, on grunting, waddling sows that stood as tall through the shoulder as some of the ponies and had to be goaded along by children with swine prods, *anything* that could carry a load of thorned nastiness.

Paving stones lined every inch of space between the long, snaking, concentric stone rings, joins made impervious to water with barrels of heated pitch. The cisterns were roofed over, forming a massive conduit that ringed the whole eighteen acres of summit, a feat of engineering the Romans themselves would have been proud to claim. And even *before* they were roofed over, they had begun to fill with rainwater from the hundreds of shallow channels dug every few inches across the entire top of the hill. Water flowed in spidery lines and snaking rivulets, pouring steadily into the cisterns.

Myrddin had ordered waterwheels built every few yards around the perimeter to lift the runoff into the cisterns from the top. A small army of boys was charged with keeping the wheels in constant motion, round the clock, with buckets mounted on timber spokes lifting the spilloff from deep, narrow troughs along the very edge of the summit, butted up against the innermost wall. The boys chanted songs in the days-long driving downpour, keeping up the rhythm of cranking the ponderous, groaning waterwheels.

Dripping buckets lifted water from ground level up to the top of the first cistern, pouring gallon after gallon down into the stone-lined channel between the first and second walls. From there, it flowed through drains down into the lower circumvallation cisterns, gradually filling up the whole, massive stonework system. When the cisterns failed to fill fast enough to suit Myrddin, he ordered wells dug around the long base of the hill, with more waterwheels to lift the thousands of gallons necessary to complete the job properly. Horses worked treadmills to keep these larger waterwheels moving, until the immense, layered conduit was finally full.

The waterwheels were immediately torn down, the timber used for roofing the houses and barracks going up all across the summit. Great wooden gates had been carefully built into the walls, as well, many more of them than necessary. Most were false gates, set along the edges of the walls in a mock facade, to fool the Saxon armies as to the purpose of those few, critical gates slated to deliver Emrys Myrddin's surprise. Runners came daily to the hill fort, gasping out the news of fighting and skirmishes all along the northern borders of Sussex and Wessex, the unexpected Briton strength forcing the Saxons to march west, right toward the trap being so carefully prepared for them. Emrys Myrddin was everywhere, directing, advising, overseeing the work day and night, only pausing to eat and rest when Covianna Nim insisted.

"You will collapse, Myrddin, if you do not eat and sleep, and where will Britain be, then? Come, lie down, I'll sing you to sleep."

At such times, she would guide him, usually stumbling with weariness, up to her rooms in the very first building finished on the summit, serving as her dispensary to treat the injuries sustained by the construction gangs. In those private rooms, she and Myrddin did a great deal more than eat and sleep. The sport they shared did him good, relaxing him and drawing him ever more delicately into her own trap.

And while he was distracted by her not inconsiderable charms, she bled him dry of every secret she could wheedle loose, pillow talk shared between lonely druidic professionals with no one else to share or understand the problems of their work. Given Myrddin's flattery-susceptible ego, larger than the whole of God's wide heavens, coupled with his long-standing infatuation with her, it was very simple to persuade him to share everything Covianna wanted to know.

He whispered the teaching epigrams between kisses, between couplings which were sometimes hard and fast, but more often slow and lazy and deeply satisfying—and always profitable. She learned the secrets of his wizardly lore, much of which consisted simply in knowing what men and women—be they superstitious peasants or kings with fine, classical educations—would do under given sets of circumstances, then uttering pronouncements calculated to achieve the desired outcome. Parable after parable slipped from his lips to her ears, deepening her understanding of how to manipulate people and situations.

He taught her healing lore not even Marguase had known, secrets picked up as a boy in Constantinople, from healers he had known before Covianna's birth. And most valuable of all, she learned the greatest secret of alchemy, long sought by her tribe of master smiths, but never found. The simplicity of it set her to laughing softly in the darkness.

"To change lead—the basest dross—into gold," he murmured, nuzzling her breast, "all that is required is the philosopher's stone."

"What stone is that? Something found only in a far country? Worth more than all the gold in Rome?"

He chuckled. "No, nothing like that. The alchemist's fabled prize is no stone at all."

"No stone at all? But—"

He tapped her temple. "The philosopher's stone is the rock-solid knowledge of *philosophy itself*. What does philosophy teach a man to do? To look at the gross and ordinary world of clay, of lead and crass stupidity, and to see within each crass and stupid thing the shining sparks of divinity waiting to be set free. And how does one set them free? By seeing them in the first place and acknowledging their existence, through the philosopher's skill of symbolic sight. Any man can change 'lead' into the 'gold' of wisdom, does he but understand this one, profoundly powerful secret."

It was the source of Emrys Myrddin's power, Covianna realized with a wondrous opening to the possibilities it made suddenly real and shining. No wonder Myrddin had been revered as a prophet even as a child, when he had seen the world through his philosopher's eyes, trained by the best minds of the East. He had seen clearly where Vortigern's weakness and greed would lead both Vortigern and the entire Briton race—and had uttered his first profound "prophecy" in symbolic terms even a slack-brained fool like Vortigern could understand. Red dragon of Britain would fight white dragon of Saxony, and Vortigern was the inevitable loser.

The very utterance of the "prophecy" had been Vortigern's undoing, leading his own sons to betray him while uniting the people behind Ambrosius Aurelianus and his closest friend, Uthyr *pen Dragon*—chosen by the "dragon," by Emrys Myrddin himself, who had invented the "dragon" whole cloth to represent the whole of the British people. It was so delightfully simple, Covianna marveled that she had not seen it sooner. It was another mark of Myrddin's genius that he had shared the source of his power with no one, not even Artorius.

Until now.

And now it was *her* secret, as well.

There was not room in all of Britain for two powerful Druids to hold this same, volatile piece of information. She smiled, whispering into his ear and nibbling at his neck, and plotted and planned and smiled up into his trusting eyes. When the fortress walls were nearly complete and Myrddin's work essentially done, Covianna put those plans into action.

"I must leave for Glastenning Tor," she told him that night. "I have stayed longer than I should at Caer-Badonicus. I worry for my kinsmen's safety. I wish . . ." She allowed her voice to trail off forlornly.

"You wish what, my dearest heart?"

She brushed fingertips against his lips, drawing a deep shudder from him where he lay joined with her. "I wish that you would come to the Tor, for just a little while, even for a day, to overlook our defenses. Your advice would be worth so much, Myrddin, for you see with eyes other men do not possess. You see the strengths and weaknesses of a place, even as Artorius sees the strengths and weaknesses of an army. And you could personally collect from the smiths of my tribe our treasure trove of fine swords and spear points, made against just such a contingency and stored away at the Tor. You could see them safely back here, to arm the defenders of Caer-Badonicus with them."

"When the work is finished here . . ." he began.

"But there is nothing further here that needs your supervision. The walls are up, the cisterns roofed over and filled, the sluice gates and the decoys built, and the houses and cattle byres are going up at a grand pace. There is no reason, really, why you could not slip away for a day or two, to help my kinsmen prepare the Tor for invasion."

"An invasion which may never come . . ."

She frowned, converting the irritation into a look of worried fear. "There is no way to know that, for sure, and I would never forgive myself if I failed to do everything in my power to protect my kinsmen. Please say you'll come."

And he did, shuddering all the while.

They left at dawn, bidding farewell to King Melwas

and King Cadorius as the rain continued to pour from leaden skies. "I'll not be gone more than a day or two," Myrddin assured them, "just long enough to see to the defense of the Tor's abbey and the townfolk at its feet. The runners coming in from Caer-Durnac assure us the Saxons are yet a week's march away, more than enough time for me to see to the Tor's defenses and return."

"God go with you, then," Cadorius clasped his arm, "and bless you for your help at Caer-Badonicus. Without you, we would have been lost, I fear. Come back to us as soon as you may."

Despite the steady rain and biting chill of the wind, Covianna enjoyed the ride home more than any other journey she could remember taking. It was perhaps twenty miles from Caer-Badonicus' windswept summit to Glastenning Tor, and considerably less than that from the Tor to the sea. Each day when the tides turned, the River Brue and the broad sweep of salt marshes meandering lazily along its low-slung, flood-prone banks, mile upon water-logged mile of them, filled up with brackish water flowing inland with a swirl of muddied currents.

With the tides and the filling of the marshes, the strange, upthrust jut of land known as Glastenning Tor rose up from the marshy lowlands, spending fully half of every day as an island, completely cut off from the rest of Britain despite nearly twenty miles between its shores and the sea. When the tidal marshes drained again, it spent the other half of its day as a high and dry hill firmly joined to the mainland once more, but surrounded by treacherous bogs, pools of brackish water, and long, landlocked oxbow lakes where salt-water fish swam in surprised dismay to find themselves cut off from the sea, easy prey to the thousands of waterfowl and wading birds and canny swamp foxes living in the marshlands.

The Tor never failed to inspire a ripple of awe down Covianna's spine. It was the Great Mother's teat, so the old stories ran, from which flowed the milky white spring dubbed Chalk Well. The whole of the Tor roared with underground water, buried rivers of it, pouring through deep caverns and spilling out into springs in a dozen or more places, here milky white, there blood-hued and iron-rich. Maps Covianna had been shown as a girl, learning from her elders the carefully hidden truths of the Tor, had revealed the great hill's sacred outlines in all their astonishing, mystical wonder. The Tor *was* the Mother, Her left breast jutting skyward where She lay on Her side, left leg outthrust in a long and elegant sweep ending in a perfectly formed human foot.

Her right leg was tucked up beneath Her, in the birthing position, with Her open birth canal spread wide, giving life to a little hillock just beyond Her sacred vulva, a hill which rose from the earth like an infant's head emerging from its Mother's womb. Bride's Mound, it was called, this infant's-head hill that was Covianna's actual birthplace. The Tor was beautiful and holy, filled with mystery, a place where Covianna's mothers and grandmothers had, for centuries, kept their greatest treasures and their sacred forges, down in the secret caverns, deep inside the body of Mother Brigit, who gave eternal birth to Virgin Bride. It was on Bride's Mound the smithies had built their reputations and their trade, not daring to profane the Mother's body with their anvils and hammers and glowing forges or the glass houses where Bride's silica-rich sands gave birth in turn to the lustrous glass for which the whole complex of hills and caverns had been named.

She smiled when she could finally trace the outlines of the great labyrinth of the Tor, an earthwork so ancient, no one in Covianna's line could remember the building of it, only that it had been, from time immemorial, the only way into and out of the Tor, with its quiet, wealthy rooms and snaking passages one had to follow—like Theseus hunting the Minotaur—in order to reach the summit. The labyrinth's pattern could be clearly seen across the wide, marshy floodplain, and smoke from the smithies rose black against the sky from Bride's Mound. Sight of her home never failed to lift Covianna's spirits. Her fingers itched to take up hammer and steel again, to forge some wondrous new blade to fit the stolen scabbard in her baggage. She chuckled aloud, imagining Artorius' rage when he discovered it missing—and apparently, at the hands of the disgustingly virtuous Morgana. Emrys Myrddin, riding beside her, smiled at the sound of her laughter.

"It is a long time, I think, since you have been home."

"Too long," she agreed. "There is much here I have longed to show you."

"I have heard wonderful tales of Glastenning Tor. I visited once, as a young man, but only the forges. It will be a pleasure to have you show me its secrets."

Laughter burbled up again, as wild and delighted as the water rushing through the heart of the Tor. "The Saxons long for the same thing, I think. I have heard the minstrels whisper that they call it Glastonbury, the glass mountain, where magic is done by the wizards and the smiths who hold the Tor."

"The Saxons," Myrddin chuckled, "consider an ordinary sword a thing of magic, forged by the gods they worship. They buy theirs, I am told, from the Franks. Which is why," he sighed, "they are so anxious to capture the southwest of Britain, to take the Tor and all your family's secrets. And why I agreed to come look over the defenses."

"For which I am forever grateful."

A cry went up as they approached the little town which lay sprawled on the flanks of the hill, spreading out down the long, slender leg of land toward the Goddess' outthrust foot. As the rain slacked off to a mere drizzle, children came running from cottage doorways, shouting the news to their parents and older siblings. Smiths emerged from the forges, wiping sweat and soot and thrusting tools into the pockets of their leather aprons. Covianna led the way along the safest path through the marshy bogs until they were close enough to be recognized.

"*Covianna Nim!*" the cry went up. "Covianna Nim's come home!"

Their horses splashed through the last of the marshes and Covianna slid from the saddle, flinging her arms round cousins and aunts and uncles amidst the noisy welcome. Her mother came running from the largest smithy on Bride's Mound, grey hair caught back in braids, face and hands streaked with soot. Tears tracked down the weathered lines in her face, losing themselves in the drizzling rain.

"My child! You've come home at last! And safe from marauders!"

They embraced long and warmly while Covianna's mother pressed kisses to her cheek, her hair, any part of her that would hold still long enough.

"Aye, Mother," she stepped back laughingly, "I've come home safe and sound, with a guest to be shown the Tor's hospitality."

Her mother gazed fondly into her eyes, then smiled. "Introduce us, Covianna. Who is this distinguished guest you've brought among us?"

She turned to Myrddin, who had dismounted and now bowed elegantly to her mother.

"It is my pleasure," Covianna purred, enjoying the

excitement in her mother's eyes, "to present the legendary Emrys Myrddin, Druid to the Dux Bellorum, Artorius. He has come to the Tor to look over our defenses. Myrddin, my mother, Vivienna of the Tor."

Her mother gasped, went pink to the ears, and dropped a deep curtsey. "You are most humbly welcome, Emrys Myrddin. We have heard much of your wisdom. You do us great honor to visit."

He took her mother's sooty hands and kissed them gently, saying, "Not at all. The honor is mine, dear lady. Your daughter is a remarkable woman, wise and skilled in the ways of healing and of forging steel. She has been a treasure to have with us in Artorius' court at Caerleul."

Vivienna beamed fondly at her daughter. "We knew, child, that you would go far, in this life. You were marked for it from birth. Now, then, come up to the abbey, I'll introduce you to the abbot and see that you are given the finest quarters on the Tor."

"I would be pleased to bear you company," he offered gallantly, giving her his arm and minding not at all the wet soot that streaked his fine tunic sleeve, although Vivienna did try to wipe off the worst of it on her skirts. They set out, walking up the narrow road while children danced around them. Older boys took charge of the horses, leading them behind and finding apples to feed them as they clopped sedately in Myrddin's wake.

All the sights and sounds and scents of home rushed forward to surround Covianna with a delightful medley of familiarity: the hot-metal smell of iron drawn red-hot from the glowing coals; the ring of hammer on anvil; the sound of men blowing through long metal pipes, shaping molten glass into delicate pitchers and cups and vases to be traded the length and breadth of Britain; the homey scents of plain cooking and newly

washed laundry. It all wafted in a wonderful mixture
from the forges and low stone cottages and glass houses
and washerwomen's huts lining the road and each
lovely scent and sight and sound whispered a glorious welcome home. Covianna relished every fine
moment of the walk.

She told herself she would never leave the Tor
again, now that she had what she wanted from the last
of her mentors. Her mother would be immensely
proud of the secrets Covianna had brought home with
her this time, proud and pleased that her daughter's
wandering days were over, at last. It was time she
settled, took a mate, and produced children to follow
in her own illustrious footsteps. She laughed softly to
herself, deciding not to take the herb she had been
using for years to prevent men's brats from sticking
to her womb. It would be quite a coup, to boast the
child of Emrys Myrddin as her own son. Or daughter. It hardly mattered.

Emrys Myrddin was saying to her mother, "As
much as it pains me to admit, I fear that I must give
you a solemn warning, Lady Vivienna. My visit is not
entirely motivated by pleasure."

Vivienna's sharp glance betrayed worry, which
Covianna's mother usually managed to hide. "The
Saxons?"

"Aye. They're on the march, as you must have heard
by now."

She nodded. "We've heard, all right. The armies of
the midlands have already marched south and the
people who live beyond these marshes," she swept a
hand outward, indicating the broad stretch of flatland
skirted round by the shaggy Mendip Hills, "have fled
already, taking their harvests and their flocks and herds
to the caves until this war is ended, one way or the
other."

"It's at Caer-Badonicus we'll stop them, Lady Vivienna, of that you may be certain. They'll not soon forget the drubbing we give them there. But you're wise to worry, for it's the Tor and the smithies they want, there's no mistaking that."

She nodded and tightened her fingers on his arm in a gesture of gratitude. "Then I am doubly pleased to make you welcome, for the runners have also brought tales of the work done at Caer-Badonicus. All Glastenning holds its breath—and for excellent reason. Many of us have cousins and brothers and sisters in Caer-Durnac, who have fled in advance of the Saxons, with tales of shocking murder and mutilations."

Myrddin's mouth went grim, a marble-hard line. "It seems to be a Saxon habit. Cutha slew every farmholder and villager within five miles and more of Penrith. The bastards outran pursuit to Dewyr and escaped across the Saxon border."

As Myrddin filled her in on the latest news, they left the low leg of land and began to climb up the path which led around the hill in a winding labyrinth of stone walls and flagged pavement. The great whorls and loops were scrupulously maintained free of weeds by a small army of monks who had taken holy orders at the abbey.

"To teach them patience," Vivienna explained with a gleam in her eyes and a lilt of laughter in her voice. They circled back and around seven times, passing monks at work in the orchards, harvesting the last of the apples and pears and repairing the labyrinth walls.

The low spires and arched windows of Glastenning Abbey rose from the very summit, dark and forbidding against the cloud-lashed sky, offensive in Covianna's eyes for squatting so leechlike on the Mother's breast. She smiled and nodded to monks she secretly loathed and daydreamed about someday having the personal power necessary to drive the Christian church out of Britain, returning her people to the ancient ways that had been preserved in her family's lore.

It would be rather nice to go down in history as Covianna the Apostate, Queen of Britain and Empress of the Celts. She had to bite back a burbling laugh at such an image, torn between outrageous humor and the self-mocking realization that such an outcome was very, very unlikely, if only because the Christians, once they'd gained a toenail's hold on a piece of turf, utterly refused to let go until they'd swallowed down the whole ruddy thing, indigestible bits along with the rest.

The trick was to be placed to take advantage of whatever change might be in the wind—and Covianna was more than half convinced that the Saxons' day had come, or soon would. Whatever miracles Artorius managed to pull out of the seat of his britches this time, the day of the old guard was done, for the world had changed and nothing Artorius did could stop that reality from crashing down on all their heads, whether it crashed on them during this battle or one next year or next decade. It was nothing more than breathing room, a delay of the inevitable disaster, that Artorius fought for, a bitter folly that was killing Britons and smashing British futures under men who would all too soon be their new masters.

What might it be worth to a Saxon king like Aelle, to have the way smoothed for a peace that would prevent needless slaughter of Briton lives? It was only when men like Aelle were crossed and humiliated, as Ancelotis had humiliated Cutha, that their tempers turned savage and butchery of innocents commenced. There had been no such slaughter when Wessex had joined ranks with the Saxon kings. Yes, much might be gained by helping the Saxons to a peaceful take-over of key Briton strongholds.

She could do nothing about Caer-Badonicus, but Glastenning Tor was another matter. And there was one more thing in the Saxons' favor, from Covianna's viewpoint. The Saxons were still a decently non-Christian group of pagan souls. She felt far more in common with the likes of Aelle than she did with the abbot who presided over the rape of the Goddess Brigit's most holy shrine. What worth could be placed on the restoration of one's faith and the destruction, stone by hated stone, of the abbey perched so hideously atop the Tor? Covianna would risk much, to see that fate brought down upon Glastenning Tor's abomination.

As they came around the last upward turn of the labyrinth, the abbey grounds opened out onto a relatively flat summit. Wind blew briskly, full of gusting rain and biting chill. The dour stone walls rose forbiddingly against the slate of sky and storm. It was not a particularly large abbey, although Covianna supposed it would be enlarged in due time, as the abbey's power and wealth continued, like cancer, to grow. A young monk Covianna didn't know, barely seventeen, if that, met them near the abbey's heavy wooden doors. "Is there trouble?" he asked, hurrying across the small plaza.

Covianna's mother reassured him, "No, not immediately. The Dux Bellorum has sent Emrys Myrddin to look over the Tor's defenses."

Relief and worry chased by turns across his young face. "I'll take you to see the abbot at once. Father Elidor is in his chamber at this hour, going over the abbey's accounts."

"That will be fine, thank you," Myrddin nodded courteously.

The monks of Glastenning Abbey had learned, long ago, the folly of trying to keep the women of Covianna's family out of the abbey when professional business was involved; their escort merely guided them inside without even a brow raised in protest. Their footsteps echoed across the stone floor. Dark walls rose around them, claustrophobic, with squat columns and ugly arches and high, narrow windows.

The windows were the abbey's only attractive feature, as most of them had been glazed in beautiful colors by the smithies of Glastenning Tor's glasshouses, who had been making colored glass for centuries, learning the skill from Roman artisans. The patterns were simple, the pieces shaped to an approximate fit and held together by strips of soft lead. Little squares and circles of white and yellow light, punctuated here and there by more expensive greens and blues and reds, fell in lovely geometric shapes where the dull, fitful daylight passed through into the darkness of the room. The masterpiece was above the altar, a mosaic in glass, depicting the death of Christ. For all its beauty, it was still abomination in Covianna's eyes, a temple dedicated to death erected on a hill sacred to the deity of life.

They stepped through a doorway behind the altar and found themselves in the monks' private quarters, a long and even uglier building adjoining the church. Tiny cubicles lined the dingy corridor, empty now, as their occupants were hard at work elsewhere. The abbot's room lay at the far end, larger than the other cells, to accommodate the abbot's worktable, accounting records, and manuscripts he was studying. Covianna could hear the quiet scratch of goose quill on parchment as Father Elidor made careful notations. Head bent, absorbed in his work, he didn't hear their approach until their guide tapped at the open door. Elidor looked up in surprise, pausing with quill suspended midair, the tip glistening with wet ink in the light cast by his oil lamp.

"Lady Vivienna has come up from the village, Father."

"Vivienna? What is the trouble?" He rose to his feet, frowning. When he glanced at Covianna, standing behind her mother's shoulder, his eyes widened. "My dear child, you've come home at last!" He hurried forward, smiling in open delight.

She accepted his embrace graciously. "It's good to be here," she murmured with perfect honesty. "I've brought Emrys Myrddin with me."

Elidor frowned as he turned to greet his unexpected guest. "I'm sorry to meet you under such circumstances. It must be drastic news, to bring you to Glastenning Abbey. How can we help?"

Myrddin clasped his arm in greeting, then said, "I would like a tour of the entire abbey, its safe rooms, lockable doors, approaches not only up the hill, but through doors and windows, weak points that would be difficult to defend. There must be room for the townfolk to shelter here, as well, should a real crisis develop." Elidor was nodding. Myrddin added, "Do any of your men know the use of arms?"

A grimace came and went. "To my sorrow, yes, all too many. There are former soldiers among us, men so distressed by the killing they've waged this past decade, they have renounced the sword and sought refuge with God. But if it comes to seeing women and children butchered, I believe even they will find it easy to lay aside the commandment to turn the other cheek, and follow instead Christ's admonition that if a man has not a sword, let him sell his cloak and buy one."

A smile, bittersweet, chased its way across Myrddin's lips. "A good thing to remember in these troubled times. Very well, the sooner we begin, the sooner you will be prepared."

The tour was thorough, with Elidor himself serving

as guide, joined by half a dozen of the senior monks, who made notes as Myrddin made specific suggestions, often sketching out the defense works to be added to the labyrinth's existing walls.

"Anything to slow them down will help," Myrddin explained, pointing out places in the looping approaches where thorny branches could be piled atop walls—leaving Covianna to wonder whether a single stand of hawthorne would be left in the south of Britain by the time this war had ended—or where pitfalls could be rigged at strategic points to send invaders plunging down onto sharpened stakes.

Elidor was frowning. "Won't wooden stakes be useless against armor?"

"One thing Artorius has gained experience of is the strength of Saxon arms and armor. Most of the soldiers they send to battle have nothing but a bit of quilted leather. Even amongst their nobility, *thegns,* they call them, armor is usually of limited quality and quantity. They are not wealthy, these Saxons, and their chieftains make gifts of weapons and mail shirts to their favorites, to be returned to the 'king' when the *thegn* dies, for such gifts are mere loans, wealth returning to the leader whenever he demands it.

"A Saxon *thegn* cannot pass on to his sons his armor and weapons, for they are not his. Nothing is his, except what his king lends him for a while. And since most of their wealth has been taken from others, and most of those others have resisted vigorously, there is not a great store of weapons or armor in the Saxons' camps. A narrow, sharpened stake set into the ground in a deadfall can pierce virtually any ring shirt made or punch through legs and arms, rendering a man helpless, or at least, unable to fight effectively. Either will suffice for our present needs."

"Indeed," Elidor nodded. "I am twice enlightened.

We had begun to fear these Saxon dogs were unstoppable, the way they've gobbled up the southern kingdoms of Britain and seek constantly to expand their borders."

"Oh, they're quite stoppable," Myrddin assured him with a nasty grin. "You would have enjoyed seeing that verminous little Cutha knocked flat on his backside by Ancelotis of Gododdin. He put to rest a fair number of unfounded rumors of just that sort. Bested him with bare hands, sent him skulking out of Caerleul like a scalded dog. The realization these bandits *can* be defeated, coupled with Cutha's ill-tempered slaughter afterward, showing us precisely what we may expect with Saxons to rule us, has sent the entire northern half of the Britons rushing to take up arms to stop these beasts for good."

The monks duly added notations on where to dig pits, to be lined with narrow, sharp-ended pole stakes. When their journey through the grounds led past well after holy well, springs gushing up from the depths of the Tor, Myrddin frowned thoughtfully. "There seems to be an immense amount of water pouring out of this hill."

"Oh, yes," Father Elidor nodded, "they flow like this year round. I've never seen them run dry, not even during a drought." He cupped his hand into the well they had paused beside, dipping up a palmful to sip, scattering droplets that lost themselves amongst the spatters of rain falling.

"A pity we can't harness it, somehow," Myrddin murmured.

Covianna began to laugh. "Oh, Myrddin, I don't think the Saxons will fall into that particular trap twice in one war."

He grimaced, then gave her a rueful smile. "No, I don't suppose they would. Has anyone ever tried to find the source of the Glastenning springs? Might there be caverns under the Tor where people could shelter?"

Covianna glanced at her mother, who was watching Myrddin through narrowed eyes, a look he missed, as Myrddin was gazing at the abbot. Elidor hesitated, clearly taken by surprise on a subject he'd obviously never considered, then dredged up an answer. "Well, we've the cold cellars, of course, beneath the abbey, where we store wines and smoked meats and other foodstuffs, and the cellars were built into a natural cavern, such as it is. It's very small and shallow. So far as I know, there's no connection with any other caverns."

Covianna's mother glanced warningly at Covianna, then said smoothly, "There are legends in our family lore, stories that the first smithies on the Tor were built by a race of dark dwarves, magical beings worshiped in the old days. The stories say the dark ones of the Tor lived in fantastical caverns deep in the hill and sold their magical weapons to men in exchange for what the dwarves wanted most: firstborn children. But these are very old stories, mere legends. If such caverns did exist, we've never found any trace of them. And our children find their way into the most amazing nooks and corners you could imagine. If the caverns were real, someone among us would have found them. Years ago, no doubt."

The abbot was smiling. "Vivienna doesn't exaggerate the children's curiosity. They do get into everything and manage to slip in everywhere."

Vivienna turned a mortified glance on the aging abbot. "Oh, dear, they've not been trouble, have they?"

"No, no," he laughed, "nothing serious. Just playing games, hiding and seeking, treasure hunts, exploring in the dead of night with a guttering candle, daring one another, all the typical games we played as children ourselves."

Covianna chuckled. "I remember my cousins

teasing me mercilessly until I gave in and tiptoed into the abbey's root cellar one midnight. There was a new moon and everything was black as pitch. My horrid cousins sneaked in behind me and barred the cellar door, leaving me stranded in the midst of the carrots and onions and turnips. I didn't sleep all night. Poor Father Gildas found me next morning, stiff with fright and wrapped up in some old sacking I found on a shelf before my candle went out. And there was absolutely no trace of another cave. Believe me, I *looked.*"

They shared a laugh, then the fitful gusts turned to a steady downpour, effectively ending the excursion. The labyrinth's walls cast long shadows down the flanks of the hill as they hurried toward shelter.

"You may wish to impose upon Father Elidor for a bed tonight," Vivienna offered as they returned to the hillcrest, "as most of us have children who would have to be shifted, but the village would never forgive me if I didn't insist that you share our supper. We'll make a real feast of it, open up the meeting hall for dancing and music."

"I am honored," Myrddin inclined his head graciously. "You are most welcome as well, Elidor."

The abbot smiled. "I, too, would be honored. Myrddin, I'll show you where to find your room tonight, in case I retire earlier than you choose."

They parted, with Myrddin and the abbot kissing both Vivienna's and Covianna's cheeks, and disappeared into the abbey while mother and daughter descended the hill together, heads bent against the stinging cold of the rain. And as she walked, Covianna dreamed of the revenge which would be hers during this lovely, wild night.

Chapter Fifteen

The moon was perfectly poised above the tallest of the Lochmaben Stones, balanced on its very edge, when Father Auliffe, abbot of Caer-Birrenswark Abbey, and Riona Damhnait, Druidess of Dalriada, jointly spoke the words uniting Medraut and Keelin in marriage.

"We are gathered to unite this couple . . ." Auliffe began, "in the sight of God . . ."

"With the blessings of the Daghda, Father of the Irish Celts," Riona added, "to join together our two great kingdoms."

Auliffe turned to Medraut, whose knees quaked visibly in the moonlight. "Do you, Medraut, King of Galwyddel and nephew to Morgana, Queen of Ynys Manaw, vow in the sight of God to love, cherish, keep, and protect your bride, Princess Keelin of Dalriada, who will be your sovereign queen, seeking no other?"

"I do so vow," the boy said, with only a slight quaver in his voice.

"And you, Keelin ni Dallan mac Dalriada," Riona spoke by turn, "agree and vow before the gods of your ancestors to honor, love, and help your husband all the days of your life, seeking no comfort, no bed but his?"

Her fingers tightened on Medraut's. "I do so vow," she whispered.

"Then," Father Auliffe said quietly, eyes bright with hope and wonder, "I declare before God the Father, God the Son, God the Holy Spirit, that the two of you are joined as one. Let no man come between thee."

"Blessings on thy heads," Riona added, "and may many happy, healthy children play at your hearth."

Keelin blushed furiously, then Medraut turned and lifted trembling hands to her face, bending to kiss her gently. Morgana found it necessary to brush wetness from her eyes and Dallan mac Dalriada blinked a little too rapidly, as well. Young Cleary came forward with the official marriage documents and the new king and queen of Galwyddel signed, laughing nervously over the trembling of their hands. Then it was done and nothing could undo it. Before she could give in to the shakes threatening her own knees, she smiled brightly and kissed her nephew and niece by turn. Dallan mac Dalriada hugged his daughter tightly, then clasped Medraut's arm in the greeting of equals.

"Take wondrous care of my child," Riona translated, "for she is all that is precious to me."

"I will do my best," Medraut vowed, voice cracking slightly, "to give you grandchildren who may be equally precious."

Lailoken, who had stayed back in the shadows during the proceedings, stepped forward with a small wine cask. "A token of my esteem for the king of Dalriada and promise of things to come. Perhaps we might drink a toast to bride and groom?"

Dallan mac Dalriada accepted it gravely, then

handed it to one of his men. Father Auliffe said heartily, "Cleary, lad, fetch out the holy communion wine I brought along, nothing but the finest from Rome will do on such an occasion. And the cups, lad."

Something about the glint of Lailoken's eyes caught Morgana's attention for just an instant, then Dallan mac Dalriada was giving orders that the wedding gift be carried back to the ship and Cleary was pouring cups and handing them round and Father Auliffe was making the first toast.

"Long and happy lives, children."

"Long and happy lives," they chorused back.

When the toasts had been made, Morgana said, "Tradition for many generations has seen couples married at this circle led to the caverns below the bluff, sacred caverns, once, and full of auspicious portents, holding as they do the happy moments of union of so many generations of Britons. I have ordered a bridal bower prepared, with a fine bed, oil lamps for lighting the grotto, and plenty of food and wine. Dallan mac Dalriada, you are graciously welcome to ride with us to Caer-Birrenswark upon the dawn, to see your child safely upon the throne of Galwyddel."

"I will stay until dawn," Dallan agreed, "but only to greet my daughter as queen. I must return to my own throne, afterward, for winter is soon upon us and many preparations have yet to be made."

"Of course," Morgana nodded, even as Keelin's lips quivered—despite her attempt to show a brave countenance. "Shall we, then, lead our heirs to their marriage bed?"

When Riona translated, Dallan mac Dalriada smiled and offered his arm. They descended once more to the shingle and Morgana led them down past the high bluff, where the sea and countless millennia of rainwater seeping through the soil had carved caves in the limestone. They paused at the entrance to the nuptial cavern long enough for Dallan mac Dalriada to pull his daughter close for one final hug. When Riona took the trembling young bride into the cavern first, to prepare her, Dallan mac Dalriada strode briskly back down the strand toward his ship.

Morgana said quietly, "See to it, Medraut, that your bride knows pleasure before you allow yourself to taste it and you will have begun your marriage wisely. Hands, lips, whispers, and all of it exceedingly gentle and patient."

He gulped. "I will try, Aunt."

"See that you do." She embraced him warmly. "I am deeply proud in you, Medraut. I will ride to the cottage nearest Lochmaben circle, where the captain of your fine fishing sloop has invited us to spend the night, and will see you again in the morning. Send Riona after me and we'll go there together."

As she turned to leave, glancing back over one shoulder, she prayed that she had done the right thing, in this. Whatever the outcome, she had acted for the best. There was nothing else to be done—except lie awake and wonder what Artorius truly would say.

The night was waning its way toward dawn when Covianna slipped into the abbey. She had not come by the normal route, up the path through the labyrinth, but rather through a narrow fissure which was concealed behind the main hearth of her mother's forge house, a fissure hidden by the enormous bellows and a panel of rock placed as a door to further close off the opening to those not permitted to know the full secrets of Glastenning Tor. Her mother's forge house stood at the base of the hill, with no other buildings between its rear wall and the beginning of the labyrinth—and the beginning of the secret passage

Covianna followed, lifting her skirts clear of the dampness and trickling water underfoot.

The passage led upwards along the selfsame path as the labyrinth's walls, having been cut beneath them. The lowest stone of the walls served as ceiling for the passageway. It was cramped and narrow, forcing her to bend nearly double most of the way, but led her steadily upwards in safety, an escape route her remote ancestors had built centuries before the coming of the Romans, so the legends of her family said.

Whoever had built it, near the summit, the underground path divided, one branch to her left leading down toward the deep caverns of the Tor, used for centuries as shelter in time of siege; the other path led upward, toward the hidden exit inside the abbey itself, whose builders and architects had come from Covianna's own ancestors, intent on preserving their secrets intact from any and all comers, including the priests of the new religion.

Particularly from the priests of the new religion.

When at last she emerged, taking the right-hand, upward-sloping turn, Covianna found herself in the lovely Mary Chapel, situated in the very center of the Great Mother's Holy Vulva, a placement that made Covianna smile in wry humor. The fools who ran the abbey had not the faintest idea that their "Mary Chapel," devoted to Mary Queen of Heaven and Mother of the Christ Child, concealed a passage down the very birth canal of the far older Holy Brigit, Goddess of the Tor.

Covianna shook out her skirts and straightened her back, which ached from the long, bent-over climb. The oil lamp she carried sent golden light splashing across the altar, behind which was the ancient eggstone of the old shrine. Intricately carved, the eggstone was topped by a hollow where ancient priestesses had sat, menstruating lifeblood onto the stone while uttering oracular prophecies.

She set her lamp in the hollow of the stone, no longer needing its light to make her way and not wishing to waken anyone except Myrddin. She smiled in anticipation. This was not the first trip she had made, tonight, along the secret pathway. Her previous three trips had served to transport everything she would need to spring the trap on her chosen victim. It waited, patiently, below the earth for his arrival.

Covianna whispered along the corridor leading past the monks' pitiful little cells, the silence broken only by the mouse-soft hush of her skirts and the occasional shattering snore from some overfed inhabitant. Emrys Myrddin had been given the guest chamber beside the abbot's room, reserved for visiting dignitaries. The door was only partially closed, allowing her to slide inside without a betraying creak of iron hinges.

A trickle of light from a high, narrow window fell like a sword blade across the bed. She could see the soft rise and fall of the woolen blanket across Myrddin's chest. For just a moment, she regretted the necessity of destroying such a brilliant mind, not to mention the most skilled lover she'd ever lain with; but only for a moment. Marguase's shade cried out for justice and this man's death was the first step in obtaining it. Pulse thundering, Covianna tiptoed across and used a long strand of her hair to tickle Myrddin awake.

Myrddin's eyelids flickered, then he focused on her face. A tiny furrow appeared between his brows. "Trouble?" he breathed.

She smiled reassuringly. "Not a bit. I've something to show you."

He leaned up on one elbow, so that the blanket slid to his waist. "Show me? In the middle of the night?"

" 'Tis the safest time."

Myrddin's eyes widened. "You've found the caverns beneath the Tor? I *knew* they must exist!"

Covianna breathed out a chuckle. "Oh, aye, they exist, all right. I've known for years how to reach them. So have all the clan heads of my family line. We're just chary of those we share the secret with, as I'm sure you must understand, given your own training."

The corners of his eyes crinkled. "Indeed. Let me get my boots and cloak."

A moment later, she was leading him through the silent abbey, down to the Mary Chapel, and through the opening, rescuing her lamp from the eggstone. "This way," she murmured, waiting for him to pass before closing the hidden exit. "The tunnels have existed for centuries, so far as we know. It's a bit cramped."

They bent low, following the passageway down to the split, then turning downward for the journey to the first of the caverns. Lamplight flickered across dressed stone, casting distorted shadows as they crept ever downward into the earth. A glow of light from ahead beckoned them forward. "I've been into the cavern already," she murmured by way of explanation when he commented on the fact, "to set everything up. It's far more spectacular when you can see everything in the first instant." Within moments, the walls and ceiling opened out into a magnificent stone chamber nearly thirty feet high. Myrddin gasped.

Glittering stalactites dripped from the ceiling in thousands of points like the teeth of dragons, mirrored by the sharp points of stalagmites reaching toward the roof of the cave. Rock glittered in blood-red and golden hues, glistening with ever-present water which poured and splashed down massive columns of rock. Shimmers of white crystal like hoarfrost surrounded deep, black pools along the floor. The roar of underground torrents vibrated the floor and the very air of the room, from deeper within the hill; at the far end of the cavern, a spectacular waterfall plunged from the ceiling and vanished into the bowels of the deeper caves, adding its volume to the water which gushed to the surface in the Tor's sacred springs. Lit torches burned every few feet, thrust into iron brackets some ancestor had driven into the walls.

"There's a path into the deeper caverns," she breathed softly, hardly able to speak in a less reverential tone. This was one spot where familiarity did not breed casual disregard. "Come, I'll show you."

She led the way across the cave, pointing out the black opening where the cavern descended along the edge of a bottomless sink. Myrddin peered into the hole, down which the roar of water could be heard. "Does the cavern ever flood?"

"Not this high, so far as anyone has ever recorded. Of course, most of what we know about the history of these caves is preserved only in our family's most secret lore and we've lost bits and pieces through untimely deaths, over the centuries. The deeper parts of the cave flood with the seasons, of course, but most of these upper chambers are relatively dry."

"And the monks know nothing of this?" He swept an awed gesture at the glittering beauty of the cave.

"Not a thing," she said cheerfully. "We made certain the cave used for the abbey's cold storage was closed off when the abbey was built. By my ancestors, I might add," she chuckled.

"Is the chapel the only way in?"

"No, there's a passage just beneath the walls of the labyrinth, which opens out at the bottom of the hill."

"Inside one of the forge houses?" he guessed. "It would be the only place you could hide the entrance from the youngsters."

Oh, yes, he was far too clever, was Emrys Myrddin.

She had little doubt that, left to his own devices and with no more clue than the existence of the springs, he would have poked and prodded until discovering the way down. She smiled. "Indeed. In a true emergency, of course, we could shelter everyone from the abbey and the village. Which my people have done before, in times of great peril. I wanted to put your mind at ease, before you leave in the morning."

"I only regret I can't stay longer."

"Yes. A pity," she agreed. "I also wanted to show you where we forge our most sacred blades. Artorius' sword, Caliburn, was forged here."

"In the belly of the dragon," Myrddin murmured, glancing at the dragons' teeth stalactites overhead. "How symbolically fitting."

"We put great store by symbolism in my family."

They made a sharp turn where the walls narrowed down to a passage a mere three feet wide, then emerged in the showplace of Covianna's ancestral clan. Myrddin let go a shocked sound.

"It is impressive, isn't it?" she asked smugly.

He simply stared, mouth coming adrift. Before them stretched a black river, into which thundered the cataract from the chamber above. Water spilled out of the ceiling in an endless roar, catching the light of torches she'd carried down and lit earlier, gleaming like a thousand fireflies in the starlight. Ribbons of stone flowed along the edges of the ceiling, looking like so many long, curling strips of bacon hung for smoking. Near the center of the cavern, the river widened out into a black lake some fifty or sixty feet across. In the center of the lake stood a stone island, ringed by glittering white crystalline walls some three quarters of an inch high. On the island stood a forge, its hearth glowing like balefire where she had patiently stoked the coals in preparation for Myrddin's visit.

A column of stone had been cut away to form a standing pedestal on which rested a massive iron anvil. Leather bellows hung above the coals, held in place by iron brackets in a neighboring flowstone column. A path of stepping stones had been laid across the lake, a pathway which would, if previous experience were any indication, soon be underwater, given the amount of rain falling above. At times, the entire island was underwater. Her timing tonight was, as ever, flawless. Her tools stood ready, waiting only her hand and Myrddin's unwitting cooperation.

"I wanted to show you everything," she murmured, slipping her hand into his. "I lit the fires and brought down all the tools I would need to finish forging a dagger blade I'm making just for you. Help me operate the bellows?"

He laughed in open delight. "It would be the greatest honor of my life, dear heart."

She kissed him, then led the way quickly across the stepping stones. She had already poured wine into two silver goblets. A full wineskin stood nearby. "A toast," she smiled, lifting them and handing the drugged goblet to Myrddin. "To victory."

He touched rims with hers, then drank deeply. "Show me what to do."

She sipped, then demonstrated how to operate the bellows. "Yes, that's perfect," she nodded as the coals hissed and flared brilliantly gold in the center.

She lifted a nearly finished dagger, which needed only a final touchup with the hammer before tempering the blade. She used heavy tongs to slide it into the coals, watching the color of the metal with a critical, practiced eye. The moment it was ready, she slid it out, laid it against the anvil, and snatched up the hammer, striking sparks and quickly working up a sweat.

"More wine?" Myrddin asked, gulping the last of

his as he pumped the bellows. That was hard work in itself.

She shook her head. "No, I'll not pause a moment until it's done. Pour another for yourself, you can leave the bellows a moment while I hammer."

He drank, then worked the bellows again at her direction, sending gusts of air across the coals. He made a hefty dent in the wineskin as she evened out the blade along its length, working more for show than because the knife needed more shaping. She was nearing the point of completion when the drugged wine began to tell on her victim. He was blinking more often and he lifted his arms with increasing difficulty when directed to operate the bellows. When he started to stagger, nearly going to his knees, Covianna flashed him a bright smile. "'Tis hard work, operating the bellows. Even young apprentices find it exhausting."

He muttered something into his beard and made an effort to hold onto the big wooden handles. She smiled to herself and waited a bit longer, putting the finishing touches on the weapon of his destruction. It didn't take long. He slid to the ground, blinking in confusion.

"Almost done," she said cheerfully. "All it needs now is the quenching."

Lifting the glowing dagger in her tongs, gripping with the strength she had gained over many years at the forge, Covianna turned and knelt. She smiled down into Myrddin's eyes—and slid the blade deep into the old man's belly.

He screamed, eyes flying wide in shock and pain.

She ruffled his hair. "Poor old fool. Don't you remember the secret of Damascus? You taught it to me, yourself."

The blade hissed and steamed in his wine-laden belly while blood poured across the haft and dripped off the end of the tongs. His mouth worked. One hand came up to grip her arm weakly.

"*Why?*"

She brushed his cheek with her fingertips. "You should never," she murmured, kissing his mouth softly, "have urged Artorius to murder Marguase. She was my first mentor and a far better alchemist than you could ever hope to be. My poor, gullible little fool." She pulled the blade out and blood gushed from the wound. He collapsed backwards, ashen from blood loss and shock.

"Don't worry, love. You won't be long in dying. Even if you managed to stop the bleeding, the water is rising."

As she spoke, she bound his wrists and ankles, tying him firmly to the base of the nearest flowstone column, dragging him across the stone floor in a long smear of blood. He cried out weakly in pain, unable to do more than shudder. She bound him with his head down, toward the water lapping at the rim of the island, less than six inches below his face.

"It'll be over your head soon," she smiled. "If you're still alive when it reaches your mouth and nose. Oh, before I forget—and just in case you're wondering— this is precisely how I forged Caliburn. Artorius' young cousin was as great a fool as you. Don't worry, darling. Once you're nicely dead, I'll come cut up the pieces and let the Goddess sweep them away, as I did with that little idiot. You deserve no less than he, after all. And who knows? Perhaps I'll give birth to your brat and send it to the afterlife to join you."

She gave him a last kiss, piled her tools and newly forged weapon into her satchel, and left him to die, laughing gaily all the way home.

Morgana and Brenna McEgan were roused from sleep perhaps an hour short of dawn by an urgent pounding on the door of the cottage where they, along with Riona Damhnait, had arranged to spend the night. The fisherman who owned the cottage, the same man who had captained the sloop which had ferried Medraut and Lailoken to Dalriada, answered the summons with alacrity, while Morgana and Riona both stumbled out of bed to see what the alarm might be.

"A thousand pardons," a young voice gasped from beyond the open door, "but I must see Queen Morgana immediately!"

It was Cleary, the young cleric who had recorded the marriage and treaty arrangements.

Morgana exchanged a worried look with the Irish Druidess before stepping into the light of the fisherman's oil lamp.

"What is it, Cleary?" she asked quietly, images of multitudinous possible disasters running through her mind.

"Father Auliffe sent me," the lad explained, voice shaking. "There's trouble, Queen Morgana, perhaps very bad trouble. I was to room with Lailoken, your new minstrel, and I thought it peculiar when he slipped away in the middle of the night. Saddled his horse, put his belongings on a packhorse, and left very fast indeed, down the coast road toward Caerleul. I might not have thought anything amiss, but a rider has come from across the border with Strathclyde, bringing dreadful news from Dalriada. Oh, Queen Morgana, I can hardly bear to tell you what's happened." The boy's eyes swam with tears and his hands shook.

She rested a hand on his arm. "Tell me."

"It was a boy, Queen Morgana, a young Briton taken into slavery across the border between Strathclyde and Dalriada. He and his whole family were taken, sold to a farmhold just outside Fortress Dunadd. He said they woke this morning to the sight of carrion crows, thousands of them, and the wind carried a sickly stench. His master rode into Dunadd and found . . ." Cleary gulped, voice trembling. "The whole town was dying, *everyone*. People in convulsions, vomiting, paralyzed, a terrible plague or . . . or . . ." he cast a mortified glance at Riona Damhnait, who had gone ashen in the lamplight, "or perhaps some terrible poison. *Everyone*, Queen Morgana, from the royal household at the fortress to the lowest fisherman's hovel.

"The boy's master promised him not only his freedom but the freedom of his whole family if he could ride overland through Briton territory and carry a message in time to King Dallan mac Dalriada." Cleary was openly weeping, now. "The abbot, Father Auliffe, fears treachery, Saxon treachery. And none of us know Lailoken so very well. Why should he ride away so quickly in the middle of the night, just before news of this disaster at Dunadd could reach us? The abbot sent me to fetch you and Riona Damhnait, while he brings King Medraut and Queen Keelin."

Morgana felt faint with shock, compounded infinitely by Brenna McEgan's utter horror. The look in Riona's eyes was one Brenna had seen only too often, a look of sanity strained by news so dreadful, by betrayal so deep, the mind could not properly take in the scope of disaster.

"Has King Dallan already sailed?" Morgana whispered, praying that he had not.

"He has. I ran to the shore first, hoping to stop him and deliver the warning. He had already said his goodbyes to Queen Keelin, saying he did not want to wait longer and miss the tide."

Brenna's memory flashed to a sharp image, of Lailoken handing a wine cask to the Irish king, of the look in the minstrel's eyes when Father Auliffe had insisted they share the communion wine, instead. The wine had been poisoned, she could see it clearly, now, when it was too late. Lailoken must be hosting Cedric Banning, there could be no other explanation for his swift departure—or the mass destruction of the entire Dalriadan capital. *How* had he accomplished it? Weapons of mass destruction were a terrorist's stock in trade—Brenna knew that only too well—but what weapon could Banning have concocted in the *sixth century*? Nerve agents or even something as ordinary as mustard gas required chemistry far beyond the reach of anything Banning could possibly have access to, here and now. She tried to focus on the symptoms, to deduce what kind of poison he might have used. Morgana, at least, knew something of poisons.

Witch's bane? she wondered grimly. *It's potent, but how could he have acquired such an immense supply and delivered it?*

"Oh, dear God," Brenna moaned, making a sudden connection between the cask of wine, the bottles she'd glimpsed in Lailoken's "peddlar's" pack, and the most toxic poison in the world—easily grown inside sealed bottles of rotten food. In the time he'd been here already, Cedric Banning could have grown more than enough to poison a whole town, and then some. "He's grown *botulism!*"

"What is this word, botulism?" Riona demanded in a hard, cold voice.

Morgana had pressed hands to her cheeks, which felt clammy and cold, even to her own fingers. Brenna had to answer, as Morgana knew nothing of it, either. "If one allows food to rot inside a sealed container, a potent poison grows in it. He must have mixed dirt in with it, to ensure the botulism would grow and produce the toxins." Morgana, grasping desperately at some explanation that would prevent further disaster to Brythonic-Irish relations, added in a shaking voice,

"If Lailoken is a Saxon agent, dear God, he *must* be a Saxon agent, they've already shown themselves capable of the worst kinds of slaughter. A man who could order infants hacked into pieces could order *anything*. And I was a fool and *trusted* Lailoken, sent him to the very people I wanted to make peace with."

She lifted ravaged eyes to meet Riona's gaze. "We must sail after Dallan mac Dalriada at once. I have to stop him or anyone else who might drink from that wine cask. Pray God he has not already tasted it. And riders must be sent after Lailoken. I want him found and brought back to me, alive and in chains." She turned to the fisherman and his family, who watched silently, eyes wide in naked horror. "Can you take us out tonight? Is your boat fast enough to catch the Irish king?"

"God will lend us wings," he choked out, "for catch him we must." He hurried away, shouting orders and sending runners to rouse his crew for immediate departure.

Morgana turned to the Irish Druidess, dreading what must be said next. Riona Damhnait held her gaze for a long, ugly moment, gauging Morgana's words and the genuineness of the emotion behind them. After a long and dangerous moment beneath a shuttered, thoroughly reptilian stare, something softened behind the other woman's eyes. Tears came, for the first time.

"I do believe you know nothing of this."

Morgana could only shake her head. "Would I be willing to sail after Dallan mac Dalriada myself, otherwise?"

"The Saxons truly are such barbarians, they would slaughter a whole town of innocents?"

Morgana wiped wetness from her cheeks. "To sow dissention between our people, to ensure we are busy fighting in the north, so they have free rein in the south? Oh, yes, I believe they would stoop to anything to destroy us. All of us."

"Then they must be stopped," she said, with such utter coldness, Morgana shivered.

Brenna recognized that sound. It was the sound of an Irish soul roused to vengeance. God help them, it was something bred into the Irish, bred into their Irish bones and blood, centuries of cold-hearted rage at wrongs committed, determination to strike back at an enemy, whatever the cost. Had Brenna inadvertently tried to prevent the birth of one set of Irish hatreds only to help spawn another? Would the mass murder of an entire Irish colony, which should have been destined to hold power in the Scottish Lowlands for centuries to come, change history sufficiently to destroy everything Brenna had known, everyone Brenna had loved? Had Banning already succeeded in carrying out his mission?

The worst of it was, Brenna realized she might never know.

Even if the Irish didn't kill her in retribution—and she held no illusions about Dallan mac Dalriada's reaction, regardless of what his Druidess might now believe—even if she survived the Irish, who could say whether time had fractured sufficiently to trap her in Morgana's mind forever? It occurred to Brenna McEgan that she might never reach home again. And in the same moment, she realized she was no longer sure what—or where—home might be.

Belfast and Londonderry?

The shot-up, bombed-out ghettoes that she herself had fled from years previously, trying to forget the killing and her own, monstrous part in it? She had tried to start over once, already, in a place that was, although just as virulently Irish, at least not involved in a perpetual self-massacre of the type which had gripped

Northern Ireland for centuries. Dublin was the home she'd known for more than ten years now, but what sort of home was it, for a Londonderry girl? She'd been living in exile for more than a decade, trying to run away from the troubles of her own countrymen. And just look at where *that* had landed her.

Running away from a society gone mad was no answer to the madness.

It only left the madmen that much freer to spill their insanity into more innocent lives.

The lesson had come late. Perhaps too late. Once learned, there was only one way in which to answer it. Immediate, drastic action was needed to prevent the lesson being taught to other wide-eyed fools like herself. There was no answer for the Northern Ireland she had fled, not short of separating the children born to both sides from their parents, from their uncles and cousins, and from one another, putting them into public creches to be raised for the next three or four generations, in some last-ditch effort to give the hatred and the blood feuds a chance to die out and let something healthier grow in its place. Either that, or they'd all wake up one fine morning to discover each side had slaughtered the other in its sleep and they'd all arrived at hell's gates together, to spend eternity snarling and blaming one another for the hell they'd all built. The devil must laugh each time another Irish fool with a bomb blew up some poor baby in his pram.

Northern Ireland wasn't dying, it was already dead, soul-deep and rotted out. And the only people who hadn't figured it out, yet, were the Northern Irish.

A small knot of people came running up the strand, even as fishermen appeared from cottages up and down the little stretch of Lochmaben coast. Medraut, his face grey as dirty ice in the moonlight, skidded to a stop in front of his aunt. Her spirits lifted, however briefly, at the way young Keelin clutched his hand, holding onto what little security she had left. It touched Morgana deeply that the child could still trust them. Would to God it remained so.

"You've heard the news from Father Auliffe?" Morgana asked quietly. "We depart the moment the fishermen hoist sail, to try and catch Dallan mac Dalriada's ship. My poor child," she turned to Keelin, whose eyes were reddened from weeping. "Would to God I could undo what the Saxons have done, and me the gullible idiot who let them in to do it."

Keelin struggled for a moment to keep up a brave front, then spotted Riona Damhnait and collapsed into her kinswoman's arms, sobbing. Medraut hovered helplessly, wanting to comfort her, afraid she would reject the offer, wanting to strike at something, anything, to undo this monstrous damage. He turned finally to Morgana, anger seething through him like storm-slashed lightning. "Send me after that bastard Lailoken, Aunt! I'll rip out his heart with these hands" he held up curved claws, fingers rigid with rage, "and feed it as he deserves to my grieving bride!"

"Nay, Medraut. He will be brought to us alive and unharmed."

"But—"

"The Irish, lad, will want him."

Unholy glee shone abruptly in the boy's eyes, reminding her sickeningly of his mother, Marguase, the late and unlamented, she who had almost been queen of Ynys Manaw, had the darkness not taken her soul. Morgana determined to do all that was possible to keep that darkness from consuming Medraut, as well. "Lailoken will be found, Medraut. Found and returned to stand trial under Brythonic law and then handed over for trial by Irish law. He will pay for what he has unleashed. Never doubt that. But your task, nephew, and mine is another matter altogether."

She had his attention now, at least. The ragged pacing and hyperactive, supercharged energy flooding out of him came to a brief standstill. "What is our task, Aunt? I don't know enough to rule Galwyddel at a time like this."

"There is no better time, lad, with war threatening from the south and now an almost certainty from the north. There is but one thing we can do, Medraut. We sail after Dallan mac Dalriada and try to persuade him that we, too, are deeply betrayed by a Saxon spy we did not suspect until far too late."

She saw it pass through his eyes, the realization that they were honor-bound to warn the Irish king, that he would probably order them killed in a hideous, slow manner befitting the crime, saw him look that death square in the eye and accept it. He nodded slowly. "Yes. It is the only honorable thing to do."

Her throat tightened, seeing that. If Dallan mac Dalriada allowed them to live, Medraut would make a fine king, indeed. She rested a hand on his arm, unable to speak. He nodded again, not needing her words. Then he turned to his sobbing bride and gently gathered her close, stroking her hair. "We sail to catch your father and deliver the warning. You must be strong, my love, for the agony will strike his heart far more deeply, even, than yours, for he will feel the whole responsibility for failing them."

She lifted a sodden, red-eyed gaze, lips trembling. "Yes," she whispered, gulping to try and contain her grief. "He will. The gods have made you wise, Medraut." She rested her brow against his chest for a moment. "I want to go home, husband, but there is no home to return to. What manner of beast is this Lailoken, to do such a thing?"

"He is a Saxon," the boy said helplessly. "It is the only answer I can offer."

The slender princess of Dalriada lifted her gaze once more and even Medraut froze at the look in the girl's eyes. "Then the Saxons must die."

She spoke briefly in Gael to Riona Damhnait, who nodded.

"They say Brythonic queens lead warriors in battle," Keelin said in a cold, hard little voice. "It is time I learned the custom of my husband's people. Come, Medraut, let us prepare our respective peoples for war."

"Yes." He turned to find Father Auliffe standing behind Morgana. "Father, you and Cleary must organize the fisherfolk of Lochmaben to spread the alarm. Galwyddel rides to war. Warn Strathclyde to strengthen the garrisons along the northern border in case we fail to persuade Dallan mac Dalriada of British innocence, but send the bulk of our own fighting strength south, against the Saxons. I will not permit such butchers to remain a threat to our people. *Any* of our people," he added, drawing Keelin firmly to his side.

Auliffe hesitated only a fraction of a second, recognizing as clearly as Morgana that the reins of power had just been transferred to the new king of Galwyddel and his queen. The aging abbot nodded. "I grieve for all of us," the priest said quietly. "It shall be done. Go, my king, and try to prevent further death among our new kinsmen."

Less than a quarter of an hour later, they were aboard the fishing sloop, crewed by grim-faced men who knew the risk as well as their passengers, and accepted that risk for their new king and queen's sake. Morgana watched and wept and stared out to sea, raking the dark horizon for the faintest hint of moon-touched sails.

Chapter Sixteen

Trevor Stirling and Ancelotis caught up with Artorius just a few miles short of Caer-Birrenswark, by riding three good horses into the ground, switching mounts at three of the fortified towns in Galwyddel. Artorius had done the same thing, they discovered, but was traveling at a slightly less frantic pace, which gave Stirling and the king of Gododdin the chance they desperately needed to catch Artorius up. They passed a column of foot soldiers heading south out of Galwyddel, presumably the men Morgana had sent to Caer-Badonicus, and—of greater surprise—they met Lailoken, the minstrel, who was also heading south.

"Have you seen the Dux Bellorum?" Ancelotis asked, flagging the minstrel down.

Lailoken gave him a searching look, then nodded, pointing back the way he'd come. "Aye, perhaps ten miles further on. He was moving fast. Is there trouble?"

"I've a message for him. They said in Caerleul you rode out with Queen Morgana?"

"That I did," the minstrel nodded, "but I left her these several days past. She had private business away from Caer-Birrenswark and when a queen is not in residence, there's little enough work for a court minstrel."

"You don't know where she's gone, then?"

"That I don't, I'm afraid. Myself, I'm riding south, to join kinsmen."

A glint of some private mirth the minstrel did not wish to share caught Stirling's attention, but Ancelotis was too distracted by worry to notice. "Godspeed to you then, and the less said of this, the better."

"I am the soul of discretion," the minstrel murmured, sweeping a bow from the waist, a bow that held an elusive, mocking quality, disturbing Trevor Stirling once again, but Ancelotis was already putting heels to his horse's flanks, sending them galloping down Artorius' trail. Only ten miles more to catch him and Ancelotis was waiting for nothing and no one.

Their fourth horse was beginning to show the strain, when the Dux Bellorum finally came into sight. Ancelotis pulled loose the signal horn strapped to his saddle and gave a good, loud blast that carried a long way. Artorius pulled up and turned in the saddle, peering back with one hand raised to shade his eyes. They came thundering down the final stretch of road, the lathered horse blowing with distended nostrils.

"What news?" Artorius asked tersely as Ancelotis pulled his mount to a sliding stop.

"The same that sent you racing for Caer-Birrenswark," Ancelotis replied, voice grim. "I'll not believe ill of Morgana, whatever you've been told. Nor will Thaney, who begged me to ride after you."

Artorius' glare made summer storms seem mild. "This is my affair! As Dux Bellorum—"

"If you were here as Dux Bellorum, the *cataphracti* would be riding at your heels."

The jibe scored; Artorius flushed a dark red. "Morgana is my stepsister, which makes it a personal matter."

"And she is *my* sister-in-law, which makes it a personal matter to me, as well."

The measuring look Artorius leveled at him only served to stiffen Ancelotis' resolve and left Stirling very glad, indeed, that this man was not his declared enemy. At length, Artorius let go a weary sigh and turned his gaze to stare down the road toward Caer-Birrenswark, the uppermost tower of which could just be seen across the treetops. "I am desperately hoping history will not repeat. It would be agony to condemn Morgana, as I once was forced to condemn Marguase."

"Morgana is no poisoner. Nor will I believe her a traitor without a great deal more proof than whatever letter Covianna handed you."

A startled look broke loose. "Thaney knew about that?"

"Oh, yes. She persuaded the minstrel to confess to it, after you left Caerleul in such a tearing hurry, without a word to anyone."

Artorius snorted. "I pity the poor minstrel, then. Your niece is a woman I would not care to cross."

Ancelotis grinned. "In that, we are fully agreed. May I see the letter?"

The Dux Bellorum hesitated, then fished into a leather satchel strapped behind his saddle and handed over a folded bit of vellum. Ancelotis read it quickly, while Stirling attempted to make out what it said. He could understand spoken Brythonic, thanks to the

merging of his mind with Ancelotis', but the written
form still baffled him. Ancelotis translated silently,
leaving Stirling groaning under his breath. It looked
very bad, indeed, if this were an accurate rendering
of the conversation Covianna claimed to have overheard. Alliance with the Irish, through a marriage
between Medraut and the heiress to Dalriada . . . Little
wonder Artorius had rushed north to try and stop
Morgana from committing irrevocable folly.

He had just handed back the scrap of vellum when
several fast-moving horsemen appeared from the
direction of Caer-Birrenswark. Artorius muttered,
"More bad news, it looks like," an assessment Ancelotis
was forced to agree with, particularly when the riders came close enough to identify as soldiers of
Galwyddel's *cataphracti.* When their officer recognized
the Dux Bellorum, they drew to a halt to greet
Artorius. The man spoke without preamble.

"Have you seen Lailoken, the minstrel?"

A queasy sensation hit Stirling square in the gut as
Ancelotis answered. "I spoke briefly with him, some
ten miles further back." He gestured down the road
that led toward Caerleul.

"Then we may yet catch the bastard. King Medraut
sent us to fetch the god-cursed traitor back for trial."

Even as Ancelotis gasped, the Dux Bellorum said
in a soft and dangerous voice, "King Medraut? Mean
you not Queen Morgana?"

The officer hesitated, clearly upset by that piece of
news, as well as whatever disaster Lailoken might have
unleashed. The man cleared his throat, then said, "No,
it was King Medraut who gave the orders to find the
minstrel. The abbot of Caer-Birrenswark himself drew
up the agreement to transfer the throne of Galwyddel
to Medraut. That news was startling enough, but the
lad, er, the new king has also married."

An unhappy look darkened the man's eyes. "It seems utter insanity, but Father Auliffe has lent the support of the Holy Church to Medraut's marriage and I cannot imagine a man less likely to support treason. Medraut has married the heiress to Dalriada, you see, and the abbot swears it is a good alliance with nothing of treachery in either the girl or her father. The hope was to secure the northern border between Strathclyde and Dalriada against invasion. And it might have worked, truly it might, only . . ." He hesitated.

"Only what?" Artorius growled, eyes dark and grim.

"Only Lailoken has betrayed all of Britain. He's a Saxon agent, in the pay of King Aelle."

"Lailoken, a Saxon *spy?*" Ancelotis asked, eyes widening in astonishment. "How can that possibly be proved? I've seen the man in my brother Lot's court and he spent a week or so entertaining the soldiers of Caer-Iudeu. You saw him yourself, Artorius, at Rheged's festivals. He's a comic buffoon and a passable minstrel, but a spy?"

The officer nodded, eyes bleak. "A Saxon spy and much else as well, I fear. There is far worse news than Medraut's marriage to Keelin of Dalriada. Lailoken is a poisoner. A monstrous saboteur. While he and Medraut visited Fortress Dunadd to arrange the marriage with King Dallan mac Dalriada, he poisoned the entire city, poisoned the wells, at least that's what Father Auliffe and Queen Morgana suspect. A Briton slave escaped across the border into Strathclyde and rode for Galwyddel with the news that all of Dunadd is dead, down to the infants at their mothers' breasts. Vomiting, convulsions, paralysis—it was no natural plague that killed those poor bastards." Distress roughened the man's voice.

The image struck Trevor Stirling with a familiar sense of horror, even as Ancelotis and Artorius went stiff with shock. Biological warfare was a reality Stirling had witnessed before, in the twenty-first century, but neither the king of Gododdin nor the Dux Bellorum had any experience with such atrocity.

"*The whole town?*" Artorius whispered. "My God, Dalriada will massacre every Briton in Strathclyde before marching into Galwyddel!"

"Not if we can catch Lailoken and hand him over to the Irish," the officer muttered. "Queen Morgana and King Medraut have taken ship to try and catch Dallan mac Dalriada before he returns home, to try and convince him it was Saxon treachery, not Briton. Queen Keelin and her Druidess have gone with them, to try and prevent utter disaster."

Artorius just shut his eyes. "Oh, God, watch over her," he groaned.

Ancelotis muttered agreement, while Stirling tried to sort out a confusing issue that puzzled him immensely. The murder of an entire town by some form of biological weapon was entirely in keeping with an agent of the Irish Republican Army. *But why would Brenna McEgan massacre the Irish?* It made no sane sense. The IRA terrorist had come here to further Irish interests, so why destroy the very Irish settlers who were destined to form the political and social structure of the entire Scottish Lowlands?

If McEgan had poisoned Caerleul, or even Artorius, it would have been perfectly understandable. But not Dalriada. And if Brenna McEgan had not killed every soul in the Irish colony's capital, *who had?* The Saxons? It was difficult to credit such a notion, when the sixth century's natives were completely unfamiliar with the ways in which a whole settlement could be taken out with chemical or biological agents.

Artorius was asking, "And Morgana has already left for Dalriada? You're sure of that?"

The officer nodded. "Father Auliffe said she took sail from the Lochmaben coast, by way of a fishing sloop, trying to catch up with Dallan mac Dalriada's ship."

"Whether or not she succeeds," Ancelotis said quietly, "there is nothing you and I can do to change what will happen between her and the king of Dalriada. All we can do is strengthen the northern garrisons against invasion and turn our own attention to the Saxon threat in the south."

"King Medraut has already ordered riders north to warn Strathclyde of the danger to the border forts. Just in case."

"Then we must ride south," Artorius said heavily. "And pray God the Irish believe her. For myself, I must suspend judgement against Morgana and Medraut until the war with the Saxons has been decided, one way or the other."

"Agreed," Ancelotis murmured, half sick with grief and worry.

They turned their horses about and set out in pursuit of Lailoken. They had gone perhaps three miles when one of the men back in the line of *cataphracti* broke into song, a stirring, cadence-rich marching tune which brought the hairs on Stirling's arms and nape standing straight up. He drew rein sharply, trying to locate the singer.

"Where did you hear that?" he demanded.

The soldier blinked in surprise. "One of the minstrels was whistling it at Caer-Birrenswark. I hadn't heard it before and asked him to teach it to me. It's good for the riding, don't you think?"

"Oh, yes, it's a snappy little tune," Stirling agreed darkly. "Let me guess? He learned the tune from Lailoken?"

The man stared in absolute shock. "Aye, that's what

he said. He'd been to Caerleul and learnt it there, from Lailoken. How did you know? Is it a Saxon tune, then?" the man asked worriedly.

"In a manner of speaking." Stirling was cursing himself as the worst fool ever to put on the uniform of the SAS. All the little clues he had failed to notice before had fallen neatly into place the instant he heard that particular song. It was a marching song, all right. An *Orange* marching song. One of the Orangemen's favorites, in fact. It wouldn't even be written for more than a millennium and a half. If Lailoken had been singing it, he could have learned it from only one soul: Cedric Banning. The man whose British affectations had struck Trevor Stirling as odd, that first night, the kind of snobbery a status-seeking colonial might display—or a very clever man wishing to pass himself off as one.

And he'd worn a *paisley* scarf, must have been laughing at Stirling the whole time they'd sat in that pub, wearing such a blatant, insulting clue and watching the SAS officer blunder his way right into the trap Banning had set up. Brenna McEgan hadn't killed Terrance Beckett. Banning had. McEgan must have been planted by the IRA as a countermeasure against an *Orange* terror plot. The bruises on her face—and on Banning's knuckles—floated into his mind's eye, another humiliating clue he'd ignored. McEgan must have walked into the lab right on the heels of the murder. And Banning, clever bastard, had led Stirling straight down the garden path with that note about her ties to *Cumann Na Mbann*.

It was entirely possible that she *had* been part of that terrorist group. It was also entirely possible that she was innocent of everything Stirling—and London—had suspected of her. And Cedric Banning had excellent reason to poison an entire Irish city. Stirling wondered who, exactly, had tipped off London that an IRA mole had infiltrated the lab staff? Banning himself? Trying—with embarrassing success—to divert attention from his own agenda? It hardly mattered, now that the damage had been done.

The question of *how* he'd done it was answered shortly enough. Moving at a steady gallop, they covered the remaining miles rapidly, only to discover that their quarry was no longer on the road. He had bolted, abandoning his packhorse, which they found grazing at the verge of the Roman highway, snatching up greedy mouthfuls of grass. A search of the horse's panniers brought to light several wine bottles and ceramic jars, all carefully stoppered, with the corks and sealed lids bound down with twists of heavy twine.

Artorius held one of the glass bottles up, peering curiously at the lumps visible inside. "It looks like chunks of meat and rotten vegetables."

"Don't open any of them!" Stirling warned sharply, seeing all too clearly how Banning had committed the atrocity at Fortress Dunadd. *Botulism toxin.* He felt an utter and complete fool, with no way to undo the damage already wrought. Damage which might well have destroyed Stirling's entire future, with no way to tell until the equipment shut down at the end of a year—and no guarantee that it even existed any longer, *to* be shut down. From this end of history, there literally was no way to tell.

Worse, yet, was the damage Banning could still do. Using botulism, the man could literally poison every Irish town and farmhold from Londonderry to County Kerry and further south, to Cork. All he'd need was a cover story—and what better cover than a traveling minstrel, bringing news of a marriage of alliance between Dalriada and Galwyddel? He wouldn't even have to mention it had ended in treachery, since no one in his wake would survive long enough to find out differently.

Stirling had to shut his eyes against the vision of all Ireland dying, leaving the island wide open for Saxon invasion. Banning was an Orangeman and the Orangemen were descended from pure Anglo-Saxon stock. An Orangeman could take no better revenge than to utterly annihilate the entire Irish population, while simultaneously stirring up war between Dalriada and Galwyddel—at a time when his Saxon ancestors were laying waste to the entire south of England. Divide British attention between war at both ends of the island and the Saxons would conquer it all, the entire British Isles, in one fell swoop. Frosting on the cake would be a few bottles of death emptied into the wells of strategically important Briton strongholds.

The question was, which way had Lailoken and his unseen guest bolted? West, to Ireland? To spread the word of alliance and treachery, while quietly leaving mass murder in his wake? Or south, to join his Saxon kinfolk and take to Aelle and Cutha the secret of biological warfare contained in these monstrous little bottles?

In low, terse tones, Stirling told Artorius as much as he could, without compromising Ancelotis' status as his host. Artorius listened in black silence, then spat to one side.

"We'll have to split our forces, meager as they are. Two riders west, toward the coast, two east, in case he's bolted for Dewyr, as Cutha did. The rest of us will ride south, toward Caer-Badonicus. And pray God we catch him before he reaches his paymasters."

Staring utter disaster in the face, whichever way Lailoken had bolted, they mounted their war-horses in silence and set out in grim pursuit.

❖   ❖   ❖

Dawn's first hint of oyster light had touched the eastern sky when one of the sailors who'd climbed the mast to act as lookout spotted sails dead ahead.

"I see them!" he shouted, pointing. "He's landward of us, rounding the tip of Kintyre!"

Morgana's heart lurched into her throat and Brenna gripped the gunwale, fingers turning white in the crepuscular light. At her side, Keelin clutched Medraut's hand and braced herself against the wild pitching of the boat as the captain turned the tiller, sending them on a tack that would take them on a shorter and faster route, seaward of the longer, looping journey Dallan mac Dalriada's crew had chosen, keeping closer to land. The Irish king's sails rose up out of the sea as they narrowed the gap, plowing deep into the troughs while the sails rattled and snapped taut again on the new course.

Brenna wished mightily for a pair of radios or even a signal cannon to flag the other ship's attention and was too distraught to try and explain to Morgana what either device was, much less how they worked. As they drew steadily closer, Brenna realized the only thing that had allowed them to catch up was the lighter, smaller boat they rode in, much faster across the water than Dallan mac Dalriada's larger and heavier warship. Like the Greeks at Salamis, whose smaller, faster boats had wrecked the massive Persian navy, the Briton fishing sloop rapidly overtook the Irish ship, finally drawing within shouting distance as they both rounded the tip of the Kintyre Peninsula.

Riona Damhnait had already taught the sloop's captain the words to shout, as deeper male voices carried farther across water than women's voices ever could. The captain bellowed out the message, which drew startled reactions from the Irish crew. A moment later, they had dropped a sea anchor overboard, slowing their

speed enough to match pace with the slower Irish ship.
Dallan mac Dalriada appeared at the ship's rail, shouting
a question across. Riona answered, shouting as loudly
as she could, while the sailors of both craft flung ropes
across, snugging the ships together and running burlap
bags filled with sand over the sides to act as bumpers,
so the hulls didn't grind one another to splinters.

"Help me across, Medraut," Morgana said, swallowing down nausea that had very little to do with the
wild pitching of the deck under their feet. "And help
your bride and Riona, as well."

A moment later, all four stood on Dallan mac
Dalriada's deck, while Keelin flung herself into her
father's arms and sobbed out their awful news. The
Irish king washed white with shock, holding his daughter tightly while he flung questions at his Druidess.
Riona spoke rapidly, urgently, hands sketching gestures
in the cold, wet dawnlight as she relayed the message
which had come by way of the young Briton slave. His
face clouded over with black rage as he listened. When
he snarled some order, sending his men toward the
Britons, weapons drawn, Keelin flung herself into
Medraut's arms and spoke shrilly, nearly hysterical in
her effort to stop whatever her father had just ordered.
Given the black looks the crew sent their way, neither
Morgana nor Brenna McEgan had any illusions as to
the nature of that command.

Keelin braced herself at bay, arms thrown wide to
protect Morgana and Medraut, like a wild vixen run
to earth and snarling at the hounds who snapped at
her helpless kits. Even Riona stared in surprise at the
violence of the girl's response to Medraut's abrupt
danger. What Medraut did next sent Morgana's heart
plunging straight into the sea. He unslung his sword
and dropped it onto the wet deck, took Keelin gently
by the shoulders, and lifted her aside. He then stepped

forward and faced the wild-eyed king straight on. Without turning his gaze away from Dallan mac Dalriada's for so much as a half-second, he said to Riona Damhnait, "Please tell my father-in-law that I will gladly die by his hand, if it is his will. But my death will accomplish nothing, not even vengeance, if he attacks Britain and allows the true culprits, the Saxons, to escape unscathed, laughing in their beards at blind Irish rage."

Brenna was absolutely convinced that she and Medraut were about to die.

She could do nothing but whimper in the back of her shared throat when Morgana stepped to Medraut's side and said, "Please tell King Dallan that I, Morgana of Ynys Manaw, have placed myself and all that I love in his hands, risking everything to bring this warning. Has he or any man aboard this ship drunk from Lailoken's wine cask?"

Dallan's eyes widened. "Wine cask?"

The words were pure Gael, but—unmistakably—he had said, "Wine cask?"

The translation came when Riona sagged in relief so profound, she nearly slid to the decks, braced at the last instant by an alert sailor who caught her from a nasty fall. "Your God has looked upon us, Morgana," the Druidess whispered, staggering back to her feet, "for no one has yet tasted the gift."

Keelin was speaking urgently now, so urgently, her father could not get in a single word of protest or negation. Judging by the expressions and gestures, she was telling her father that Medraut and Morgana had themselves insisted upon accompanying Keelin on this voyage, knowing full well they might be executed for it, that she had come to love Medraut for the honorable and courageous young man he was, that Medraut would fight to the death whole armies of Saxons, to protect his new Dalriadan Irish kinfolk, those the Saxon treachery had left alive. And judging by the tears sparkling in the dawnlight on her cheeks and the thunderous black look on her father's face, those kinfolk were very few in number now, and therefore doubly precious.

The king's reply, when it came, needed no translation. *I ought to have my head examined,* that look said. He gestured and two of the sailors bound Medraut's wrists behind him, and Morgana's as well, while Irish sailors spilled over into the British fishing sloop and tied the hands of every man aboard her. But they had not been gutted on sight, which was more than Morgana, at least, had expected.

"Ask the king if he has a dog aboard this ship," Morgana said, turning her gaze to meet the Druidess' unhappy gaze. "Or better still, a rat. Feed the creature some of the wine from Lailoken's cask. If it contains the botulism toxins, the animal will be dead within twelve to twenty hours. And he will have enough proof to hang whomever he considers guilty for the atrocity at Dunadd."

Dallan mac Dalriada snarled out a reply. Keelin shrieked, "Nay!" and threw herself in front of Medraut again. Impasse. One that did not last long. At a bellow from her father, two burly sailors dragged the girl away, fighting and clawing, even biting them in her desperation to escape and prevent Medraut's untimely slaughter. That he had won not only the girl's heart, but her unswerving loyalty, was not lost on Dallan mac Dalriada. It was equally clear that the Irish king had no idea what to do about it, a hurt and bewildered and angry parent doing his best to protect his child while his entire world crashed down about his ears.

When he finally gave a curt order that sent Medraut and Morgana below the deck, dragged down into the cramped cargo space—cold and damp and unutterably wretched with dirt and foul smells of dead fish and live rats—Keelin broke free, striking her father with both fists in a paroxysm of raging emotion, then collapsed in Riona's arms, sobbing uncontrollably.

A heavy wooden hatch slammed down across the only exit from their watery prison, robbing them of further sight of Keelin's wild grief, which was just as well, for Medraut's sake. The boy trembled where they lay crammed together between ship's hull and a heavy case of something that thumped and rattled like shifting crowbars. Ingots of iron, no doubt, ferried north to be forged into weapons.

Battered and bruised, Morgana lay still, the ropes hurting her wrists, and tried to catch the sound of Irish voices arguing in Gael. It was, like the German spoken by the men of Saxony, a language one ought to understand, if one simply listened hard enough to catch the similarities of phrase and slightly odd pronunciation of familiar words.

Medraut whispered, "I've learnt enough Gael to know a little of what's being said. Dallan mac Dalriada is ordering rats brought to him, along with Lailoken's wine cask. He's going to try it, Aunt."

"Pray God he believes Keelin and his Druidess, for Riona Damhnait is no fool and it's clear he knows that. He's also turning for home," Morgana muttered as the ship wallowed and rolled and took up a new tack, but without turning around to sail back south. "He'll go straight to Dunadd to verify the deaths himself. God pity us when we arrive, Medraut, for I very much doubt that Dallan mac Dalriada will."

"I'm sorry," Medraut choked out, his whisper a badly shaken child's apology for creating an unwanted mess.

"No, never be sorry, Medraut, for doing the right and honorable thing."

"No," he countered her at once, "I'm not sorry for coming. I'm sorry for allowing you to come along, as well. For that, I am twice the fool and will regret it as long as the Irish allow us to live."

She wished there were some comforting thing, anything, she might say to the boy.

There was not a single, useful word in her weary and battered brain.

So she laid her head against a pile of coiled rope and waited for the rats—and doubtless soon thereafter, the prisoners—to die. The day passed in agonizing slowness, the most physically miserable day of Morgana's life, not as painful as childbirth, but bone-jarring as the ship plowed through heavy seas, rolling and bashing them against one another and the contents of the cramped space below deck. Nausea tore her throat, occasionally leaving her helpless in the throes of uncontrollable heaves. Medraut tried to brace her at such times, using his shoulder to help lift her over his own body, as their hands were bound tightly behind them.

Brenna McEgan, unused to travel by water, suffered in silence. She had never taken up the sport of sailing and preferred air travel for the short hop between Dublin and London or Dublin and Edinburgh. While Morgana *had* made the sea journey from Ynys Manaw to the mainland many times, she had never traveled locked in a tiny, dark space unable to see sky and waves. Medraut, too, was messily ill several times, mumbling abject apologies as they took turns trying to assist one another. They were given no food, which was probably a mercy, and no water, either, which was an added cruelty. Not that Morgana could have swallowed any without disastrous consequences, but she would've dearly loved to rinse the sour taste from her mouth.

What felt like an entire lifetime later, night

descended, robbing them of the few meager cracks
of light that found their way between boards and joins.
The total darkness was suffocating. When the ship
wallowed heavily, coming around on a new heading,
Medraut murmured, "We must be entering Dunadd
Harbor. It feels like the right amount of time to've
reached it."

"I wonder," Morgana said bitterly, unable to keep
the sound out of her voice, "if the rats have died yet."

"At least they haven't forced us to drink from the
cask. I've halfway expected him to order it."

Morgana shivered. "He may yet."

A distantly heard splash reached their ears and the
ship pitched and yawed and came to a rocking standstill, tethered by her anchor line. They could hear
voices overhead, shouting in Gaelic, and other voices
replying faintly. "They must have brought the fishing
sloop along," Medraut said in a faintly surprised tone.

Morgana forced a chuckle. "What, fail to secure a
free ship and several new slaves for himself? Your
father-in-law is no fool, nephew. He will," she added
darkly, "have need of a few slaves, to replace the men
and women Lailoken murdered. Winter is nearly upon
them and this blow bids fair to destroy his whole
colony."

Overhead, the hatch cover was lifted clear, allowing torchlight to spill into their eyes. As Morgana
squinted against the light, a sailor slid down and lifted
her into the hands of another man who hauled her up
onto the deck. Medraut was hoisted out, in turn, while
a third sailor busied himself untying her wrists. She
rubbed the chafed skin and bruises gingerly, wincing
and trying to keep her balance, more weakened by
thirst, battering, and fear than she'd realized.

Medraut stood glaring at their captors, shaking with
visible rage as he pulled Morgana protectively to his

side. For once, she was more than happy to lean against him. As her eyes adjusted to the torchlight, she made out Dallan mac Dalriada's thickset figure and beyond him, Keelin and Riona Damhnait. Keelin bit her lip when she saw the bruises and stains on their clothing from the seasickness.

Dallan mac Dalriada gave a rough-voiced order and they were prodded none too gently into a small boat which had been lowered over the ship's rail and bobbed on the water, making the task of entering it difficult— particularly with all her limbs still trembling. She and Medraut were herded into the bow, while Dallan mac Dalriada, his daughter, and his Druidess sat in the center, leaving the stern for the sailor who rowed them across black water toward an utterly silent town. Waning moonlight picked out the whitewashed walls of cottages, and gleamed ominously along the darkened watchtower of the fortress above the village.

The offshore wind carried a stench so foul, Morgana found herself swallowing convulsively over sharp nausea. She gripped the rough wood hard, trying to distract her senses from that hideous smell. Not a dog barked as their little boat scraped ashore and Medraut jumped out to steady her onto the strand. They waited silently on the beach while the boat went back for several of the ship's crew, who carried torches. Morgana bent to tear strips of cloth from her skirt, wetting them and tying them over her nose and mouth against the foulness on the air. She handed one to Medraut, who hastily copied her example. Even Riona and Keelin accepted the strips she offered, poor Keelin near to vomiting.

A dull anger burned in Morgana's breast that Dallan mac Dalriada would subject his daughter to the horror waiting in this village, where literally everyone she knew and loved lay rotting in the streets. Even from this distance, she could see bodies lying at grotesque angles, some of them visibly gnawed on by scavengers.

The moment the crewmen arrived with the torches, Dallan mac Dalriada prodded them into motion. They walked numbly through street after street, encountering at least a few graves already dug, where survivors from the outlying farmholds had begun the grim work of burying the dead. Keelin began to cry within a few short minutes, stumbling along in her father's wake as he stalked straight through the town and up the long ramp to the fortress gates. What Morgana could see of Medraut's face above the mask was ashen in the torch-light, with beads of cold sweat shining along his brow. Morgana steeled herself not to look too closely into the shadows as they passed open cottage doorways and narrow little alleyways between houses and shops.

When they finally reached the fortress gate, they found bloated dogs, horses with their legs stiffened, grotesque in the moonlight, and pathetic little bundles of fur that had once been pampered housecats. Keelin fell to her knees over one of the cats, sobbing beneath her makeshift mask and uttering a little cry of protest when Riona urged her back to her feet. Morgana's heart broke, watching the distraught girl, but dared not offer comfort; Medraut's eyes shone with unshed tears, even as his jaw muscles clenched in rhythm with the fists he tightened every few seconds. Staring at the charnel-house ruin of the great courtyard, Brenna McEgan whispered silently, *Lailoken and Banning must have poisoned every well in town, it couldn't have been anything else, to kill the animals as well as the people.*

Morgana, lips trembling beneath her own mask, could not even reply, lost in an agony of grief. She could not even ask what sort of hatred Brenna's world bred, to create such men, when her own world and time had created the likes of Cutha. The Saxon prince had merely used a sword instead of poison. The devastation was just as bad, either way.

Inside the great hall, they found servants lying where they'd collapsed, trying to assist the noble ladies and lords of the royal household. As the torchlight revealed the scope of destruction, Keelin uttered a wild shriek and darted forward, cradling a child's body to her breast and weeping uncontrollably. Medraut's voice came out strangled over a string of curses as he dared Dallan mac Dalriada's wrath to rush to Keelin's side, gathering her close and stroking her hair, very gently prying the dead child from the girl's hands.

"We must bury her, Keelin," he choked out. "Please, you must let her go, there's nothing you can do for her and I would sooner die here and now than see you struck down by contagion from holding what is left of her."

The sobbing girl refused to loosen her hold on the child's body until Riona and Dallan mac Dalriada stepped in to separate them by force. One of the sailors carried the broken little body away, hurrying at the king's urgent gesture. Keelin uttered a wailing protest, then turned and collapsed. Not in her father's arms, but in Medraut's. Dallan mac Dalriada's eyes widened in shock as his child clung to her new husband, shuddering and weeping, moaning what must have been the child's name over and over.

Morgana saw the shift in the Irish king's eyes, that moment of stunned recognition when he realized his child truly did not believe the Britons responsible. And she saw the doubt come surging into his face as well, the first doubt that Keelin and Riona Damhnait just might be correct in that belief. Medraut was stroking his young wife's hair, rocking her gently, helpless in the face of her wild grief and weeping for that helplessness.

Dallan mac Dalriada stumbled toward the nearest chair, which happened to be his own throne, next to the hearth, and sank down onto the cold stone. Wetness shone on his own face, now. He choked out something in a low voice, speaking at some considerable length. When he had finished speaking, Riona touched Morgana's wrist.

"My king would have you know the depth of his regret for treating you so ill, this day. We captured a number of rats, forcing them to drink Lailoken's wine as you suggested, poured it down their throats while holding open their jaws. They *all* died, just at sunset. He pondered long and hard on this, during the final hours of our journey home, thinking if you had meant treachery against his life, you surely would not have come chasing after him with a warning. Why would you have brought such terrible news yourself, with your nephew in your company, if you had ordered the poisoning of Dunadd?

"Then he thought perhaps you are very clever, intending him to think these things, while plotting yet more destruction while he was distracted by grief. He begs forgiveness, begs you to understand all that he has lost, kinsmen and brave people who trusted him and his father before him, men and women who came to this wild new land, many of them only within the last year, trusting his word that they would be safe to build their homes and raise their families here. Your ship he restores freely, and the brave men who knew what they risked in bringing you with the warning. King Dallan mac Dalriada asks only one thing more of Queen Morgana and King Medraut."

"Name it," Morgana said quietly.

Riona's eyes were hard as flint in the firelight.

"Help him kill the Saxons."

Chapter Seventeen

Trevor Stirling was getting used to forced marches, short sleep, and foul weather.

The SAS should train half so hard, he grumbled, although he did so with a fair dose of wry humor.

Aye, Ancelotis sighed, *war is no business for the faint of heart, nor those weak of constitution.*

It was an unexpected compliment and one Stirling valued, considering the source—Ancelotis' unhappily broad experience of warfare at a level and brutality which still had the power to raise the fine hairs on the nape of his borrowed neck. He and his host had ridden far ahead of Artorius and the bulk of the army rushing south as fast as their infantry could travel. Ancelotis and Stirling were accompanied by more than a hundred *cataphracti* from Ancelotis' own Gododdin, men headed south toward Caer-Badonicus in answer to the summons he'd sent out several days previously.

The Sarmatian bows most of them carried were

heavy-pull compound bows made of horn in the Scythian style, perfect, deadly weapons for a force of heavy cavalry. The Romans had learned at great cost— an entire legion, slaughtered to the last man—what such bows could accomplish against infantry. Those bows gave Stirling ideas. Really nasty ideas. And he ought to arrive at Caer-Badonicus in plenty of time to implement them.

"Ride ahead with word that we are on the march," Artorius had told him shortly after finding Lailoken's abandoned packhorse. "We'll need some kind of signal to let you know when we've come close enough to Caer-Badonicus to break the Saxons' siege with our infantry as well as the rest of our cavalry."

Stirling considered the possibilities for a moment. He knew multiple ways to send coded signals, but which of them were most easily adapted to current conditions? "Have you any polished mirrors?" he asked thoughtfully.

Artorius' brows flicked upward in surprise. "Mirrors? I suppose I could lay hands on a polished bronze mirror, readily enough. Why?"

"Light flashing from a mirror travels a long way. You could devise a simple code and use sunlight on the mirror to send us the message you're close by."

Artorius tugged at his lower lip for a moment. "I seem to recall reading, many years ago, as a boy under Myrddin's tutelage, that one of the Roman emperors used a mirror to send long coded messages from the mainland to one of the islands, Sicily or Sardinia, I can't recall which, now. And the Visigoths who've taken over Rome use signal fires, it's said, occluded by some barrier like a blanket, to flash out numerical patterns. They keep codebooks to translate the number flashes into words."

"Perfect," Stirling nodded. "When you reach a point

within a few miles of Caer-Badonicus, use the mirror flashes if it's by day or an occluded fire if by night." He couldn't help chuckling, thinking about Rudyard Kipling again, the poem about the young British officer stationed in India, using the heliograph to flash messages to his "darling poppsy-wop," warning his bride against General Banks, that "most immoral man"—a warning inadvertently seen and decoded by none other than the general himself.

"We'll use a simple numerical replacement system," Artorius decided with a grin. One flash is 'A,' two are 'B' and so on, through the Latin alphabet. Look for the signals from the highest of the Mendip Hills. Flashes from there will be seen easily from the summit of Caer-Badonicus. And you can signal back where the Saxons' greatest troop concentration is camped."

Stirling chuckled. "With pleasure."

"Watch the northern horizon for the signal then, and when it comes, you'll know relief is only a few miles away. Cadorius and Melwas must fight a holding action if the Saxons reach Caer-Badonicus ahead of our main force. Which I suspect they will. King Aelle of Sussex would be a fool to delay, once Cutha's brought news of our disarray in the north. God help us, two kings dead and a queen . . ." Artorius hesitated, spat to one side, then muttered, "Enough said about Morgana. God help us, even Ganhumara worries me less."

Stirling's host would have liked to say something comforting, but Ganhumara was trouble everywhere she turned her attention. Ancelotis of Gododdin was too honest a man to mouth platitudes nobody believed, so he and Stirling took their leave silently, to begin yet another body-numbing forced march. Stirling had no idea where Caer-Badonicus was—its location remained one of the twenty-first century's greatest

Arthurian mysteries—nor how many horses he would have to change out along the way. Not too many, he hoped, for the armies moving ahead of them surely would have rounded up every stray cart horse and fat pony to be found.

I hope you have some idea where we're going, Stirling groused, trying in vain to ease himself in the saddle, stiff and aching from sitting too long in one position. *"South" covers a lot of territory.*

Stirling's attitude only amused Ancelotis, who was a well-educated man, by sixth-century standards. *Don't fret,* Ancelotis advised, *we Britons know how to locate a place accurately enough, even if you don't. It's the roads, lad, the Roman roads, that tell us how far south or west or northeast to ride after a marked junction. Every man of us—and most of the women, for that matter—knows the maps of these wondrous roads, even if he learns nothing else from his priests or Druids. It's the roads that tie us together, bind us into one people. Without them, we couldn't hope to mass this kind of force on such short notice.*

Stirling's brows twitched upward. He'd never thought of using roads in symbolic terms before, as a metaphor of power and unification. He was simply too accustomed to their presence as a network of tools to get a person where he wanted to go in the shortest amount of time possible, given the physical terrain and its obstacles. He felt a little foolish, particularly since a good officer took very careful account of such things as logistics, how to move men and war materiel from one point to another in the most efficient manner possible.

Ancelotis nodded. *You've the right of that. It pays a man well to remember that the Romans, a people of very small physical stature, for the most part, still conquered a very large chunk of the known world and held it for centuries upon centuries, with fast and good roads to move their legions and supply trains. 'Tis the roads, right enough, that are the saving of Britain, as much as Artorius' skills at organizing a battle.*

The idea that stole into Stirling's mind, unbidden and startling, was the abrupt connection he made between the "people of the dragon," as Myrddin had dubbed the Britons, and the long network of dragonlike scutes that comprised the top layer of Roman paving stones. Those "dragon's scales" stretched from the Antonine Wall south to Cerniw, from the western shores to the eastern lands now held by the Saxons of Sussex and Wessex. Having seen the might of Roman engineering in other cities and having studied military accounts like Caesar's *Gallic War*, Stirling appreciated with sudden, startling clarity precisely what such roads could mean to a people like the Britons, widely scattered and in desperate need of unity.

And Emrys Myrddin had seen it while still a child, warning Vortigern of the danger he was unleashing against the People of the Red Dragon. A proud people connected politically and culturally via *roads*, long stone dragons that wound through mountains, sailed across open plains, slipped silently through deep and treacherous forests, spanned gorges and lonely, echoing valleys.

The power of the British tutelary dragon did, indeed, lie in these roads, good military highways that a cavalcade could traverse at a fast and steady pace. Roads of war. *Red* roads. Red dragons. Emrys Myrddin had named the dragon the tutelary beast of Britain's rightful kings—or, more accurately—her war leaders: Ambrosius Aurelianus, the last Roman among them, Uthyr Pendragon the Sarmatian, and his son Artorius.

In a very real sense, the men and women who had built the Roman roads under the direction of Roman

engineers and Roman officers had not only built the
blood-red dragon, they had been born from it. Born
as one unified people who understood themselves to
be Britons, a far-flung but important portion of the
Roman empire, the last civilized bastion in the West.
It was a psychological shift that lifted them out of
tribalism and re-created them as one nation, regardless of tribe of birth. The dragon of Britain—the blazing emblem of Artorius—the half-Sarmatian Dux
Bellorum, was nothing less than the mighty Roman
roads of war.

Emrys Myrddin's genius in tying the symbolism—
and the Britons—together left Stirling in awe.
Ancelotis, who had never given the matter much
thought, either, marveled. *You're sure it's not a Druid
you are, from the Otherworld? 'Tis certain you think
like one, Stirling of Caer-Iudeu.*

*Huh. I'm no more a Druid than this horse we're
riding. But I do know a thing or two about psychol-
ogy and symbolism. Let's just agree to name Emrys
Myrddin the genius he is, eh?*

Ancelotis agreed as they raced along the back of
Emrys Myrddin's dragon, accompanied by the *cataphracti* who had joined Ancelotis, traveling in a thunder
of hooves against the ancient Roman paving stones.
As they rode, Stirling tried to reconcile the sixth
century's appalling lack of exactitude with his twenty-
first-century desire for laser pin-point accuracies and
satellite image-mapping systems, literally accurate down
to the fraction of a millimeter. He mourned the loss
of technology so precise that it was used, among other
things, to map the rate of continental drift across the
tectonic plates. With one decent satellite photo, Stirling
could have pinpointed the exact location of the Saxon
army boiling up from Sussex and Wessex toward the
southwest of England, using that knowledge to gauge

their speed, their likeliest route, and their numerical strength. He would have been content with something as relatively primitive as aerial reconnaissance from a hot-air balloon.

You're sure you can't pinpoint Caer-Badonicus more precisely? he fretted silently.

Ancelotis tried to come up with landmarks his twenty-first-century guest might recognize. *I've never been there, understand, but I'm told it's near the border between Glastenning and Caer-Durnac, farther south than Roman Bath. It's west of Stonehenge,* Ancelotis added, *but a good way east from the Cheddar Caves.* As Stirling listened, he pinned imaginary flags into his mental map of the south of England, triangulating from those three points and coming up with Salisbury Plain. Where in that broad sweep of flat land would one put a critically strategic hill fort? Then he saw it, a probable location that elicited a startled grunt. *Cadbury Hill?*

As he thought about it, Stirling's smile faded, replaced with a thoughtful frown. Such a location for Caer-Badonicus made sense. An army trying to take— or hold—the southwestern portion of England would be forced to guard against any detachment of troops camped on that hilltop. Failure to do so would result in lightning attacks from the ancient hill fort's summit, requiring a full-scale siege to dislodge, and a siege of that magnitude would tie up resources the kings of Sussex and Wessex could ill afford for any length of time beyond a few days.

What he could have done with gunpowder and a few small mortars on that hilltop didn't bear thinking about, since there was no time to locate the ingredients and experiment with the formula, never mind cast the mortars—or even a few hand cannons—from iron or bronze. Of course, if they survived the battle at Badon Hill, there would be ample time to experiment, provided he could obtain the ingredients. Charcoal was easy and saltpeter could be found at the bottom of manure and compost piles, crystallizing out of the muck, but what about sulphur? Wasn't that found in association with hot springs and volcanic vents? Were there any sulphur deposits in Britain? The only hot springs in Britain were at Bath—and Stirling had never heard mention of sulphur deposits associated with the springs. What he needed was a nice, cooperative volcano. And that was one thing Britain simply didn't have.

Thoughts of volcanoes triggered another whisper at the back of his memory, something important he couldn't quite put his finger on. Something important to British history, linked oddly with Arthurian lore, and he couldn't remember now what it was. Stirling frowned, while Ancelotis puzzled over the tantalizing glimpses into the future resident in Stirling's memories. Ancelotis knew virtually nothing about volcanoes, outside of their connection with ancient Greek and Roman myth, things like Vulcan at his forge deep in the heart of Mt. Etna or Pliny the Younger's eyewitness account of Vesuvius, the day it erupted to bury Pompeii and Herculaneum. Why was he remembering a connection between volcanos and Arthurian legend?

Well, if Stirling couldn't figure *that* out, what did he know about volcanoes in general? They tended to cluster along the edges of tectonic plates grinding past or diving under one another—he knew that much at least—and they appeared along the midoceanic ridges, as well, which were tectonic plates pulling apart, stirring up a froth of magma from the mantle, which spewed up periodically in spectacular volcanic eruptions. The mid-Atlantic ridge had produced Iceland and the mid-Pacific ridge had produced a whole necklace of volcanic islands, like Hawaii in the northern hemisphere and Easter Island in the southern hemisphere.

The rim of the Pacific Ocean had been dubbed the Ring of Fire, with volcanoes from the western shores of South America and the grand volcanoes of Chile and Peru, north to the Pacific Northwest of North America and volcanoes like Mt. St. Helens, across to Japan with its highly active volcanoes and earthquakes, south past China and down into Indonesia, where the world-famous nineteenth-century blast from Krakatoa had blown an entire island into oblivion.

That particular eruption had been heard halfway across the Pacific by the admiral of the British fleet stationed in India, who'd thought the fleet was under attack by naval guns. The explosion which had destroyed most of the island had also blasted so much rock and dust into the atmosphere, there had been a literal "volcanic winter" that year—a whole year with no summer, with dark skies and snow on the ground even in temperate and warm southern zones, and crop failures turning productive agricultural belts into wastelands—

Stirling gasped.

The wasteland!

One of the most powerful, recurring images of Arthurian lore. A land so blighted, nothing could grow, a land so sick, crops died, cattle died, and people starved to death as the land failed to produce life— a condition blamed, mythically, on the impotence and injury of the king. The wasteland was part of the Arthurian Grail lore, with the cup of Christ healing the formerly pagan king's deep physical, psychic, and spiritual wounds—and with the healing of the king came the healing of the land. He'd seen the twentieth-century movie, *Excalibur,* with its extraordinary sequence of the land bursting into blossom once more, one of the most beautiful movie images ever filmed.

And that image jolted loose Stirling's memory, the newspaper article he'd read on the train, heading for Edinburgh and the time-travel lab. Krakatoa hadn't blown up just once. There'd been a previous eruption— *in the sixth century* A.D. One that made the nineteenth-century explosion look like a champagne cork popping loose. Stirling narrowed his eyes, trying to recall exactly what that article had said. So far as he could remember, the Pacific volcano had blown itself to spectacular bits somewhere between the year 536 and 539 A.D., creating worldwide ecological devastation so severe, crops had failed and ecosystems had crashed for more than ten years. A whole *decade* of world-spanning wasteland. Crop failures had triggered mass migrations of people across the face of the whole earth and wars of bloody genocide had been fought over land that was still producing even marginal amounts of food.

The article had mentioned something about Irish lake fortresses. Two whole villages built on stilts in the centers of lakes as war between clans and island-wide starvation made such watery retreats the only safe places for people to live, subsisting on fish caught through the floors of the lake-straddling villages. And there was a connection, too, with the beginning of the plague years.

Something about temperature changes causing plague to spread into zones that had previously been immune, carried by traders from Constantinople as far as Britain. Plague had wiped out such an immense percentage of Britain's population that the Saxons, Angles, and Jutes— who had *not* been trading with Constantinople and therefore had not been weakened by the disease—had essentially waltzed in and taken over from a people nearly dead of hunger and epidemics.

There was a terrifying parallel between the end of "King Arthur's" golden years, a reign of thirty-nine to forty years after his twelfth victory at Badon Hill, and the timing of that volcanic explosion, somewhere between A.D. 536 and A.D. 539. Even with Artorius victorious at Caer-Badonicus, the Britons were doomed to lose the war to the Saxons, all because one volcanic explosion on the other side of the planet would destroy their crops, their cattle, and their strength as a unified people.

It was a vision so horrifying, Stirling found it impossible *not* to try and save these people from it, or at least to cushion the blow poised to fall thirty-nine years from now.

Stirling's abrupt desire to try a deliberate alteration to history far greater than the damage already wrought by Lailoken and Cedric Banning was a physical ache inside him. Dared he risk it? And what could he possibly do, even if he did decide to interfere as Banning had done? Ancelotis—stunned, amazed, and appalled by turns at Stirling's memories, suppositions, and foreknowledge that spilled like sea-foam into their shared awareness—whispered, *Stirling, if these things be true, and I misdoubt them not, then we must act to save our people. And we must act quickly—but how is one man or even a handful of men to prevent something like an island blowing itself apart?*

Huh, Stirling grunted. *You can't. There's nothing in this world—or out of it, for that matter—that can stop a volcano from doing whatever it wants, whenever it pleases. The only thing you can do is get out of its way.*

True, Ancelotis growled, *but if you know a disaster is coming, you can at least prepare for it. Look at what Egypt managed, with no more warning than Joseph's interpretation of the pharaoh's dream. Seven lean cows devouring seven fat cows, seven blighted stalks of grain devouring seven fat ones. With warning, they built granaries and saved the people from starvation.*

Ancelotis' eyes widened slightly. *Ye Gods. The Grail! A circular cup of life. If a man were to build circular cups to hold the abundance of the next thirty-nine years . . .*

It was a beautifully simple plan.

And in the later versions of Arthurian myth, Lancelot had wandered the land as a religious hermit, doing penance for his disastrous adultery with Guinevere. What if Lancelot wandered the land, instead, as an organizer of strategic supplies, using religion and the parable of Joseph and the seven years of famine as a "sign from God" that the people of Britain were meant to lay aside foodstuffs against future emergency? Stirling realized with a chill that it would probably work. And it would probably change history irrevocably.

And with Cedric Banning's interference in Dalriada having doubtless already damaged time's fractural planes, the notion of stepping in to prevent further devastation from falling on these people was singularly attractive. He might never get home again, if he tried. And he might never get home, anyway, if Banning's mass murder of the Dalriadan Irish had changed history sufficiently. He wouldn't know the answer to that for nearly a year. If that year came and went and he was still trapped here, with history too fractured to return to his plane of origin, there would be plenty of time to prepare for the wasteland years. Close to four full decades.

It was rare that one man, in place at precisely the right time, could alter the fate of thousands of people with one simple action. Stirling knew he would likely never be given another chance to match it. The thought of returning to the twenty-first century without even trying was utterly repugnant. He had taken an oath to defend his people—and in a very real sense, these Britons *were* his people, his ancestors on the

Welsh side, if not the Scottish side. To refuse to act seemed to Stirling cowardice of the greatest magnitude, a betrayal of all he believed in and had fought for, since joining the SAS to fight terrorism and the other forms of twenty-first-century madness threatening civilization itself.

Here, in the sixth century, he was embroiled in yet another war to protect civilization. He didn't think it was possible to walk away from this one, when damage had already been done by perpetrators from that other, once-and-future war. He could no more walk away from this than he'd been able to walk away from that flat in Belfast, without carrying the child of an IRA terrorist to safety through a burning building. *God forgive me*, he sent a tiny prayer winging heavenward, *but I have to try. I wouldn't be fully human, if I didn't.*

Ancelotis of Gododdin, thankful for any help his guest from the twenty-first century could render, expressed a gratitude too deep for words, a gratitude which wrapped around their shared heart like healing balm. It felt, God help him, like the right choice.

But first, they had to survive the battle of Badon Hill.

As they entered the broad expanse of the Salisbury Plain, the weather grew steadily worse, with fields of half-harvested, rotting crops churned into slurry where farmers—desperate for silage to feed their herds—had turned cattle loose to graze on what was left of the ruined crops. Stirling shivered. Ancelotis was worried, too. Very much so. As they rode through the southern reaches of Glastenning, they passed whole villages standing empty, their inhabitants having already fled for safety in the distant, cave-riddled Mendip Hills.

Stirling had never actually been to Cadbury Hill. He knew about it, of course; only the dullest, least diligent of British schoolchildren failed to learn *something* about Cadbury Hill and its ancient fortress. But he'd never actually seen it, save in photographs, and the impact of mere photos was virtually nil compared to riding across a rain-battered landscape of flat fields toward an immense fortified shape that rose up from the flatland like a great, grey battleship riding a stormy sea. Prickles ran down Stirling's borrowed back. Even Ancelotis, who had seen plenty of other massive hill forts in the north, shared Stirling's sense of awe.

'Tis a veritable city, Ancelotis breathed silently. *I've seen nothing like it! Why, there's no wondering at all why the Saxons mean to strip us of its ownership. An army could hold out there for weeks, months, perhaps, if supplies were properly laid in, ahead of the need.*

Concentric rings of stone circled the summit, five of them, lost at times in the low-scudding rainclouds that raced across the plain, their underbellies torn open by the hill fort's pike-studded walls. By the time they reached the base of the hill, its summit towering five hundred feet straight up, darkness was nearly upon them. Cookfires, sheltered beneath canvas tent flaps to protect them from the rain, blazed in a ragged river of light where workmen and wagoners and soldiers had paused in their work for the night. Ancelotis and his contingent of *cataphracti* were greeted by a perimeter guard riding diligent patrol despite the foul weather and darkness.

"Where can I find King Cadorius and Emrys Myrddin?" Ancelotis asked the guard.

"You'll find Cadorius at the summit, along with King Melwas," the man pointed toward the walls high overhead, "but Emrys Myrddin has gone to Glastenning Tor with Covianna Nim. He left near dawn this morning, although we expect him back within a day or two."

Ancelotis frowned. It wasn't like Myrddin to abandon a task before completion. "Was there news of

attack at the Tor, that Emrys Myrddin's presence was
required there?"

"If there was, we've heard nothing of it. The kings
might know more."

Ancelotis intended to ask them.

A five-hundred-foot climb up a steep, muddy hillside in a blinding downpour was not Stirling's notion
of a good time; such a climb made in utter darkness
proved treacherous in the extreme. Ancelotis instructed
the rank-and-file cavalrymen from Gododdin to find
a sheltered spot to bivouac until he could meet with
Cadorius about battle strategies. The ranking officers
of the *cataphracti* followed Ancelotis as he reined his
horse around and began to climb. The horses slipped
and slid and groped for footing while the riders kept
their animals centered more or less steadily along a
steep path that led toward one of the wooden gates
set into the outermost wall. The gate would have been
completely invisible, but for the sheltered lantern set
atop one post, marking the way in. Ancelotis and
Stirling were challenged by sentries, who swung the
gate open just enough to let Stirling, Ancelotis' officers,
and their shivering horses slip through.

What lay on the other side startled him.

There was no open space between one wall and the
next. The gate opened into a narrow trench which ran
along the inner edge of the outermost wall.

"I'll lead you through," one of the sentries said
quietly, picking up a lamp, its flame protected from
the rain by thin sheets of mineral mica, nearly as clear
as glass and far less prone to breakage. "The horses
will put a foot wrong, else, and end with broken legs—
or worse."

Stirling needed the guide, too, as they snaked
through a maze of narrow passages and gates leading
gradually inward as well as around the upper slopes

of the summit. There was just enough room for the horses to crowd their way through, single file. Sentries had been posted every yard or so along the route. By his guide's lantern light, Stirling and Ancelotis could just make out broad, flat paving stones that formed a roof of sorts, covering most of the width of ground between the five walls. These hidden roofs were invisible from lower down the hill's slope because they were recessed some twelve or thirteen inches below the walls' uppermost edges.

"What's inside these?" Ancelotis asked as they snaked their way past the fourth wall, crossing to another gate that took them around the northern slope of the hill toward a gate in the fifth and final wall. A fierce wind battered them, sweeping across from the northwest, a cold wind blowing in from the North Atlantic, driving rain squalls ahead of it. "And why are there other wooden gates with no apparent function?"

The sentry turned his head to call back, "It's Emrys Myrddin's surprise for the Saxons. These," he patted the stone "roof" with one hand, "are full of water. Cisterns to hold the rain pouring off the summit and even more water brought up from the plain by waterwheels."

Water? Stirling frowned. With that much water stored, the Britons must be preparing to hold out for several months under the Saxons' anticipated siege, a prospect he found somewhat less than delightful. Then he made the connection between all that water and the false wooden gates set into the walls. *Sluice gates! Ye gods, the man's a genius!* Even Ancelotis grinned, albeit wearily.

They finally reached the final gate which would lead them out onto the hill fort's open summit. Beyond this, Stirling could make out the shape of buildings, dark structures made of stone and brick, serving as barracks rooms, storage for supplies and weapons, shelters for civilians, workshops for the armorers whose hammers still rang and clashed despite the increasing lateness of the evening. There were few windows, but doors stood partially open here and there, giving them glimpses of the work under way within.

Stirling had never seen so many blacksmiths in one place in his life. Several of the structures proved to be stables for the cavalry horses and holding pens for livestock—pigs and goats, mostly, along with chickens and geese, too many to easily count in the darkness. Smokehouses and slaughtering pens sent an unpleasant mix of smells drifting through the wet night, where the hogs were being converted with efficient industry into sausages, hams, rendered lard, and pigskin leather.

They found the kings of Glastenning and Dumnonia in the centermost building, which boasted a squat, brick watchtower that would be perfect, Stirling realized, for scanning the northern hills for Artorius' signal. Stirling and the officers of Gododdin's *cataphracti* slid out of wet saddles, turning their horses over to half-grown boys who led them off to a nearby stable. Ancelotis pushed open a wooden door, stepping into a roomful of warmth, where a cheerful fire crackled in a hearth set into the northern wall. Wood lay stacked along the entire width of that wall, piled higher than Stirling's head. Another wall bore a large oxhide with a map of southern Britain drawn carefully in black ink, marked with important river crossings, hill forts, towns, and the borders of the southern kingdoms— including those currently held by the Saxons. Cadorius paused in whatever discussion was under way and received them with a glad armclasp, although his face was haggard from strain and lack of sleep.

"You are most well come, Ancelotis, most well come,

indeed! But is Artorius not with you?" he added, peering at the *cataphracti* officers at Ancelotis' back.

"No, he rides with the bulk of the army, including the infantry, which will slow him considerably. He is perhaps a full week's march behind me, maybe as much as eight or nine days, given the condition of the roads in this weather."

Cadorius frowned. "Then he will reach us well after the Saxons do. We expect the Saxon army to lay siege within five days, at most. Refugees are flooding into Glastenning ahead of them."

"The sentries tell me Emrys Myrddin has gone to Glastenning Tor?"

Cadorius nodded, gesturing to a servant, who brought hot stew and wine. As Ancelotis tackled the meal with enthusiasm, Cadorius brought him up to date.

"Melwas and I didn't want him to leave Caer-Badonicus, but he insisted. Covianna was afraid for her kinsmen, who would be unprepared if the Saxons broke through here. Myrddin agreed to ride with her to the Tor, to offer his suggestions for defenses. My greatest worry for his safety is the bandits on the roads, taking advantage of all this turmoil, looting empty villages and abandoned farmholds. Such cutthroats care nothing for which set of masters they rob. And we win this war, I'll be after cleaning them out with fire and hangmen's ropes."

"What of our defenses here? Are we ready to meet the enemy?"

Cadorius nodded. "We've laid in a good supply of food. Water," he added with a snort of wry humor, glancing at the ceiling where rain rattled and danced, "is not a problem. A week to nine days, you said, before Artorius arrives? We could hold them off at least ten times that long, and we've deliberately built of stone and brick, as much as possible, so they can't burn us out with fire arrows. We could use some of our shelters, for there wasn't time to roof *everything* in stone shingles. But we're nowhere nearly as vulnerable as the defenseless villages they've used that tactic against."

"I've some ideas of my own, to add to the defenses." Stirling nodded toward the officers of his *cataphracti*, men with Asiatic features, who watched and ate in alert silence, many of them wearing the Sarmatian tribal badge embroidered on their tunics, a naked sword thrust through a stone. "There's no force in all of Western Europe to match my Sarmatian bowmen. Come the dawn, I'll work out a few nasty surprises for the Saxons, to teach them the damage Sarmatian archers can inflict."

The officers grinned, several of them lifting fingers to brow in a jaunty salute. "It will be a pleasure," one of them chuckled, "a very distinct pleasure."

"There's little more to be done, tonight," Ancelotis nodded in satisfaction, mopping up the last of the stew with a hunk of bread. "If you've spare cots someplace, my officers and I need to steal at least a few hours' sleep. We've been riding hard these last few days, and the lack of rest is catching up to us."

Cadorius had a servant guide them across the windblasted summit toward the barracks. The *cataphracti* officers were shown to quarters with others of their rank and Ancelotis left them making plans to check on their men, to be sure the rest of Gododdin's forces had found a good spot to bed down and had found plenty to eat. Ancelotis and Stirling were escorted to another building, where the royalty of half a dozen Briton kingdoms had taken refuge for the duration. Ancelotis recognized several princes, sent by harried fathers to direct the troops lent to Glastenning for the coming conflict. There was even a scattering of royal daughters and queens who preferred the safety of the hill fort to the uncertainty of the Lowlands. Ancelotis halted in dismay when Ganhumara gave a glad little cry and rushed forward, flinging herself into his arms.

"Thank God, you've come in time!"

He placed firm hands on her shoulders, forcibly moving her a step backwards. She peered up through long, coppery lashes, feigning hurt with a masterful pout. "Is this any way to greet the queen of Caer-Guendoleu?"

"What are you doing here?" Ancelotis demanded bluntly.

She tossed her long hair across one shoulder. "If you must know, I was kidnaped."

"Kidnaped?" he echoed, disbelieving.

"By Melwas! Cadorius rescued me. Oh, he was so gallant!"

Ancelotis glowered down at her. "I refuse to believe that King Melwas was so great a fool as to kidnap you, Ganhumara. Let the story stand as a salve to your reputation, if you must, but do not attempt to fool *me* with it. I would strongly suggest you find some way to beg your husband's humble pardon for your continued foolhardiness when he arrives."

Ganhumara's eyes flashed, defiant and proud. "I will beg *nothing* from Artorius!" she hissed. "He is nothing but the son of commoners and whores! Never will I forgive my father for binding me in marriage to a half-blood bastard of a *Sarmatian*!"

She whirled and stalked away, stiff with rage.

Ancelotis scrubbed his face, too weary to deal with her tempers and peccadillos.

"Is she always like that?" a quiet voice at his elbow startled him.

He found a troubled, grey-eyed gaze locked on the

retreating queen of Caer-Guendoleu, a quiet gaze which turned to meet his forthrightly. Ancelotis didn't recognize her, but she wore a torque of royalty, so he supposed her to be of the royal house of one of the southern kings.

"Unfortunately, yes. She is. And often worse."

"Then I pity Artorius. The Dux Bellorum has enough to worry him, without a wife like that to damage the peace even further."

"I must beg your humble pardon," Ancelotis murmured, "but I do not know you, dear lady. I am Ancelotis of Gododdin," he added.

Her lips twitched into a slight smile. "Yes. The news of your arrival spread like wildfire through brambles. It gave us heart, when all has been gloom for so long. I am Iona, last survivor of the royal house of Ynys Weith."

Ancelotis' eyes widened. "Dear God, I thought the whole family dead! I thank God in heaven that you were spared. But how?"

Tears welled up in her eyes. "The Saxons came in the night, led by traitors among the fisherfolk. They slaughtered my whole family as we slept. A servant, one of the old men from the stables who had seen the Saxons arrive, dragged me from my bed, threw old clothes across my nightdress, hid me in the kitchen. I crouched for hours in the hearth, covered with ash and shaking with terror. The Saxons came through the kitchen, guzzling wine and ale until they could scarcely stagger to the cesspits."

Princess Iona was trembling. The look in her eyes chilled Ancelotis' blood. "Just before cockcrow, the stableman led me down to the strand, where loyal fishermen hid me beneath their nets and took me to safety in Caer-Durnac. When the Saxons came across the border into Caer-Durnac, I fled into the marshes, where I hid for months, eating raw fish and learning to survive by my wits." She gazed down at her hands, visibly roughened and red, even by lamplight. "It took more courage than I thought I had left, to come out of those marshes and seek asylum with Cadorius and Melwas. But I had to come, to warn the other royal houses of Britain what the Saxons are capable of, when they set their sights on a victim."

Ancelotis reached up with gentle fingertips to wipe tears from her cheeks. "Thank you, Iona, for your courage. And for reminding us that creatures like Ganhumara are the rare exception, among Britain's royal ladies. I sorrow for your losses. Please consider Gododdin a place of refuge for you, should you ever need a home."

The tears came faster, but she managed a tremulous smile. "I am honored, Ancelotis of Gododdin. Thank you. And I fear I have kept you too long from your bed. If there is anything I can do, on the morrow, to help you and your men prepare, please ask it of me."

He offered her a formal bow, then found an unoccupied cot and collapsed onto the straw-filled tick, asleep within moments. Morning found him outside the circumvallation, walking the steep, muddy hillside in the company of the Sarmatian commanders of Gododdin's *cataphracti*. Stirling pointed down the lee side of the hill. "According to Cadorius, Emrys Myrddin expects the bulk of the Saxons to camp along here, protected from the weather. Frankly, I agree. What I want is for someone to pace off known distances from the outermost wall, beginning with the farthest range of a bowshot and coming back toward the wall in stepped increments, three paces at a time. Put up small wooden posts to mark the known distances."

"For what purpose?" one of his officers asked, brow furrowed in puzzlement.

Stirling grinned. "You'll see shortly. Put several men in charge of the work out here. Then join me inside the walls again."

As they hiked in through the mazelike passages between the walls, Ancelotis muttered silently, *Just what are you up to? I don't understand it, either.*

Stirling explained. *The Sarmatian cavalry archers are very good for our purposes. The flight of an arrow is very much akin to the flight of a bullet or cannon ball—and artillery ballistics is something I bloody well know. What I'm going to do is teach our Sarmatians some drills, things I know that will increase their effectiveness, a way of shooting at targets they can't see.*

What sort of drills? Ancelotis asked, unsure what artillery and firearms might even *be*; despite the memory images in Stirling's mind, it was difficult for the sixth-century king to grasp the concepts and distances an ordinary rifle or mortar could throw a projectile, never mind the speeds such projectiles could reach. Before he could answer, the officers of his *cataphracti* joined him inside the wall, so Stirling explained it to everyone at once. "How many bowmen are with us?" he began.

"Seventy, at least," one of the officers answered.

"And they shoot at individual targets, one at a time, from horseback?"

The officers nodded, expressions puzzled. "It's the way Sarmatians have fought for centuries."

"Very effectively," Stirling agreed. "But there are other ways of firing a bow than aiming directly at a target, especially since we'll have battlements to use as shelter."

Puzzlement turned to utter bafflement.

"May I?" Stirling asked, nodding to the nearest heavy compound bow, made of horn and wood and requiring a strong man, indeed, to pull it. The Sarmatian handed over his bow and a quiver of arrows. "Very good. What I'm going to teach you is a way to hit something you cannot see, do so without exposing yourself to enemy spears or javelins, by coordinating your shots."

He notched an arrow and pulled the powerful bow, drawing the string back to his chest, rather than his ear, in the older style of shooting that Sarmatians and other ancient archers had used—a technique that would remain in force until the advent of the Welsh longbow. Rather than aiming directly at the wall, three paces away, Stirling aimed high above it, eyeballing the angle and projecting the parabola of the arrow's flight.

He released the bow with a *whap!* and watched the arrow speed skyward. It arced upward and out across the walls, the curve descending steeply at the end of the foreshortened parabola. The arrow vanished somewhere downslope, well beyond the wall.

He turned to find the officer unimpressed.

Stirling chuckled and handed the bow back to its owner. "Shall we see how far it flew before landing?" They found the arrow several yards downslope, sticking up like a spike in the muddy ground.

"How can a man control it, though?" one of the officers asked, staring from the wall to the arrow embedded in the mud. "How would you know how high to aim, to have the arrow drop precisely where you wanted it to go?"

"That's what the posts out here are for, to mark known distances from the wall. I'll want several tall wooden poles erected inside the walls, with bands marked on them. And I'll want marker stones inside the walls, as well, so that if a man stands on the stone and aims past one of the painted rings on a pole, he'll know exactly how far that arrow will travel and where it will come down, with close approximation, relative to the marker posts out here. Then we'll drill to make sure we can hit those marks every time."

"Even so, it will be impossible to hit your enemy with any real accuracy if we can't see them because we're behind the walls!"

"Ah, but we'll have one man up top, a forward observer acting as the eyes for all the rest of us who'll be shooting at exactly the same time and exactly the same place."

Understanding dawned. "God above, it's *elegant*!"

They put every archer in Gododdin's *cataphracti* to work, cutting and setting poles every few yards along the innermost wall, painting narrow bands every few inches along the poles, setting stones in a line with those poles, and cutting marker posts which they placed beyond the walls to mark the farthest and nearest ranges of arrows when shot past the upper- and lower-most bands. Once the markers had been placed, the archers began practicing, with Stirling once again demonstrating.

"If I aim just to the left of the white band at the top, my arrow will fall very close to the post nearest the wall." He let an arrow fly and had a boy leap onto the outermost wall to call where it had landed. The boy shouted, "You're a foot beyond the post!"

Three more arrows and Stirling had put the shot within six inches of the post he could not see, nearest the outermost wall. "Mark this spot with a stone," he nodded in satisfaction, "and do the same for every pole we've put up along the line." He gestured. "Devise a shooting order, so that every man knows his place beside his comrades and always shoots from the same spot, whether he stands on a stone or to the left or right of the markers."

Stirling promised a keg of ale and a gold coin to the five archers who, at the end of a week, placed their shots consistently closest to the outside marker posts. The contest spurred the Sarmatians to a friendly competition of skill that sharpened their accuracy with amazing rapidity. Ancelotis was delighted, while Cadorius and Melwas regarded the king of Gododdin as a military genius.

"It won't be as effective if the Saxons approach in a thin skirmish line, but I've another idea or two that will bunch them up a bit, to give the archers a nice, broad target to drop arrows on, from overhead. Now, about these other ideas I have in mind, I'll need the best men we have, men who can move swiftly and silently in the darkness. And I'll need cordage, the largest, longest skeins or balls of it to be found in the southwestern kingdoms."

"Cordage?" Cadorius frowned in confusion.

Stirling grinned. "Trust me."

By week's end, Stirling was satisfied that they were as ready for the Saxons as they would ever be—and not a moment too soon, for a runner arrived in the middle of the night on a badly lathered horse, gasping out his message. "The Saxons are nearly upon us! They'll reach Caer-Badonicus by dawn!"

Final preparations took on frantic speed as the last of the horses hauled the final supplies up the hill. What the Britons could neither carry up to the hill fort nor send farther north, out of harm's way, they burned to further deprive the Saxons. It was a grim business, one that Stirling would have given much to avoid, but he knew only too well the cost of trying to walk away from madmen bent on destruction. The madmen followed, until you and everything you valued had been smashed into oblivion. Whether he acted rightly or wrongly with regard to the future timeline which had birthed him, he had no way to know. He knew only that here, in this now, he had only one real choice. He would stop the spread of darkness or die trying.

Stirling slept poorly that night and was awakened from fitful slumber by a commotion of voices. He groped for his sword before he was even fully awake; then a familiar voice, a woman's voice, drifted through the small crowd that had gathered to greet a new-comer.

"No," Covianna Nim was saying, "I can't imagine where Emrys Myrddin might be. He left the Tor three or four days ago."

Stirling and Ancelotis rose to find Covianna Nim looking half asleep and disheveled from what had obviously been a hard ride.

"Why did you come back to Caer-Badonicus?" Ganhumara asked. "Not that I'm dismayed to see you," the young queen added hastily, "for you must know I'm delighted to have a friend here, but I don't understand. They said you were dreadfully anxious about your family at the Tor."

"And I was," Covianna replied smoothly, stifling a yawn. "We've done all we can to strengthen the Tor's defenses and my clan wanted to send a master smith to Caer-Badonicus to help with the defense here. I was the logical choice, with my training in the healing arts, as well. Please, I'm dreadfully weary. I'll tell you all you want to know in the morning."

Ancelotis grunted once, then stumbled back to bed, asleep before the commotion of Covianna's arrival had fully died down. He didn't wake again until dawn, when a brassy signal trumpet sent its warning through the entire encampment atop Badon Hill. Ancelotis splashed cold water into his face, meeting grim glances from royal princes who had led troops here during the previous weeks and days. Half a dozen servants made the rounds with bread smoking hot from the ovens, served with slabs of cheese and cold ham.

Ancelotis bolted down the meal, buckling on armor and sword belt while still chewing. Leather creaked against ring-mail shirts and scale armor as the men prepared grimly for battle. Their sisters and mothers laid out spare weapons, heated enormous kettles of water over half a dozen hearths built into the room, prepared linens for bandages and set out ointments, salves, and glass vials of unknown medicines. Surgeons' tools—scalpels, bronze tweezers, saws for amputating mangled limbs—were dropped into boiling water to be held in clean readiness against all-too-probable need.

Ancelotis left the women to their preparations, harboring a secret feeling that their tasks were even harder than those of the men, knowing they sent loved ones out to be maimed or killed and quietly hugging terror and distress to their breasts while doing what was necessary to save lives. Stirling muttered silently, *You may just be right about that.* In his experience, gathered unpleasantly in the streets of Belfast, women were not only stronger than their menfolk, they were braver, as well, attempting to carry forward the business of living while their men were busy slaughtering one another.

It was a kind of courage Stirling didn't fully understand and found somewhat awe-inspiring to watch, that picking up of shattered lives, the bravery required for women who had seen the effect of bombs to choose, consciously and with a perhaps misplaced sense of hope, the decision to bring new lives into existence in the midst of societal suicide. It hurt, watching these women prepare for battle that might see the men they loved best maimed or killed by day's end.

Lips thinned to a marbled line, Stirling strode out

into the grey morning, almost relishing the slap of icy rain and wind against his face. His cloak snapped and whipped around in the gusts, like a living thing gone mad. Mud squelched underfoot and the bleating of penned goats drifted on the wind. Everywhere he turned his gaze, Stirling saw men in armor, officers shouting directions, soldiers piling up caches of weapons, swords and long-necked iron *pila,* pikes and leaf-bladed spears by the hundreds, war axes and Roman-style short swords stacked beside piles of daggers.

A moment later, they had reached the southeastern slope, where Cadorius and Melwas had gathered around them the royalty of Britain. Ancelotis joined the group with a nod of greeting and watched silently as a great, boiling mass of men and horses coalesced on the horizon. It was an eerie, hideous sight, as though the driving rain had solidified into the shape of the enemy. Hundreds of men, a vast carpet of spearpoints and javelins and pikes, with a baggage train of supply wagons that reached farther than the eye could discern, even from the immense height of the hilltop.

"That," Cadorius said quietly, "is what we must hold back until the Dux Bellorum arrives with the greatest bulk of our own army."

Casting a practiced eye over the opposing force, Ancelotis estimated their strength at close to double a thousand men at arms, plus camp followers: wagoners, armorers, cooks and barber surgeons, signal men with curved ram's-horn trumpets whose calls drifted to them on the rain-slashed wind.

"They have learned a trick or two from their Briton captives," Melwas murmured, hearing those signal trumpeters. "That's no Saxon strategy, to march in formation under the direction of disciplined officers."

Cadorius glanced around, nodding grimly. "Aye, you've the right of that, Melwas. Cerdic and Creoda know well enough the strength of such organization. Filthy *gewisse,* all of them."

The term translated in Ancelotis' mind as "traitors."

"Let us hope," Ancelotis muttered, "that Cerdic's Saxon allies forget to *maintain* their discipline in the heat of battle."

They watched in silence as the Saxon army spread like plague across the Salisbury Plain half a thousand feet below. Most of them were on foot, poorly armored, but in a siege such as this, horses would be of little use to the Saxons, in any case. On horseback or not, armored or not, the Saxons had the advantage of sheer numbers, close to three times the number of Briton defenders on this hilltop. Stirling and Ancelotis and the others watched them come, watched them reach the base of the immense hill, watched the spiked carpet of men and weapons break like foam across a rocky seacoast, parting around the base of Badon Hill to surround it with a ring of glittering weapons.

At least, Stirling muttered to himself, *they don't have siege engines.*

The Saxon kings were in no apparent hurry to attack. An unpleasant, fluttering sensation rose from the pit of his stomach as Stirling watched the Saxons cut off escape routes one by one. At a nod from Cadorius, Stirling and his host walked the whole long perimeter of the innermost wall, studying troop deployments, squinting into the brutal teeth of the wind as the Saxons dispatched small squadrons along the muddy roads leading from Caer-Badonicus to the nearest villages.

They would find little of value in those villages, which had been abandoned for a radius of five miles around. The Saxons would find no food, no livestock, no slaves to force into building their siegeworks, nothing but a few very nasty surprises in the form of covered pit traps dug beneath barn and cottage floors. The Britons had camouflaged their man-traps with layers of dirt and straw or rushes across tightly stretched panels of woolen sailcloth, dyed brown with walnut hulls to match the color of their earthen coverings. Like Burmese tiger traps, the stake-studded pits waited for unwary predators to step into them. Very soon, the Saxons would discover just how high a price they must pay for attempting to conquer Salisbury Plain.

Down at the base of the hill, foot soldiers were busy erecting camps in a loose circle, a living noose of men, spears, and swords. They began digging trenches, as well, throwing up an earthen rampart to shield them somewhat from missiles hurled from above. Ancelotis muttered a few choice oaths, watching. "That bastard Cerdic is earning his blood money, no doubt of that." He spat disgustedly to one side, earning a grunt of agreement from King Melwas, who had joined him.

"That's a move yon bastards have never tried before," Melwas growled. "And I've fought them enough times to know."

Stirling watched and wished bitterly for better weapons than they had. *What we could do with just one good machine gun . . . Might as well ask for attack helicopters and cruise missiles, while I'm at it.*

Melwas frowned. "I see nothing like a tent a king would use down there. Not even one fit for a royal prince. The Saxons may be barbarians, but their so-called royalty are quick to demand the comforts of civilization and complain loudly when deprived of them."

Ancelotis grunted. "Try the lee of the hill. It's where I'd set up, were I King Aelle or Cerdic."

Melwas' glance was keen. "Emrys Myrddin said much the same thing."

"With good reason." Stirling grinned as fierce gusts of rain ripped through the Saxon encampment, playing hob with their attempts to set up sleeping tents.

Melwas smiled in dark humor. "They'll be cold and wet and exhausted before a few hours have passed. And unless I miss my guess, they'll have as much trouble as our own men did keeping cookfires going anywhere but the lee of the hill."

An army fighting on cold, unpalatable rations was an unhappy army, resentful and discouraged. With the countryside laid bare in advance of their arrival, they'd find little more than dirt to add to their already strained supply of rations. He smiled in cold pleasure at the notion. Having seen enough for the moment, Ancelotis and Melwas left instructions for the men standing perimeter watch to report anything out of the ordinary in the Saxons' preparations, then headed back for the lee side, to study further developments there.

"They look to be throwing the bulk of their men downslope of here," Ancelotis told Cadorius, who was issuing orders on their own troop deployments.

Cadorius nodded. "It's as we expected, then. I've assigned Dumnonia left flank guard along the lee," he pointed to a stretch of wall some hundred feet distant, "and, Melwas, I'll want Glastenning on the right flank. Ancelotis, you and your Sarmatian archers will take the center, as we agreed and planned for." He nodded toward the banded poles set up at carefully measured intervals along the lee side of the summit. "We'll scatter the other kingdoms around the perimeter." He was scratching a rough map in the mud, sheltering it with his body as he crouched down to work.

Even with the number of men they already had, the

summit and its sprawling perimeter walls were so large, the defenders would be spread dangerously thin. And they would have precious little but women and children in reserve, should Artorius be delayed on the march south.

I mislike it, Ancelotis said privately to Stirling. *I mislike it a very great deal.*

Stirling wasn't particularly keen on it, either. "We'll have to watch for shifts in their deployment, day and night," he said aloud for Cadorius' benefit. "The children could fill in the gaps as lookouts, particularly the older lads, and give our men more rest for the actual fighting. A sudden surge along one of the more thinly defended stretches, and they'd be among us before we knew they were climbing. Particularly after dark."

"After dark?" Cadorius grunted while Melwas' eyes shot wide.

Even Ancelotis was taken by surprise.

It was something, Stirling supposed, to startle three kings, each of them with more than a decade's bitter experience in combat. Yet the notion of a night sortie astonished them. Stirling grinned. "Why d'you think I wanted the specially trained men and the cordage? You do remember what the Oracle at Delphi said, don't you?"

Melwas frowned in puzzlement, but Cadorius had begun to chuckle. "Oh, aye. A grand story that was, I remember my own father reading it out to me in the Greek. I've forgotten which historian it was, but the story I recall very well, indeed."

Melwas looked from Stirling to Cadorius and back again. "I've not heard it."

"For a shipload of gold," the Dumnonian king chuckled, "the poor bastard was told by the Oracle of Apollo, 'You will destroy a great empire.' Sure of victory, he returned home to the war with Persia. And when the autumn came, and the time for the harvest was due, the fool retired from the field, for that was how war was fought in those days, everyone on both sides of a conflict going home to bring in the crops. Only the Persians followed him. Shocked the entire known world, waging war at harvest time. Sacked the capital, took over the gold fields, and put the vanquished king in chains, so he could repent at length on the empire he'd destroyed. His own."

Stirling nodded. "The Persians changed forever the way war would be fought, with that maneuver."

Melwas was grinning. "Fighting a night sortie will be just as great a shock to the Saxons, I'm thinking. Marvelous idea, Ancelotis."

Ancelotis, as startled as the others by the notion, laughed aloud. "Oh, aye, isn't it just, now?"

The others chuckled at the play on words.

The Saxons spent several hours erecting siege works, ditching the entire circumference of the hill and readying caches of weapons, spears and pikes, mostly. Swords were scarce amongst them, a fact which still surprised Stirling, for all that he'd heard the others discuss it. Briton forces watched in eerie silence as Germanic voices shouted far down the slope. One group climbed halfway up the lee side, dragging timbers and tools with them under the cover of a bristling shield wall of armed warriors.

"What in the devil's unholy name are they doing?" Melwas wondered aloud. "Erecting some kind of siege engine?"

"I think not," Ancelotis frowned. "A platform on which to mount one, perhaps."

"Should we discourage them from building it?"

The younger king was showing signs of impatience as the preparations dragged endlessly. Cadorius, who also stood frowning down at the activity two hundred fifty feet below them, answered the sub-king's question. "No, Melwas, I believe we'll let them build it, unhindered. The weaker we seem at the beginning, the likelier they are to err through overconfidence later. We give up nothing, for we can demolish it at our leisure, with any number of methods."

Stirling glanced at smoking braziers blazing at the bottom of firepits all along the inner perimeter, the fires protected from the weather not only by the depth of the pits, but also roofed over with small awnings and further protected by trenches the children had dug to allow any rainwater that did get in to drain away before it drowned the coals. Vats and iron cauldrons simmered over the fires, filled with rendered animal fat, much of it from the pigs and cattle slaughtered to feed them all.

And near each firepit stood a Roman-style catapult, standing ready to deliver the melted grease in each of those kettles and cauldrons. Cadorius, who followed Stirling's glance, said, "We've also prepared Greek fire, from the formula Emrys Myrddin obtained as a boy in Constantinople. With Greek fire, we can burn anything on this hill, whether it rains or no—and I am mortally certain the Saxons don't have the secret of it, to hurl back at us."

Stirling's brows had twitched upward in astonishment. The formula for "Greek fire"—an incendiary substance Greek warships had used to set fire to a Persian fleet—had been lost for millennia. Somehow, it didn't surprise Stirling that Emrys Myrddin should have added that particular secret to his truly vast collection of useful information. Ancelotis wondered uneasily where the Druidic councillor might be, for he had not returned to Caer-Badonicus and Covianna Nim claimed he'd left Glastenning Tor several days previously. Had he ridden north, to meet with Artorius on the march? Whatever the answer, Ancelotis hugged his impatience to himself and watched the Saxons.

The purpose of their platform became clear shortly before dusk, when the Saxons hauled up and erected a large pavilion tent on it, protected from the summit by a wooden wall which they'd driven into the hillside. That wooden palisade stood higher than a man, acting as a shield for the men who climbed laboriously up the first two hundred fifty feet from the broad plain, obviously intending to shelter in the tent. The broad expanse of cloth shuddered and rippled with the gusts of wind and rain, but the shield wall and the hill's own mass protected the platform, tent, and occupants from the worst of the weather.

"There's Cutha," Stirling said abruptly, as a small cadre of well-armored men climbed a muddy path up to the platform.

"And King Aelle beside him," Cadorius nodded. "They've brought their highest-ranking *eoldormen* and *thegns* with them, besides their *athelings,* princes of the blood. Speaking of which, Cerdic looks a bit pale, doesn't he?"

If the king of Wessex was pale, his son was ashen. Creoda kept glancing fearfully at the silent Briton defenders, bristling with weapons like an American porcupine.

"It's one thing," Ancelotis said thoughtfully, "to take a kingdom by treachery, killing off only the royal family, but quite another for a Briton traitor to order Briton troops into battle against Briton soldiers, to slaughter Briton women and children who've sheltered here. He must be wondering, even now, if his men will obey him when put to the test."

"And Aelle is wondering, right along with him," Melwas muttered. "Have you noticed, men wearing Briton armor, with Briton-made weapons, are held back from the front lines? Aelle's keeping them back as first reserves, putting loyal Saxons in the front ranks and more of his own men behind the Britons, to be sure of them."

Stirling hadn't noticed—neither had Ancelotis—but the young sub-king of Glastenning was correct. King Aelle clearly distrusted his *gewisse* Britons. The Saxons' high command disappeared from view into the royal pavilion. The conference they held there lasted well past darkness, with the occupants' shadows flickering, ghostlike, on the tent's walls and ceiling as the men within moved about, gesticulating occasionally to make some point. Stirling allowed himself a tight smile. Any one of his Sarmatian archers could have taken out the men inside that tent simply by aiming at those moving shadows. He filed away the plan for later execution, another piece of the plans firming up in his mind.

When it became clear that no attack would be launched this night, Cadorius suggested, "Sleep is what will do us the best good. Our sentries will watch for any possible treachery in the night, but I'm thinking they haven't completed enough of their preparations to launch an attack just yet. They're new to siege warfare and I'm thinking they'll want to be thorough about it, rather than risk haste and defeat themselves from poor preparations."

Ancelotis agreed, although Stirling would have preferred to remain on guard through the night, with his different perspective and expectations about when battles were waged. As it happened, however, Cadorius and Ancelotis were right in their assessment. They spent a quiet night, sleeping through most of it without interruption or alarms. Dawn found them on the walls again, watching as Saxon troops labored to build other relay camps halfway up the hill, laying in stashes of lightweight javelins to supplement the heavier spears and pikes the infantry would use as thrusting weapons.

Clearly, they meant to fight from their platforms as much as possible, saving themselves the added effort of climbing the entire five hundred feet from plain to summit every time they made a charge at the Britons' perimeter walls. And still the Briton defenders watched in stony silence, doing nothing to interfere or discourage the work, hiding their own strength and hoarding their finite supplies.

The silence was finally broken just after midday, while Stirling was washing down the last mouthfuls of bread and cheese with a cup of ale. A runner came skidding into the barracks where Britain's royalty were quartered, gasping out, "The Saxons are sending up a rider under flag of truce!" Cadorius and Ancelotis exchanged glances, then they were on their feet, snatching up heavy wooden shields on the way, in case of Saxon treachery. By the time they reached the spot above the Saxons' royal pavillion, the rider had nearly reached the outermost wall. Cadorius growled under his breath. "Creoda!"

It was, indeed, the nervous princeling of Wessex.

"Greetings, *gewisse*!" Cadorius called out strongly. "What message do you bear us from your foreign masters?"

The prince of Wessex lost what color remained in his face, lips clamping tightly at the double insult. "I bear a message from King Cerdic of Wessex!" the young man shouted back.

"And what does the usurping murderer of Wessex have to say that would possibly be of interest to loyal Briton kings?"

Creoda's ashen features flooded scarlet. "My father, king of Wessex, urges you to abandon this folly!" He swept a gesture at the walls of the newly strengthened hill fort. "We can starve you out at our leisure! Would you condemn the women and children who've mistaken your hospitality for safety, when Wessex guarantees their safety should you bow to reason and surrender quietly?"

Before any of the Briton kings could frame an answer, a woman's voice split the silence.

"Do not presume to speak of Saxon guarantees to me!"

It was Princess Iona, standing tall and proud atop the innermost wall, dark hair flying wild in the wind, grey eyes burning with rage. Creoda gasped, recognizing her.

"Yes, you might well be astonished to see me alive!" she snarled down at him. "I know whose gold it was paid the traitors of Ynys Weith! Firsthand, I've seen how Saxon dogs greet innocent Briton women and children. They spitted my infant sisters and cousins on their swords and drank wine from my father's skull! You reek of death and foul murder, traitor. Begone from my sight. Return to Aelle of Sussex and busy yourself licking his arse once more, since that is what you do best! Let this be the answer of Britain!"

She snatched up a javelin from an astonished foot soldier and hurled it with all her strength. An instant later, Creoda's horse reared with a savage scream, with the javelin buried in the animal's neck. The horse toppled, kicking and screaming as it died. Creoda, hurled to the ground, rolled and slid ignominiously through the mud. A thunderous cheer rose spontaneously from Briton throats, rolling like an avalanche down across the mud-soaked princeling.

Iona, trembling atop the wall, spat once in Creoda's direction, then turned her back. Ancelotis leaped forward, assisting her down to the ground. She was shaking violently now, barely able to keep her feet, and tears spilled loose, blinding her. Ancelotis guided her gently back toward the barracks, relieved when Covianna Nim came hurrying forward.

"Help her," Ancelotis said quietly. "She must have some relief of the grief that has wounded her heart so deeply."

"Come, Iona," Covianna Nim said soothingly, "let me help you rest."

Ancelotis was on his way back to Cadorius and the others when a scream of ram's-horn trumpets shattered the raw morning. The sound came not from the Saxons' command pavilion, but from the northern slope. He ran forward, just in time to see a group of five heavily armored riders burst down the hillside through the northern gate, horses thundering toward the Saxon lines.

"What in hell—?" Stirling gasped.

The riders met infantry with a shock of lances on shields. The first wave of Saxons went down, but infantrymen poured in from the flanks, cutting off the riders' escape. One of the Britons went down, hacked to death by Saxon war axes. The others tried again for a breakout and were blocked at every turn. When the infantry tried to drag the cavalrymen from their saddles, the Briton war-horses screamed and lashed out with flinty hooves, kicking and biting to clear a path back up the hill. The remaining four riders spurred their horses up the steep slope, having failed to break through the Saxon lines. Spears whistled after them, bringing down two of the war-horses. Their riders rolled clear of the wounded animals, then clawed their way upward, until all four were safely back inside the gates.

"What in God's name was that in aid of?" Stirling demanded.

Cadorius spoke behind him. "To convince the Saxons

we are desperate to break out a message for help—
and are too weak to do so."

Stirling tightened his jaw muscles, then nodded. He,
too, had ordered men to their deaths. Necessity never
made it easy, however, and Cadorius' eyes reflected
the same pain Stirling and Ancelotis felt so keenly. "So
it begins," Stirling said through clenched teeth. "A cat-
and-mouse tradeoff of blows."

"Take heart," Cadorius said quietly, laying an arm
across his tense shoulders. "They can do us little damage and Iona's proud defiance has stirred the men's
blood far better than you or I could have done."

That, at least, was nothing more than raw truth.

And so they waited the Saxons out, midday stretching interminably toward a cold blustery dusk, while the
Saxon army continued its work, throwing up fighting
platforms around the circumference of Badon Hill.
Four times more did Cadorius send riders thundering downhill, attempting breakout, testing Saxon
strength and responsiveness, testing their signaling
systems and how well they worked together as infantry. And four times more were the Briton riders turned
back, with greater ease and swifter responsiveness as
the day wore endlessly on and the Saxons, too, began
to hit their stride as a functional battle unit. Cadorius
said little, Ancelotis even less. Stirling bided his time,
waiting for the proper moment to spring the first of
their surprises.

By dusk of the second day of siege, the civilians atop
Badon Hill were beginning to show signs of strain.
"Why don't they attack?" Stirling overheard a woman
asking one of the off-duty soldiers, who was gulping
down a bowl of stew. "They outnumber us, why don't
they attack?"

Ancelotis paused. "To wear down our nerves," he
said quietly.

The woman, dressed as a farmholder, turned in surprise—and gasped when she recognized him. "My apologies, King Ancelotis," she stammered.

"No." He smiled, resting a hand on her shoulder. "It is a fair question and deserves answer. They hope to fray our patience, to leave us so jittery we'll lose all effectiveness when their charge does come at our walls."

Her eyes flashed. "Filthy curs! They'll not succeed with such tricks!"

Ancelotis smiled as she stormed off, shouting the news to the other women, sending the word of Saxon perfidiousness through the encamped refugees. Stirling chuckled. *Brilliant, Ancelotis. Absolutely brilliant. You've put the fighting spirit right back into them.*

Aye, he sighed. *Now if we can just keep their spirits high . . .*

Stirling waited until full darkness had descended, walking through the camp to give the high sign to the men he had selected a week previously and trained so carefully by day and night. The rain ended shortly after dark, the wind blowing rents in the clouds, through which glittering cold constellations could be seen. How long the clear weather would last, there was no way of knowing, but Stirling did not intend to waste the opportunity.

At least there was no moon to light the summit and upper slopes. His men gathered quietly in the darkness, waiting for the signal to begin their first nighttime raid. The Saxons far below crawled into tents for the night, leaving banked coals smouldering in the darkness like dragons' eyes. Sentries could just barely be made out, stolidly making their way past silent campfires, occluding the light as they passed.

"You know the drill," Stirling murmured. "Give it another quarter hour, to let them settle into sleep, then we'll begin."

Stirling walked the walls, studying the terrain below, the pattern of campfires, nodding to himself. Yes, they'd laid themselves out almost precisely as he'd expected. Silence had fallen over both camps now, as the frozen stars winked and glittered overhead, wisps of wind-torn cloud racing past. It was a wet wind, nonetheless, promising more rain off the cold North Atlantic—within hours, if Ancelotis were any judge of the weather.

The quarter hour passed swiftly, leaving Stirling's palms damp and his heart thudding with adrenaline. He'd made plenty of night sorties, both in training and actual combat, but pre-battle jitters were simply part of the package. He nodded to his men, whispering out the signal to begin. The Briton soldiers he'd trained so carefully in commando tactics began the raid by tying one end of an enormous ball of whip-thin, strong cordage to each of the several gates leading out through the outermost wall.

In groups of ten, they slipped out through those gates, each man letting the guideline slide through his fingers in the darkness. Stirling led one party toward the royal pavilion. When they reached the end of the first skein, some one hundred and sixty feet from the summit, the commando immediately behind Stirling tied the beginning of his skein to the end of Stirling's and they continued their silent descent.

Each band descending the hillside included one Sarmatian archer with a quiver of deadly arrows slung across one shoulder. As they approached the royal pavilion—which was not Stirling's goal, not tonight— they paused long enough for the archer to find and target the night sentry on duty outside the kings' tent. A soft slap of bowstring and a hiss of arrow's flight were followed by a muffled gasp of pain and the thud of a man's body striking the ground. Stirling was on top of him an instant later, cutting the wounded man's throat to finish silencing him. Blood, hot and terrible, flowed across his hands, which he wiped on his woolen trousers to prevent his grip on dagger and guideline from slipping.

Stirling signaled with one hand and they continued the perilous descent, down toward the flat plain at the foot of Caer-Badonicus. They tied ten separate lines to the end of the final skein, so that each of the commandos could find his way back swiftly, then split up, creeping low through the camp. Stirling's goal for the night was multifold, but his main target was the line of horses and supply wagons dimly visible as hulking black shadows at the edge of the Saxons' camp. They crept around tents where Saxons snored and turned restively in their sleep. Stirling would have given a great deal for a simple set of starlight goggles, but that kind of technology was sixteen centuries in the future, so he did the best he could with ambient starlight and the smouldering coals of the campfires.

The archer creeping along at Stirling's heels took down another sentry, catching this one through the throat with his deadly aim. The man thrashed down with a choked gurgle and went still after no more than two feeble kicks of his feet. Heart pounding, Stirling eased past the body, gaining at last the line where the Saxons' supply wagons had been parked for the duration of the siege. The draft horses had been tied for the night just beyond the heavily laden wagons. He held his long dagger in his teeth, ignoring the coppery taste from the blood of the Saxon he'd killed with it, and slipped open the satchel strapped to his back.

He lifted out one of the clay pots inside, upending its mixture of pitch, sulphur, tow, frankincense, and sawdust across the nearest wagon's contents, then crept to the next wagon in line, repeating the action until

Emrys Myrddin's combustible compound had drenched the contents of ten Saxon wagons. That done, Stirling slipped around to the picket line of horses, hushing them as they whickered, patting velvety noses and thick-muscled necks. He cut the lines with his dagger, then slipped back to the nearest campfire, where he paused, waiting for the signal from the summit.

A moment later it came, as each of the teams tugged on their guidelines, signaling their readiness. Light flashed from the top of the watchtower, lantern light that glowed like a star in the inky darkness. Stirling grinned, then thrust his torch into the coals. It caught with a flare of red-gold light. Sprinting now, he ran from wagon to wagon, setting Myrddin's surprise alight. Flames roared in a great whoosh as the Greek fire ignited. Horses screamed, plunging away from the sudden spread of flames, running in panic, bolting with their cut tether lines across the great, dark plain.

Stirling let go a bloodcurdling yell and dashed back through the Saxons' camp, setting fire to tents as he ran. Wagons blazed for hundreds of yards along the Saxons' outer perimeter, spelling utter ruin for the besieging army. Grinning like a madman, Stirling fired more tents, gained the guideline, and shouted, "To the walls! To the walls, my bonny Britons!" Men came running through the blazing camp, Saxons milling in terror and confusion, Briton soldiers making a purposeful dash for the trailing guidelines.

"Move, move, move!"

Men scrambled past, climbing the muddy hillside. Overhead, the Saxon kings had burst out of their pavilion tent. Stirling's Sarmatian archer lit an arrow wrapped with oil-soaked rushes and fired high into the night air. The flaming missile whistled through the blackness and landed squarely atop the kings' tent. Fire spread in greedy tongues and rivers across the top of the cloth pavilion. Shouts of anger and panic spread through the group milling inside. Stirling's men climbed at a fast jog, bursting amongst the confused Saxons with whoops of savage glee. The kings scattered into the night, shouting for assistance.

"Leave them to run!" Stirling bellowed, urging his men back toward the summit.

Within minutes, they were safely back inside the walls, while below, fire blazed in a gaudy ring all the way around the base of Badon Hill. Cadorius was waiting to pound his back in delight. "By God's holy beard, you've done it! Look at them!"

Saxons were running in wild confusion, silhouetted against the blazing camp, trying with ragged, disjointed coordination to catch the scattering horses, to douse the flames consuming their supplies, their tents, and their caches of weapons. Britons, roused from sleep by the wild shouts below, were cheering in the night, whistling and laughing in open merriment. Stirling couldn't stop grinning, although he did pause long enough to order a trumpeter to blow the rally signal. Deep notes sang out across the hill fort's walls, a summons which brought Stirling's raiders running to report.

Of the fifty men he'd sent down in teams of ten, forty-eight had returned safely. One had been killed, his body dragged back by his comrades for proper burial. Another had been wounded and was receiving care from the camp's healers. The glow in his men's eyes closed Stirling's throat for a moment. In all his years of service to king and country, not one soldier had ever looked at him with such proud confidence in his leadership. *Go back?* a portion of his mind whispered to itself. *Go back, when I'm needed here and now?* Memory of the butchered women and children left to rot by Cutha and his Saxon cutthroats floated behind Stirling's eyelids. No. He could not go back. Not now. Not ever.

He hoped to God his family and his commander in the SAS would understand.

"I am deeply proud in your courage and skill this night," Stirling said in a voice that shook a little. "I have never served with finer men. It is my privilege and honor to fight at your side."

A roar went up from the watching Britons.

Princess Iona, cheeks wet and grey eyes brilliant in the firelight, smiled through her tears, then moved quietly away, clearly wanting to be alone with her grief. Stirling watched her go. Nothing he did, nothing these brave men did, could ever undo the damage the Saxons had already wrought. But they could prevent further butchery. Stirling swore an oath to God and whatever host of angels might be listening.

I will not fail these people. To the last of my strength, the last breath in my body, I will not fail them. This, I swear by all I hold holy.

Vow cast, Stirling saw his men well fed, plied with good wine, and then sought his bed, knowing full well the vengeance the Saxons would wreak, come the dawn.

Chapter Eighteen

Morgana had never been to Ireland.

When the Irish coast rose out of the stormy grey sea, frissons of mingled apprehension and excitement shot through her, while Brenna McEgan gazed at that coast with such homesick longing, it brought tears to their shared eyes. They arrived in a grand flotilla of Dalriadan warships, manned by every able-bodied *Scotti* farmholder and fisherman left alive. The disaster visited upon Dunadd had not touched the countryside, thank God, the farmholds being too scattered for Banning to have reached their vulnerable water supplies.

Enraged Dalriadans had answered the king's summons from miles around, gathering nearly three hundred strong to pursue vengeance. King Dallan mac Dalriada had insisted, however, that they sail first to Eire, to raise more sword hands from their Irish kinfolk. And so they had turned their prows west, across the narrow North Channel toward lands that one day would be called County Antrim and County Down.

Brenna had listened very hard to the conversation of the Irish sailors and soldiers on Dallan mac Dalriada's flagship. Her grandmother had taught her a fair bit of Gaelic. She'd forgotten much of it over the years, but listening to the *Scotti* clansmen, it began to return to her, although many of the words and most of the pronunciations were unfamiliar. By the time they sailed into the upper reaches of Belfast Lough, the broad estuary which speared some ten miles inland from the coast, Brenna was picking up whole conversations.

Tears prickled in her eyes again when Belfast rose out of the mists, a thriving settlement of several thousand, judging by the smoke curling up from cottage hearths. The achingly familiar profile of Cave Hill rose like a sentinel north of the town. Brenna had explored the hill during school holidays, catching a ride with older cousins who had licenses to drive. Five artificial caves had been dug into that craggy hill by Neolithic inhabitants, for what purpose, only those long-dead people could have explained. They'd seemed magical caves to Brenna and her cousins, three of whom had since died in the violent Troubles, two of them not even making it to their twentieth birthdays.

South of the town, some three miles from the harbor, Brenna could just make out the shape of the Giant's Ring, one of the most impressive ancient monuments anywhere in Ireland. Nearly six hundred sixty feet in diameter, the standing stones were enclosed by an earthen bank fifteen feet high and more than twenty feet across. The dolmen at the center stood guard over a Stone Age burial site. She wondered what the Iron Age Irish chieftains ruling Belfast village used it for? In later centuries, it had become a popular spot for horse racing.

A crowd had gathered at the harbor by the time
Dallan mac Dalriada gave orders to drop the anchor
stone overboard. He shouted across the water, greeting someone by name. A murmur of surprise ran
through the onlookers as the Dalriadan king leaped
over the gunwales into hip-deep water, wading ashore
to clasp arms with a tall, stocky Irishman wearing a
torque of high rank. Brenna listened closely as sailors ran a ladder over the side for the ladies to climb
down into a coracle being rowed out to ferry them in.

"What brings you to Belfast?" the tall man was asking. "Trouble, by the look of it."

"Grim trouble indeed, cousin. All Dunadd is dead."

Shock washed white over the tall man's features.
"Daghda help us, what's happened? Not plague?"

Dallan mac Dalriada shook his head. "Worse.
Saxons."

The Belfast chieftain blinked. "Saxons?"

"Aye, Saxon dogs with treachery behind every false
smile. But there is more news even, than Saxon plots
against Irish interests." He turned to beckon Morgana,
Medraut, and his daughter forward. "You'll remember
my daughter?"

"Fondly." He embraced Keelin and kissed her cheek.
"You've grown, child, lovelier every time I see you."

Keelin brushed a kiss across his whiskered cheek.
"It is good to see you again, Bradaigh mac Art."

Brenna shot an intent glance in Bradaigh mac Art's
direction. This was the Iron Age chieftain whose
stronghold was still called MacArt's Fort in the twenty-
first century? She had little time to ponder it, however, as Dallan mac Dalriada was beginning formal
introductions.

"Cousin, my daughter has married this week past,
in what may prove the most advantageous marriage in
the history of our clan. It is my honor to present King

Medraut of Galwyddel, husband to my child, and Queen Morgana of Ynys Manaw, sister to Medraut's late mother."

Bradaigh mac Art's eyes shot wide. He stared from Medraut to Morgana and back to Dallan mac Dalriada. "Have you taken leave of your senses, man?" he cried. "Married her off to a *Briton*?"

"I thank you for your gracious welcome," Brenna said icily, in near-flawless Gaelic. "I am so pleased that my nephew can lay claim to such well-mannered kinsmen."

A deathly silence fell across the Irish crowd. Bradaigh mac Art's jaw had dropped and even Dallan mac Dalriada started in surprise. Dawning delight shone in Keelin's eyes, then she swung back to face her father's cousin, firmly clasping her husband's hand.

"Your rudeness shames our clan," the girl said in a voice nearly as cold as Brenna's. "When you have recovered a civil tongue, I may be moved to sit beneath your roof!" She switched to Brythonic. "Come, husband, I will not stay on Belfast Beach and be insulted further by my own kinsmen."

She strode straight into the water and Medraut, glaring briefly at Bradaigh mac Art, followed, lifting her out of the waves and wading toward the ladder still hanging over the side of her father's ship. Morgana turned to follow, only to halt at Bradaigh's cry.

"Wait! Please forgive the insult to your honor, Queen Morgana, King Medraut. We have so long been enemies, the news took me by considerable shock."

Morgana swung back around to find the clan chieftain of Belfast holding out his open hand, cheeks stained red with embarrassment. After a moment's pause, Morgana stepped gravely forward to clasp the proffered hand. Calling upon Brenna's reacquired—if somewhat shaky—proficiency in Gaelic, she said, "It is my fondest hope, Bradaigh mac Art, that the sons and daughters of Ireland count Britons as kinsmen and allies from this day onward."

"Alliance does present intriguing possibilities," the tall clan chieftain nodded thoughtfully.

A moment later, Medraut had waded ashore and offered his open hand to Bradaigh. They clasped forearms in the greeting of equals and the Irishman offered apologies, one to Medraut and another to his young cousin Keelin, whose frosty gaze thawed somewhat at his obvious sincerity.

"Come up to the fortress, please, and tell me what's happened at Dunadd, that you've made alliance with Britons and speak of Saxon treachery."

Dallan mac Dalriada explained their grim news as they walked toward the great fortress rising up at the center of the town. Medraut glanced at Morgana and said in a low voice, "I didn't know you spoke Gaelic, Aunt."

Brenna twitched her lips as Morgana replied softly, "There is much you have yet to learn about me, nephew. Be thankful that our new kinsmen will never underestimate us again."

Bradaigh mac Art's hospitality, once stung into motion, proved cordial in every possible manner. The clan chieftain plied them with good Irish ale and steaming platters of roast boar, geese stuffed with apples, and fresh-baked bread, the dark Irish bread Brenna had grown up loving and had missed during the months in Beckett's lab in the Scottish Lowlands.

While they ate, Dallan mac Dalriada explained the monstrous act of destruction wrought by the Saxons' agent, Lailoken. "It is my intention, cousin, to sail with as many men-at-arms as I can raise by sunset tomorrow. All Britain marches to battle against these Saxon dogs. With Queen Morgana's help in securing safe conduct through Briton-held lands, I will lead an Irish army to strike the Saxons' southern flank. We'll take them by surprise and cut off their escape while Artorius and the Briton *cataphracti* smash them from the north."

Bradaigh tugged thoughtfully at his lower lip. "Where think you this battle will occur?"

Morgana leaned forward to answer. "My brother, Artorius, plans to meet the Saxons at Caer-Badonicus, a fortified hill in the south of Britain. We have left more than enough troops to guard the northern and western borders," she added with a slight smile, "but Artorius will ride south with at least a thousand men under arms, or I very much misjudge Briton fighting strength. And there are many more already at Caer-Badonicus."

"More than a thousand men-at-arms?" Bradaigh echoed, visibly startled.

"Artorius," Morgana nodded, "is Dux Bellorum. Every king in Britain owes him allegiance, supporting my brother's battle plans with their finest troops. The Romans may be gone from Britain, but Britons are still finely organized under Roman structures of command. The Saxons will soon learn this at great cost."

Bradaigh tugged at his lower lip again. "And your request, cousin?" he asked Dallan mac Dalriada.

"Sword arms to increase the fighting strength of Dalriada. How many men can you send with me to drive these Saxons dogs into the sea and drown them?"

"By the son of Beli Mawr, I'll raise a hundred men to send with you by tomorrow night's tide, and fast ships to carry them. And I pledge upon my sacred honor," he added, glancing into Morgana's eyes, "no Irishman within fifty miles of Belfast will raise sword against any son of Britain nor raid British shores for plunder."

"I am glad to hear it. Medraut has already sent word through Galwyddel that the Irish of Dalriada are now their kinsmen and must be accorded the respect rightfully due a king's cousins."

Bradaigh mac Art raised his goblet, finely wrought from silver, in a toast. "To the alliance then, Ireland and Britain joined by blood and friendship—and victory over our mutual enemy, the dogs of Saxony."

The toast was drunk solemnly around the table.

Then Bradaigh mac Art called for runners to be sent out through the countryside, summoning every firstborn male householder to war. Brenna watched with a chill down her spine. It was now far too late to call back what she had set in motion. Then a rueful little smile twitched at her lips. It was, at the very least, a miracle of diplomacy. And a very good beginning.

A distant wail of rams' horns sounded far below, the sound carrying through the grey dawn, in a vast ring surrounding Badon Hill. Stirling drained the last of his breakfast ale and tossed away his cup, drawing his sword and taking his place among the men of Gododdin, with Cadorius' contingent on one flank and Melwas on the other.

"First rank, to your places!" he shouted, even as other Briton kings, princes, and high-ranking officers were bellowing instructions to their own men. Far below, another blast on the rams' horns sent hundreds of men rushing forward, spears and pikes held at the ready. Stirling saw no archers at all. But there were javelins in plenty, causing him to duck back down as the first wave of lightweight, sharp-pointed missiles came whistling across the walls. Briton shields went up in a clattering wall of quarter-inch oak. Javelin points thwacked into them, some embedding themselves deeply, others glancing off and skipping across the heads of the defenders to clatter against the stone walls behind their first rank.

At Stirling's shouted command, echoed up and down the Briton lines, a mass of iron-headed *pila* darkened the sky, hurtling down into the Saxons' shields. The soft iron heads struck, biting deeply into enemy shields, then bent under the weight of their own shafts, tangling one shield with another and tripping the foremost rank of attackers. Men went down in yelling confusion, stepped on and across by the men behind them. Another wave of *pila* whistled down, slowing the Saxon charge, but not stopping it. On they came, shouting from behind their shields, heavy spears tucked beneath armpits for stability in the charge.

Saxons and Britons came together at the edge of the outermost wall, with a shock of spears against shields and a roar of bellowing male voices. Men shouted foul curses and stabbed and jabbed with spearpoints, trying to pierce the overlapping walls of wooden shields on both sides of the thick stone barrier. When the second wave of Saxons hit the wall, driving back the defenders, trumpets sang out the retreat, sending Britons scrambling back toward the fourth wall. Even as the Saxons roared forward, Briton axemen were chopping through catapult ropes, sending gallons of sizzling-hot, melted fat soaring out over the walls. Liquid grease fell like rain across the Saxons' front ranks. Men screamed, dropping shields and spears to claw at scalded faces, beards, clothing. The Britons turned and surged forward with an unholy shout, driving the staggering Saxons back across the outer wall and leaving bodies piled underfoot.

The Saxons, shaken, retreated down the hillslope, pausing in the shelter of their wooden palisades. Stirling could hear the shouts of their leaders, kings and their *atheling* sons, high-ranking *eoldormen* and noble-birth *thegns*, exhorting their men to overcome such shameful cowardice and make the charge a second time. Stirling climbed to a lookout perch atop the innermost wall and peered downward, then grunted.

"Send word to Cadorius and Melwas, they're putting the *gewisse* Britons in the first ranks this time, rather than risk their own."

A glance back toward their own rear lines showed him the women busy tending Briton wounded, but there were far fewer than he'd expected after such a clash, which heartened him considerably and left Ancelotis jubilant. Then the signal horns called the charge again and the enemy's front ranks pounded up the hill once more. Any serious worries Stirling had, that they faced Britons this time, evaporated when the defenders struck with even greater ferocity than before. *Never underestimate the power of hatred, when a man stands face-to-face with a traitor,* Ancelotis grunted, scanning their lines from Cadorius's contingent on his far left flank to Melwas's on his far right.

They drove the attacking *gewisse* back with a steady hail of javelins and *pila*. As the traitors of Wessex fell, their front lines wavered and collapsed backwards, until the entire charge faltered and reversed itself back down the hill. Stirling, leaping once more to his vantage point atop the inner wall, could see King Aelle and Cerdic of Wessex snarling at one another beside the platform where their charred pavilion had been replaced with a much shabbier affair. For the next hour, the Saxons licked their wounds and rethought their strategy.

And the Britons of Caer-Badonicus waited patiently.

Then the lookout atop the high watchtower called out, "They're shifting troops northward!"

Stirling raced up the ladder to see for himself what the Saxons were up to. They were shifting, all right, moving the bulk of their men to the spot where Briton defenses were weakest, along their northeastern flank. Stirling whistled sharply, fingers between his teeth, and caught Cadorius' attention. Stirling waved to his left, held up five fingers and pointed to their reserves. Cadorius nodded, bellowing orders. The Briton reserves, some fifty men from the rear ranks of the Glastenning, Gododdin, and Dumnonia contingents, ran for the northeastern flank, forming up behind the front-line defenders, while catapults were winched around to face the third charge. When it came, they were ready, much to the Saxons' consternation.

As the front lines came together again with a shock of weapons on shields, the second ranks leaped to the top of the fourth wall. Javelins and deadly *pila* hurled down from that angle forced the Saxons to lift their shields high, to guard against the deadly rain. Whereupon the front line of defenders launched a blistering attack with spears and javelins under the edges of their high-held shields. Blood ran thick as the Saxons staggered. Then a sudden shift along the Saxons' rear echelons signaled a new line of attack and Briton trumpets sang out a warning.

The Dumnonian reserves Stirling had dispatched reeled under sudden attack along their thinned ranks. Saxons poured across the outermost wall in a solid wave of spearpoints and oaken shields. Stirling skinned back down the ladder, shouting for the Gododdin center to pivot and strike the Saxons along their flank. For long, terrible minutes, all was confusion between the outermost and fourth walls. The lines swayed, crumpled, fell back to the third wall, while Saxons howled and leaped across the Briton dead. Then the catapults slapped with a crack like doom, and blazing oil, set alight before being hurled, fell in a fiery rain across the Saxons' shields. Men screamed, their leather jerkins and quilted tunics set ablaze by the flaming grease.

The contingent from Gododdin let fly a rain of arrows, like shooting pigs in a barrel. The Saxons stumbled, the momentum of their charge broken. Briton defenders poured in from both flanks, catching the Saxons along their vulnerable sides, trapping most of them between the third and fifth walls. And when the Britons drew swords and began to hack and hew at legs, arms, necks, unarmored heads, anything within reach of their deadly British blades, the Saxons fell back in total disarray, unable to match the Britons with the smaller daggers they carried—if they carried any blade at all. Most did not. Spears broken, shields afire and cast down in terror, the Saxons broke and ran. Or died under Briton blades. What remained was ground into bloody paste in the mud.

Stirling thrust and hacked at the retreating Saxons right alongside his Gododdin warriors, shouting encouragement. When the last of the survivors had fled down the hill, Stirling leaned against the third wall, gasping for breath, and scrubbed filth from his face with the back of one hand. His fingers trembled as the adrenaline rush wore off, leaving him shaking with exhaustion. Grim-faced soldiers were stripping the Saxon dead of weapons, tossing the bodies over the walls to roll them after their luckier companions downhill. Wounded Britons limped for the aid stations back amongst the women, where a glance showed Covianna Nim directing a whole host of nurses to tend the injured.

Cadorius limped his way, as spattered with gore and filth as Stirling.

"God be praised," the king of Dumnonia gasped, "I thank the Almighty you were in position to sound that warning. I didn't see their shift in time to respond."

"The Dumnonian lines held," Stirling insisted, cleaning his sword on the tunic of a dead Saxon. "Gododdin only gave them the breather they needed to regroup and hold fast, which they did. With more bravery than I've ever seen in battle, and that is no lie."

Cadorius smiled wearily. "Then let us agree to praise one another's men to the skies and be grateful that we've men left alive to praise."

"Agreed," Stirling said, offering his hand.

Cadorius clasped his forearm, then hugged him with a rougher embrace. "Come, let us see to our wounded while yon bastards try to talk their men into making another try at us!"

The Saxons gave them a respite of two hours, which they all needed, then charged the walls from the southwestern flank this time. Britons scrambled to strengthen the defenses, only to snarl curses as Saxon slingers hurled live coals onto wooden roof shingles and thatched barracks inside the hill fort. Smoke and flames blazed up from a dozen spots while soldiers dodged the children who scrambled with pails of water to douse the flames. Confusion engulfed the whole compound while the Saxon charge shattered the southwestern shield wall and poured into the hill fort itself. Stirling found himself in a desperate hand-to-hand fight for his life, slashing and stabbing with his sword, shouting orders through the chaos, trying to regroup his men in a wedge formation.

"Rally to me!" he shouted, "Rally to me! For Artorius and Britain!"

A rumbling thunder drove through the confusion. Stirling could spare no time even to glance around to see what it might be. An instant later, a mass of cavalry smashed into the Saxon lines, *cataphracti* mounted on armored chargers, lances held low for full-bore charge. The heavy horses shattered the Saxons' front ranks. Half a hundred of Britain's finest cavalry rode down the infantry beneath flint-hard hooves. Men screamed, horses snorted and trumpeted, lances shattered on shields and skewered yelling men on every side. More Saxons were pouring over the walls, but the momentum slowed as the cavalry drove straight through their ranks. More Britons came pouring in from the flanks, driving the Saxons slowly back across the innermost wall, across the second, the third, and finally the fourth and fifth walls. Briton dead lay trampled beside Saxon invaders, while smoke rose ominously into the sky at their backs.

Stirling waited to be certain the Saxons were, in fact, being driven back before turning his attention to the fires blazing up from the compound. Livestock bellowed and tried to break out of burning pens. Women and children hurled buckets of water onto the flames, while soldiers used axes to cut supports out from under burning roofs, toppling the structures before the flames could spread. By the time the last fires had been doused, they'd lost two months' worth of supplies, most of the grain for the horses, and shelters for nearly a third of their civilians. Cadorius, cursing under his breath, stalked through the camp shouting orders for temporary shelters to be rigged for the women and children, while Stirling and Melwas ordered the butchering and dressing of the livestock that had perished before the flames could be doused.

As the sun dropped behind the distant Mendip Hills, a single rider rode up from the Saxons' main encampment, under another flag of truce. Cadorius and Ancelotis waited in terse silence while Melwas ordered the civilians back, out of sight. The courier was not Creoda this time, but Cutha. His arrogant face wore a smug expression as he reined around beside the outermost wall, trying to survey the destruction within.

"Ancelotis, I see you have tasted the beginning of my vengeance!" he shouted across the walls.

Ancelotis didn't even bother to answer.

"I come bearing a message from my father, king of Sussex. Pay heed, for we will not repeat ourselves and we will offer you mercy only once. Surrender Caer-Badonicus to us and we will allow your women and children to leave the fortress in safety. Defy us and we will deliver to them the same mercy I showed the whores of Penrith!"

Melwas, striding up to join them, clenched both fists and started forward with a snarl of hatred. Cadorius grabbed his arm and slung the younger king to a forcible halt. "No. Let the jackal speak."

Cutha smirked at them from across the five walls. "Give this jackal your decision, old man."

Cadorius stared levelly into the Saxon's eyes. "I will answer the puppy of Sussex when it suits me. Return here in a quarter hour and I will give you an answer."

Cutha's lips twitched and he lifted fingertips in a mocking salute. "By all means, confer with your brother kings."

He set spurs to his horse's flanks and the animal leaped away, tossing its head unhappily at the steep descent. Cadorius turned a brooding gaze toward Ancelotis. "We have lost much that we needed to hold out."

"Artorius will come. He cannot be far away, now. Tell Cutha when he returns that you must persuade others to surrender, as the safety of the women and children is your greatest personal desire."

Cadorius' eyes flashed. "Surrender is the furthest thought from my mind, Ancelotis!"

"And from mine. But two can play the game of lies that Cutha delights in so greatly. Unless I am very much mistaken, we can strike them a blow at dawn they'll not soon forget."

Cadorius frowned, clearly unhappy, but nodded.

"Very well. After these past few days, I trust your judgement and cunning implicitly."

When Cutha returned, Cadorius called his answer across. "It is in my mind to accept your offer of clemency, Saxon, but my brother kings need more persuasion. Grant me the night to confer with them and I will give you our combined answer with the dawn. But look you, I will not give such a reply to mere princelings and go-betweens. If Aelle of Sussex wants to hear terms of surrender, he must come to these walls and take them in his own person."

Cutha's smirk was a mortal insult. "Of course. My father, King of the Saxons, will greet you at dawn. Take very great care that you do not disappoint him." He put spurs to his horse's flanks and galloped recklessly down the steep hillside once more. Melwas sent an obscene gesture after him, then spat out, "Terms of surrender?"

Cadorius smiled tightly. "You will please note that I carefully did not say *whose*."

A bark of laughter broke from the younger king. "Very well. Let us go and discuss how to force the Saxons to their knees."

Ancelotis and the other kings made the rounds of the hill fort, making sure the wounded were being properly succored, seeing to it the children and women were fed, overseeing the repairs to structures only damaged while work crews labored to clear the charred wreckage of destroyed structures out of the way, should rapid troop movements be required again. They had just retired to the assembly hall for discussion of the Saxons' ultimatum when the lookout in the tower high overhead gave a shout and came skinning down the ladder, bursting a moment later into the room.

"Come quick!" he gasped, snatching at Ancelotis' arm. "A signal light!"

Ancelotis raced outside, climbing the ladder in haste. The lookout shinnied up behind him and pointed to the northwest, where a light blazed in the darkness atop the highest of the Mendip Hills. The light flickered in a definite pattern. Ancelotis counted flashes, translating numbers in his head.

"Artorius is camped at the edge of the Salisbury Plain," he said tersely. "He plans a charge at the Saxons' northeastern flank at dawn. Besides infantry numbering five hundred, he's brought more than a thousand heavy cavalry. Fetch me a lamp, quickly."

The sentry vanished into the darkness, returning a few moments later with a lit oil lamp. Stirling shielded the light with the edge of his cloak while his host took a moment to compose his reply, then used a corner of the woolen cloak to occlude the lamp in his own coded series of numerical flashes.

"Dawn charge acknowledged. Saxon command halfway to summit, southeast flank. Greatest force to southeast, two thousand strong. They are without supplies and grow evil-tempered. Aelle demands surrender by dawn. Signal your departure, we will coordinate surprise attack."

The light flashed back from Mendip's heights. "Message acknowledged. We ride at dawn."

When Stirling turned, he found Cadorius perched on the top rung of the ladder, peering northward, his cloak whipping like a maddened snake in the rising wind.

"What is it?" Cadorius asked tersely.

Ancelotis pointed. "Artorius' signal, in code. He camps at the edge of Salisbury Plain and will charge the Saxon flank at first light."

"That's the best news I've had in days."

Ancelotis chuckled, albeit a trifle grimly. "Indeed. Come, we still have much to prepare. And I, for one, could do with a hot meal and a cup of ale to wash it down with, if anything fit to eat survived the fire."

Cadorius smiled wanly in the starlight. "A keg or two, at any rate."

They downed hot stew while issuing orders for a double watch through the night, to prevent the Saxons from copying their own night-sortie tactics. "We'll need to bunch them up, in the morning," Stirling said around a mouthful of boiled beef, "which shouldn't be too difficult, under the circumstances. I'm willing to bet Cerdic and Creoda, not to mention Cutha, will insist on being present for the surrender. And they'll bring a fair number of their ranking *eoldormen* and *thegns* with them, as a show to their own troops, demonstrating their high status."

Melwas snorted. "Aelle doesn't travel *anywhere* without at least twenty of his picked favorites riding guard around him. Doesn't even trust his own peasants, that one."

"Which works to our advantage," Cadorius nodded. "At one blow, we can cripple their entire leadership."

"Precisely. Covianna—" Ancelotis glanced across to where the master healer sat at the edge of their council. "How goes it with our wounded?"

She answered gravely, "Not so badly as I had feared. Some two score and ten have suffered serious wounds that may yet prove fatal. We've had to take shattered arms and legs in a few cases, but no more than eighteen have been so maimed, to my knowledge." She bit one lip. "The worst is perhaps three dozen men with the onion sickness, for whom I can do nothing. No healer in Britain could save them."

Onion sickness? Stirling frowned. *What the deuce is that?*

Ancelotis answered grimly, *The women feed onion soup to men with gut wounds. If the scent of onion*

*comes out the open wound, the bowel has been pen-
etrated. Such men will die sometime within the next
two to three days. In the old days, victims with the
onion sickness were given merciful release with a knife
at the throat. Since the coming of Christ, such mercy
is called murder, so the poor wretches die slowly. Their
sole comfort is the hope of heaven, rather than hell.
The women dose them liberally with alcohol and herbs,
to keep them as comfortable as possible while they wait
for death.*

Stirling winced inwardly. In the twenty-first century,
even a fourth-year medical student knew enough
surgical procedures to save such men. In the sixth
century, however . . . "Thank you, Covianna. I'm sure
you will do whatever you can to ease their last hours."

She bowed her head in silent assent.

Cadorius said, "We've lost some hundred more,
killed at the walls. Our fighting strength is down to
slightly more than five hundred men-at-arms. How
fared your archers, Ancelotis?"

"Very well, indeed. I lost one archer in the night
operation and two more at the walls during that last
charge. That leaves three score and nine remaining.
More than enough to gift the Saxon commanders with
our barbed reply."

Grim smiles ran through the council chamber.

"In that case," Cadorius grunted, rising to his feet,
"the best thing we can do for our troops and ourselves
is get a fair night's sleep. Even with Artorius on the
horizon and the tricks we've prepared for the bastards,
tomorrow will not be an easy day."

Of that, Stirling was absolutely certain.

Chapter Nineteen

The clans of Belfast added four warships to Dallan mac Dalriada's flotilla.

Foul weather dogged them all the way down the long reach of the Irish Sea, past the jutting coastline of Wales and south to the storm-battered tip of Cornwall. Brenna managed well enough until they rounded the long, narrow arm of land that comprised the Cornish coast. The bulk of Ireland itself had sheltered them from the worst of the storms, but once past the southern edge of County Cork, the full fury of the Atlantic burst across their ships. Squalls black with rain swept across the Irish convoy, buffeting them with terrific wind and towering waves. Nausea struck Brenna and Morgana so completely, even fear of capsizing in the maddened sea held no real terror. Medraut was a bit green, as well, although he bore up under the rough weather better than Morgana and her unseen guest.

"We'll go ashore at the border of Caer-Durnac," Medraut shouted above the roar of wind and thunder. "March inland from somewhere along the edge of Lynne Bay!"

That ought to put them right about Weymouth, if Brenna remembered her English geography accurately. From there it was twenty-five, perhaps thirty miles to the hill fort Morgana called Caer-Badonicus, which victorious Saxons and their descendants still referred to as Cadbury. "Wonderful," Morgana moaned, too ill to muster any enthusiasm at all. "If I survive this wretched seasickness, I'll build a church at Weymouth Bay and dedicate it to Holy Mary, Mother of Mercy."

Medraut grinned. "A fine idea. Here, let me pull this blanket round your shoulders."

He fussed solicitously until she waved him away. "Go, lad, go and help your father-in-law guide us safely to shore."

Keelin, disgustingly hale and hearty despite the pounding of the waves and the incessant pitching and yawing of their little ship—which bulked no more than forty feet from stem to stern—placed a bucket at Morgana's side and periodically emptied it over the gunwales. By the time they reached Weymouth Bay, destined by Brenna's time to become one of Britain's most favored seaside resorts, Morgana was exhausted. Once out of the worst of the battering wind and waves, the Irish flotilla made fine speed across the wide harbor, throwing anchors overboard within a yard of shore. Medraut and Dallan mac Dalriada had to lift her over the side and carry her to solid ground. She felt like kissing the stony beach. She did sink down to sit above the tideline while the Irish offloaded horses and weapons.

When an armed delegation from Weymouth village spurred toward them, shouting the alarm at sight of the Irish fleet, Morgana staggered to her feet again, groaning the necessity for movement. Morgana leaned against Medraut as they stepped forward to greet the men of Weymouth, old men and half-grown lads, she realized, faces chalky with fear at yet another disastrous invasion. When the approaching war party came within javelin range, Morgana swallowed back nausea and shouted across the open beach.

"Hold fast, men of Weymouth! I am Morgana, Queen of Ynys Manaw and sister to Artorius, the Dux Bellorum of all Britain. My nephew Medraut, King of Galwyddel, has brought allies to drive back the Saxons." She swept a hand toward the Irish, who were still offloading war-horses and equipment.

Medraut added in a strong, clear voice, "These men are now my kinsmen, for I have wed Keelin of Dalriada and made her Queen of Galwyddel. Her kinsmen and mine have journeyed with us from Dalriada and Belfast, to lend Irish strength to our own, for the Saxons have foully attacked the Irish as well as our own British kingdoms. All Dunadd lies dead to Saxon perfidy. The Irish would take dire vengeance upon men who kill the coward's way, with poison that strikes down innocent babes as well as warriors grown. Vouchsafe us passage through Caer-Durnac and we'll drive the Saxons all the way to the sea."

Consternation passed visibly across the old mens' faces, while the lads stared at their elders in open confusion. One of the oldest riders stroked his long, white beard while staring into Morgana's eyes. "And does Morgana of Ynys Manaw guarantee that yon Irish bastards won't burn our homes round our ears and carry our children into slavery?"

"Dallan mac Dalriada of Dunadd and Bradaigh mac Art of Belfast could have held all Galwyddel and Ynys Manaw to ransom during this week past, for Medraut and I went among them alone and unarmed, under truce of marriage. They treated us with honor and pledged to add their swords to our own in blood-feud with the Saxons who murdered their kinsmen at Fortress Dunadd. I swear before Christ and Holy Mother Mary that I believe them to be honest allies of Britain. I would not have brought them, else."

The old men of Weymouth village conferred quietly among themselves, then their white-bearded spokesman gave Dallan mac Dalriada a formal bow and put away his sword. "We bid you welcome then, and Godspeed to your journey. Weymouth will send a guide to show you the fastest route north to Caer-Badonicus, where the Saxon armies of Sussex and Wessex have laid siege."

"My grateful thanks," Medraut nodded graciously, a sentiment Morgana repeated as well.

Within a quarter hour of arrival, the Irish army— more than four hundred strong—set out in a thunder of hooves across the chalk hills and open downlands of Dorset, past thatched cottages built of chalk and flint, cottages and tiny villages that were ominously devoid of males between the ages of ten and seventy. Whipping through the villages, charging across the broad downs, with their grassy, rolling hills and vast herds of sheep, they raced overland at the gallop, past the Giant of Cerne Abbas, an immense male figure cut deeply into the white chalk of the hillside, with a gnarled war club held high above his head. Whoever had carved that immense chalk man, their warlike valor was desperately needed by the Britons who now ruled this land. As the white chalk man fell away behind their fast-moving cavalcade, Morgana prayed they would arrive at Caer-Badonicus in time. And that Artorius would find it in his heart to forgive her.

❖   ❖   ❖

Dawn's first hint of grey had barely touched the eastern sky when Stirling climbed the ladder up to the watchtower.

"There it is again," the lookout whispered, taking care that his voice didn't carry. He pointed north, toward the Mendip Hills. Wishing mightily for a pair of ordinary binoculars, Stirling peered northward. The horizon was still too dark to make out anything like actual movement, but the signal light atop the highest hill flashed out an unmistakable message:

Charge under way . . . charge under way . . .

"Send the response code," Stirling said quietly.

The lookout's lamp flashed briefly in the near darkness, carefully shielded from all directions except the direct line of sight with Artorius' signalman. Straining his ears to the utmost, tipping his head slightly to put his best ear toward the invisible cavalrymen, Stirling finally detected a faint rumbling sound, like very distant thunder—which could all too easily be taken for the real thing, since lightning flashed and jittered across the northwestern sky. In the encampment below, Saxon soldiers had barely begun to stir out of their tents, clearly reluctant to crawl out into the drizzling cold rain that had begun falling during the night.

All the better, Stirling nodded to himself.

The lookout hissed, "Look you to the south! The Saxon kings are climbing up."

Stirling turned swiftly. They were, indeed, climbing. Swiftly so. *On horseback!* That was a stroke of luck Stirling hadn't counted on. He grinned. "Bloody marvelous! The fools don't want to muddy their finery, slogging up here on foot! And they've brought their ranking *eoldormen* and *thegns,* as I'd hoped. Call down which marker post they're nearest when they decide to stop. And yell out the moment you actually *see*

Artorius and our *cataphracti*. In this battle, timing's *everything.*"

The lookout saluted sharply. "Yes, sir!"

Stirling skinned down the ladder to find Cadorius, Melwas, and a number of Briton princes waiting at the foot of the tower. "On their way," Stirling said tersely.

Cadorius nodded, heading toward the rendezvous point. They passed three score and nine Sarmatian archers who waited silently, crouched down on one knee so as to remain completely invisible to the approaching Saxons. They sheltered their bowstrings beneath cloaks to protect them from the wet weather until time to fire. Stirling paused to murmur, "The lookout will call down the number of the marker they stop nearest. Aim accordingly."

Nine and sixty stone-still Asian faces nodded silently, a blood-chilling sight. Warriors carved of granite, prepared to come to life at the merest whisper from above . . .

As the Briton kings reached the innermost wall, an arrogant Saxon voice shouted, "Britons of Caer-Badonicus! Why do your kings not show themselves?"

Cadorius climbed up, Stirling and Ancelotis to his left, Melwas to his right. The king of Dumnonia stared coldly down at the Saxons, who could not see the men crouched low in the narrow spaces between the layered walls, ready to snatch open the wooden sluice gates. Of all the gates—real and false—built into the fortress walls, only these crucial five were lined up one in front of the other. Once opened, God Himself couldn't stop the pent-up water behind them from roaring free. Ropes quivered, held taut by the gate teams, five men to each side. Lying prone across the roofing stones other soldiers waited, ready to drag up the crossbars holding the floodgates rigidly closed. Enough rain had fallen—and continued to fall—that the slight loss of water trickling from beneath those tight-wedged gates looked like simple runoff seeping down the muddy hillside.

"Well?" the Saxon spokesman challenged Cadorius, sneering through his great, gaudy blond mustaches. "What say you, kings of Britain?"

Stirling and Ancelotis could just see the Saxons' upper bodies, along with their horses' heads and twitching ears. They'd called their halt near marker post three, an innocuous looking stub of wood barely visible above the muddy ground, which had been chopped by mens' boots and horses' hooves into a fine and filthy slurry. A very faint "Line on three . . ." drifted down from the watchtower, the sound so faint it couldn't possibly have carried to the Saxons, who had halted some fifty yards or so downslope. Stirling held three fingers up behind his back, to be sure every archer knew the proper aim point.

Cadorius, watching the silent preparations at his feet, shouted across, "Who among you will hear our terms?"

One of the *eoldormen,* a man neither Stirling nor Ancelotis recognized, sent back a jeering laugh. "*Your* terms? You do not dictate terms to the kings of Sussex and Wessex, Briton! We dictate them to you."

"Very well," Cadorius nodded, doing a creditable job of a man determined to remain reasonable at any cost. "What terms do you offer?"

The *eoldorman* turned slightly in his saddle. "What say you, mighty King Aelle of Sussex?"

The Saxon king swept them with a withering, dismissive glance. "If they would save the lives of their womenfolk, let them send the females out first. Along with any children below the age of five. Let this be the first demonstration of Saxon power—and Saxon clemency."

Behind Stirling's shoulder, Melwas muttered, "He means to butcher them before our eyes."

Cadorius' answer came out flat with apparent dejection. "You offer us no other sane choice. Very well, I will give orders to summon our women and children. And I will unbar the gates, to let them pass."

Aelle inclined his iron-helmed head in assent as grey light gradually brightened the eastern sky with long, bloody streaks of crimson, ominous predictor of more rain. Cadorius turned toward the inner compound. "Gather the womenfolk up and their babes, as well— we will send them out under a flag of surrender."

Waiting men "relayed" the command, buying a few more precious seconds while women added shrill voices to the commotion they were carefully engineering inside the compound. The Saxons sat their horses in jaunty confidence, most of them wearing smirks, clearly enjoying every moment of their triumph, which had come at a remarkably low cost in Saxon lives. Oh, yes, they were most assuredly enjoying this moment. Tension tightened through Stirling's every muscle, every sinew, waiting, waiting for the final signal—

High overhead, the watchtower sentry blew the ram's horn.

Artorius was in sight.

"NOW!" Stirling bellowed. He dropped flat. The others threw themselves down beside him. Wooden bars, snatched from their brackets, sailed into the air. The teams on the gates hauled in unison, dragging ponderous sluice doors wide open. Five wooden gates slammed into five stone walls. Gate teams scrambled for safety as the pent-up water burst free, like the gushing spillway of a dam. Muddy water frothed and flattened into a wave that spread across the whole side of Badon Hill.

Horses reared and snorted in panic as the flood smashed into them, fetlock-deep and splashing up to the horses' knees in places. The churned-up mud, already saturated from weeks of rain, liquefied instantly underfoot, like slurry thrown off a potter's wheel. Several animals lost their footing and crashed to the ground, lunging and screaming in terror and pain. Hapless riders were hurled through space to land badly in the mud and brambles, or, even worse for them, they lay pinned beneath their wounded mounts, dragged downhill with bone-crushing force as their horses skidded downward in the muck. Other horses bolted, kicking and sunfishing in their desperation to escape the shifting, slick mud. Water sucked semisolid ground out from under flailing legs. Equine panic redoubled as wounded men and downed horses thrashed and bellowed their inelegant way toward the plain five hundred feet below. In the space of thirty seconds, surprise turned into chaos and—with lightning's jagged quickflash—chaos spilled into utter rout.

Ancelotis gave the high sign. Three score and nine Sarmatian archers let fly. Arrows fell in a thick black rain. Wounded horses, already panic-stricken, bucked and pitched. More riders came adrift. Another flight of arrows slashed through armor and flesh, through mail shirts, through arms and legs and horses' fleeing hindquarters. "Fall back!" someone was shouting from within the mass of shaken Saxons. "Fall back—for the love of Frigga, *fall back!*"

Men slipped and scrambled through the deadly black rain. Saxon kings and royal princes cartwheeled and skidded through the muck. At the base of the hill, Saxon infantry scurried like confused ants. Someone was blowing the signal to charge. Someone else was frantically gesturing troops out of the flood's path. Water hit the wooden wall shielding the royal pavilion, parted in a great splash, and roared down into the camp below. Whole tents were swept away, their anchoring pegs yanked out of the softened, muddy ground. Saxons splashed after them, trying to rescue weapons washed away with the rest of the flotsam.

"Look!" Melwas cried.

He was pointing to the northeast corner of the hill.

Saxons were running in wild confusion, a whole mass of them fleeing in a mob. Some tried to climb the hill, others ran straight out onto the plain. A fierce exultation swept through Stirling. Ancelotis let out a wild shout. "They're running! Bastards are *running*! *We've broken them!*"

An instant later, a thousand galloping horses burst into view. Thunder rolled across the Salisbury Plain, four thousand flying hooves shaking the very ground. Artorius was visible in the vanguard, his white stallion snorting at full charge, his golden armor gleaming in the early light, the red dragon banner snapping like a ribbon of blood. The cavalry charge cut through the mass of fleeing Saxons, mowing them down like rye before a scythe. Hundreds of Saxons went down beneath the *cataphracti*'s hooves. None of those who fell so much as stirred when the cavalcade swept past. Britons up and down the wall were shouting, hurling javelins into the clustered Saxons foolish enough to seek safety by climbing toward the fortress. A flight of Sarmatian arrows blackened the sky once more, bringing down more.

"Charge!" Cadorius shouted. "Sound the charge! *Cataphracti*, to horse!"

The watchtower lookout sounded a long blast. A wave of Briton infantry poured over the walls. Women and children led horses forward, running with them toward other gates snatched open by foot soldiers manning the walls. Cavalrymen vaulted into the saddle and charged through them, carefully keeping to solid ground on either side of the slurry that had spelled ruin to the Saxons' hopes. Ancelotis shouted, "Archers! Keep your ranks closed up! Advance in a group! Continue massed fire!"

He leaped onto the nearest horse, not caring whose it was, and plunged through the open gates, leading Gododdin in the charge. The Saxon kings and their shaken sons cowered against the wooden shield wall of their command platform. Covered in mud, eyes wild, horses dead or galloping away riderless across the open plain, the Saxons drew swords to face down the Britons stampeding toward them.

"Alive!" Ancelotis shouted. "Take them alive!"

A moment later, Gododdin had surrounded them, hemming them round with a glittering wall of British steel. Ancelotis gave them a mocking salute with his own sword.

"You seem to have lost an army," Ancelotis favored them with a cold smile. He gestured slightly with the tip. "Unless it is your wish to die immediately, throw down your weapons and your arrogant pride and beg the kings of Britain—whom you have greatly wronged—for mercy on your shivering wives and daughters."

King Aelle of Sussex, barely recognizable through muddy filth, blood, and shock, snarled, "What guarantees do you give us for our safety, do we acquiesce?"

"Guarantees?" Ancelotis raised his brows. "What guarantees did your murderous son and the odious, craven fool with him offer the village of Penrith? Or the farmholds within five miles of the standing stones? We guaranteed Cutha and Creoda safe passage and they repaid it by spitting infants on pikes and hacking toddling babes into scattered pieces for the crows to eat. Shall I return your courtesy back to you in full measure?"

Aelle lost color beneath the grime. Not, Stirling

realized with utter contempt, because the news of the massacre was a surprise, but because Aelle finally realized that an accounting was due for their atrocities—and that he, as much as his son, would be held accountable for it. Stirling could see it in his eyes, that moment of sick horror when he realized the Britons were fully capable of slaughtering *his* daughters. Even Cutha looked pale around his tight-clenched mouth, pale with shock and hatred and the burning desire to sever British heads from British necks in a war he had already lost.

Ancelotis smiled down into their eyes.

"Yield up all that we demand," he said softly, "or your wives and daughters will learn the true meaning of terror. You have shown us too much of Saxon butchery to expect pity on your women and your squalling infants. Not from men whose families you have slaughtered like lambs under the axe. You have sown hatred and now you reap it in full measure. Surrender here and now, or I vow to you, there will be no stopping our soldiers in their drunken rampages across the lands you've stolen. They will defile your daughters and feed your infants to their dogs and smile while they do it. What say you, curs of Saxony? Shall I loose the hounds of Britain against your families? Or leash them and show the mercy you have failed to show any of us and ours?"

For tense moments, silence gripped the huddled knot of men at his horse's feet. The Britons hemming them in tested the keenness of their blades and smiled into the prisoners' eyes. *Come,* those blazing looks whispered, *come let me part your ribs with the kiss of steel . . .*

King Aelle had not taken his gaze from Stirling's. He stared, pride warring with shock and exhaustion and the realization that he could salvage nothing by his own hand. A sigh finally shivered loose and he broke his long silence.

"Let me speak for Sussex, then," he began hoarsely, "and beg from you better mercy on my people than my fool of a son showed yours." He let his sword thunk into the mud. The splash darkened the blade with muck. Cutha's mouth worked once, twice, while his hand tightened like the grip of a vise around the pommel of his sword. His father turned on him with a snarl. "Don't be a bigger fool than you were at birth! Throw down the sword—for it is no longer yours to hold. I take it back, sword, pommel, and gold rings of honor. I strip you of them before Woden and all his Valkyries, for you are unworthy in my sight and a curse to every Saxon who treads soil upon this earth."

Cutha's face washed grey with shock. He collapsed back against the wooden wall, shaking violently. The sword slid from unnerved fingers, splashing down beside his father's. His father had just repudiated him before everyone who was likely to matter in Cutha's life. To take back the sword, to be disgraced by its loss, by the loss of the rings of fealty, rings of reward for fine service—such humiliation overbalanced him, left his eyes wide and staring.

Shunned, Stirling warned Ancelotis silently, *shunned and broken. He'll be deadlier than any wolverine when that shock wears off. Consumed with hatred, blaming everyone but himself. Watch that bastard closely in future—if the kings of Britain allow him to live.*

Ancelotis grunted. *If the king of Gododdin has any say in the matter, Cutha will be hanged for a murderer from the nearest oak.*

The others—Creoda, his father Cerdic, their few surviving *eoldormen* and *thegns*—let their weapons fall in formal surrender. "Bind their hands with rope," Ancelotis said tersely. "Behind them, please. Drag them up to the fortress. We'll want to question them closely—" He broke off, startled, as movement out across the southeastern plain caught his attention. From his vantage point two hundred fifty feet up the hillside, he could see a long way across the open ground to the southeast.

Beyond Artorius and the *cataphracti*, beyond the straggling lines of the smashed Saxon supply train, beyond the running, panic-stricken Saxon infantry, a living carpet flowed across the plain. Horses at the full gallop. An army's worth of them. Headed straight for Caer-Badonicus. And Ancelotis could not for the life of him figure out whose army it might be. The Saxon kings, following his gaze, turned to peer across the plain.

"Your reinforcements?" Melwas demanded harshly.

King Aelle shook his head, obviously confused. "No. Would to Woden they were, but they are not men under my command. Nor under Cerdic's."

"Then who—?" Ancelotis realized in a lightning flash of utter horror who they *must* be. "Dear God. Take these men up to the fort and guard them. Archers, to horse, ride with me!"

He kicked his horse into a flat-out run, plunging wildly down the sodden, mud-churned slope. Out on the Salisbury Plain, the fleeing Saxon infantry had stumbled and stalled in their headlong flight from Artorius. The front ranks began to shift direction, running back toward the British lines, scattering to the sides, trying to escape two cavalry charges that rushed toward one another on a direct collision course.

Spurring madly, Stirling and his host caught up with Artorius—who had slowed in open puzzlement—just as the leading edge of Saxons, men who'd fled British steel just moments previously, crashed in amongst them, screaming for mercy, many of them flinging themselves to the ground, prostrate before Artorius' white stallion.

"Oh, dear God," Artorius breathed as Ancelotis reined to a halt beside him.

They could see the approaching army's battle flags. Ancelotis knew those flags, knew them as well as Artorius did. The bottom fell out of Stirling's gut, splashed into the mud at his horse's feet, and tried to crawl away with the wounded, exhausted Saxons. *"Ireland!"*

Artorius opened his mouth to give the shout to charge, when the Irish cavalcade drew abrupt rein and halted, hundreds of them, just out of javelin distance. For long moments, an eerie, unnerving hush fell across the field of death, with neither side moving. Then a small knot of riders detached themselves from the main body of Irish troops. A white scrap of cloth fluttered in the wet wind as they rode slowly forward, horses dancing sideways in the adrenaline rush of the fore-shortened charge. After a tense moment, Stirling could make out five riders, three women and two men, it looked like. A moment longer and they were close enough to recognize faces.

"*Morgana!*" The word was wrung from Artorius.

He spurred forward, gesturing the *cataphracti* to wait. Ancelotis was right on his heels.

They met halfway between the two armies, with cowering Saxons lying prone in the mud all around them, desperate to avoid rousing fatal attention. Morgana rode like a woman carved of granite, face pale and haggard with exhaustion and strain. Medraut was with her. Ancelotis wondered at the glow in the boy's eyes, an inner fire he had never before seen in the boy. The other man with them wore Irish insignia of royal rank, as did one of the ladies, a girl barely Medraut's age. Father and daughter, Stirling realized abruptly, tracing similarity of features and proud carriage. The other woman was a quiet, sharp-eyed soul who had the look and demeanor of a highly placed court councillor.

"Greetings, stepbrother," Morgana said quietly, spine straight as a church steeple. "I bring allies of Britain." She gestured with one graceful hand. "King Dallan mac Dalriada. Riona Damhnait, a Druidess of his privy council. Keelin, daughter of Dallan mac Dalriada and wife to Medraut, King of Galwyddel by my lawfully recorded order. He has made the Princess of Dalriada a Queen of Galwyddel, binding our two peoples into one. Before you speak," she lifted a slim hand in a commanding gesture that closed Artorius' lips over the protest balanced there, "know that the Saxons have committed atrocity in Irish-held lands and attempted to shift blame for it onto Britons."

Lailoken . . .

Stirling found himself wondering where that bastard might be, along with his unseen guest.

Morgana, reiterating the story of poisoned wells at Fortress Dunadd, which he and Artorius already knew, added, "The Dalriadan Irish and their kin from Belfast seek alliance with any force strong enough to hurl Saxon swine into the sea. Dallan mac Dalriada begs the favor of joining their not inconsiderable force to ours to keep both our islands safe from Saxon ravages." Her eyes glowed with fiery pride and a defiance that left Artorius pale and silent. "It would," she murmured, "at the very least, secure much of our northern border and a very large portion of our western seacoast."

Artorius sat blinking for long moments. He finally brought himself sufficiently out of shock to say, "I cannot trust Irish treachery, Morgana."

"Brother," she said gently, "they have already given us the greatest hostage they possess: Keelin, of the royal house of the *Scotti* clan, last of her father's direct line. They have held Medraut and me in their power for more than a week now, could have killed us and launched an attack against Galwyddel, against Ynys Manaw and Strathclyde, against any Briton kingdom they chose, with our armies distracted by this Saxon menace to the south. They chose, instead, to seek alliance against a common enemy."

Ancelotis and Stirling, both of them deeply curious about Morgana's new allies, studied the face of the Irish king. They saw pride there, strength, and pain, but nothing of treachery. And Keelin—God help, queen of Galwyddel—had reached across to grip Medraut's hand. The look he gave her was so gentle, so protective, Ancelotis could not hold suspicion in his hands. He turned to Artorius.

"This is a matter for the kings and queens of Britain to discuss in council," he said quietly. "If I may suggest it, allow the Irish army to camp here, keeping the Saxons imprisoned between us, and hold a dialogue with King Dallan mac Dalriada and Queen Keelin in the meeting hall at Caer-Badonicus. Would to God Emrys Myrddin were not missing. We could use his guidance."

"Missing?" Artorius asked sharply.

Ancelotis explained.

"I mislike it," the Dux Bellorum muttered. "I mislike it intensely." Ancelotis wasn't entirely certain whether he spoke of Emrys Myrddin's disappearance or his new in-laws. Both, probably.

"Very well, let us see to these wretches' confinement, then seek the council chamber."

Chapter Twenty

Morgana was aware of narrow scrutiny from all sides as she rode through Caer-Badonicus' open gates with Irish kings and high-ranking noblemen at her back. Whispers and muted sounds of shock followed their progress. By the time she swung down from the saddle, she was weary enough that standing was an effort. King Cadorius greeted her with outstretched hands and a kiss on the cheek, a far more gracious welcome than she'd been expecting.

"I will not ask," he murmured, "until council has been convened. Please introduce me to your guests."

The introductions went round, formal and stiff and wary on all sides. Curious women and children clustered to stare while Briton soldiers manning the walls, still alert despite the resounding victory, stood ramrod stiff, studiously facing their duty posts; but she could tell just how intently they were listening. Cadorius welcomed the Irish king and his daughter with quiet respect, gesturing Medraut and his wife into the meeting hall. For a long moment, Morgana didn't even want to move. Then Ancelotis came up close behind her shoulder.

What he breathed softly into her ear, for her hearing alone, sent shock and terror skittering through her veins. "Brenna McEgan?"

She lurched around, heart pounding. The muddy ground slid and shook underfoot. The look in Ancelotis' eyes shocked her even more deeply than his words. He was trying to *smile.*

"Dr. McEgan," he said softly, in *English,* "I owe you the deepest apology it is possible to offer. Cedric Banning played me for a fool and fouled up both our lives rather spectacularly. Please believe me when I say SAS officers do not appreciate being manipulated into suspecting the wrong party."

Brenna's lips parted, trembling, but no sound emerged past the constriction in her throat.

"Will you answer one question?" he asked softly.

She nodded, still unable to find her voice.

"*Were* you *Cumann Na Mbann?*"

Her eyes stung with salt. She nodded, bit her lip. "I watched an Orange bomb blow up my sister, my niece. I was young, so full of rage and hurt . . . I left them, eventually, when I realized the hate was turning me into the same thing I was fighting. Left for Dublin and made a clean break. I'd no contact with the IRA for years. Until this." She blotted her eyes with shaking hands. "My grandmother was the one who convinced me I was the only one who could get close to him, close enough to find out what his plan was and stop him. I had the professional credentials to join the team.

"I'm convinced Banning engineered the motor crack-up that killed the team members he and I were hired to replace. I found out that he'd arrived just after the

accident, chatted up Dr. Beckett, met him at the pub
and convinced him to put Banning on the team. It was
a good bit more difficult getting *me* in. I still don't
know who pulled all the necessary strings, but the
strangest part of it was, at least some of the people
who made it possible were Belfast Protestants."

Stirling's brows shot up.

"Aye," she said softly, "it *was* a bit of a shock. The
Orangemen had gone to the Provos to ask their help.
Banning had gone wildcat on them, disappeared, vowing to destroy all Britain for what he saw as betrayal.
London had vowed the election would take place as
scheduled, even when it was clear there'd be a Catholic
majority for the voting. He knew that majority would
vote for reunification with the Irish Republic, destroying his country. He vowed to destroy Britain for it.
He'd gone too far even for the Orange marching
societies and paramilitaries and they wanted help
finding him."

"Which the Provos did?"

She nodded. "They could have simply shot him or
blown up his car, but when they realized what he
was after, what the project was all about, both sides
realized this was one job *neither* the Provos nor the
Orange paramilitaries wanted publicized. And shooting
or blowing up a research scientist in a remote little
village in the Scottish Lowlands would've drawn publicity down on everybody's heads."

"So they sent you in to stop him? To kill him?"

She shook her head. "No. To identify him and
determine what his plans might be. There was an IRA
team waiting for my signal, to let them know I'd
learned what I needed—whether or not the project
was actually viable, whether or not he actually intended
to sabotage it, to try and alter history. I was to signal
them, so that if the danger was real they could arrange

something that would seem accidental, damaging his car so he collided with a tree, lost his brakes, something that wouldn't be an obvious IRA hit."

The man Brenna had feared would kill her rubbed the back of his neck in a rueful gesture. "And he got the drop on both of us, instead." His eyes went dark, then, as Ancelotis' unseen guest sought to confirm the worst. "And he truly poisoned a whole town in Dalriada?"

Tears stung her eyes again. "I went there, Medraut and I did. With Dallan mac Dalriada and Medraut's bride. I saw with my own eyes what he'd done to Dunadd. He poisoned the wells with botulism toxin."

Stirling nodded. "We found Lailoken's packhorse, trying to track him, after we rode into Galwyddel and heard the news. There were several bottles in the panniers."

"You *knew* it was Lailoken?"

"Oh, yes. Artorius and I rode for Caer-Birrenswark to try and stop the wedding—"

"How did you know about that?"

Captain Stirling's borrowed lips quirked. "Thaney discovered that a minstrel had forwarded a letter from Covianna Nim to Artorius, a message betraying your plan. Artorius rode out of Caerleul at a dead gallop, without speaking a word. Thaney told me, or rather my host, what had happened. Begged us to stop Artorius, to protect you. Thaney thinks the world of Morgana, you know."

Her eyes misted.

"Anyway, we went tearing after Artorius. We ran slap into a party of soldiers trying to track Lailoken for the murders."

"And Covianna Nim betrayed us to Artorius? She must have heard us talking to Medraut, right after Morgana and I caught him in Ganhumara's arms."

Ancelotis—it was fascinating, watching the shift in the face shared by the king of Gododdin and his host, as one or the other personality came to the fore—just groaned. "Ganhumara?" he cried, adding in Brythonic, "A liaison between those two is the last thing we need!"

"That's been rather thoroughly squashed," Morgana said firmly, also in Brythonic. "Trust me for that much, at least."

One corner of Ancelotis' mouth twitched. "Morgana, you know I trust you implicitly. And I'm coming rapidly to trust you, as well, Dr. McEgan," Stirling added in English, with a twinkle in his eyes.

She smiled wanly. "I'm glad to hear it. Particularly as I could've done away with you ages ago, had I meant you harm."

Stirling groaned this time. "Oh, God, how inept was I?"

"No more so than I, just a bit more, ah, publicly."

"The challenge match with Cutha?"

She chuckled. "According to Morgana, the Britons have a number of highly effective close-combat techniques, but I've seen aikido. It's rather unmistakable."

"So it is."

"I don't suppose Lailoken's been found among the prisoners? The Irish want him rather badly."

"I'll just bet they do. And frankly, I can't imagine a more fitting application of the king's justice. We'll give the order to search the dead and the prisoners. Meanwhile, we've a council of kings and queens to convene." He offered his crooked arm.

Brenna McEgan, who never in her wildest imaginings had considered it possible for *friendship* to be offered her by an SAS officer, smiled in rueful amazement and slipped her hand into the crook of his elbow. Perhaps—just perhaps—there was hope, after all? If not for their own future, the timeline of their mutual origin, perhaps for *this* one? She intended to try with all her heart. And for the first time in many, many years, she was no longer alone in the attempt.

They found Lailoken alive, huddled with the Saxon army in the remains of their washed-out camp. When he was dragged into the council chamber, struggling and covered with mud, the minstrel took one look at Dallan mac Dalriada and screamed, trying violently to free himself. The grim-faced soldiers who'd hauled him up the hill shoved him to his knees. Several princes arrived hard on his heels, out of breath from hurrying up from the battlefield. Artorius gestured them to seats, while studiously ignoring Ganhumara, who sat in stony silence to his left.

"Thank you for arriving so promptly for council," Artorius said quietly. "We have much to discuss. Royal princes, your fathers have deputized you as their official representatives for this battle. The council I have called is very much a part of that battle. What we decide here will affect Britain for the next hundred years."

Stirling glanced from one face to the next, seeing no dismay, only grim resolution to do what was necessary to make the correct decisions. Even the queens and princesses, many of whom had seen battle first-hand and several of whom had led troops into battle, wore the cold, closed expressions of leaders on whom the lives of thousands of innocents depended. It was a sight Trevor Stirling had never seen before, one that sent chills up his borrowed spine: a room full of world-class leaders, tempered like fine steel by harsh reality, united in purpose, determined to safeguard the interests of their people, their way of life.

And, moreover, to do so through the power of the vote in lawful council. Lailoken's unseen guest, Cedric

Banning—world-class terrorist fighting no less urgently to safeguard the interests of *his* culture—stood in vivid, revolting contrast, a man willing to subvert law, to murder not only thousands of civilians in an "enemy" city, but billions of innocents in the world whose future he had come here to destroy.

Banning's fate would be decided in this council chamber.

By rule of law.

Artorius spoke again. "The Saxons have been defeated. Utterly. Their kings have surrendered and are held prisoner in our custody. This council must decide the terms under which their kingdoms must be surrendered, as well. We have defeated two thousand of their men-at-arms, but thousands more Saxon settlers remain, from Ceint to Caer-Durnac. This council must draw up the terms of how these Saxons are to be ruled—or exiled, sent back to Saxony and Jutland where their grandfathers were born. This council also must decide the future of Briton relations with Ireland and Dalriada."

A low buzz went around the room. Word of the marriage of alliance had spread through the settlement like wildfire. Medraut sat very straight, very proud, with Keelin's hand clasped in his own, claiming her openly with just a touch of defiance in his stare. Keelin, too, sat with chin high, very young, very beautiful, but with a haunting look of grief in her eyes that nothing, not even time, could ever erase. She perhaps didn't realize it, but that wounded pain behind eyes that had seen more death and atrocity than any human being should ever have to witness firsthand, was the most powerful argument anyone could have presented in favor of the alliance she and Medraut were trying to forge.

"And finally," Artorius said coldly, staring down at Lailoken, "we have the matter of a Saxon spy, a traitor

to Britain, guilty of murdering an entire Dalriadan city
with foul poison. It is in my mind that he tested his
bottles of death against the Dalriadan Irish to provoke
an Irish invasion of Briton kingdoms at a time when
he knew the bulk of Britain's fighting forces
were rushing south. It is also in my mind that he fully
intended to spread his gift of death to every major city
in Britain *and* Ireland, every hill fort, every village,
every farmhold he could reach—and that his Saxon
allies would do the same, using the same method. I
accuse Lailoken, Saxon spy and traitor, of conspiracy
to commit genocide against the Irish and British
peoples. This council will deliberate his guilt and
determine what sentence to hand down."

Lailoken's dirty face, smeared with mud and his own
blood, washed a sickly hue. He kept his gaze on the
floor, where it belonged, unable to face those he had
so grievously wronged. What Cedric Banning was
thinking, Stirling had no idea—but intended to find
out. Artorius asked for the roll of royal houses to be
called. The kings and queens and princes of Britain
answered for the people and lands they represented,
until every kingdom had been accounted for—even
Ynys Weith, answered for by Princess Iona in a strong,
clear voice.

"Let the first matter before this council be the fate
of the Saxons." Artorius gestured and the Saxon kings
and princes were marched into the chamber, wrists
bound, clothing matted with filth. "Aelle and Cutha
of Sussex. Cerdic and Creoda of Wessex, *gewisse* traitors to Britain, who slaughtered the royal families of
the kingdoms they have overrun. What say you, kings
and queens of Britain, to their fate?"

Debate was brutally brief. Recommendations were
universally grim. At the end of the tally, the vote was
unanimous for beheading Cutha, who stared straight

ahead and remained stone-silent throughout his sentencing. Opinions varied on whether to hang Creoda by the neck until dead, or simply burn out his eyes and let him wander as a beggar for the rest of his days. The princeling fell blubbering to his knees. "Please— I never killed any of those poor souls at Penrith, it was Cutha's doing, him and those brutes of his—"

Cadorius glared down at him. "Your crime is worse than Cutha's in my eyes, *gewisse*. You brought them among us, under oath of truce. You collaborated with them, scheming to insinuate yourself into Rheged's council, in the very council hall where Artorius and the high councils meet. You are a weak, spineless, sniveling thing, wretched beyond loathing. When your allies slaughtered all Penrith, did you lift a hand to stop them from butchering innocent babes?"

The princeling's lips trembled, wet and pathetic. "I— I feared too greatly they would turn upon me—"

"*Yet you brought these jackals among us!*" Cadorius roared to his feet, bringing his fists down so hard the table jumped and Creoda fell to his knees. "*You* brought them! *Knowing* you could neither control them nor enforce their honorable behavior. Fool, you are ten times the traitor for unleashing *that* on people whose blood flows through your veins! You disgust me." Cadorius spat on the floor, wringing a flinch and a moan from the ashen young man. "Hanging is too quick a mercy for his like. Blind the bastard and let him repent his folly at leisure." When Cerdic began to plead for mercy on his son's behalf, Cadorius stopped him with a single backhanded blow.

"That," he said through clenched teeth, "is for the murders of Princess Iona's entire family at Ynys Weith! Dear friends of mine, married to my own beloved cousins. I leave your fate to *her* discretion, for among us, none is so grievously wronged by your greed than she."

Iona rose with slow dignity, grey eyes as haunted by grief and horror as Queen Keelin's. She stood gazing down at Cerdic for a long time, her face like cut marble, her lips thin and hard. Keelin, at least, still had her father. Iona had lost everyone. Everything. Except herself. Her eyes were chilly as the winter Atlantic, stormy seas clashing and rolling behind those eyes, behind that long, utterly silent gaze. Cerdic flushed, ran icy pale, began to tremble. When she finally spoke, her voice was scarcely a whisper, yet as clear and strange as warped faerie bells in the twisted midnight glen.

"Show him the courtesy he showed to me. Send him naked into the winter marshes to hunt for his survival with nothing but his ragged nails and teeth. Let him eat fish raw from the bones while his hands bleed from the brambles he's pulled up to make a hand-knotted net to trap his wet and scaly dinner in, without so much as a knife to cut the thorny stems. Let him sleep in rotten rushes with the crabs and the mice to nibble at his frozen toes. And send him thus, exiled from human civilization, of which he knows *nothing*, lawfully deprived of all he holds dearest."

Cerdic had begun to tremble.

"Let his daughters and the infant grandchildren playing in his grand hall be taken as hostages. Let him trade places with me for the year I cowered and crawled in those self-same marshes. But grant his loved ones the mercy he failed to grant mine, for I will never demand that his kinsmen be slaughtered without pity, as mine were. Let the kings and queens of Britain decide how they will gift his family, should he *ever* try to leave those marshes. I wash my hands of the House of Cerdic and pray God has yet some mercy to spare in His rage over what you have done."

It was, Stirling realized slowly, while harsh in its

demand for justice, still the most humane punishment yet suggested. All the more surprising, given what Iona had so grievously lost. As though reading his mind, Brenna McEgan murmured in a low English whisper, "Good for her. She's refusing to sink to their level. That child has more courage and more compassion than any five men in this room."

He shot her a startled glance, then nodded. She was right. More than right. It was a hopeful sign, one he almost dared believe would prevail. Artorius put the matter to a vote and within moments, Cerdic's fate had been sealed—along with his family's. Cadorius, commander of the besieged defenders at Badon Hill and highest-ranking monarch of the southern kingdoms, gave pronouncement on Cerdic's head.

Staring coldly down at the defeated Briton traitor who had crowned himself king with Saxon gold and treachery, Cadorius said, "You will be stripped of land, rank, title, and possessions. You will be sent into the salt marshes of Dumnonia's Irish-facing coast, away from your people, away from anyone who might give you pity or shelter, to live there by your wits, or die as God wills. If you so choose, you may take your son with you, once this council has carried out his sentence. He may share your exile, to remind you of the blind folly in your own dark hearts. Your children and grandchildren will be brought to Dumnonia, where they will remain my guests. So long as neither of you sets foot outside those marshes again, they will be treated with courtesy and respect. More than this, the kings and queens of Britain will not grant. Unlike God, our mercy has reached its limits. Do not ask for more."

The Saxons were taken away, heads bowed in utter defeat.

Artorius called for mulled wine to be passed round, symbolically washing the bitter taste of vengeance from their mouths before moving to the next item of business. Tension ebbed away and a low murmur of voices broke out as people rose and stretched their legs, strolled in conversation, sipped at the heated wine servants brought in clay pitchers. Covianna Nim brought a goblet of the steaming, spiced beverage to Artorius, smiling as she spoke in a low voice. He chuckled softly and drank with evident thirst. Morgana was frowning at the younger woman, a mixture of worry and hostility in that long, narrow-eyed stare. Ancelotis, alert to the fact that Covianna Nim had been the one to betray Morgana's intention to Artorius, decided to join her conversation with the Dux Bellorum.

"Have you received any word of Emrys Myrddin's whereabouts?" Ancelotis asked as he strolled up, while watching Covianna closely.

Lovely eyes widened slightly. "No, I haven't. I can't understand what's happened to him. He was so eager to return to Caer-Badonicus when he left the Tor, to oversee final preparations here. I fear bandits may have overpowered him. Or Saxon scouting parties."

Ancelotis narrowed his eyes. The likelihood of Saxons sending a reconnaissance party as far as Glastenning Tor was almost nonexistent, given its distance west and north of Caer-Badonicus. And Badon Hill was—so far as anyone had been able to determine—the farthest west and north any Saxon force had penetrated. "Bandits, more likely," he said coolly. "We'll have to scour the countryside for them, burn them out."

She lowered long, ash-blonde lashes, sipping at her own cup of wine. "Yes, we will. A dreadful business."

Something about her, something Stirling couldn't put a finger on any more than Ancelotis could, was raising his hackles, for no reason he could fathom.

Perhaps it was only that she had given Artorius that letter, accusing Morgana of treason. Which was, Ancelotis thought darkly, gut tightening down in dread, the next order of business on the council's agenda. And there was almost nothing he could do to protect her— or Brenna McEgan—if this council decided Morgana was also guilty of treason to Britain. Smuggle her out, perhaps, to live with the Irish . . .

The council reconvened with a shuffling of feet and a refilling of goblets as servants hurried around with more pitchers of wine. When everyone had returned to their seats, Artorius spoke again. "We have among us guests from the north and west, from Dalriada and Belfast, guests who have been as greatly wronged by the Saxons as we have, here in Britain. At our last high council, we debated the wisdom of making contact with the Irish of Dalriada and found ourselves divided on the matter." A brief smile came and went on the Dux Bellorum's deeply gullied face. Listening in surprise, Ancelotis dared to hope for the first time that Artorius might possibly support Morgana in this.

Artorius gestured to the Irish delegation. "Kings and Queens of the Briton High Council, I formally present to you Dallan mac Dalriada, King of the Irish *Scotti* clan, and Queen Keelin, daughter and heiress to Dallan mac Dalriada and bride of Medraut, newly crowned King of Galwyddel."

A stir of surprise ran round the room, as the wild rumors were formally confirmed.

"Riona Damhnait, Druidess to King Dallan mac Dalriada, will translate his greeting."

The Druidess rose gracefully, hair caught back in a jeweled net that scattered light in bright sparkles. "I speak for Dallan mac Dalriada, King of the *Scotri* of Dalriada. Greetings to you, my neighbors and now my kinsmen. The history of our respective peoples has been a violent one, with warfare between us for many generations. Yet we are more like one another than any of us realized, until the coming of the Saxons. This threat touches our hearts deeply, for Saxon treachery has destroyed the capital of Dalriada, four thousand souls murdered by poison poured into the town's wells.

"This creature," she gestured contemptuously toward Lailoken, huddled now along one edge of the room, between his guards, "wormed his way into the confidence of Briton queens and kings, offered himself as go-between in the matter of alliance between Briton Galwyddel and Irish Dalriada. I embraced this alliance with joy, seeing the good it would do all our peoples, Briton and Irish alike, for we all face a rising threat from the Jutland Danes, the Saxons, the Angles from Denmark's Angeln Peninsula, and their cousins of Frisia. I gave my only child, my greatest treasure, in marriage to the king of Galwyddel, to forge an alliance I believed necessary for the safety of both our peoples.

"When this foul poisoner fled," Lailoken withered beneath her cold contempt, trying to cower down through the floor, "betraying Briton and Irish alike, Queen Morgana and King Medraut risked death to warn us of the treachery he had committed. They could have remained silent, could have allowed me to drink from a final, poisoned gift, but rushed to prevent yet more deaths and the senseless blaming of innocents that would surely have occurred, had not their honor driven them to act with greater courage than any I have ever witnessed."

A stir ran through the room, at that, surprise at the candor and the compliments.

The Druidess let the buzz of hushed reaction die down, then continued gravely. "My king, Dallan mac

Dalriada says, the murder of four thousand Dalriadan Irish only strengthened my resolve to destroy this Saxon threat to both our peoples. I raised an army from the countryside around Dunadd, sailed for the town of Belfast, where kinsmen joined us to meet these Saxons in battle. And when Artorius' charge scattered the Saxons ahead of him on the plain, we were waiting; Artorius' hammer crushing them against our Irish anvil, preventing their escape. Together, Briton and Irish soldiers kept these Saxons from regrouping elsewhere with a fighting force still capable of waging war."

That point, at least, could not be argued. Stirling had seen it almost at once, so had Ancelotis. Given the look in Artorius' eyes, he could see the truth in it, as well. Without the Irish "anvil" stopping their headlong retreat, the Saxons might well have escaped to regroup elsewhere—making another battle and another after that, for months or years, painfully necessary. Together, they had accomplished something profound.

Riona Damhnait gazed at each of the tables in turn, each of the kings and queens and princes, each of the princesses and royal advisors seated beside and behind them. "We ask only two things of this council. Give this alliance a chance. Honor the pledge these young people have made to one another and to peace between our peoples. Give us a chance to exchange artisans and craftsmen, to send home any Britons who were taken from their homelands while we were enemies, with compensation for them and their families. Give us a chance to marry Irish widows to Briton landsmen, to knit up the damage wrought by war, give us all the chance to build something better in its place. And give us the traitor, Lailoken. I, Dallan mac Dalriada, King of the *Scotti* clan of Dalriada, thank you for the chance to ask these things, and for the hospitality and honor you have shown us."

The Druidess returned to her seat.

For a moment, absolute silence reigned.

The explosion of voices rattled dust from the rafters. Artorius was on his feet, banging the hilt of his sword against the table, shouting for silence. "*Is this the way Britons greet guests and allies?*" he snarled into the babble of angry words. "You shame us, shame the good names of your royal families and clans!"

Mutters finally died away into silence once again. Artorius glared around the room, pinning each and every one of them with an icy stare. Cadorius had the good grace to look troubled. But young Clinoch of Strathclyde was on his feet, literally shaking with rage.

"*Ally ourselves with the butchers of Dalriada?*" the boy spat. "We've fought them across our borders longer than I have been alive! They killed my grandfather's brothers, they've taken our people into slavery, plundered our fishing and trading fleets, and you would ask me to break bread with them? To call them allies? *Kinsmen?*"

Before anyone could answer the boy's vitriolic burst of hatred, Keelin rose to face him, pale to her very lips. She promptly astonished everyone in the room by speaking fluent Brythonic.

"Honored Clinoch, King of Strathclyde, our nearest Briton neighbor, I beg you to remember that I, too, have lost kinsmen in the wars between Strathclyde and Dalriada. My uncles, my grandfathers, both of my own beloved brothers were killed in the fighting. And our fleets have been attacked by Strathclyde's, as well, sometimes with cause, in retribution for raids, but sometimes not. There has been wrong on *both* sides of this war. Yet when Medraut of Galwyddel came to Dunadd and offered alliance, I put aside the grief for my own much-loved brothers. I recognized the great courage it took for him to sail into Dunadd Harbor, to ask for this alliance. I married Medraut, with all the anguish of the past between us, because I believed it was the best, the *only* way, to ensure that no one else from his people or mine *ever* grieves the loss of loved ones in a war that we have the power to stop, now and forever."

Tears were running openly down her cheeks. Medraut, visibly stricken, drew her close, his tenderness and care so open and honest, a low hum ran through the assembly, softening expressions and defusing much of the tension that had tightened so dangerously through the room. Clinoch of Strathclyde stood silently for long moments, jaw clenched as he, too, fought powerful emotion. *Children,* Stirling realized with a pang, *these three passionate souls deciding the fate of all Britain, are mere children.* Clinoch was barely fifteen, Medraut and Keelin no more than sixteen and seventeen. It was, perhaps, only fitting that the future of Britain rested in the grief and pride and courage of her children.

In a gesture that surprised everyone, perhaps except Stirling, Princess Iona of Ynys Weith rose with outstretched hands, clasping Keelin's trembling fingers in her own. "I know the grief you feel, know it to the depth of my heart. The Saxons have wounded us deeply. I, Princess Iona of Ynys Weith, formally greet you as sister."

She embraced the trembling Irishwoman, kissed her cheek, then turned and faced Clinoch of Strathclyde. "Your father is but a few weeks in the ground, Clinoch, but remember that it was not Dalriada who murdered him."

"If the Irish had not driven the Picts from their homeland—"

"You would not now be king, faced with a choice that will affect your grandchildren's grandchildren.

Would you throw away the chance to stop war between them and Keelin's great-grandchildren? When you have been given the chance to build peace, instead? To strengthen your borders against enemies of both Strathclyde and Dalriada? To pull men needed badly elsewhere away from a border that no longer needs guarding? You have younger sisters, do you not?"

He nodded, face a mask of anguish.

"Would you have them grow to womanhood, wed, and watch their sons march to war, knowing that you could have spoken the word that would send them north as kinsmen and guests, instead?"

Bright water glistened in his eyes. "Would you have me forget the wrongs done us?"

"Would you have me forget the butchery of my family? It was in my hands, the fate of Cerdic and all his kinsmen. A man who drank ale from my father's skull and laughed while he did so."

Clinoch flinched. So did many others listening in silent judgement.

"Clinoch," Iona stepped toward him, hand extended, "I know the pain you hold in your heart. But I will never sink to the level of my family's murderers. That victory, I will not grant them. My soul is too precious to stain it with hatred and murder. And Clinoch, it is not the *Scotti* of Dalriada who have done your family, your people their greatest harm. Please, remember that and think long and hard on the way your answer here, today, will harm or stain *your* soul, and the souls of those who look to you for their best protection."

The brightness in the boy's eyes had spilled over, tracking down his face. He gulped once, fighting to retain control, no longer a child, not yet a man, with the weight of decision cruel and heavy on his young shoulders. He looked into Iona's eyes, looked into Keelin's and Medraut's, sipped air, willfully stilled his unsteady lips. "It is not in my heart to inflict war on my people. I have not your strength, Iona, to greet them as kinsmen, but for the sake of Strathclyde, for the sake of my people, I will give this alliance a chance."

Iona embraced him gently, while Keelin's eyelids came clenching down over more tears.

In such a highly charged atmosphere, not even those most adamantly opposed to alliance could cheapen the gesture made by Clinoch and Iona. The voting went swiftly. Ganhumara sent Keelin a dark look of utter jealousy, but under the eyes of all Britain—and her husband—even she voted to let the alliance stand. Morgana seemed stunned by the outcome, clearly having expected to be censured, at the very least, if not convicted of treason during time of war. More heated wine went round, with Covianna Nim once again carrying a goblet to Artorius. Toasts were made and answered, congratulations offered on the marriage, and articles of treaty debated and ratified, providing for trade, exchange of artisans, even the establishment of missions by Briton Christian priests.

As the final details were recorded, Artorius called once again for the council's attention.

"We have one final order of business. Bring the traitor, Lailoken."

He was hauled forward by his guards, eyes downcast.

"Have you anything to say in your defense, Saxon?"

The man looked up, eyes wild with fear. "It was the demon made me do it! The demon in my head, whispering secrets, promising revenge on the Irish butchers who murdered my wife, my children . . ."

"He's mad," someone muttered.

Stirling watched with a chill in his blood, pitying the Briton minstrel whose life had been shattered by the Orangeman from sixteen centuries in Lailoken's future. Ancelotis, too, felt a complex blend of pity and revulsion, having had his own life wrenched inside out by Stirling's arrival. The look in Morgana's eyes was ghastly. She rose to her feet and spoke, gaze locked on the minstrel as though facing Grendel.

"Cedric Banning," she said in coldly in English, causing Stirling to suppress a gasp, "what have you to say to me?"

The man's head jerked up, as though wrenched by a giant, unseen hand. Shock washed across Lailoken's face. Then he snarled, hatred twisting his features. *"Filthy Irish bitch! I should have broken your neck that night in the lab!"*

She held his gaze levelly, neither speaking nor moving.

Banning spat at her, eyes mad with a sparking insanity that left Stirling ill. "I'm only sorry I hadn't the chance to poison every well in Ireland!" Banning laughed, the sound wild and mad. "Get home if you can, McEgan. And if you can't, take your exile as a last gift of the Orangemen of Ulster!"

Stirling, rising swiftly to stand beside her, said softly, "Who do you think told the IRA and the SAS to hunt for you?"

The denial balanced on Banning's lips died there when Stirling held his gaze levelly, staring down at Banning with all the loathing he could summon. He saw it form, the realization that his own had betrayed him, the slipping of what little solid ground remained under the man's feet. The caved-in, sick look in Banning's eyes, might, under other circumstances, have moved him to pity. But Banning had chosen hatred and death at every step along his life's path, had allowed his anger and desire for revenge to fester until he'd murdered his own sanity with it. Faced with such a creature, there was only one humane course open to Stirling—or to anyone else in like circumstances.

Voice soft in the uncertain hush of the council chamber, Stirling said, "In the name of His Majesty's British government, I charge you with terrorism and mass murder, Cedric Banning. If I had access to a gun, I would consider ordering you shot by firing squad. That is the way the Orange paramilitaries deal with traitors to their own, isn't it?"

A terrible sound broke loose, timbers cracking under the weight of a glacier. Banning began to tremble violently. His lips, wet and quivering, glistened horribly in the light. The looks of utter revulsion sent his way by the silent, stunned audience were lost on the man, whose gaze had not left Stirling's face.

"This"—Stirling swept a gesture at the council, men and women staring in puzzled silence at the three of them, speaking a language no one else understood—"is the trial by law you are entitled to receive. Take whatever comfort you can find in the knowledge that the murder of every soul in Dunadd may have accomplished what you set out to do. You may well have fractured history for all time, destroying several billion innocents in the process. We," he gestured to himself and Brenna McEgan, "won't know that for a year, if ever. But you, Cedric Banning, *you* will never know. You will never be given the chance to find out. May God pity your soul, for the rest of us do not."

Switching to Brythonic, Ancelotis said coldly, "He has confessed his intention to murder as many Irish and British souls as possible. Gododdin votes to hand him to the Irish for whatever punishment they find most appropriate."

At the head table, Artorius—clearly wanting to know what language they'd been speaking and why—sent

Ancelotis a hooded look, but he merely nodded and called for the council's vote. The final tally was unanimous. "Lailoken," the Dux Bellorum said in an icy, iron voice, "you are formally remanded to the custody of Dallan mac Dalriada, who will carry out the death sentence both our peoples have rendered upon your head. If you request it, a Christian priest will accompany you to perform last rites."

Banning laughed wildly, gasped out in English, "Oh, God, it's too precious, the Dark Ages baboon's offering me *papist rites*!"

Artorius frowned, glancing at Ancelotis.

"He doesn't want a priest."

"Ah."

When the king of Dalriada gestured his ranking officers to take charge of the prisoner, Banning spat on them, laughing insanely one moment, cursing them the next, until he was dragged unceremoniously from the room. Artorius rubbed his eyes wearily. "I thank you, kings and queens of Britain, for your wisdom in this council. It is time for us to look to our homes and our harvests and the coming winter. We will meet again tomorrow to settle the matter of reoccupying Saxon-held lands."

The council—and the war—had finally come to a close.

At least, Stirling qualified it, until the next time the Saxons grew bold enough and strong enough to try it again. And he knew only too well that they would, again and again. He met Brenna McEgan's eyes, read in them exactly the same weary resolution he felt, to stay and fight for these people as long as they possibly could. It was, perhaps, a form of atonement the two of them could offer these people, for the destruction the twenty-first century had unleashed in their midst. As the council broke up into a genuine celebration, with wine flowing freely and laughter taking the place of grim debate, Stirling felt more hopeful than he had since his abrupt arrival, a few short weeks and a lifetime ago.

Chapter Twenty-One

Covianna Nim remained close by Artorius through-out the long celebration, plying him with plenty of spiced wine, smiling into his eyes and waiting for the signs to make themselves visible. When he began to grow sleepy, excusing himself for the evening, she smiled softly, making certain Ganhumara was well occupied with young men with whom to further shred her reputation. Covianna slipped out of the meeting hall to follow Artorius, who had begun staggering as though drunk on the way to his room in the building next door.

He wobbled his way toward the bed he and Ganhumara would eventually be sharing for the night, unsteady on his feet and wiping sweat from his face. She waited until he'd disappeared inside, waited until a lamp shone softly within, then hurried away to her own chamber, rescuing a long, slim package wrapped carefully in folds of wool. She slipped it under her cloak, reaching Artorius' room moments later. Looking carefully about to be sure no one observed, Covianna eased open Artorius' door and stepped inside, pulling it closed behind her.

The Dux Bellorum turned in slow surprise.

"Covianna?" He frowned, voice already slurring.

"You seemed unwell when you left the celebration," she murmured. "I wanted to be certain you were all right, as it's only too plain your wife neither cares nor troubles herself over your welfare."

Pain ran through his eyes, then he collapsed in slow motion onto the edge of his bed. "I thank you for caring. It's kind of you." He was blinking in confusion. "I've had too much wine, s'all. Need to sleep it off . . ."

"Of course." She smiled. "Let me tell you a story, to help you sleep." She crossed the room, brushed heavy hair back from his brow, hiding the package beneath her cloak. "It's an old story, Artorius. One you should appreciate." She trailed a fingertip down his face. "Many, many years ago, there was someone very special in my life. A teacher, a mentor, who taught me many ancient arts."

He was frowning up at her, eyes tracking with difficulty.

"I loved her as greatly as my own mother," Covianna whispered, nibbling his earlobe with her lips. "She taught me everything of worth in my life. The use of herbs, the use of power, of the ways to blind and bind a man." Covianna smiled down into Artorius' eyes. "Can you imagine, Artorius, what it was like when she died?"

He worked his mouth with difficulty, speech more slurred than ever. "Muss've been . . . painful . . ."

"Oh, yes. Most painful. Do you know how she died, Artorius?"

He was shaking his head, tried to scrub his face with one hand. When he was unable to lift it, he sat staring in rising dismay and dawning fright.

Covianna whispered intimately, "She was murdered, Artorius. Oh, it was done with all the pomp of law, but it was murder, cruel and cold, nonetheless." Covianna stepped back a pace, smiling down into his eyes. "You really should not have condemned Marguase, Artorius. She was worth ten of you. Twenty."

Shock detonated behind his eyes. "Marguase?" It came out a hoarse rasp. "But—how—"

"She came to Glastenning Tor, when I was but a child. I worshiped her. Learned every wondrous secret she had to share. She chose me—*me*—as her acolyte, out of all the girls she could have taken, instead. Oh, I have waited a long, long time for this night."

He was trying to rise, succeeded only in falling to the floor. She laughed softly at the look of naked horror on his face. When he dragged his sword free of its new scabbard, hunching along on elbows and shoulders, trying to put distance between them, she drew out the package hidden in her cloak. "Did you miss this when I stole it away?" she asked merrily. His eyes widened, recognizing it. "Have you never wondered why you have *always* been victorious? Why those who oppose your sword arm inevitably die? 'Tisn't the sword, Artorius, nor yet the skill of the arm behind it."

She tapped the sheath. "I made this, as I made Caliburn, and there is as much witchcraft in the scabbard as there is death in the sword. The lining, Artorius, that's the secret of your wondrous, invincible power." She laughed, derision in every droplet of sound falling from her lips. "Oh, you pitiful fool. I've been most careful to join each of the high councils that have voted on war. And before each battle those councils sanctioned, I renewed the 'magic' of Caliburn's sheath. Mistletoe, Artorius. Sap of the mistletoe, the Druids' weed, mixed with oil and soaked into the lining of the sheath. Do you know the secret of the Druids' weed?"

He shook his head, eyes wide with horror he could neither escape nor conceal.

"Coat a blade with mistletoe and you will never stop the bleeding from any cut it makes. Even the smallest nick will bleed for hours. *That* is the secret of your prowess, my dear and mighty Dux Bellorum!" She laughed again, delighting in the blow to his manhood, to his self-value as a warrior, a blow that left a sick and empty look in his eyes. "Oh, I learned many secrets from Marguase. And even more from Emrys Myrddin. It was Myrddin taught me the secret of Damascus. Do you know how Caliburn was quenched, to give it that wondrously fine temper?"

He was panting, trying in utter desperation to lift the sword.

"You must remember, surely, your poor little cousin who vanished? Taken by pirates, most people said? I entertained the little fool at my forge, Artorius, deep in the heart of Glastenning Tor. Down in the sacred caverns my grandmothers have used for centuries. Showed him the secret of Damascus steel, there. Fed him full of ale, then quenched the blade in his drunkard's belly."

His mouth worked, soundlessly, the look in his eyes ghastly beyond words. Delicious. A victory she would relish every moment of her life.

"The pieces of him lie scattered beneath the Tor, but don't fret on his account. He's not alone any longer. The advisor who persuaded you to denounce Marguase lies beside him. A pity, really. Emrys Myrddin was the only man I ever met who knew *anything* about pleasing a woman in bed. And I shall miss his conversation and wit, truly I shall. But he sealed his fate years ago, when he condemned the lovely Marguase to death by slow drowning. I returned the favor, deep in the Tor's sacred caverns, where by now he's rotting as he so richly deserves. And now, Artorius, *you* will join my dance of death. My revenge lies complete in your destruction. The poison paralyzes slowly, doesn't it? Utterly delightful, that look in your wounded little eyes."

He lay gasping, trying to lift the sword, barely able to draw breath now.

She stepped nearer. "The time has come, Artorius, to return Caliburn to my hand. You will *not* be needing it any longer."

She stooped to pluck the blade from his hands—

And he moved, convulsively. The sword lurched upward, too fast to avoid. *"Take it back, then!"* he hissed. *"I return it freely!"*

The shock of pain was so intense, she couldn't even draw breath to scream. The blade had rammed deep into her belly. She clutched at it. Tried to pluck it loose. He shoved hard, lunging in one final spasm of strength. The blade twisted inside her vitals. Her scream burst loose this time, smoking hot through her womb. Shouts and running footsteps reached her ears, but dimly, so dimly and far, far away . . .

He's killed me! The thought ran like icewater through her mind. *The brainless little bastard's killed me . . .*

Then the darkness closed down like the waters of an icy lake over her head, until all that remained was the feel of that smoking sword slipping from her dying hand.

Morgana was dancing, skirts whirling as Ancelotis laughingly drew her to join the merrymakers, when the meeting hall door crashed open.

"Morgana!" A wild-eyed soldier stood in the doorway. "Where's Queen Morgana?"

She whirled, fright shocking her heart into sudden stillness. "Here," she gasped. "What is it? What's wrong?"

"It's Artorius! He's collapsed! Says he's been poisoned!"

Shock washed through her whole body. Then she was running, shouting for Medraut to fetch her satchel. Ancelotis ran with her, bellowing at the others to stay where they were, to give the healer a chance to work. The soldier led them to Artorius' room, where another stunning sight greeted them. Covianna Nim lay dead beside him, Caliburn buried in her gut. Artorius looked up, eyes dark with terror and grief.

"She was Marguase's . . . chosen pupil," he croaked, voice badly slurred. "No one knew it. Killed Emrys Myrddin . . . killed him at Glastenning Tor. Morgan . . . *Can you help me?* It's a poison that paralyzes, she said . . ."

"Search the bitch!" Morgana snapped at Ancelotis, over one shoulder. "See if she's still carrying the stuff. She must have dropped it into the wine. And fetch her potions and herbs, I must see what's there!" She didn't dare voice aloud the half wish, half prayer that Covianna might have brought with her an antidote to protect *herself*. Then Morgana was on her knees, testing his pulse, peering into his eyes. Medraut arrived in a skidding run, stood gasping, eyes wide with fright at what lay on the floor at his feet. Ancelotis, badly shaken, searched the dead woman, pulled something from a jeweled pouch at Covianna's waist, handed it over. Morgana unstoppered the small pottery vial, sniffed. "Fetch me a cup, a lamp, *anything* to hold liquid."

Medraut snatched up a wooden cup from Artorius' table and handed it over, while Ancelotis ran from the room, bellowing orders to fetch the poisoner's herb satchel. Morgana poured a bit of the stuff into the cup, tilted it to the light to see more clearly its color, how it smelled, how it clung to the sides of the cup. A feeling of utter dread turned her blood cold when she recognized it.

"Oh, dear God, yes, I know what this is. 'Tis rare. The bitch must have traded for it all the way to Constantinople. My satchel, Medraut."

She raked through the packets and bottles with shaking hands. "Bring me another cup and a stack of bowls. And a cauldron of boiling water. Burn that." She indicated the cup, now contaminated with Covianna's poison.

Ancelotis returned with Covianna's heavy satchel, which Morgana searched carefully as a soldier in the doorway sprinted away to do her bidding. While Morgana plucked at knotted twine to open packets and unstoppered clay vials to sniff at their contents, her unseen guest spoke urgently.

Have him eat crushed charcoal to absorb what's still in his stomach, then induce vomiting, so he'll bring up whatever's left of it with the charcoal. And force liquids, try to flush his blood and kidneys with water, to dilute the poison he's already absorbed.

Aye! Morgana gasped, then said aloud, "Ancelotis, send someone to fetch charcoal. Make him eat it, crushed finely. Then pour this," she handed over a bottle of wormwood from her own supplies, "down his throat until he vomits."

Someone ran from the room, feet slapping against the wet ground. Mere seconds later, a girl's voice, breathless from running, asked, "Is this enough?"

It was Keelin, eyes wide and distressed, face streaked with tears, carrying a basket piled high with charcoal and ash.

"Aye, crush the charcoal and get a good double handful down him."

Keelin tipped the basket onto the floor for Medraut to pulverize. Morgana left them to their work as she continued her search of Covianna's lethal little collection of herbal death. She was beginning to despair when she found it, a small packet of carefully dried leaves that she knew at once, although Brenna McEgan didn't recognize the plant.

What is it? Brenna asked as Morgana gave a glad cry.

Echoing her hidden guest, Ancelotis asked tersely, "What is it?"

"An herb as rare as the poison, itself. Devil's Bane, the Nine Ladies called it, for it undoes the devil's work when a man has swallowed poison of this kind. Covianna must have paid a king's ransom to obtain these leaves. No one has even *seen* this plant growing wild since my childhood. My teachers had a precious supply of them at Ynys Manaw, not many more leaves than in Covianna's packet, and the cost was dear, indeed." She peered at the doorway. *"Where is that hot water?"* she added urgently.

A soldier arrived with a heavy iron kettle. Steaming water slopped over the sides. He'd brought a silver goblet, as well, carried tucked under one arm, and had dropped several bowls into the kettle to carry them more easily.

"Set it there, quickly, man!"

Morgana closed her eyes for a moment, praying, then set to work. She scooped out the bowls, draining most of them, then carefully measured the water remaining in the last one. Morgana shook the precious leaves into her palm, gauging the amount needed against available supply and Artorius' body weight and mass. There would be enough for three full-strength doses, and perhaps two second and third doses steeped from each of those three, but no more. It shook her to realize she might well hold the last supply of this wondrous drug anywhere in the world. She looked into Artorius' eyes, sunken in a face the color of the grey rainclouds overhead, and prayed it was enough.

"Give him the wormwood," she said tersely as she dropped the first batch of leaves into the steaming water. A sharp, aromatic fragrance rose from the bowl. Artorius made a choking, gagging sound as Ancelotis fed him the emetic, then forcible retching filled the room. Keelin hastily slid a bucket under his face and held his head gently while he vomited. Ancelotis poured more wormwood down him while the leaves bled their lifesaving medicine into the hot water, turning it dark. More vomiting ensued. Morgana checked Artorius' pulse again and carefully refrained from biting her lips.

Not good, Brenna muttered silently. *Not good at all . . .*

But better than it was before he swallowed the charcoal and wormwood, Morgana retorted. Aloud, she added, "That's good, that should be enough, I think." She checked the contents of the bucket and nodded sharply. "Calm his stomach with a few sips of water, now. He must, at all cost, hold down this medicine. Should he throw it up, again, all is lost."

It was Keelin who got the water down him, murmuring soothingly when Artorius choked and swallowed convulsively. It was Keelin who gripped his hand and wiped sweat and sour vomit from his face. Medraut hauled away the noxious bucket, while Ancelotis crouched to one side, waiting with pain etched into his face. The moment Morgana deemed it safe to try, she poured the medicine into the silver goblet and held it to Artorius' lips, herself.

"Slowly," she murmured, dribbling the liquid into his mouth.

He grimaced and tightened his grip around poor Keelin's fingers until her hand turned purple, but he kept the bitter stuff down.

"More, now," Morgana soothed. "You need the whole bowlful, brother, and time is critical." She got all of it down him, praised him for holding it in his belly, then added more water to the leaves at the bottom of the bowl, determined to wring as much from each precious batch as possible. While they steeped, longer this time, she gave him an infusion of foxglove to strengthen his heart and calm his pulse, which was thready beneath her seeking fingertips. She watched him so closely that sight and sound of everything else faded away. His color, a ghastly shade of grey, gradually lightened to an ash-white pallor. Violent shudders began to rock through him as she poured the second bowl of Devil's Bane down him. He gulped, shuddered, groaned and got more of it down.

"What—?" Artorius began, voice shockingly weak.

Morgana placed gentle fingertips across his lips. "Hush, brother, you must save all your strength to fight the poison, to give the medicine its best chance to work." She dredged up a smile from somewhere down near her feet, she had to reach down so deeply to find it, and tried—with Brenna McEgan's help—to answer his unvoiced question, to explain what was happening inside his body. "The poison paralyzes, attacking the body's way of communicating with itself. The muscles don't know how to respond to commands from the brain, commands which come down tiny, threadlike fibres all through the body. The brain uses these threads to give commands to the rest of the body. It's these threads the poison attacks, making it impossible to move."

As Brenna spoke, Morgana began to realize this was a subject of far greater complexity than even she, a master healer, understood. Yet Brenna McEgan made it comprehensible, not only to her, but to Artorius. Morgana's step-brother understood exactly what paralysis of an army's communications network meant on the field of battle. *Well done*, Morgana thanked her unseen guest with tears in her eyes. *You've given him something he can focus on, something he can understand, to fight against.*

He fought to whisper out one question, anyway. "Is it an antidote?"

She bit one lip, hating the look that came into his eyes, seeing her hesitate. "It's the best I can offer. The best anyone can offer. 'Tis a miracle she had the herb, at all, and I know of nothing else that *could* help, considering what she's given you. What I don't know is how much she's used, how strong it was, how long it's had to work in your system. Here, get another cupful down, stepbrother, and all the water you can drink, to flush the toxins."

Keelin, kneeling beside him to wipe sweat from his face every few moments, whispered, "What can I do to help?"

"You already have helped, child, more than you know." Not just in her care of Artorius, or her quickness to fetch back the charcoal, or even her tenderness with his illness, but she had helped the alliance, as well. She had shown Briton royalty, crowded around the doorway to wait for news, that the alliance really did have a chance. No one watching the girl's concerned care of the Dux Bellorum could continue harboring suspicion against her. There simply wasn't an ounce of guile anywhere in her. The quiet look of pride in Medraut's eyes as he watched his bride brought more tears to Morgana's eyes.

Morgana gave the girl a brief smile. "You can join me in vigil, as well. We must sit with him through the night. Ancelotis, lift him into bed. Help him, Medraut. And someone needs to remove that carrion from my stepbrother's room." She gestured toward Covianna Nim's body, refusing even to look at the remains of a woman who had taken in Marguase's hatred, her craving for power, and used it to destroy, just as Marguase had done so long ago.

She also never slackened her grip on Artorius' pulse, which beat weakly, but with more strength than before, as they shifted him. Despite his efforts to help, the paralysis was horrifyingly apparent, causing Morgana's breath to catch in her throat. *Oh, stepbrother,* she moaned silently, her heart breaking within her breast, *years, it will take, trying to restore your strength, if God wills that you remain with us in this world.* As they lifted and carried him to bed, Keelin snatched aside the blankets on his sleeping cot and Medraut tugged off Artorius' boots, easing his feet beneath the covers. They settled him carefully, slipping off his vomit-stained tunic and trousers, then Morgana pulled blankets and furs up, seating herself beside him and holding his wrist lightly, one finger on the pulse point at all times.

Men arrived to lift Covianna's body, yanking loose Artorius' sword first, wiping it on the dead woman's skirts before carrying her out. Ganhumara arrived as Covianna was dragged outside, staring wide-eyed at the bloodied remains of a woman she had called friend. She then stood slim and proud in the doorway, her hair a copper waterfall around her shoulders, her eyes narrowed as she swept her gaze across her husband.

"Will he live?" she asked coolly.

Morgana flicked a glance upward into her eyes. "How is it that Medraut and Keelin arrived well before you? Artorius is your husband. At least have the decency to act the part of his wife when he lies ill and helpless."

Fire stung the younger woman's cheeks. "*How dare you speak to me that way?*"

Morgana strode across the room and cracked a hand across her face, hard. "*How dare you behave that way?*"

Ganhumara clutched her cheek, eyes wide in shock and pain.

Morgana clenched her fists to stop herself from tearing the other woman's hair out by the roots. "My stepbrother would have done better had he married a common *whore*! Get out. Your presence is neither needed nor desired."

Ganhumara stared into Morgana's eyes, disbelief warring with utter astonishment; then she sent a pleading look toward Medraut, holding out one slender hand.

His mouth twisted in contempt. "I was a fool ever to think you desirable. Take your wiles and your scheming ways out of my sight. And pray to God your husband lives, for if he does not, the victory won today will be erased as though it had never taken place. Think *hard* on how well it would please you to lie in a Saxon's bed. Or bear a Saxon's bastard in your sweet little belly."

Tears flooded Ganhumara's eyes. She uttered a single sob, then turned and fled into the darkness. Morgana watched her go, then hurried back to Artorius. He fumbled weakly for her hand. "I'm sorry," she whispered, gripping his fingers tightly and wishing she could unsay everything that had just been said. "I'm sorry you had to hear that."

He shook his head slowly, fighting to move his head against the weakness. "She is young," he breathed out sadly, "young and foolish. As we all once were. And she has been as . . . disappointed in our marriage as I." A sigh shuddered loose. "Don't trouble your heart over her, Morgana. She is my problem. If God permits me to live."

Tears stung Morgana's eyes. "I will stay by your side and *fight* for your life, as long as it takes. Rest now, save your strength. We'll sit with you, I vow it."

He tightened his fingers around hers, then closed his eyes and lay quietly. The night was endless, stretching out cold and bitter toward the small hours of morning. Morgana fed Artorius more of the medicine, praying each time she did so that the poison would do no further damage. Dallan mac Dalriada and Riona Damhnait came to the doorway for a few moments, murmuring in low voices to Keelin, who whispered the news to them, tears streaming down her cheeks. They left quietly, leaving her to sit vigil beside Morgana.

Very few people in the hill fort slept that night. Bonfires were built high and messengers were sent round every hour with word of Artorius' condition. Artorius was one of the few who *did* sleep, resting quietly and lying so still he scarcely seemed to be breathing. With painful slowness, his pulse gradually strengthened beneath Morgana's fingertips. His color improved. The waxen grey tint slowly left his skin, which flushed with a rosier, healthier hue. By dawn, Morgana was certain.

"He's past the crisis," she murmured, leaning against Ancelotis. "He will live."

Word raced through the hill fort, through the camps below, on the plain, where a great shout went up from the assembled armies of Britain. Morgana sent Medraut and Keelin away to bed, reeling on their feet. When they'd gone, Ancelotis murmured, "You're exhausted as well, Morgana. You must get some rest."

"Bring another bed then, and place it beside his. I will not leave him. Not even for a moment."

Ancelotis hesitated. "Tell me truly, Morgana. Will he *recover?*"

She met his eyes, bit one lip. "I don't know. The poison paralyzes, weakens the muscles. It will take time, perhaps a great deal of time, to rebuild his strength, to teach him to use those damaged muscles again."

"How long? How long will you and I need to stay by his side? To . . . protect these people?"

She could see the worry burning in his eyes, knew that it was Stirling, as much as Ancelotis, who was asking. She phrased the answer in English. "It may take years. I—" She hesitated. "I'm afraid I don't know Arthurian lore very well, never mind the history behind it. Do *you* know how many years were supposed to pass between this battle and Artorius' last one, the battle he was to be killed in?"

Stirling replied, also in English. "From Badon Hill to Camlann? Thirty-five, maybe forty years. And, Brenna, it isn't just the Saxons we need to worry about, getting ready for Camlann. There's more than just the loss of their war leader that led to the Britons' destruction. There's this ruddy volcano that's going to erupt. I read about it on the train, on the way up from London. You've heard about the explosion of Krakatoa in the 1800s, I'm sure? Well, it blew apart in AD 536 or so, as well. So violently, it caused weather disruption like nuclear winter for ten *years.* The crops will fail, Brenna, worldwide. And when that happens, the Briton kingdoms will fall, weakened by starvation and plague."

Brenna's eyes widened. "My God. The *wasteland* . . ."

He nodded gravely. "If I am still here, thirty-six years from now, I will do everything in my power to make sure they're ready for it." He managed a smile. "They say Lancelot became a wandering hermit, preaching Christianity everywhere he went. I think Ancelotis and I may take up that challenge, when Gwalchmai is old enough to take his throne. And there's much we can do before then, as well. I'd like to spread the word about Joseph and the seven fat and lean cows, that lovely parable about being prepared for famine. I may not have the holy grail to heal the king and bring the land back to life, but I can at least urge these people to build granaries in every town, every village, every hill fort."

She touched his cheek, wonderingly. "You will, too, won't you?" She found herself swallowing hard. "You can't know how very sorry I am, that I didn't meet you a long time ago, Trevor Stirling."

Very, very gently, he kissed her lips. "And you can't know how very glad I am, that I met you when I did. Even if I did spend several weeks thinking you were the enemy."

He waited for the smile that touched her eyes, happy to see it displace some of the terrible bleakness. He sighed then and glanced toward Artorius. "Where will you take him for his rehabilitation?"

"Ynys Manaw. The Nine Ladies who taught me the healing arts will help me care for him." She chuckled. "You know, we Irish call the Isle of Man the 'Apple Isle' in Gaelic."

Very softly, Trevor Stirling began to laugh.

It was the most joyous sound Brenna McEgan had ever heard.

Epilogue

In a laboratory tucked away in the Lowlands of Scotland, an aging, white-haired man stepped out of his car and crossed the graveled car park to a heavy steel door. He slid a card through the reader, pulled the door open, stepped inside. He had not been back to this place in many, many years, but the sight which waited for him beyond the bustle of technicians, the scientists and scholars working under close military supervision, brought painful memories rushing back.

There had once been three bodies lying in the quiet little transfer room, hooked into the computers that had sent their minds plunging back through the centuries. Cedric Banning was dead, long since. He had died within weeks of his departure, in fact, suffering a massive coronary and stroke that killed him almost instantly. Ogilvie had not mourned Banning's death. The information they had dug up on his background had turned Ogilvie grey with cold horror. No, he would never mourn that one's death.

But Brenna McEgan and Trevor Stirling . . .

When Colonel Ogilvie stepped into the transfer

room, saw them lying there, still as death, their hair greyed, their faces wrinkled with age, muscles wasted from nearly four decades of coma, tears came to his eyes. They had not come home. Not even when the computers had finally been shut down, a year after their departure. Time had fractured, so the scientists had told him forty years previously, spawning a new timeline in which they were trapped, leaving their bodies in this timeline, to slowly age without them.

Ogilvie stood silent for a long time, just looking at them. The uniform Stirling's body still wore had been decorated, long ago, with a Victoria Cross, an honor Ogilvie himself had placed with trembling hands. Another Victoria Cross shone beneath Brenna McEgan's long, greying hair, awarded by special act of Parliament at the request of His Majesty. No woman, no man could have risked more for king, for country.

Very slowly, with tears in his eyes, Ogilvie saluted them.

Then he turned to leave, his last mission before retirement finally completed.

Wherever they were, he wished them well.

TIME SCOUTS CAN DO

In the early part of the 21st century disaster struck—an experiment went wrong, bad wrong. The Accident almost destroyed the universe, and ripples in time washed over the Earth. Soon, the people of the depopulated post-disaster Earth learned that things were going to be a little different.... They'd be able to travel into the past, utilizing remnant time strings. It took brave pioneers to map the time gates: you can zap yourself out of existence with a careless jump, to say nothing of getting killed by some rowdy downtimer who doesn't like people who can't speak his language. So elaborate rules are evolved and Time Travel stations become big business.

But wild and wooly pioneers aren't the most likely people to follow rules... Which makes for great adventures as Time Scouts Kit Carson, Skeeter Jackson, and Margo Carson explore Jack the Ripper's London, the Wild West of the '49 Gold Rush, Edo Japan, the Roman Empire and more.

❧❧❧

"Engaging, fast moving, historically literate, and filled with Asprin's expertise on the techniques and philosophy of personal combat, this is first-class action SF."   —*Booklist*

"The characters ... are appealing and their adventures exciting ..."   —*Science Fiction Chronicle*

❧❧❧

The Time Scout series
by Robert Asprin & Linda Evans

Time Scout	87698-8	$5.99	___
Wagers of Sin	87730-5	$5.99	___
Ripping Time	57867-7	$6.99	___
The House that Jack Built	31965-5	$6.99	___
For King & Country (HC)	7434-3539-7	$24.00	___

If not available through your local bookstore send this coupon and a check or money order for the cover price(s) + $1.50 s/h to Baen Books, Dept. BA, P.O. Box 1403, Riverdale, NY 10471. Delivery can take up to eight weeks.

NAME: _____

ADDRESS: _____

_____

I have enclosed a check or money order in the amount of $ _____

American freedom and justice versus the tyrannies of the seventeenth century

❧

1632 *by Eric Flint*

Paperback • 31972-8   **$7.99** ____

"This gripping and expertly detailed account of an episode of time travel that changes history is a treat for lovers of action-SF or alternate history...it distinguishes Flint as an SF author of particular note, one who can entertain and edify in equal, and major, measure."

—*Publishers Weekly*, **starred review**

1633 *by David Weber & Eric Flint*

Hardcover • 7434-3542-7   **$26.00** ____

The greatest naval war in European history is about to erupt. Like it or not, Gustavus Adolphus will have to rely on Mike Stearns and the technical wizardry of his obstreperous Americans to save the King of Sweden from ruin, but caught in the conflagration are two American diplomatic missions abroad. . . .

If not available through your local bookstore send this coupon and a check or money order for the cover price(s) + $1.50 s/h to Baen Books, Dept. BA, P.O. Box 1403, Riverdale, NY 10471. Delivery can take up to eight weeks.

NAME: _____

ADDRESS: _____

_____

I have enclosed a check or money order in the amount of $ _____

DAVID WEBER's
HONOR HARRINGTON SERIES

On Basilisk Station	(HC) 57793-X / $18.00	☐
	(PB) 72163-1 / $6.99	☐
The Honor of the Queen	72172-0 / $7.99	☐
The Short Victorious War	87596-5 / $6.99	☐
Field of Dishonor	87624-4 / $6.99	☐
Flag in Exile	(PB) 87681-3 / $7.99	☐
Honor Among Enemies	(PB) 87783-6 / $7.99	☐
In Enemy Hands	(HC) 87793-3 / $22.00	☐
	(PB) 57770-0 / $7.99	☐
Echoes of Honor	(HC) 87892-1 / $24.00	☐
	(PB) 57833-2 / $7.99	☐
Ashes of Victory	(HC) 57854-5 / $25.00	☐
	(PB) 31977-9 / $7.99	☐
War of Honor	(HC) 7434-3545-1 / $26.00	☐

ANTHOLOGIES

More Than Honor	87857-3 / $6.99	☐
Worlds of Honor	57855-3 / $6.99	☐
Changer of Worlds	7434-3520-6 / $7.99	☐
Service of the Sword	(HC) 7434-3599-0 / $26.00	☐

If not available through your local bookstore send this coupon and a check or money order for the cover price(s) + $1.50 s/h to Baen Books, Dept. BA, P.O. Box 1403, Riverdale, NY 10471. Delivery can take up to 8 weeks.

NAME: _____

ADDRESS: _____

_____

I have enclosed a check or money order in the amt. of $_____

The Strangest Civil War Novel You've Ever Read!

Novels of Alternate History & Fantasy from the Master of the Form

HARRY TURTLEDOVE

SENTRY PEAK (PB) 31846-2 $7.99 ☐

MARCHING THROUGH PEACHTREE
(HC) 31843-8 $21.00 ☐
(PB) 7434-3609-1 $7.99 ☐

ADVANCE & RETREAT (HC) 7434-3576-1 $27.00 ☐

"Harry Turtledove has established himself as the grand master of alternate history." —Poul Anderson

"One of alternate history's authentic modern masters."
—*Booklist*

"One of the finest explorers of alternate histories ever."
—*Locus*

And don't miss:
Thessalonica 87761-5 $5.99 ☐
The Case of the Toxic Spell Dump 72196-8 $6.99 ☐
Wisdom of the Fox 57838-3 $6.99 ☐
Alternate Generals 87886-7 $5.99 ☐

If not available at your local bookstore, fill out this coupon and send a check or money order for the cover price(s) plus $1.50 s/h to Baen Books, Dept. BA, P.O. Box 1403, Riverdale, NY 10471. Delivery can take up to ten weeks.

NAME: _____

ADDRESS: _____

_____

I have enclosed a check or money order in the amount of $ _____

Got questions? We've got answers at

BAEN'S BAR!

Here's what some of our members have to say:

"Ever wanted to get involved in a newsgroup but were frightened off by rude know-it-alls? Stop by Baen's Bar. Our know-it-alls are the friendly, helpful type—and some write the hottest SF around."
> —**Melody L** *melodyl@ccnmail.com*

"Baen's Bar . . . where you just might find people who understand what you are talking about!"
> —**Tom Perry** *perry@airswitch.net*

"Lots of gentle teasing and numerous puns, mixed with various recipes for food and fun."
> —**Ginger Tansey** *makautz@prodigy.net*

"Join the fun at Baen's Bar, where you can discuss the latest in books, Treecat Sign Language, ramifications of cloning, how military uniforms have changed, help an author do research, fuss about differences between American and European measurements—and top it off with being able to talk to the people who write and publish what you love."
> —**Sun Shadow** *sun2shadow@hotmail.com*

"Thanks for a lovely first year at the Bar, where the only thing that's been intoxicating is conversation."
> —**Al Jorgensen** *awjorgen@wolf.co.net*

  Join BAEN'S BAR at
WWW.BAEN.COM
"Bring your brain!"